STORM OF DESIRE

"I should have known that night," Justin said softly. "I should have recognized you. God, how I wanted you—from the first moment I saw you. I've never wanted anything the way I wanted you that night—the way I want you now . . ."

Dyanna trembled, seeing the fire of desire in his golden gaze. "No," she whispered, but she knew at that moment it was inevitable.

"Yes," he replied, and then she was in his arms, held, cradled, caressed.

Dyanna gazed up at him, her beautiful aqua eyes filled with the wonder of his face above hers. She was fascinated by him, caught in his spell, drawn to him—the moth drawn too near the flame of his passion.

"Wonderful escapist fiction. Sandra DuBay fulfills all her readers' fantasies!"—*Romantic Times*

Sandra DuBay

LEISURE BOOKS NEW YORK CITY

A LEISURE BOOK

January 1989

Published by

Dorchester Publishing Co., Inc.
276 Fifth Avenue
New York, NY 10001

Printed in the United States of America

Prologue

Portsmouth, England
1780

Justin, Sixth Earl DeVille, awoke slowly, gingerly, his aching head screaming in protest, his amber-colored eyes slitted against the mid-morning sunshine that glowed behind the green velvet draperies at the mullioned windows. The hand that lay against his stubbled cheek was hot and moist. He shifted his arm to relieve the uncomfortable pressure, but it remained even when his own calloused, sun-bronzed hands were in plain sight before his out-of-focus gaze.

Turning his head on the pillow, he saw the tumble of golden curls that covered the pillow beside his own. Groaning, he pushed away the stranger's hand and rose from the velvet-hung fourposter.

He swayed slightly as he drew himself to his full six feet three inches. It seemed as if he could still feel the motion of his ship even though he was on dry land and had been since his vessel, the *Golden Falcon*, made port the day before.

"Bertran!" he shouted, then winced as the word seemed to echo and re-echo along the wine-soaked corridors of his brain.

"Milord?" Justin's Swiss valet appeared in the doorway. As always, he was cool and unruffled. He appeared not to notice the litter of wine bottles surrounding the rumpled bed, nor the buxom blonde still draped across it.

"What time is it?"

"A quarter past twelve, milord," Bertran replied as he brought his master's velvet robe and held it for him to slip on.

Scowling, Justin knotted the sash. "A quarter past twelve! I should have been back on the ship hours ago! Get rid of—" He pointed toward the bed but, as he did, he noticed the delicate foot dangling over the bed's edge.

Almost dreading what he might find, Justin lifted the sheet. The foot, he found, was attached to the shapely leg of some unknown brunette who was otherwise buried beneath the tangled bedding. He glanced at Bertran, who regarded him with the same look of unperturbed serenity as before.

"Get rid of them both," he told the valet.

"Give them some money and send them away."

"As you wish, milord."

"But first . . ." Justin drew a deep breath and raised a hand to his throbbing head. "First get me a hot bath."

Later—bathed, shaved, and fortified by Bertran's vile-tasting but effective secret hangover cure—Justin sat in a chair near the window of the sitting room of the inn's finest suite. Outside, in the harbor, his ship rode at anchor. He smiled as he gazed at her. Her hull scarred, her sails badly in need of mending, she was marked by the long months at the mercy of the Atlantic. But he loved her as he loved the sea itself.

He was a privateer, some said—a pirate, others whispered. Whichever it was, he was phenomenally successful. He had made himself rich and restored the family fortune lost in the service of the Crown during the Civil War more than a century before. He was master of his own ship. He had a fine house in London, and he had Wildwood, the great manor house he was building near the fire-blackened ruins that had once been Castle DeVille, his family's ancestral seat.

He sighed as he leaned back in his chair. It had been hard to leave America. The raw newness and magnificent promise of a country still in its infancy touched that place in his heart that yearned for challenge and adventure. But his fortune came from the sea and the letter of marque—that invaluable piece of paper that gave him the right to plunder the riches of England's enemies—obliged him to reaffirm his allegiance from time to time to the government that had issued it.

Still, he thought as he stretched his long legs, flexing the muscles beneath the taut russet cloth of his breeches and wiggling his toes inside his knee-high jackboots, as much as he loved the sea and loved America, it was good to be in England in the spring. Nowhere else on earth seemed so green and alive at that time of year.

"Milord?" Bertran stood in the doorway. "A messenger from London. From your solicitor."

Justin took the packet the valet offered. "It didn't take him long to get down to business. I wrote to tell him when I expected to arrive, but—"

His brow furrowed as his long-lashed, orange-brown eyes skimmed the letter attached to a thick sheaf of papers. "Damnation!"

"Bad news, milord?"

"A death," Justin replied, reading on. "A friend from my youth." He let out his breath in a long sigh. "Rayburn McBride."

"My sympathies, milord."

A wistful smile quirked Justin's lips. "We went to Oxford together. And we were sent down from Oxford together."

"A true friendship," the valet remarked drily.

Justin smiled reminiscently. Being thrown out of school was nothing unusual for Rayburn. He was a wild one, some years older than Justin. All the McBrides were reckless, impetuous. Rayburn had had two brothers— both older, both of whom had died of their own foolishness, so Rayburn was their father's heir. It seemed he'd be the last of the McBrides. No one believed he could settle down and make an acceptable husband. But he fell in love and married Elizabeth Conway, the only child of the Earl of Lincoln. She was a great heiress, and she loved him, wildness and all. They eloped and the change in him was miraculous. Elizabeth bore him a child.

Then, a few years later, Elizabeth died in a carriage accident. McBride had been driving and, rightly or wrongly, blamed himself for his wife's death. After that he went back to his old ways with a vengeance. He was like a man possessed. It seemed he was committing suicide by inches.

Justin glanced at the papers in his hand. It appeared that he had succeeded.

His mind swept back through the years, remembering times long past. They had made a splendid couple. Rayburn was a handsome

5

man for all his dissipation, and his wife was held to be the greatest beauty of her generation. Her hair was the color of moonlight, her eyes like aquamarines. The old Earl, her father, never forgave her for throwing herself away on Rayburn McBride—or 'Rakehell McBride' as he was usually called. He and Elizabeth were still estranged when she died. He lost his own wife, Elizabeth's mother, not long after, and became a recluse. No doubt he was dead as well. It was a sorry tale.

"Rakehell's daughter—Dyanna—is heiress to both the McBride estates and those of her grandfather, old Lincoln," Justin told his valet. "Good God! What a fortune." He turned to the next page. "She is to inherit upon her twenty-first birthday or her marriage. Until then, her estate is to be held in trust and she is to be given an allowance overseen by her guardian—"

Heedless of the papers lying in his lap, Justin thrust himself to his feet. "God's teeth!"

Bertran stepped back, momentarily shocked from his habitual composure. "Sir!"

"I am the girl's guardian! Rakehell willed his brat to me, God damn his black soul!"

"Congratulations, milord."

Justin shot him a withering glare, but his valet's expression was blandly respectful. "I can't play nursemaid to some schoolgirl! I don't know how old she is, but it will surely be years before she's of age. I'm not a governess

6

or a maiden aunt!" He consulted the letter. "It says she's at school. She'll just have to stay there until they find someone else to be her guard-dog. That's all there is to it!" He ran a hand through his thick, dark gold hair. "Pack for me, Bertran. I'm going to settle this McBride business at once so I can get on with my own affairs. And then—"

He was interrupted by the opening of the bedchamber door. His two bedmates appeared, smiling, and came to him, twining their clinging arms about his neck and stretching up to kiss him.

"If you need anything, milord," the blonde cooed, "just ask the innkeeper."

"Anything at all, milord," the brunette added.

Justin smiled wanly as they flounced out the door. He had wanted a woman badly by the time his ship had docked in Portsmouth—but even he hadn't realized just how badly.

"Must have been quite a night," he murmured as Bertran left to go about his master's packing. "I wish to hell I could remember it."

Chapter One

The Misses Pettigrew Academy
for Select Young Ladies
1780

The Honorable Dyanna McBride lay across her narrow bed in the small, austere room she shared with another inmate of the Pettigrew Academy. Neither the beauty of the late afternoon sunshine nor the sweet fragrance of the spring blossoms wafting from the overgrown gardens touched her. For she was lost—happily, contentedly lost in the pages of one of the books that were her comfort, her friends, the birthplaces of her every dream and fantasy.

As she turned the pages to begin reading it yet again, her fingers caressed the lettering worked into the scuffed leather of the cover:

9

Sandra DuBay

The Trials and Triumphs
of
Jenny Flynn
An Orphan

Snuggling deep into the worn coverlet of her bed, Dyanna turned past the title page to the beginning of the story and read the words that were engraved in her memory and had been since she'd first discovered the book in her grandfather's library years before:

Book I
Like most women whose names are spoken in hushed murmurs behind the spread fans of their more fortunate sisters, my downfall was brought about through the offices of a man. His name was and is (though I can scarce relate it without feeling a shudder of the utmost repugnance) Ebenezer Greatrakes.
When my mother and father, personages of no little consequence and respectable means, were taken from this life, this man, Greatrakes, was left my guardian. As I was merely an innocent child and he a gentleman respected by his colleagues who little suspected the true wickedness that lay beneath his air of kindness and refinement, my upbringing and well-being was left entirely in his hands.
Thereafter I lived in his household, the

10

support of which came, in the main, out of my inheritance. I was less a ward than a dependent; my days were passed in circumstances little better than those of the lowliest scullery maid. It was not until I had attained enough years to be called a young woman rather than a child that Greatrakes deigned to notice me.

Though the details of my seduction are far too sordid and scandalous for me to commit to paper, suffice it to say that Ebenezer Greatrakes relieved me of my innocence and virtue with as cavalier an air as he had determined to relieve me of my inheritance.

Afterward, his coldness toward me, the arrogant callousness with which he regarded me, the victim of his unprincipled lusts, wounded me far more deeply than even the loss of that precious maidenhood that is every young woman's treasure.

To no avail did I remonstrate with him. My tears could not move him; my threats of exposure only angered him and prompted him to immure me in the country, closely guarded by servants—villains—in his employ. I was left to languish in the depths of Devonshire while he, in London, plundered my birthright at his leisure.

The long, lonely days turned to weeks,

*the weeks to months. Winter passed, cold
and dark like my wounded heart. I
lapsed into a melancholia from which it
was feared I might not recover. (Which
news, I have no doubt, was greeted with
glee by the villain, Greatrakes. Were I to
die, he would have the spending of my
fortune without the trouble of my
person.)*

*But then, with the coming of Spring,
my bleak melancholy lifted. My heart, its
bruises healed by that universal balm,
Time, was filled with a new
determination. It was as if the long dark
night had at last ended and the coming
of the dawn was full of hope. With a
certainty that was equal parts optimism
and anger, I knew there was only one
course of action open to me: I must
escape my gaolers and . . .*

"Here you are, Dyanna. I should have
known where to find you."

Dyanna looked up from her book at the girl
who had just opened the door.

"The old ladies want you in the morning
room," Miss Kitty Fitzsimmons, Dyanna's
roommate, announced.

Groaning, Dyanna slid off her narrow bed
and smoothed the skirts of her grey linen
gown—the uniform of the Pettigrew Academy. Her hands captured an errant lock of

12

shimmering silver blonde hair and tucked it back into the neatly coiled knot near the crown. Austerity and simplicity were bywords at the academy despite the fact that all of the girls placed in the Misses Pettigrews' care came from wealthy, if not aristocratic, families.

"What do they want?" Dyanna asked as she slipped her feet into the simple leather slippers which, along with a pair of boots for inclement weather, were the only footwear allowed.

Kitty shrugged her narrow shoulders. "How would I know? I have my own troubles to worry about."

Dyanna left quickly, eager to avoid a recitation of Kitty's much-vaunted 'troubles.' Kitty's real trouble, so far as Dyanna could see, was the fact that no man, however low his station or advanced his age, was allowed within shouting distance of the Pettigrew girls. After having formed an attachment with both her noble father's steward and his head groom, Kitty had been found attempting to embark for the wilds of North America in pursuit of a young lieutenant who had, so she said, promised to marry her. After that unhappy incident, Miss Kitty Fitzsimmons had found herself dispatched to the Pettigrew Academy.

"For Select Young Ladies," Dyanna mused aloud as she made her way along the ancient stone cloister that had once, in the time-shrouded past, been part of an abbey. All the fine-sounding title meant was that the girls who were placed there were too incorrigible to be kept at home and too blue-blooded to be tossed into the streets. They were more prisoners than students, for they never went home on holidays nor were they left for long without supervision. If they ventured beyond the confines of the walled grounds it was under the watchful eyes of one of the no-nonsense matrons who kept order among the collection of hoydens and ne'er-do-wells—girls like Kitty Fitzsimmons who were far too fond of the wrong sort of male company and girls like Dyanna who, left on her own for too long, had grown up without the genteel guidance of a governess or female relation.

Dyanna was not incorrigible, simply untutored. She was not, by nature, bad, although the celebrated McBride wildness had its prominent place in her personality. She was simply untaught in the intricate rules that governed the behavior of a girl of her breeding and prospects.

The heels of her slippers tapped on the worn stones of the cloister, echoing and re-echoing in the beautiful fan vaulting of the ancient passage. She was sorry when she reached the end, reluctant to leave the peaceful solitude of the cloister for the unknown that awaited her in the morning room. No one ever got good news in the morning room. She did not expect to be the first.

She tapped at the door and was admitted to a dimly lit chamber. The brilliant sunshine of the day was barred entry by the heavy damask draperies drawn across the leaded windows. Eyes downcast, Dyanna crossed the faded carpet toward the pair of spreading black silk skirts.

"Good afternoon, Dyanna," a thin, unpleasantly nasal voice said.

She raised her eyes. Miss Adelaide Pettigrew regarded her with that look of grim disapproval she reserved for her students. They were, in her opinion and without exception, wicked, fallen creatures with scant hope of redemption. By opening her ancestral home to them, she believed, with a self-righteous certainty, that she was earning her way into heaven.

"Sit down, dear," a second voice, eerily similar to the first, invited her. Abigail Pettigrew smiled gently at Dyanna, who sank onto the edge of a sofa opposite the sisters.

"Sit, Dyanna," Adelaide ordered sharply, "do not perch."

Obediently, Dyanna pushed herself backward on the sofa until her back touched the tapestry upholstery.

"We have some bad news for you, I'm afraid," Miss Abigail began.

Dyanna's aqua eyes flitted from one narrow, ferret-like face to the other. "Bad news?"

15

Adelaide pursed her lips, annoyed that her sister should try to usurp her right to tell Dyanna the reason she had been summoned. After all, she was the elder, if only by a matter of minutes. Her younger twin had no business trying to steal her thunder.

"It is your father, Dyanna," she said quickly, before Abigail could continue. "I'm afraid he is dead."

Dyanna blinked. "Dead?" she said blandly. "When?"

"Not long since," Abigail told her. "It was an unfortunate riding accident."

"I see. The funeral?" Dyanna felt a glimmer of hope. She might be released from behind those forbidding walls to attend—

"Has already taken place," Adelaide informed her, dashing her hopes. "You will, of course, be provided with mourning attire."

Dyanna let her mind drift. That she felt no swelling surge of grief came as no surprise. She'd hardly known her father, could scarcely remember him. She'd still been in leading strings when her mother died. All she remembered of that time were emotions—the feeling of black doom that descended over what had been a happy home filled with love. One of her earliest, mistiest memories was of her nurse trying, between her tears, to explain to a three-year-old child why her mama did not come to kiss her good-night. "She is an angel now," Nanna had said, but that made no

16

sense. After all, hadn't Papa always said Mama was an angel?

Dyanna had longed to ask her father all those troubling questions, but he had shut himself away. "Maddened with grief," as the servants whispered. After that, Dyanna had caught but fleeting glimpses of him. Once, when she'd seen him from her nursery window sprawled on a bench in the garden below, she'd slipped away from her nurse and gone to him. He had frightened her with his blank stare, his pasty white face. He had seemed not to know her at first, and then he had turned from her, had bellowed for her to be taken away out of his sight.

He had gone away not long after that. Gone back to his wild ways in London, the maids gossiped, not bothering to whisper in Dyanna's presence, for they thought a three-year-old far too young to listen or comprehend. She had never seen him again.

The years that followed had been a strange mixture of happiness and melancholy. She'd grown up wild on her father's estate. Without their master's presence, the servants fell into indolence. They used the house as their own and allowed their master's daughter to grow up amongst the kitchen maids and stableboys and, later, with the children of the gypsy bands that camped on the fringes of the McBride lands, confident that they could poach as they pleased without fear of arrest.

17

Dyanna was twelve by the time her maternal grandfather, the Earl of Lincoln, came for her. Emerging at last from the double grief of his daughter's death and that of his wife, he had come for his granddaughter, had come to try to salvage what remained of his heritage — his last descendent, his heiress.

But instead of the cultured young lady of breeding he had expected, he found a wild little hoyden who, with her thick silvery curls cascading down her back, her simple peasant's garb, her bare feet and her sun-browned face, behaved more like a gypsy child than the daughter of two great and noble houses.

She could not read, he discovered; she could not write; she knew nothing of etiquette or music or art; she rode the horses of her father's stable astride and barebacked rather than being perched decorously on a side-saddle; and her language would make a bosun blush.

The old earl was horrified. Without waiting for his son-in-law's permission, he closed the house. Leaving only a few of his own trusted servants to keep away robbers and squatters, he took his granddaughter away with him to Blaykling Castle, the ancestral home of the Earls of Lincoln.

There Dyanna was transformed by an army of governesses, tutors, dancing masters, music teachers, and riding instructors. She was laced into corsets and hoops for the first time; she was drilled in art, in etiquette, in French and Italian. In the earl's splendid stables she learned to ride like a lady, in a proper habit, on a precarious, dainty sidesaddle.

But it was reading that was the earl's greatest gift to his granddaughter. The day she discovered the cavernous, two-story library of Blaykling Castle was the day it seemed her life began. It was there she learned about faraway lands, about history, about adventures beyond her wildest dreams. It was there she found, amongst the romantic novels her late grandmother had loved, her favorite heroine— Jenny Flynn.

She'd spent three years at Blaykling, three happy years, occasionally slipping away to the village that nestled in the shadow of the great castle. There she had left off her new airs and graces and frolicked with the village boys and girls as freely as she had on her father's estate.

But then her grandfather had died and Dyanna, once more, was left alone.

Her father, summoned from his mad, downward spiral in the brothels and gaming hells of London, had met with the old earl's solicitors. Without troubling to set eyes on the daughter he had not seen in twelve years, he asked if the McBride wildness was apparent in his only offspring. Assured that it was, he had consigned her to the Pettigrew Academy and then returned to London, giving her not a moment's further thought from then until the day of his death.

"What will become of me now?" Dyanna wondered aloud.

Adelaide, interrupted in mid-discourse, glared at Dyanna. "If you had been attending rather than letting your senses run a'woolgathering as usual—" She drew herself up indignantly. "As I was saying. You will come into your inheritance when you are twenty-one or on the day of your marriage, whichever comes first. Until then, you will receive an allowance and your estates will be overseen by your guardian."

"Guardian!" Dyanna cried. The leering, wicked face of her beloved Jenny's nemesis, Ebenezer Greatrakes, loomed threateningly in Dyanna's imagination. "But who is to be my guardian?"

"If you had been listening!" Angrily, Adelaide consulted her papers. "Lord DeVille— Earl DeVille—has been appointed."

"Who is he?" Dyanna demanded.

"A longtime friend of your father's, dear," Abigail told her.

"Will I be leaving this"—she checked herself. "—the Academy?"

The obvious eagerness in her voice irritated Adelaide beyond measure.

"You are to remain with us for the present,"

she snapped. "It will be for your guardian to decide."

"What is he—"

"You may return to your room, Dyanna." Adelaide was maliciously glad to dismiss the girl with her questions unanswered.

"But—"

"Mourning attire will be provided for you. The dressmaker in the village has your measurements and a mourning ensemble will be ordered. The bill will be sent to your guardian. Now go along, Dyanna."

Rising, Dyanna dropped the ladies a curtsy and left the room. But once outside, she pressed her ear close to the rough panels of the ancient door.

"She was not the picture of grief," Adelaide observed acidly.

"After all, sister," Abigail, ever the gentler soul, reminded her, "she hardly knew her father. They do say she grieved mightily over her grandfather, Lord Lincoln."

"Humph. In any case, I do not understand why you were so adamant that she not be told the truth of her father's death. Riding accident, indeed. He was drunk! So drunk he fell from his horse and drowned in a ditch. Incapable of saving even his own miserable life. It was not for nothing they called him Rakehell McBride! And his daughter is like him, you mark my words. The McBride wildness! Wildness, indeed. It's madness, more like—depravity!"

"Perhaps her guardian will be able to—"

"Her guardian!" Adelaide screeched. "Justin DeVille! You know what they say about the DeVilles. Wicked. Evil. Worse than the McBrides! Remember his father? The stories! They said he murdered his wife! They said he was in league with the Devil! No doubt his son is like him. He'll plunder Dyanna's inheritance and seduce her into the bargain. No doubt he will—"

Adelaide's next words were lost on Dyanna, who started as a door nearby slammed shut. Lifting her skirts, she fled on tiptoe back down the cloister, back to her room which was, mercifully, deserted.

Seated on the wide stone sill of the tall lancet window, she idly followed its wooden tracery with her finger while her mind dwelt on Adelaide Pettigrew's venomous revelations.

"Wicked. Evil," she had said. A murderer.

Closing her eyes, Dyanna leaned her head back against the window frame. How could her father, even lacking in paternal feeling as he was, leave her in the clutches of such a man? A man who would rob her. Seduce her, too, if Adelaide could be believed. A monster's son. Why, the man was no better than Ebenezer Greatrakes himself!

"What will I do?" she asked herself. "He

22

will keep me shut away here while he robs me of my inheritance. When I come of age I will be penniless. Then he will laugh at my misery and leave me to make my own way in the world. I'll be abandoned on the streets like a common—"

Scowling, she shook herself out of her miserable self-pity. She was acting like a missish, mawkish little girl. She should be ashamed of herself! This was certainly not how Jenny Flynn had acted when confronted by an evil guardian who was out to fleece her of her last brass farthing!

From beneath her mattress, Dyanna pulled the treasured volume. Opening it to where the frayed and creased scarlet ribbon marker lay, she went on from where she had left off earlier:

> *"There was only one course of action open to me: I must escape my gaolers and make my way to London, there to confront the vile, loathsome man who had robbed me of my virtue, my innocence, and my birthright. Such wickedness as his would not go unpunished. I vowed, at that moment, to be the instrument of Ebenezer Greatrakes' destruction."*

Sighing, Dyanna closed the book and laid it aside. That was it. She would do as Jenny had done. She would not simply allow the cad, DeVille, to rob her. She would not!

Saucy mouth set with determination, blue eyes glittering with excitement, Dyanna lay back on her bed in the gathering twilight and began formulating her plans for escape.

Chapter Two

Curiosity forced Justin to break his journey to London and order his coachman to stop and ask directions to the Pettigrew Academy. It was as he walked along the stone cloister, the heels of his tall leather boots ringing on the worn and ancient stones, that he began to have doubts about Dyanna.

After all, he reasoned, tucking his three-cornered hat beneath his arm, the place was like some genteel prison—a cleaner, less cruel version of Newgate. How could a girl possessed of any small share of the wild spirit that had driven Rakehell McBride to his untimely death allow herself to be immured in such a place? She must take after her mother, he decided, a meek, biddable, gentle creature.

But perhaps that was for the best. She would take the news that she must stay until a new guardian could be found for her all the better.

A grim-faced matron left a bevy of grey-clad 'students' and ushered him into the morning room that was Adelaide Pettigrew's inner sanctum. There he found the sisters, clad in their habitual black, awaiting him.

Though they were not identical, their twinship was apparent. The chief difference between them seemed to lie in their expressions. Adelaide—the dragoness, he immediately dubbed her in his mind—glared at him as though he were the Devil Incarnate while her sister, Abigail, dimpled, her wrinkled skin flushing like a schoolgirl's, when he made her a courtly bow.

"Sit down, my Lord DeVille," Abigail said, indicating a chair nearer her own than that of her sister. "May we offer you some refreshment?"

"Nothing, my thanks, ma'am," Justin replied, flashing the younger Miss Pettigrew the gleaming smile that had melted female hearts on several continents. "I have come, as you doubtless know, on account of Miss McBride."

"You are, I believe, her guardian now," Adelaide snapped coldly, irritated as she always was to see her sister garnering the lion's share of their visitor's attention.

"For the moment," Justin acknowledged.

"Actually, I am on my way to London to meet with my solicitors. Owing to the nature of my business, it would be impossible for me to play guardian to a young girl."

Adelaide's mouth pursed mutinously. The nature of his business indeed! The man was nothing more than a pirate, whatever he liked to call himself.

Reading Adelaide's thoughts clearly in her eyes, DeVille cursed her for the sour old harridan she was. He could not help feeling a pang of sympathy for any girl unlucky enough to fall into her hands. Nonetheless, he went on:

"I feel it only fair to explain to Miss McBride my reasons for refusing her guardianship. If you would be so kind as to summon her, I will do so and then resume my journey to London."

"I am afraid, my lord, that would be impossible."

"Impossible? But why?"

Adelaide's eyes gleamed with the unmistakable relish she felt at thwarting his plans. "She is not here."

Justin glanced at Abigail and saw that the becoming flush had faded from her cheeks. Her gaze was averted, refusing to meet his.

"I don't understand," he admitted, turning his attention back to Adelaide.

"Dyanna ran away some time during the night last night. She was in her room when

27

the matron last checked, but was missing this morning."

Justin's tawny brows drew together. "And where is the search being concentrated?"

"Search, my lord?" Adelaide asked icily.

Justin leaned forward in his chair. "Surely you have organized a search."

"Not at all."

"Good God, woman!" He thrust himself to his feet, towering over both Pettigrews. "Have you any notion of the conditions that exist out there? Highwaymen, Bedlamites, murderers —And you sit here, blithely unconcerned, while a young girl of birth and breeding faces all that alone!"

"By her own choice, my lord," Adelaide reminded him. "And may I say I have pity for anyone into whose hands that little hoyden falls."

"You have no heart, madam," he snarled.

Adelaide rose, drawing herself up self-righteously. "And you, my lord, have no notion whatever of what it is like to try to steer these ungrateful little wretches down the path to respectability. Many of them are all but ruined by the time they come to us. Most have no desire to become honorable members of society. No, my lord! I will not take any part in a search for Dyanna McBride. Nor will I take responsibility for any calamity that may befall her because of her own foolishness and ingratitude!"

"Well, I shall find her!" Justin stormed.

"Damme if I don't! And when I do, I assure you she'll not be sent back to this hell-hole!"

"You're quite correct!" Adelaide flung after him, her words nearly drowned by the echoing of his footsteps on the stone floor. "She won't come back here because we will not have her!"

Slamming the iron-bound front door behind him, Justin clapped his hat on his head and leapt into his carriage.

"She's gone," he told Bertran who looked up from a book as his master appeared. "She's run away, and the miserable old spinster who runs this gaol won't lift a finger to find her."

"Fortunate for you, milord, that you are not accepting her guardianship. You will not have the task of finding her."

Justin glared at his valet as the carriage rolled out of the courtyard. "I have to find her. Until another guardian is appointed she is my responsibility."

"As you say, milord." Bertran stifled a smile. For all that Justin DeVille affected an air of arrogant unconcern for the wishes and opinions of others, he had, throughout the ten years the two men had known each other, displayed a fatal weakness for young women in unfortunate circumstances. Bertran liked to call it his master's 'damsel in distress penchant.'

"She most likely set out for London," Justin mused aloud. "Most girls would. Don't you think, Bertran?"

"Not being a girl, milord, I could not say."

"Take care, Bertran," Justin warned. "I am in no mood to be baited today." He stared thoughtfully from the window, a muscle working in his taut, clean-shaven cheek.

"It will be dark soon," he observed. "I suppose we may as well find lodgings for the night. We can ask if Dyanna's been seen. In the morning, we'll search the area before moving on toward London."

Bertran nodded his agreement and Justin ordered the coachman to stop at the first respectable-looking inn they passed.

Not so very far ahead of Justin on the London road, Dyanna trudged along. She was right to have run away, she told herself every time her feet began to ache inside her tight boots or a fly buzzed around her perspiring shoulders. What else could she do? Wait patiently at the Pettigrew Academy for her loathsome guardian to arrive? Sit by and allow herself to be robbed of her birthright and, no doubt, her virtue? There had been no other choice. She would have to get to London and seek out her father's solicitors. She would have to demand they either allow her to oversee her own inheritance—the chance of which, she knew was extremely small—or appoint as her guardian someone she trusted.

She shielded her eyes as she glanced toward the sun which was fast lowering toward the western horizon. The air was cooler now; night was coming on. It would soon be time to find a place to sleep.

Pausing, she shifted her bundle to the other arm. Of necessity, she was traveling light, bringing along only a few items of clothing, what little money she'd been allowed at school, and, of course, her treasure, her guidebook—the story of Jenny Flynn.

Lying awake the night before, waiting for her roommate to fall into a deep sleep so she could make good her escape, Dyanna had re-read the part of the book in which Jenny fled to London to confront her guardian. Her adventures with the lecherous squires who'd made their advances, the sharps who had tried to exploit her, and the highwayman— Jenny Flynn's lover—handsome, dashing, a ruined cavalier taken to the King's highway, had set Dyanna's heart racing.

Sighing as she remembered the description of her heroine's dashing lover, Dyanna trudged down the rutted highway toward London.

As the road cut a swath through a thick forest, Dyanna debated whether she should try to go on. Night was falling; she thought it might be wiser to find a bed beneath some ancient and drooping tree—or, better yet, a bed of straw in the corner of some farmer's barn.

As she turned the question over in her

mind, her thoughts were interrupted by the sound of hoofbeats. Her pulse quickened. Here it was! Adventure was approaching at a gallop and she was still less than one day away from school!

"You there!" a masculine voice commanded. "Stand and deliver!"

Dyanna dropped her bundle, pinched some color into her cheeks, and turned around. Her face fell. Instead of the handsome, dashing rogue Jenny had found, Dyanna was confronted by a skinny man astride a scrawny, swaybacked horse.

"How do you do," she said, her disappointment evident in her voice.

The man's eyes widened. "Why, you're no more'n a girl!" he exclaimed, his too-prominent Adam's apple bobbing in his bony throat. "What do you think you're about, then, bein' out alone and it gettin' dark?"

Dyanna shrugged. "Are you a highwayman?"

"That I am. But I don't expect you'd have anything worth my while in that bundle of yours."

"I'm sorry, no. Only a few clothes. I'm running away, you see. I'm looking for adventure."

"Adventure, is it?" He eyed her with grave disapproval. "If you was my daughter, I'd give you an adventure with a hickory switch!"

Dyanna lifted her chin and treated him to

her haughtiest stare. "Then I'm glad I'm not your daughter!" She frowned. "By the bye, I've heard that highwaymen rape women they come upon alone and defenseless. Are you going to rape me?"

The highwayman drew back in his saddle, obviously aghast. "Here, now! You're a dirty-minded baggage, ain't you? Just because I'm a highwayman, that don't give you call to accuse me of rapin' helpless women! I got a daughter your age!"

Dyanna nudged a stone with the toe of her boot. "Well, I do apologize. I didn't mean to insult you. It's only what I've heard."

"You probably heard talk about Dirty Ned. He used to work this stretch of road." The highwayman shook his head in sour disapproval. "Randy bugger was old Ned, and no mistake. If it'd been him here 'stead of me, you'd have had your skirts tossed over your head afore you knew what hit you."

"I would?" Dyanna chewed her lower lip. "Would you know—that is to say—does this Ned person still work some road in this area?"

"You got your mind in the sewer, ain't you! Well, just for your information, Mistress Adventure, they hung ole Ned on Tyburn Hill last summer."

"Do you know any other highwaymen like him?"

"No, I don't! An' I wouldn't be tellin' you if I did! The only thing I'll do for you is take you home with me for tonight. You can share a bed with my daughters, and in the morning I'll take you home."

Dyanna took a step backward. "But I don't want to go home! I'm going to London!"

"London, is it? What're you goin' to be, then? The town tart? Let me tell you somethin'. I been to London plenty of times and they already got more tarts there then they need!"

"Oh, fiddle! I don't care what you say! I'm going to London and I will find adventure!"

"You'll find a dose of the French pox more like! But go on if you want. And never say I didn't warn you!"

The highwayman kicked his horse and rode away. Snatching up her bundle, Dyanna stormed off into the depths of the forest. Night was falling quickly now and she needed a place to sleep.

Chapter Three

When the hoofbeats of the highwayman's rattleboned horse had faded into the distance, Dyanna returned to the edge of the rutted lane. The awakening night sounds of the forest were making her nervous. She wished she could come upon some cottage or . . .

As if in answer to her prayers, the lights of an inn appeared, glowing in the gathering darkness. Over the arch that led to the enclosed courtyard, a swinging sign was painted with an angel of blue with gilded wings. Gold letters proclaimed the place to be the "Angel Inn."

Dyanna crept cautiously through the archway. The courtyard was deserted. The sounds of laughter coming through the open windows of the taproom were muted. The Angel Inn catered primarily to travelers, there being no village close by, and its taproom was not crowded nightly by farmers and shopkeepers as a village inn's might be.

Slipping silently along the ivy-covered stone wall, she heard the soft whinny of a horse and knew she was near the stable. Relief washed over her. If she could find an empty stall, or a deserted hayloft, she could spend the night in relative comfort and start out at first light for London.

The stable was filled with shadows. A single lantern showed at the far end near an open door. The air was redolent with the smells of hay and horses and leather, though few of the stalls were occupied.

Dyanna moved slowly toward the far end of the long stable, hoping to find an empty stall where the hay was clean and fresh. But the sound of a carriage turning into the courtyard brought the inn to life and she ducked swiftly into the nearest stall, fearing the stableboys might appear and discover her.

There was no sound in the stable. It seemed no one was going to attend the carriage and its matched pair of dappled horses. Dyanna was about to leave her hiding place when a short, round figure appeared in the wide, arched stable door.

"Topham!" the woman shouted. "Topham, you lazy wretch! Where are you?"

From the lighted doorway at the opposite

end of the stable, a tall, gangly man appeared. "Here I am, Missus. Is somethin' amiss?"

"Your head'll be amiss if you don't get out here," the woman threatened. "There's a carriage in the courtyard and horses needin' stablin'. A lord's horses, mind, so take good care of 'em."

"I will, Missus, never you fear. I ain't never let no—"

The rest of his assurance was drowned by the sound of Dyanna's sneeze. In a flash she was being dragged from the stall. As she went, she kicked straw over her bundle to hide it.

"What've we got here, then?" the groom, Topham, asked, a leer in his voice to match the one in his small dark eyes.

Dyanna looked from the groom to the short, plump, grey-haired woman, and back again. "I wasn't hurting anything," she insisted. "I wasn't!"

"What was you doin' in here then?" Topham demanded.

The woman pulled Dyanna's arm out of his tight grasp. "I'll deal with her," she told him sharply. "You just get about stablin' them horses."

After the groom had gone, the woman turned back to Dyanna. "All right, my girl, what are you hidin' in here for?"

"I was looking for a place to sleep," Dyanna told her. "That's all. I was going to sleep in one of the empty stalls."

"I ain't runnin' an almshouse, you know.

This ain't a charity hospital. If you can't pay, you can't stop here."

Caution sealed Dyanna's lips on the subject of money. The golden guineas tied in a handkerchief in her bundle were her stake in London. She wasn't about to admit she had a penny. Instead, she bit her lip and forced hot, salty tears into her great blue eyes until they glittered like aquamarines.

"I only wish I could pay you," she said softly. "My father died recently, you see, and I am on my way to London to try and make my way. But a highwayman robbed me. He took everything. I . . . I . . ."

"Mrs. Cockerell!" A trembling young girl wearing a stained apron and limp mob cap came stumbling across the courtyard. "Mrs. Cockerell!"

"Oh, what is it now, Ruby?" Mrs. Cockerell snapped impatiently.

"Mr. Cockerell has shown his lordship and his man up to their rooms. He says the gentlemen want supper right away!"

"Have Meg see to it. I'm busy just now."

"Meg can't, ma'am."

"Can't? Why not?"

"She's been at the gin again."

"Crikey! What next! Well, I can't wait on 'em. Somebody's got to do the cookin'."

"What about me?" the timid girl asked hopefully.

"You! Wait on a lord! Don't be daft. This is a

pretty kettle of fish, I must say!" Her heavy brow wrinkled as she scowled. Her eyes, dark and nearly obscured by heavy lids, slid thoughtfully over Dyanna. "What your name, my girl?"

"Jenny," Dyanna lied quickly. "Jenny Flynn."

"Well, Jenny Flynn, if you'll be of some help to me, I'll give you somethin' to eat and a bed for the night. What do you say? Can you serve supper to a gentleman?"

"Oh, yes, ma'am. I'm sure I could."

"You talk like one of 'em yourself. What was your name again?"

"Jenny Flynn, ma'am." Dyanna's mind raced. "My father was estate manager to Lord Killigrew, you see. I was tutored with his lordship's children and—"

"Yes, yes." Mrs. Cockerell cut her off. "That's likely why you talk so fancy. But come along. I haven't time for the story of your life."

Dyanna followed the woman across the courtyard and into the inn. Bypassing the taproom where Mr. Cockerell was once more holding forth to a small band of cronies, they went through the kitchen and into a store-room.

From a chest, Mrs. Cockerell pulled out a wooden box and handed it to Dyanna.

"Wash your face and hands, then put this on," she instructed. "Don't spill anything onto it, mind. I only let my maids wear it when we get highborn customers. Be quick about it, hear?"

Quickly as she could, Dyanna did as Mrs. Cockerell had ordered. A basin of water was brought and she washed off the grime of a day on the hot, dusty road. From the box she pulled a round-eared muslin cap. It was made to fit close to her head even after her hair had been tucked up out of sight beneath it. The jacket and skirt, of pale rose taffeta, matched the ribbon threaded through the lace on the cap and the fabric of the shoes. A fichu of white lawn was tucked modestly into the low front of the bodice and an apron of white lawn fastened to the front of the bodice, then flared out to cover the skirt.

As she emerged into the kitchen, Dyanna was seized by Mrs. Cockerell, who swung her around for an appraising examination.

"Very nice, indeed," the woman pronounced. "Do a good job, my girl, and I just might hire you on. Now go up to number seven and find out what his lordship and his manservant might be wantin'."

Dyanna's heart pounded as she climbed the worn stairs and walked along the hallway. The wide, rough-hewn planks beneath the flowered carpet had warped with the passing of the years and the floor undulated, rising and falling along its entire length.

But Dyanna had little attention to spare for such details. Her lips curved in a pleased little smile. This, at last, was adventure. A runaway heiress passing as a maidservant. It was worthy of her heroine, Jenny Flynn, herself.

Tucking a stray curl beneath her cap, she knocked lightly on the door marked with a tarnished brass number seven.

"Yes?" a deep, masculine voice called from within.

Pressing down the latch, Dyanna opened the door.

"Beg pardon, milord," she said, stepping into the room. "Mrs. Cockerell sent me up to—"

Her words faded into nothingness as the man across the candlelit chamber turned toward her.

He was tall—taller than any man she'd ever seen. His shoulders were broad, his hips narrow, his long, muscular legs encased in brown breeches and thigh-high leather boots. His russet coat and creamy neckcloth lay over the back of a chair, but his oyster-colored waistcoat was still buttoned over his open-necked, full-sleeved linen shirt. His face, when she found the courage to steal a glance at it, was heart-stoppingly handsome. The candlelight threw shadows into the taut planes of his cheeks and made a shadow in the cleft of his chin. His hair was darkly golden, reflecting the candleglow in a thousand glimmering pinpoints. Its wavy thickness framed his face, then was drawn back into a black grosgrain ribbon at the nape of his neck.

His eyes—his black-lashed, amber-brown

eyes—swept over her and Dyanna felt her knees tremble weakly beneath her.

"Yes, my dear?" he prompted softly, the simple words sending a queer sort of shiver down Dyanna's spine. "Mrs. Cockerell sent you up to—?"

"To ask what you and your man want."

Deviltry glittered in Justin's eyes. Over Dyanna's head, he glanced toward Bertran, but the valet refused to meet his gaze.

"Just tell Mrs. Cockerell to sent up whatever she has that's ready. And her best bottle of wine."

Grasping either side of her skirt, Dyanna bobbed a curtsy. "Aye, milord," she managed, flushing scarlet beneath his amused gaze.

She turned to leave, but he called out to stop her.

"What's your name, sweetheart?"

"Jenny Flynn, milord," she replied without hesitation.

"All right, Jenny Flynn. Be sure you bring up our meal. Don't let Mrs. Cockerell send anyone else, will you?"

"I won't, milord," she promised, heart bursting with excitement.

A half-hour later, Dyanna grimaced under the weight of the laden supper tray. Turning her back to the door, she kicked at it with her heel.

The door opened and Bertran took the tray from her and carried it to the table. The aroma of roast beef and fresh-baked bread filled the room.

Pushing himself away from the hearth where he had been examining the smoke-tinged painting above the mantelpiece, Justin came toward her.

Dyanna could not help staring. His movements were fluid, feline, captivating, somehow threatening yet entrancing.

Her eyes met his and she realized he had noticed her fascination. Cheeks pinkening, she averted her gaze. "Will there be anything else, milord?" she heard herself asking.

"Have you other guests to attend to?" he asked, seating himself in a chair at the table and stretching out his long legs.

"No, milord."

"Then why don't you stay? Share my dinner. At least have a little wine. I hate to eat alone."

"Alone? But milord—" Dyanna turned just in time to see Bertran disappearing into his bedchambers on one side of the sitting room the two bedchambers shared. In his hands he carried a plate laden with food and a glass of the sweet red wine.

As the door closed behind the valet, Dyanna turned back to find Justin watching her. His handsome face wore an expression of amusement and something else—some indefinable air that touched a place deep inside Dyanna and set it aquiver.

Gratefully she sank into the chair he offered. Her knees felt rubbery and threatened to betray her. She hid her hands in the taffeta folds of her skirt to conceal their trembling.

"Hungry?" DeVille asked. When Dyanna nodded, he pushed a plate of beef and a thick slice of bread and butter toward her. There was only one wine glass so he filled it and set in within easy reach of them both.

Dyanna ate slowly, clumsily, trying to concentrate on the food and ignore the tantalizing heat of the penetrating stare he fixed her with. But her heart was pounding so hard it took her breath away. Her fingers stubbornly refused to cooperate and her throat tightened, making it hard to swallow. The wine, as she sipped it, seemed to go straight to her head, making her feel giddy, almost dizzy, and making the room, though cooled by the night breezes wafting through the open windows, seem close and stifling.

His eyes never seemed to leave her. She could feel them upon her; there was no need to look up to know he was watching her, studying her. She wanted to look at him, examine him, revel in the sheer masculine beauty of him, but she did not dare.

Taking a last sip of the rich, heady wine, she passed her napkin across her lips and laid it aside.

"Finished?" he asked, and she realized, a flush staining her cheeks, that he had stopped eating some time before.

She nodded and he rose, holding out a hand

to her. The hand in which her own was dwarfed was calloused and hard, burnt brown by the sun. It surprised her, for he was obviously a gentleman born and bred, and in her experience, limited though it was, gentlemen seldom performed the kind of manual labor necessary to produce work-toughened hands such as his.

Wordlessly, he led her across the room to the deep, velvet-cushioned window seat. He sat down, leaning into the corner, and drew her down beside him, cradling her against his chest, his arms about her.

The warm fragrance from the forest surrounding them spilled through the open window, borne on the gentle night breezes. Justin closed his eyes and breathed deeply. He sighed, content, as his fingers idly caressed Dyanna's neck just below her ear.

"There's nothing quite like an English spring," he told her softly, then smiled down into her upraised eyes, "unless it's a pretty English girl."

Dyanna shivered. The simple caress of his fingers on the delicate skin of her neck stirred her senses more than the wine she'd consumed at dinner.

"You sound as if you've been away," she said, her voice sounding strange to her own ears.

"I have. I was at sea. And in America."

"America?" Dyanna knew little of America save that it was far away across the wide and perilous ocean and, so her tutors had told her, was populated in the main by a few foolhardy Englishmen and a great many bloodthirsty savages. It sounded forbidding to her, but venturing into such a dangerous place seemed madly adventurous and elevated DeVille even further in her estimation.

"Tell me of America, milord," she begged eagerly.

"Justin," he said.

"Pardon me?"

"Justin. My name. You needn't keep calling me 'milord.'"

"Justin," she repeated obediently. "Tell me, please. Is America truly overrun with wild men who kill white settlers?"

"It happens, unfortunately. But come, this is hardly the kind of talk for a night like this, is it, my pretty?"

Dyanna turned in the circle of his arms until she was kneeling on the cushion beside him. Their faces were level and her eyes met his and were imprisoned by his dark, penetrating gaze. The candles that lit the room were burning low, but his face was no less handsome for the dimness of the light. Her heart fluttered in her breast like the beating wings of an imprisoned bird.

Reaching up, he drew off her cap and her shimmering curls tumbled free, spilling over her shoulders like rivers of molten silver. Justin hesitated as the sight of it sparked some faint memory, but he forced the thought aside. The girl who knelt before him was far too beautiful, the rising desire he felt for her much too urgent, to be quelled by some flickering shadow of the past.

"How fair you are," he murmured, his fingers cupping her face. Slowly, too slowly, they trailed down her cheek, over the delicate edge of her jaw, down the tender curve of her throat to her shoulders. He paused, his eyes boring into hers, searching, questioning: then, finding his reply in the rosy flush of her skin, in the wild pulse that throbbed in the warm hollow of her throat, in the quick, shallow breaths that raced between her moist, parted lips, his hands drew the lawn fichu free of the deep, square neck of her gown.

Dyanna gasped as his fingers brushed gently over the ivory swells of her breasts. His eyes never left her face as he opened the first few fastenings of her bodice. His hands slipped inside and caressed her, cupping the silken flesh, teasing the hardening tips.

Dyanna shuddered as his hands spanned her waist and pulled her toward him. Her head fell back and she buried her fingers in the tawny thickness of his hair as he kissed the taut, rose-pink crests of her breasts.

"Justin," she whispered, pulling his head back.

His eyes met hers for a single, searing instant before he pulled her down to him and

47

covered her lips with his own. His kiss was hard, demanding, burning with a fire that threatened to boil the very blood in her veins.

Dyanna knew she should stop him, sensed that a word from her lips would win her release, but her senses were whirling in a mad, reckless descent she was powerless to stop. Even as her mind screamed a warning, her body arched against his, her arms wound about his neck, and his lips traced the smooth, ivory column of her throat making her want more, so much more of him.

The pounding on the door was like thunder, shattering the fragile, sensual spell that held them both in thrall.

"Milord?" The low, harsh voice of Mr. Cockerell was muffled by the stout oak door. "Milord DeVille?"

"God's teeth!" DeVille snarled, as the innkeeper rattled the latch of the locked door. He gently set Dyanna aside and rose from the window seat.

"Milord DeVille?" Cockerell called again.

"I'm coming!" Justin shouted, adding, "damn you!" beneath his breath.

Moving toward the door, he didn't see the look of stark shock on Dyanna's pale face.

"DeVille?" she breathed, horrified.

"Just a moment, my sweet," he said off-handedly, "let me see what this rude bastard wants."

Dyanna stared after him as he crossed the

48

room. For a moment she was unable to move, paralyzed by shock, horrified by what had nearly happened between them. And then, impelled to action at last by the sound of the key turning in the iron lock, she fled to Justin's bedchamber and disappeared inside.

Justin, opening the door to admit the inn-keeper, smiled. So, she was going to hide in the bedroom, was she? Just as well. That was where he had intended to take her in a very few moments.

"What is it, Mr. Cockerell?" he asked impatiently.

"When ye got 'ere, milord, ye asked after a girl as had run away. Ye said she might be wearin' a grey dress. Would it be like this one, milord?" He held out Dyanna's grey dress, which she'd left in the pantry.

Justin examined the dress. It was exactly like the ones he'd seen on the students at the Pettigrew Academy.

"Yes! This could be the one. Where did you find it?"

"In the pantry, milord. It belonged to a girl my wife found in the stables. Fixin' to sleep in one of the stalls, she was. She said as how she had no money. She said 'er father'd died not long since and she was on 'er way to London to make 'er way."

"Where is this girl?" Justin demanded eagerly.

"She was up 'ere, milord." Cockerell

glanced around the room. "My wife offered 'er a meal an' a bed if she'd work as a maid for tonight, our regular maid bein' a mite the worse for gin, if you take my meanin'."

"Here? The maid? The blonde? But—" The blood drained from his face, leaving it a chalky grey. The little flicker of remembrance that had touched him at the sight of Dyanna's hair returned to him. He'd seen that pale, silver hair before, and those aqua eyes—seen them in the face of Elizabeth Conway, Viscountess McBride. She was the very image of her mother.

"Dyanna," he breathed.

"Dyanna?" Cockerell frowned. "She said her name was Jenny, milord. Jenny Flynn."

Leaving Cockerell to stare after him, confused, Justin strode to the bedchamber door and flung it open. As he'd feared, the room was empty. The hall door stood ajar in mute testimony of Dyanna's precipitous flight.

Turning back to Cockerell, Justin ordered a search of the inn, its outbuildings, and as much of the surrounding forest as possible.

But even as lanterns were being distributed to the grooms and postboys, Dyanna was stumbling away into the night-shrouded forest, her meager possessions in their haphazard bundle clutched to her heaving breast.

Chapter Four

The city of London spread out around Dyanna, its noises deafening to ears used to the softer sounds of the country, its smells flooding her nose until it seemed she could scarcely breathe. Her eyes darted left and right, exploring the windows of shops and houses, mansions and hovels. She clutched her bundle in one arm and with the other hand picked at stray wisps of straw that clung to her hair and clothing—souvenirs of the cart in which she'd begged a ride to the city. Lifting a strand of her hair to her nose, she sniffed it, hoping against hope that she did not smell like the sheep that had been her companions in the back of the cart.

After what seemed an eternity, Dyanna

found herself in Grosvenor Square. Gathering her courage, she approached the door of Number 21, the London residence of Horatio Culpepper, Marquess of Summersleigh, one-time boon companion of her grandfather, Lord Lincoln.

All around her stood the stately homes of London's most fashionable society. Fine carriages drawn by blooded horses drew up before one or another of them and disgorged elegantly dressed ladies and gentlemen, and more than one of them stole a glance or two at the disheveled girl in rose-colored taffeta who pounded at the door of Number 21 with one hand and clutched a lumpy bundle in the other.

At long last the door swung open and a tall, grey-haired man fixed her with a baleful glare.

"Begone," he ordered. "Away, I say. You'll get no handout here."

Dyanna's sea-blue eyes glittered as she treated him to her haughtiest stare. "I wish to see Lord Summersleigh," she announced icily. "You will tell his Lordship that Miss Dyanna McBride is here."

The manservant hesitated. She was dressed like a tavernmaid, but her finely-boned beauty bespoke breeding above the ordinary. Her voice, her tones and accents, were not those of the rabble that occasionally turned up— usually at the back door—begging charity.

"McBride?" he repeated.

52

"Dyanna McBride," she confirmed. "The Honorable Dyanna McBride. My father was Lord McBride. My grandfather the Earl of Lincoln." She scowled, her arched brows lowering. "I have come a long way to see the marquess, my good man, and I do not appreciate being kept waiting on the stoop like a milkmaid."

The manservant, knowledgeable as all servants were of the gossip circulating in society, knew the tales of Rakehell McBride. He was something of a London legend. Perhaps it was not so unthinkable after all to find Rakehell's daughter at the door, unchaperoned and dressed like a barmaid.

"Come in, Miss McBride," he said at last, bowing as she passed him and swept into the entrance hall. "I will tell his lordship you are here."

Dropping her bundle to the marble floor, Dyanna gazed about the long, oval room. Statues of Roman emperors stood in niches along the walls and medallions painted in rich reds and golds covered the high, domed ceiling with its cascading chandelier of sparkling crystal.

"Dyanna?" a voice called, the word softened by distance. "Dyanna McBride? Are you certain that is what she said?"

"Quite certain, m'lord," the manservant replied.

"Little Dyanna, here? In London? Alone? Bring her in, man. Be quick about it."

Dyanna pretended to study the details of the statue nearest her as the returning footsteps of the manservant drew nearer.

"Miss McBride?" he said, framed in the open doorway. "His lordship wishes you to attend him in the saloon."

Leaving her bundle in the entrance hall, Dyanna followed the servant through an exquisite anteroom hung in scarlet Spitalfields silk and into a room decorated in cream and green. It seemed as cool and clean as a new spring day.

"Dyanna?" A stooped figure in black and fawn rose from an armchair near the yawning fireplace. On his head sat an old fashioned, full-bottomed wig that cascaded in thick, brown curls to his narrow shoulders. "Little Dyanna! How long it has—"

As he spoke he turned toward where she stood bathed in the sunshine streaming through the tall Palladian windows.

"Little—" he began again, then stopped. "M'God," he breathed, lifting his quizzing glass to his right eye. "Has it been as long as this? No longer a pretty child. No, by God. You are the image of your mother. Turn around, my girl."

Slowly Dyanna did as he asked, turning in a circle before his bemused eyes. As she faced him once more, she clasped her hands behind her, feeling little more than a child eagerly awaiting the approval of a favorite uncle.

"I was wrong," the marquess decided. "You are not the image of your mother. No. You have a spark, my child, a fire that is pure McBride. Your mother was a beauty. Gad! What a beauty she was. But for all her looks she was an insipid little creature. You have her beauty. And more. But you have the spirit of your father. I'm not certain if that is good or bad."

With his quizzing glass, he motioned toward a chair facing the one he had occupied when she'd entered the saloon.

"Sit down, Dyanna, and tell me what brings you to London." He examined her gown as she moved toward the chair. "I say, your father hasn't bankrupted you, has he? You've not taken work in a tavern, I hope."

"No, my lord," Dyanna assured him.

"Here now, here now, none of that. You used to call me Uncle Horatio."

"Very well, then, Uncle Horatio," Dyanna amended, warming to the old man who, along with her grandfather, treated her like a pet more than a child. "I've run away from school, Uncle."

"Run away? But why?"

"My father is dead."

"I know, child. Pity, that. But he'd been heading in that direction since your mother died."

Dyanna nodded, acknowledging the truth in the remark. "He left me and my estate in the care of a guardian, and, so Miss Pettigrew told me, I was to remain at school. Oh, Uncle, I hate that school!"

"And this guardian," the Marquess said sourly, thoroughly annoyed that he, as Dyanna's grandfather's best friend had not been given the care of Dyanna and her fortune, "he will not provide you with a home?"

"He is a monster of a monstrous family. A pirate and worse! He means me ill, Uncle. I know it!"

"Here now, child! He has told you this?"

"No. But I heard the Misses Pettigrew speaking of him."

"Who is he? It may be I know him. He may not be as black as those two old spinsters paint him."

"He is Justin DeVille. Lord DeVille."

"Good God! The Devil you say!"

"Then it is true!" Dyanna cried. "You know him to be a villain!"

"No, no. Calm yourself. I know only the name DeVille by reputation. I knew his father, Sebastian DeVille, most casually. Of the son, I know only that he is a privateer. Successful, as I've heard. Of his character, I know nothing."

"Nor I," Dyanna admitted. "But he is to be my guardian until I am of age or until I marry. I cannot bear it, Uncle. I cannot! Please, help me."

"I can do nothing to set your father's will aside. You are his heiress. You are not of age.

You are his to dispose of as he wishes. My only advice would be to marry as soon as possible."

"And pass from my guardian's rule to my husband's," Dyanna murmured sourly.

"Pass from the rule of a guardian not of your choosing to that of a husband of your choice. There is a deal of difference between 'em as I see it, child."

Dyanna nodded. "I see the sense in what you say, Uncle. But the fact remains that I must give myself into Lord DeVille's care in the meanwhile."

"That you must. Is he in London, I wonder?"

"If not, he soon will be, I'm sure," Dyanna said cryptically, wondering how close on her heels the handsome Lord DeVille might be following.

"Then I will have my solicitors contact him. In the meanwhile, you must stay here, at Summersleigh House. I shall invite my grandson to dinner tonight. It will do you good to make the acquaintance of someone closer to your own age."

Flushing, Dyanna plucked at the skirt of her rose taffeta gown. "I'm afraid I have not the clothes to make a decent showing at even a private dinner, sir. All I have is this and what I managed to bring away from school." She wrinkled her nose. "Grey linen."

"Never fear. I shall send the housekeeper

out to see what she can find for you. I'm confident she will be able to find something that will do until other arrangements can be made."

Impulsively, Dyanna went to the marquess's chair and knelt beside it.

"I knew you would help me, dearest Uncle," she said feelingly.

The marquess let a thick strand of her pale silver hair slide through his fingers. "Your grandfather was my closest friend, my dear. Your mother was like a daughter to me. I only wish I could have done more for you after your grandfather's death." He pinched her cheek lightly. "Now I think you should be about finding something to wear for dinner. Let me call a maid to take you upstairs."

Rising from his chair, the marquess went to the fireplace and tugged the embroidered silk bell-pull that hung beside it.

As he stood there, awaiting the maid's arrival, he wrinkled his long, hooked nose and sniffed the air.

"I'll have to set someone to cleaning this room. Damme if it don't smell like a sheep pen in here."

Blushing, Dyanna said nothing. She dropped a curtsy to the old marquess and turned to follow the maid out of the saloon. Under her breath, she cursed her woolly traveling companions.

Chapter Five

"It's monstrous, I tell you. Monstrous!" Lord Geoffrey Culpepper repeated for the seventh time.

Seated on a gilded sofa at a discreet distance from Dyanna, the Marquess's grandson —his heir since the death of Geoffrey's father, the Marquess's only son—fixed his grandfather's guest with sympathetic eyes.

Dyanna toyed with the ruffling of her pale green silk skirts. When the Marquess had asked her to stay, she had not expected him to entertain her by summoning company. Moreover, when he had said the wisest course for her would be to marry as quickly as possible, she had not expected him to produce a suitor that very night. But that was precisely what Lord Geoffrey Culpepper seemed to be.

"As I was telling Dyanna," the marquess said, "she should marry, and soon. I don't hold with a young girl's fortune and care being left in the hands of an outsider. Family! Such concerns belong in one's own family."

Dyanna thought it tactful not to remind the marquess that the death of her father had left her without a family. She knew the old gentleman regarded himself as a sort of uncle once removed. She feared it might hurt his feelings to remind him that there were, in fact, no blood ties between them.

"Marriage," Geoffrey pronounced grandly, an elegant sweep of his hand dislodging a lock of his gleaming, dark brown hair. "I own that I have never considered it." He turned his liquid gaze once more toward Dyanna. "I wonder now if that was because I had never found a lady worthy of my love."

"I am certain you shall find her, sir," Dyanna said quickly. "Someday."

Seizing her hand in his, Geoffrey raised it to his lips. "At the risk of appearing impetuous, Miss McBride, I wonder if I may not have found her already."

One glance at the marquess's beaming face told Dyanna she could expect no rescue from her fond 'uncle.'

As if reading her thoughts, the marquess rose. "I regret, children, I am no longer of a

60

constitution to enjoy late hours. I shall bid you both good-night and retire."

"I also—" Dyanna began quickly, but the marquess's raised hand silenced her.

"I won't hear of it, m'dear," he said. "You've been shut away from society too long. Stay and enjoy Geoffrey's company. Geoffrey, I expect you to entertain this pretty young lady."

"I shall do my best, Grandfather," Geoffrey promised, sweeping the old marquess an elegant bow.

"Good-night, m'dear," the marquess said fondly, kissing Dyanna lightly on the temple.

"Good-night, my lord," Dyanna murmured. "And thank you for your hospitality."

"It is the least I could do."

With a pleased smile for the handsome pair before him, the elderly gentleman left the room, pointedly closing the tall, gleaming doors behind him.

An awkward silence reigned for some moments while Geoffrey and Dyanna each waited for the other to open a conversation. At last, Dyanna said:

"Your grandfather is very kind, sir."

"Exceedingly," Geoffrey agreed. "To us both."

"I do not take your meaning."

Geoffrey brushed a speck from the sleeve of his lilac velvet frock coat. "He has given you shelter and the promise of friendship, Miss

McBride. And he has brought you into my life. We are both the beneficiaries of his kindness. I hope our acquaintance will be a lengthy one."

Dyanna swallowed hard. Geoffrey was an attractive man in a foppish sort of way. But she felt none of the confusing, tantalizing feelings that had assailed her from the moment she first laid eyes on Justin DeVille at the Angel Inn. What could it mean? She did not quite dare think of it.

"I wonder," Geoffrey said, strolling to the tall windows that overlooked the small, walled garden behind the house, "how your father could have left you in the clutches of a DeVille."

Dyanna lifted her shoulders. "I know nothing of the matter, sir, save that they were friends of long standing. I have heard the Lord DeVille is a privateer, but—"

"I was not merely speaking of Justin DeVille," Geoffrey interrupted, turning toward her, his hands clasped behind his back. "I meant any DeVille. There are dark legends attached to that family. Legends that may be more fact than fiction."

"I met Lord DeVille once," Dyanna admitted, a rosy stain pinkening her cheeks as she remembered what had passed between them at the Angel Inn. "He is an exceedingly handsome man."

"Looks do not signify, my dear," Geoffrey

chided, more than a touch of annoyance in his tone. "Does it not say in the Bible that Lucifer himself was the most beautiful of the angels before the fall?"

"Lord DeVille was most charming. I find it difficult to believe his blood as tainted as you say." Dyanna stopped, wondering at herself for her defense of her guardian. "Although," she added hurriedly, "Miss Pettigrew, one of the mistresses of the school I attended, did compare Lord Justin's father to the Devil."

"As well she might," Geoffrey decreed. "You know they called Sebastian DeVille Lord Lucifer."

Dyanna's ever-fertile imagination snapped to attention. "Lord Lucifer?" she repeated, eyes wide.

"Oh, yes. In his day, there was much speculation about him. They said he was a sorcerer. A necromancer. He was as notorious as Sir Francis Dashwood and his Hell Fire Club. In Devonshire, Sebastian DeVille is a part of the local folklore. They say that in Cheswyck—the village that lies near the DeVille lands— mothers of disobedient children tell them Lord Lucifer will get them if they don't behave."

Dyanna shivered, a thrill coursing down her spine. Here was every Gothick novel she'd ever read come to life! Here was excitement far beyond anything Jenny Flynn had known.

"Was he truly as wicked as all that?" she

asked, a breathless hush in her voice. "Were the rumors true?"

"He was the stuff of novels, apparently," Geoffrey assured her, wondering if the thought of being delivered into the clutches of the son of such a monster might not frighten Dyanna into accepting a proposal. "I'll wager you like novels, don't you? Gothick novels full of specters and curses."

Dyanna felt the hot blush that pinkened her cheeks. "Yes," she admitted guiltily. "I do. I expect you think me foolish."

"Not at all. I suspect more people read them than will ever admit it. I was merely going to say that there was such a book written, so it was said, about Sebastian DeVille. It was reputed to be a thinly disguised account of his foul deeds."

"Really?" Dyanna breathed. "What was it called?"

Geoffrey expertly feigned reluctance. "I should not have mentioned it. Please forgive me. Lord DeVille is your guardian, after all, and doubtless has suffered enough over his father's soiled reputation. And, after all, it was only rumor which named Sebatian DeVille the model for the novel's wicked Lord Lucifer Wolfe."

"Even so," Dyanna persisted. "I wish I could see the book."

"There may be a copy here," Geoffrey mused. "But no, it would be wrong of me to show it to you. I could not be responsible for coloring your opinion of your guardian's family by giving you a book which is likely no more than the gleanings of some author's fevered imagination."

"It has been so long since I had a new novel to read," Dyanna murmured, pouting prettily. "Please let me see it, Geoffrey."

"How can I resist such a pretty request?" he smiled. "But you must promise to treat it as a work of fiction and remember it is only malicious rumor that names Lord Justin's father as the model for the character."

Solemnly, Dyanna promised, but Geoffrey knew that the wheels of her imagination were already in motion, turning Justin's father into some dark and monstrous creature. Taking up a candle, Geoffrey led the way to the library.

The library of Summersleigh House had a closed, abandoned air that told Dyanna without words that the marquess and his family were not much given to reading. She waited in the shaft of light spilling through the open door while Geoffrey lit the tall, dusty wax tapers of a five-branched candelabrum.

"Let me see," he murmured thoughtfully as Dyanna joined him beside a gilded library table topped with a polished slab of green malachite. "I saw the book in here once. Where was it?"

"Perhaps someone moved it," Dyanna suggested, though the dust that frosted the shelves and the books made it seem unlikely that even the marquess's maids had seen this room recently.

"Moved it?" Geoffrey asked, squinting as he peered at row after row of finely bound volumes. "Whyever should anyone do that?"

"If they read it, they may not have put it back in the same—"

"My dear Miss McBride, these books were bought by my grandfather years ago, when he refurbished Summersleigh House. I doubt if more than a dozen have been taken from their original places since and even fewer new volumes have been added. Ah—" He plucked a thin volume bound in scarlet leather from a shelf. "Here it is."

Dyanna took the book from his outstretched hand. On the spine, in tarnished gold letters, she read:

The Life and Death of Wicked
Lord Lucifer Wolfe

"Lord Lucifer Wolfe," Dyanna repeated. "You did say they called Sebastian DeVille 'Lord Lucifer,' didn't you?"

"Now Dyanna, you promised to read it only as a work of fiction and forget the rumors," Geoffrey reminded her, secretly delighted that she seemed so susceptible to suggestion. "Just because they called the former Lord DeVille 'Lord Lucifer' does not make him guilty of all the misdeeds of the man in this book. He is not, after all, here to defend himself and it is not fair of us to libel him—even now, so long after his apparent death.''

"Apparent death?'' Dyanna repeated, hugging the slim book to her breast.

"Yes. He disappeared, you see. One night there was a terrible storm. Lightning struck Castle DeVille—the DeVille country seat. The lightning set the castle ablaze. In the morning, the smoldering ruins were searched as thoroughly as possible, but Sebastian DeVille was nowhere to be found. It was presumed he perished in the fire, but his body was never recovered. Local legend has it that he had made a pact with the Devil, and Satan came at the height of the storm and took Sebastian away to Hell.'' He paused, gazing down into Dyanna's wide-eyed, fascinated face. "But then, of course, country folk are notoriously superstitious, are they not?''

"And Justin,'' Dyanna could not resist asking, "where was he when all this was happening?''

"Oh, he was there. He was a young child. Sebastian's wife, Lady Barbara DeVille, was the daughter of a baronet who had made his fortune in trade. He married her for her fortune and to have an heir. Gossip said he treated her cruelly, that he flaunted his infidelities beneath her nose. She died in a fall from the highest tower of the castle.'' Geoffrey stifled a smile as the audible intake of Dyanna's breath. "Some said,'' he went on, his tone low and intimate, "that she jumped. Some said she was pushed, though opinions vary as to whether her murderer was Sebastian himself, or his mistress."

Dyanna's pent-up breath was expelled in a long 'ooooh' of horrified surprise. "His mistress!"

"Hmmm. Georgiana, Lady Naysmith. Her husband's lands adjoined the DeVille lands."

"How evil it all seems," Dyanna whispered.

Taking her arm, Geoffrey led her to a chair near the elegant, if grimy, bowed window. Beneath his hand, he could feel her trembling.

"Now, Dyanna, we don't know if any of it is true. As I said, it is all rumors and gossip, which we both know are often false and malicious. And this"—he indicated the book that lay in her lap—"is merely a story. It may be that none of it has anything to do with Lord Justin's family—excepting, of course, that both Lord and Lady DeVille perished under mysterious circumstances."

"If Lord Sebastian actually did perish," Dyanna whispered.

"The courts were satisfied that he had and so must we be. When Justin came of age, he inherited his father's titles and lands."

Dyanna chewed her lip and Geoffrey frowned, apparently troubled but secretly delighted that the tales of Justin's notorious family should have such an obvious and pro-

Certainly not," Geoffrey agreed, thinking

found effect on her. "Perhaps it would be better if you did not read—"

"No!" Dyanna clutched the book tighter as he reached for it. "I want to read it, Geoffrey. I must."

Geoffrey's heart fluttered. Even though he had tried to dissuade her from connecting the villainous Lord Lucifer Wolfe with Justin's father, he knew she would subconsciously attribute Sebastian DeVille—and, he hoped, Justin—with the wickedness related in the book. If her mind were filled with terror at the thought of being given over to a man whose family history was so blackened with shame, it might be easier to convince her to marry him. She was a beautiful girl, heiress to an immense fortune. He could not risk losing her.

"If you insist." He took her hand and held it gently. "But remember, even if the rumors about Sebastian DeVille are true, Justin is not to blame for what went before. Doubtless he is a good man, honest and kind. You must not allow this book to prejudice you against him when you don't even know him."

Dyanna's sea-blue eyes glittered with unshed tears. "How very good you are, Geoffrey," she murmured. "I promise to give Justin the benefit of the doubt. After all, the wildness of my father's family is well known, but that does not mean that I have inherited it."

"Certainly not," Geoffrey agreed, thinking

to himself that any well-bred girl who could pack a rag-tag bundle and set out alone for London was no timid flower. She was a wild one—a true McBride. But if she chose not to believe it, he would not contradict her. There would be time enough later, after she was his, to break that spirit and tame that wildness.

He noticed that she was gazing longingly at the book, even lifting the cover to steal a glance at the frontispiece.

"I think it is time I took my leave," he suggested tactfully. "It is getting late and you must be tired after your long journey."

"I am tired," she agreed, too quickly, wishing only to retire to her room and begin reading the fascinating, dreadful tale of Lord Lucifer Wolfe.

"Then I will bid you sweet dreams."

Lifting her hand to his lips, Geoffrey kissed it tenderly, his eyes fixed upon hers in a glance filled with meaning and unconcealed longing. "Until tomorrow."

"Until tomorrow, Geoffrey," Dyanna whispered, trying without much success to match his tone.

Demurely she walked with him to the grand entrance hall and stood, a sweet smile curving her full lips, until he had disappeared out the door. Then and only then did she catch up her billowing skirts and petticoats and race up the grand, curving staircase to her room.

Chapter Six

Dyanna lay on the canopied bed in her room, bathed in the golden glow of a single candle, the fascinating book cradled in her hands. The book about Jenny Flynn she'd been so careful to bring with her from the Academy lay forgotten in a drawer. This new tale was far more interesting.

As she always did before beginning what promised to be a particularly interesting read, Dyanna hesitated. She knew that the sooner she started the book, the sooner she would finish, and all the delicious anticipation would be behind her. Still, her curiosity was far stronger than her desire to savor the waiting. With eager fingers she opened the book and turned past the title page where she read:

Sandra DuBay

The Life and Death of Wicked
Lord Lucifer Wolfe
-A True Story-
By A LADY

Turning a few more pages, she read the
opening lines:

> *"The village of Rottinghurst cowered in
> the shadow of Wolfe Hall like a mongrel
> dog brought to heel by a cruel master. It
> huddled there as it had for centuries. Not
> war nor plague nor time could ease the
> web of fear the Hall wove about the
> village and its inhabitants. The turnings
> of the world mattered little to the
> villagers. For their world was ruled by the
> changeable whims of Lord Lucifer Wolfe,
> the Wicked Earl of Legend, the Monster
> of Wolfe Hall."*

Dyanna thought of what Geoffrey had said
—that the book was said to be a thinly disguised account of the evil actions of Sebastian
DeVille, Justin's father. But surely, if that were
true, some legal action would have been
brought against the author. Surely Justin
would not have allowed his father to be portrayed in such a scandalous light. Unless, she
told herself, unless there was enough truth to
make legal action futile. She stroked the leather cover. She meant to savor the book, truth or

72

not, and discover what kind of man Justin's father was reputed to have been. In doing so, she hoped to learn what kind of man Justin might be.

A yawn overtook her, a reminder that she had not had more than a few hours' sleep in the past three days.

There seemed no use trying to read any more, much as she wanted to. The words blurred before her exhausted eyes and the sentences could not penetrate her dulled senses.

Sliding the book far beneath the topmost feather mattress, Dyanna blew out the candle and slipped between the lavender-scented sheets. With another great yawn, she abandoned herself to sleep and to dreams of Justin. Dressed in black, his angelically fair masculine beauty became diabolical; he swept through the ruins of a burnt-out castle, a caped cloak swirling about him, pursuing her for dark reasons even her unconscious mind dared not contemplate.

The following morning dawned clear and warm. Dyanna awoke late to the sound of birdsong and the clip-clop of horses' hooves from outside in the square.

Stifling a yawn, she slid her hand beneath the mattress and retrieved the book from where she'd hidden it the night before.

Turning over the first few crisp, yellowed pages, she took up where she'd left off:

"Lord Lucifer Wolfe was a handsome man, dreadfully handsome as only the truly wicked can be. He gave his allegiance to no mortal man. His sovereign Lord was the Prince of Darkness. His religion was the Black Arts. His piercing golden eyes could look into the heart, the very soul, of the most pious of men. He could divine the mind's most secret thoughts. His was the power to fascinate . . ."

A light knock at the door was followed by the appearance of a muslin-capped girl whose unruly titian curls strayed about the shoulders of her demure grey gown.

"Morning, miss," she said cheerfully. "It is near eleven and Mrs. Critchley said you'd be awake by now."

"Mrs. Critchley?" Dyanna repeated.

"The housekeeper, miss."

"And who are you?"

The girl bobbed a curtsy. "Putney, miss. Charlotte Putney. I'm to be your maid, if it pleases you."

"It does please me, Charlotte," Dyanna decided, liking the spark of vitality in the girl's bright blue eyes. "Very much."

"Would you be wantin' breakfast now, miss?"

"No. But I would like a bath."

"It's been ordered. It's nearly ready."

Climbing out of bed, Dyanna pulled on the

dressing gown that matched the nightdress she'd found laid out for her on the bed. With a last longing look at the book, she left for the sweetly scented bath that awaited her down the hall.

When she re-entered the room, her damp hair pinned atop her head, Dyanna found Charlotte curled in a chair, reading. It was obvious she found the book as fascinating as Dyanna had, for she appeared not to notice her mistress's return. One finger was thrust into her mouth and she gnawed at the ragged nail as she read, her eyes wide as saucers.

"Charlotte?" Dyanna said quietly.

With a shrill little scream, the maid dropped the book and thrust herself to her feet.

Dyanna laughed. "I didn't mean to frighten you," she lied blithely.

"Oh, miss! What a story! That man must be the Devil himself!"

"A close acquaintance at the very least," Dyanna agreed, sitting at her dressing table.

"Thank the good Lord 'tis only a story."

"Actually, it is not only a story," Dyanna disagreed, watching in the lace-draped mirror as Charlotte went to work on her hair. "Supposedly, it is based on a real person. The father of a gentleman—well, a person of my acquaintance."

The maid shuddered. "I hope he never comes here, Miss."

"I hope so too," Dyanna agreed fervently.

Falling into a reverie, Dyanna could not help wondering how much of what she'd read was true and how much was simply libel and slander invented by people with nothing better to do than create and spread gossip. It was not impossible that most of it was the latter, though certainly there were men like Lord Lucifer Wolfe. Less than twenty years had passed since Sir Francis Dashwood and his Hell Fire Club had practiced Devil-worship at Medmenham Abbey.

And there were men with the power to fascinate. Dyanna had read accounts of the famous Austrian, Friedrich Mesmer, who put people into trances in which they could be bent to his will. He had even gone so far as to claim he could cure disease by suggestion alone.

But if Geoffrey's book were to be believed, Sebastian DeVille—or his fictional counterpart, Lord Lucifer Wolfe—had powers far beyond even these, powers bestowed upon him by Satan himself. Dark, supernatural powers. But surely that couldn't be?

Both she and the skittish Charlotte started as Maria, the maid who had shown Dyanna to her room the night before, appeared in the opened door.

"Pardon, miss, but his lordship asks that you attend him in the saloon. There is a gentleman here asking for you."

"A gentleman? Lord Geoffrey?"

"Oh, no, miss. Another gentleman." Maria rolled her cornflower blue eyes. "So handsome! Tall, with dark golden hair and eyes that send shivers down—"

"His name, Maria! Tell me quickly!"

The maid seemed startled by Dyanna's near-panic. "Why, I believe it was DeVille, miss. Yes, that was it. Lord DeVille."

The room seemed to tilt around Dyanna. She felt Charlotte's hand at her elbow, steadying her.

"Are you ill, miss?" she asked, exchanging a curious glance with Maria. "Should we send for—"?

"No. No one," Dyanna interrupted. "I'm quite all right. It was only . . . " She waved a dismissing hand. "Tell his lordship I'll be down directly, Maria."

The older maid left and Dyanna rose and went to the wardrobe where a selection of the clothing she'd been given had been arranged for her use.

"Justin," she whispered. "How did he find me? Could it—could it possibly be true—?"

Her eyes went to the book on the chair. Could Justin's father truly have possessed supernatural powers? Could Justin also . . . ? No! It couldn't be! And yet, he was here, below, waiting for her.

Having been raised in the country where old wives' tales were accepted as fact and superstitions were taken seriously, Dyanna had heard, since her earliest years amongst the villagers and gypsies, tales of witches and warlocks, of demons and sorcerers. Nor were such beliefs confined to the poor. There was scarcely a great manor house or castle in England that did not boast its Grey Lady or Phantom Monk or haunted room. Few aristocratic families were without some tradition of death—the appearance of a mournful specter, the tolling of a long-silent clock, the approach of the coach of bones that foretold the death of a family member. Suicides were still buried at a crossroads, a stake through their hearts to keep their restless spirits from rising and wandering the night.

Dyanna had shivered with delicious horror at those tales. She'd believed them with the unquestioning faith of country folk who were less cynical than their worldly city cousins. As she'd grown older, she'd come to view them with a healthy skepticism, though her interest in Gothick novels was surely an extension of those early beliefs. But now, faced with Justin's uncanny appearance, she wondered if she might not have been left in the clutches of some sorcerer from whom she could neither run nor hide.

"Is he the one, miss?" Charlotte asked, her voice hushed, as she helped Dyanna into a gown of pink muslin.

"Yes," Dyanna breathed. "He's the one.

He's come for me, Charlotte. I am his ward. I am at his mercy."

"Oh, miss! Surely his lordship and Lord Geoffrey will never let him take you."

"There is nothing they can do, I fear. I must go with him."

Charlotte hesitated, then fumbled with the neck of her gown. With trembling fingers, she drew out the only remembrance she had from her long-dead mother. From a long gold chain depended an exquisite gold crucifix. Slipping it over Dyanna's head, she tucked the crucifix down inside the rose-ribboned neckline of Dyanna's gown.

The two young women gazed at each other for a tense moment and then, with a brief hug, Dyanna left her maid. Squaring her shoulders, she left the room and marched down the corridor toward the stairs.

Below, in the saloon, Justin listened half-heartedly while the marquess lectured him on the duties and responsibilities of a guardian. His golden eyes roamed the room, admiring the furnishings, storing details of a cornice, a mantel, a chandelier, to be incorporated into the building of Wildwood.

There had been nothing supernatural or diabolical about his discovery of Dyanna's whereabouts. The information had come to him through that most reliable of sources—backstairs gossip.

One of the marquess's footmen had slipped away the night before and gone to his favorite pub, the Pear Tree. There he could not help repeating the story of the Honorable Miss McBride for the edification of one and all. The story, much repeated and embellished, had been overheard by one of the footmen of the Duke of Queensberry, who happened to be a neighbor of Lord DeVille in Piccadilly. Upon arriving home, the footman had told the butler, who had told the Duke's valet, who was a friend of Bertran, Justin's own valet. Having lost no time in imparting the information, Bertran revealed to his master the whereabouts of his errant ward. Soon after breakfast, Justin began preparations for retrieving Dyanna.

He was now, as the clock struck mid-day, beginning to wish he had left well enough alone. The marquess droned on and on. It was some time before Justin realized he had stopped speaking and had fixed him with an expectant stare.

"I beg your pardon, my lord?" Justin said quickly.

"You were not attending," the marquess scolded. "This is important, m'boy. I said, I wish you to consider relinquishing Dyanna's guardianship to me. After all, her grandfather was my greatest friend. If her father had not borne a grudge against his father-in-law, I have no doubt I should have been named

Dyanna's guardian. Certainly, had Rakehell died before Lord Lincoln, her care would have been left to me."

"No doubt, my lord," Justin admitted freely. "But the fact remains that it was not."

"Still, it was to me Dyanna came for shelter. I should think that would carry some weight with you. And only think, sir. You are a young man. Unmarried. You have spent much of your time at sea. Surely Dyanna would be better here, in London, where she could enter society and meet the kind of people her breeding and heritage—"

"Yes, yes, my lord," Justin interrupted wearily. "I understand what it is you are saying."

"Then you will consider my proposal, sir?" the marquess persisted. He had earmarked Dyanna for Geoffrey from the moment she'd appeared at Summersleigh House. Her fortune would go far toward restoring various properties that would one day be Geoffrey's. And, much as the old gentleman hated to admit it, even in the privacy of his own thoughts, the young pup did seem to have a way of letting money slip through his fingers. A fabulously rich wife was precisely what was needed. The thought of a catch of Dyanna's potential going to live beneath the roof of a man of Justin DeVille's looks and his family's reputation was a serious threat to the marquess's plans.

Justin sighed. Perhaps the marquess was

right, he thought. After all, the primary responsibility of a guardian was to see one's ward launched in society, guided into marriage with a suitable husband. For himself, he had no taste for London society. The mad whirl of the Season held no attraction for him. To attend the balls and dinners and breakfasts and theaters and operas for the express purpose of exposing Dyanna to throngs of eligible males was distasteful to him. And yet, would it not be unfair of him to refuse her such opportunities merely because of his own aversions?

"I see the sense of what you are saying, my lord," he allowed at last. "The matter is worthy of long and serious thought. I will tell you now, however, that the thought of relinquishing Dyanna's guardianship is—"

The saloon door opened on a soft knock, and Dyanna appeared. The pliant, pale pink muslin of her gown whispered over the carpet as she entered the room. The rose satin bows that ran down the front of her gown gleamed as she passed through a shaft of sunlight. Stopping before the marquess and the earl, she sank into a deep and graceful curtsy. As she bent, the long, shimmering ringlets into which Charlotte had coaxed her silvery hair fell forward over her shoulders. They brushed her breasts, which swelled tantalizingly against the low, round neckline of her gown.

Justin swallowed hard as his tawny eyes

followed the gleaming lines of the fine gold chain that disappeared into the lush, ivory valley of her breasts. As Dyanna rose, he caught the briefest glimpse of her aqua-blue eyes before they were concealed by the thick, curling lashes of her lowered lids.

He could not take his eyes off the vision before him. He had never seen a more beautiful woman. He had thought her lovely at the Angel Inn but now . . . now . . . He knew he could not give her up. He knew that he could not allow someone else to keep her, see her, shelter her beneath another roof. The sudden violence of his possessiveness shocked even him.

"You were saying, sir," the marquess prompted eagerly, leaning forward in his chair. "The thought of relinquishing Dyanna's guardianship is—?"

"Is out of the question," Justin finished softly. "I was appointed her guardian, my lord, and I intend to remain so." He turned an unrelenting stare at the elderly aristocrat. "Dyanna is my ward. And if you will instruct your servants to pack whatever belongings she has, I will take her home now."

Chapter Seven

As they rode along South Audley Street toward Piccadilly, Dyanna stole a sideways glance at Justin. The marquess had not tried to hide his reluctance to let her go, even though he knew he could not legally stop Justin. That the old lord had insisted Dyanna take the small but lovely wardrobe his housekeeper had managed to obtain for her was a mark of his kindness, his genuine affection for her, Dyanna thought. The gowns and accessories would tide her over until a dressmaker could provide her with her own things. The two small trunks rode in the carriage behind them and, guarding them, rode Charlotte, whom the marquess had insisted accompany Dyanna over Justin's protests that he had maidservants aplenty to see to the needs of his ward.

But the mystery that remained, the question that plagued Dyanna, was how Justin had found her so quickly.

Nervously threading the ribbons trimming her feathered bonnet through her fingers, Dyanna took a deep breath and said:

"My lord?"

Justin arched his brows, though his gaze never wavered from the street before them. "Hmmm?"

"How did you find me?"

A deep crevice appeared in his taut, tanned cheek as he smiled. A low chuckle rumbled deep in his throat.

"I have my ways, my dear," he said cryptically.

Dyanna's eyes narrowed as she thought of the book tucked in among the clothing in one of the little trunks.

"What ways?" she asked, holding her breath.

Justin hesitated, loath to tell her the information had come to him via a network of gossiping servants.

"Oh," he said at last, his tone airy, "I looked into my crystal ball and there you were."

Dyanna felt her heart thud sickeningly in her chest. Glancing over her shoulder at Charlotte, she saw the girl surreptitiously crossing herself.

Wondering at her silence, Justin looked at

his ward. To his surprise, he found her deathly pale and obviously shaken.

"Dyanna," he said, amused, "I was only teasing you."

She said nothing, but as they turned in between the grand iron gates of DeVille House, she wondered at the vagaries of a fate that enabled her to make the perilous journey to London unscathed, only to deliver her into the hands of such an unnerving man.

The carriage drew up before the elegantly pilastered entrance of DeVille House. Justin leapt down and, before Dyanna knew what was happening, his hands were at her waist, lifting her out of the carriage and setting her on her feet.

Together they mounted the steps and swept into an entrance hall whose floor was a breathtaking mosaic of multi-colored marble. DeVille stopped as a man in black appeared before them. He bowed grandly, bending low before them as though to Majesty itself.

"Dyanna," Justin said, stifling the smile that no doubt would have wounded the man's pompous dignity to the quick, "this gentleman is Ipswich, my butler. Ipswich, Miss Dyanna McBride. My ward."

"The honor is mine entirely, miss," Ipswich said. "Please feel free to call upon me at any time. I am here to serve you."

"Thank you, Ipswich," Dyanna said. Like Justin, she was more than willing to allow the plump man in black the airs he so obviously

Sandra DuBay

believed befitted his position at the top of the
household hierarchy.

"Your pardon, milord, but a gentleman has
called upon you. From your solicitor. He is
waiting in the morning room."

An impatient scowl flitted across Justin's
sharply planed face. "I'm sorry, Dyanna," he
said. "I had hoped to see you settled in myself.
But apparently I must attend to business.
Ipswich will show you and your maid to your
rooms."

"Honored," Ipswich concurred. "If you
will follow me, miss."

Trailed by Charlotte, Dyanna followed the
butler up a gracefully curving staircase and
down a wide corridor brightly lit by the sunshine spilling through a tall Palladian window
at the end. It was near this window, at the last
door, that Ipswich stopped. Pressing down the
ornately scrolled latch, he swung the door
open and stepped back to allow Dyanna to
enter first.

The sitting room into which she stepped
was furnished delicately, beautifully, in the
finest of taste. It was obviously meant as a
lady's room. The delicate furniture, the ornate but exquisite ornaments that lay scattered on tables and shelves, the pretty pastoral
scenes hanging on the pale yellow silk walls,
were undeniably feminine.

"It is beautiful," she said honestly. Churl-
ishly eager though she might be to find fault

with anything having to do with Justin DeVille, she had to admit it was the loveliest room she could imagine.

"His lordship will be pleased," Ipswich declared, crossing the room quickly, as though afraid to tread too heavily on the rose and blue and cream beauty of the antique French carpet. "This is the bedchamber, miss."

Dyanna followed him to the double doors that led from the sitting room to the bedroom. An 'oh!' of delight and surprise escaped her as she stepped past the butler and into the bedchamber.

The room was a long oval, its gently curving walls painted a rose so pale it was more like the delicate blush of a porcelain-smooth cheek. The ornate plasterwork that encircled the doorframes and windows was outlined in gold leaf. The ceiling, so deeply coved as to appear almost domed, had as its centerpiece a painting of Venus attended by cherubs and adored by a handsome and ardent young lover.

The furniture in the room was, without exception, beautiful, delicate, and gilded. The bed which dominated the room was hung with pale pink silk shot through with golden threads. The draperies descended from a gilded crown and were held aloft at the corners of the bed by fat golden cherubs. The same glimmering, shimmering fabric adorned the chairs and the windows. Over the fireplace, with its white marble mantel, hung a painting not dissimilar to the one in the ceiling.

"It's breathtaking," Dyanna whispered, noting the way the crystal lusters of the candelabra scattered about the room caught and reflected the light.

"His lordship will be most gratified," Ipswich vowed. "Now, if you will follow me"—he cast a pointed look at Charlotte—"I will show you where your mistress's belongings are to be kept."

Charlotte followed the butler through yet another door. As they disappeared into what Dyanna assumed must be the dressing room, Dyanna untied the ribbons of her bonnet and laid it aside with her pelisse. In the mirror of the shell-shaped dressing table, she tidied her hair.

She sighed, sinking onto the golden shell that was the dressing table's bench. Her eyes followed the long, graceful curve of the room, pausing here and there to examine some table or chair or objet d'art more closely.

It was so beautiful, far lovelier than anything she'd ever known. She felt like a princess in a palace. The thought of waking up each morning in such a magnificent chamber filled her with delight. And yet . . . Should she be happy here? Did she dare ignore what she'd heard about the man in whose hands her future rested? Surely no wicked fiend such as the one described in Geoffrey's aunt's book could create such beauty.

Ipswich returned and paused before her. "Your maid is acquainting herself with the dressing room, miss. Your trunks were brought up the backstairs. Is there anything you require?"

"Nothing, thank you," Dyanna assured him.

But as he bowed and moved toward the sitting room door, she called out to him:

"Ipswich?"

He turned, an eyebrow cocked expectantly. "Miss?"

"This house. Has it been long in Lord DeVille's family?"

"It was built, Miss, in 1715 or thereabouts, by his lordship's great-grandfather. It has been in the family since, with the exception of some twenty years—1750 to 1770—during which time it was the London residence of the Viscount Cholmley."

"How did he acquire it?"

"In a game of cards, Miss, with his lordship's father."

The thought of Sebastian DeVille's betting his magnificent London residence on the turn of a card did not overly surprise Dyanna.

"I see," she murmured. "And then Lord Cholmley sold it to the present Lord DeVille?"

"Not at all. In fact, Lord Cholmley spurned milord's every offer to buy the house. He had done all this redecorating, you see." With a sweep of his hand, he indicated the splendor surrounding them.

So much for giving the DeVilles credit for the decor, Dyanna thought wryly.

"But Lord DeVille did, eventually, convince Lord Cholmley to sell?"

"Not precisely," Ipswich said. "Lord Cholmley dropped dead. It was quite a shock. He seemed such a vital, healthy man. Lady Cholmley said the house was haunted. She refused to live here."

"And so she sold it to Lord DeVille?"

"No. She wanted it to go to her husband's heir—a cousin, so I remember, from Northumberland. Or was it Yorkshire? In any event, shortly thereafter, Lady Cholmley went mad."

"Mad!" Dyanna shivered. "Was there madness in her family?"

"No one seemed to think so. In fact, there were those who said it was as if a witch had cast a spell—"

"Ipswich!"

Both the butler and Dyanna jumped, shocked by Justin's exclamation. He stood there, framed in the doorway, his brow furled with grim disapproval.

"I hardly think the young lady could be interested in such lurid tales, Ipswich," he said tightly.

"Your pardon, my lord. Excuse me, miss. Excuse me, milord."

Dyanna's eyes followed the butler as he

made his hurried retreat from the suite. When she heard the sitting room door close behind him, she turned her attention to Justin.

She could not help being struck, as she had been both at the Angel Inn and again at Summersleigh House, by Justin's looks. His tawny golden coloring was enhanced by the bright blue of his coat, which fitted to perfection over a buff waistcoat and trousers. His black boots were polished to a shine that rivaled the glitter of his coat's golden buttons, and even the spill of lace at his neck and wrists could not detract from the air of masculinity that surrounded him.

"You mustn't punish Ipswich," Dyanna told him, rising from the dressing table. "I asked him about the house."

"Even so, there are some matters which are best allowed to fade into the past," Justin replied, a hint of ice in his tone. His eyes scanned the room before coming to rest on Dyanna's face. "Are you satisfied with your rooms?"

"They're beautiful," she told him freely. "I've never seen anything so lovely as this room."

"A beautiful setting for an exquisite jewel," he replied, and Dyanna wondered if she detected a note of mockery in his words.

Flushing, she turned away. There was an awkward silence before Justin said:

"I have to go out for a little while. I just

thought I'd see if you were getting settled before I left."

"I'm fine," she answered softly. "Charlotte is unpacking my things."

"We'll have to see about a wardrobe for you. You can't content yourself with so few gowns."

"I suppose not."

Dyanna felt his gaze boring into her back, but her tongue was maddeningly tied. He bewildered her, frightened her, and yet attracted her. She wanted to run and hide from those piercing eyes and yet, when she heard his footsteps leave the room, she felt a sudden desire to run to the window and see if she could see him drive off in his carriage.

Wandering out to the sitting room, she sank into an armchair. Leaning her head against its carved, gilded back, she closed her eyes wearily and tried in vain to push the image of his face from her mind.

The minutes ticked by, counted by the tortoiseshell and chased-gilt clock on the table near the bow windows which overlooked Piccadilly. Lost in her reverie Dyanna did not even hear the knock on the door. Charlotte swept past her to answer it.

"Inform your mistress that a gentleman is here to see her."

"A gentleman?" Dyanna asked before Charlotte could convey the message. "Who is it, Ipswich?"

"He gives his name as Lord Geoffrey Culpepper, miss."

"Geoffrey!"

Dyanna exchanged a delighted glance with Charlotte as she thrust herself to her feet. "Where is he?"

"In the red salon, miss," the butler replied uneasily. Having run afoul of his master's temper once already that morning, Ipswich wished the young gentleman caller had appeared while his lordship was at home to give or withhold his permission for the visit. "This way."

Dyanna followed him down the stairs and thanked him when he indicated the door to the red salon. Opening it, she found herself on the threshold of a chamber whose walls were hung with crimson Spitalfields silk. All around the long, rectangular room, portraits hung in their gilded frames. But Dyanna had no eyes for Justin's forebears, interesting as they might prove at some other time. All she saw at that moment was Geoffrey, resplendent in scarlet and silver, standing near the black marble fireplace.

"Geoffrey!" she called, hurrying toward him.

"Dyanna," he breathed, taking her hands in his and kissing her lightly on the cheek. "I can't tell you how furious I was to find that you'd left us. My grandfather never should have allowed DeVille to take you away."

"There was nothing he could do to prevent it," Dyanna soothed him, drawing her hands from his too-tight grasp. "My father's will gives Jus—Lord DeVille—complete authority."

"Even so . . ."

She pressed her fingertips to his lips to still his protests. "We must make the best of things, Geoffrey."

"Make the best of things! Surely you cannot be happy here! Not knowing the sort of people these DeVilles are!"

"Of course I am not happy. But for the present, there is nothing to be done. And Charlotte is here with me. Lord Summersleigh insisted she come along."

"That's some consolation, I suppose," he allowed grudgingly. "If DeVille mistreats you, Charlotte can be depended upon to get word to Grandfather or myself."

"I shouldn't think he would mistreat me," Dyanna reasoned. "You know, the rooms he has given me are quite extraordinarily lovely."

"Just take care, my sweet, that he does not lull you into dropping your guard. It concerns me that he might spoil you with kindness at first so that he might later take advantage of you."

"How black you paint him," Dyanna murmured.

Geoffrey sighed. "I fear for your safety. Is that so cruel? So unfair of me?"

96

"Of course it isn't," she hastened to assure him. "I'm grateful for your concern."

"Gratitude is not the emotion I desire most from you." His eyes filled with adoration. "I want to take you away from here. I want to protect you." Closing his eyes, he turned away as though overwhelmed by his emotions. "Forgive me, Dyanna, I know it is too soon for me to be saying these things to you, but—"

"Geoffrey," she said softly, touched. "How good you are to me."

He turned back toward her, a mixture of relief and hope springing into his face. Covering the distance between them in two short strides, he took her gently into his arms.

Dyanna slid her arms about his waist. Her cheek lay in the crisp folds of his cravat and the coolness of a ruby stud chilled the corner of her mouth. She had never felt so cherished, so cared for, in all her life.

Together they stood, their arms around each other, until a voice from the doorway tore them apart.

"I don't believe I gave you leave to come courting my ward, sir," The words fairly dripped icy disdain.

Her cheeks blazing crimson, Dyanna turned from Geoffrey and found herself skewered by Justin's furious golden glare.

Chapter Eight

Dyanna stood in the red salon, tight-lipped with anger, as Justin dismissed Geoffrey as if he were some impertinent tradesman who had overstayed his welcome. She glared at Justin as the hoofbeats of Geoffrey's horse faded into the distance.

"How dare you!" she hissed, her fury whipped to even greater heights by the cool, unperturbed stare Justin directed toward her. "Am I not to be allowed friends, then, my lord? Am I to be immured in this house like a prisoner?"

"If necessary," Justin confirmed.

"My father made you my guardian, sir. Not my gaoler!"

"Your father entrusted me with your well-being. I presume that means moral well-being as well as physical well-being."

"Moral!" Dyanna jammed her fists into the soft gathers of muslin at her hips. "How prim and proper you are, my lord! This must be your London guise. I don't imagine you are quite so priggish when you are off a'pirating."

"Privateering," Justin corrected her icily.

"Your pardon, milord," she mocked him with a saucy little curtsy. "Privateering. And I know for certain you are not so stiff-necked when you are in the country. For I do seem to recall a tavern maid you were well on your way to seducing at the Angel Inn."

"That was different."

"Different?" she widened her eyes in taunting surprise. "My! You do have a convenient set of morals. When I was a tavern maid, it was all right for me to dally with you. But now that I am a lady—" She glared fiercely at him as he smothered a derisive chuckle. "A lady!" she repeated. "It is not permitted for me to receive a friend in my guardian's home."

"Are you finished?"

"For the moment."

Hands clasped behind his back, Justin crossed the room to the lace-curtained, bowed window. He was furious but he'd long ago learned to hide his emotions. He pondered his words for a long moment, then turned to face her.

"Dyanna," he said softly, in the cool, emo-

"Miss?" The maid appeared in the bedroom doorway.

"Lock the hall door quickly. Before Lord DeVille can get—"

But it was too late. Propelled by Justin's savage thrust, the sitting room door slammed back against the wall with a crash. Justin stood framed in the doorway, eyes glittering like topazes. He looked like an avenging angel —or a hellborn demon.

Dyanna did not stop to ponder which. Picking up her skirts, she ran for the bedchamber. As she passed Charlotte, she caught the girl's arm and dragged her along into the adjoining room. Together they slammed the double doors and twisted the key in the lock.

"Dyanna!" Justin's roar sent shivers down her spine.

"He's going to kill us," Charlotte whispered, plainly terrified.

"Of course he's not," Dyanna insisted. But as the doors shook with the impact of his fists, she was not as confident as she sounded.

"Open this door, Dyanna," he said calmly, almost coolly. His voice was deceptively mild, but there was an undertone to his words that promised—or was it threatened?—dire consequences if his errant ward did not obey.

"Go away!" she called back. "Leave me alone!"

"I said, open the door. Now!"

Dyanna said nothing as she stood in the

center of the bedroom, her hands clasping the trembling hands of her maid.

"He'll go away," she whispered to the quivering servant beside her. "He'll go away and calm down and then, perhaps—"

The stillness of the moment was shattered by the splintering of rose wood as Justin slammed his booted foot against the center of the double doors. Charlotte screamed as they flew open, whipping back to crash into the curving walls. She took one look at Justin who stood in the doorway, fists clenched, knuckles white, face flushed with anger. Then, abandoning her mistress to her fate, Charlotte fled into the dressing room.

Dyanna swallowed hard as she heard the click of the key in the lock of the dressing room door. Her wide, black-lashed, sea-blue eyes, never left Justin's face. She watched him, wary as the vixen before the huntsman's hounds, as he moved into the room.

"Do not ever—ever!—lock a door against me in my own house again," Justin snarled. "Do you understand me? Do you!"

"Yes," Dyanna breathed. She too was trembling now, though not with the nervous fear that had shaken the timid Charlotte. Hers was a far more visceral fear—the terror that descended when one was in fear—real or imagined—of one's very life. "I understand."

"I am your guardian, Dyanna," he went on, moving closer, careful to block her most obvious avenue of escape, the broken doors which hung sadly on their bent hinges. "It is not a position I asked for, but it is one I have decided to accept. And do you know why?"

"No," Dyanna answered honestly. "I cannot imagine. I suspect it is because you and my father—"

The small, impatient shake of Justin's head stilled her speculations. "It has nothing to do with your father. It has to do with your mother."

A frown creased Dyanna's forehead. "My mother?"

"I don't imagine you remember your mother well. You could not have been more than two or three when she died. But I remember her." The memories Justin summoned to mind softened the rage that had twisted his handsome features earlier. "I remember her very well. She was a beautiful creature. The most beautiful woman of her generation, they said. You look very like her. But there, unfortunately, the resemblance ends. Your mother, you see, was a lady. Something, it is obvious, you are not."

"The McBride wildness has left its mark," she said with a philosophic shrug.

"The McBride Wildness," he sneered. "That is a convenient excuse, nothing more. If your mother and your mother's mother and her mother had been whores, would that mean you would have to be one as well?"

White-hot temper flared in Dyanna's eyes, but for once she held her tongue. It was Justin's first victory, though neither recognized it. She bit back the razor-sharp retort that sprang to her lips, and instead asked simply:

"What is your point, my lord?"

"My point, Dyanna, is this: You are the last descendant of two noble houses. The Conways, Earls of Lincoln, and the Viscounts McBride have both come to their culmination in you. I think there is nothing so sad as watching the greatness of the past degenerate, wither, and die until nothing is left but a single, blighted blossom. I am responsible for you. I am determined to see that the noble houses that bred you and the ancient bloodlines that are mingled in your veins are not shamed by your foolishness—your willfulness."

"Such high and mighty words," Dyanna flung back, "particularly when one considers your—"

She stopped, suddenly realizing the folly of exposing too much of what she knew.

Justin stood very still. He could guess the gist of what she had been about to say. It didn't surprise him. The rumors and scandal surrounding his father had haunted him most of his life. He let the moment pass. He did not want their confrontation steered in another, futile, direction.

"In any event," he went on, coolly unruffled, "I will not tolerate behavior that could put you outside the pale. You will become a lady, Dyanna, a lady of whom your mother would have been proud. Scenes such as that tantrum downstairs will not be tolerated."

"What will you do?" she asked skeptically. "Send me to bed without supper? Lock me in my room?" Arching a taunting brow, she directed a meaningful look toward the broken doors with their useless locks.

Justin allowed himself a small smile. "I'm quite certain both those methods have been tried in the past. I'm equally certain of their futility."

"Then what will you do?"

With the sleek swiftness of some night predator, Justin had Dyanna's finely boned wrist in his iron grasp. Though she struggled against him, she was no match for the strength that months at sea had built into his tall, broad-shouldered body.

"Let me go, damn you to hell!" she shrieked. "Charlotte! Charlotte!"

"That mouse won't help you," Justin snarled as he sat on the edge of the bed and tried to pull her across his knees.

"Bertran!" she screamed in desperation. "Help me!"

Justin muttered an oath. If nothing else, Dyanna's long years of running wild on her father's and grandfather's estates had made her stronger, more lithe and agile than most gently reared girls of her station. She struggled and twisted, redoubling her efforts when she felt the first slap of his hand against her backside. It was not until then that she realized that, at almost eighteen years of age, she was in imminent danger of getting her first spanking.

"Don't you dare!" she growled, her eyes flashing with hot blue fires of purest loathing. "Don't you dare!"

Justin's anger and determination were fueled by his frustration at finding that she was so thickly padded with skirts and petticoats as to be untouchable. His efforts were met by little more than layer upon layer of fluffy muslin and springy lace.

Furious, he turned, rising, and threw her down on her stomach across the bed. Before she could writhe away from him, he had braced his knee in the small of her back and was digging at the yards of fabric with both hands.

Dyanna kicked her heels at him but there was nothing she could do. In the end, she could only claw at the gold and pink coverlet of the bed and shriek as he administered his punishment with little between his flesh and hers save the diaphanous silk of her chemise.

When he'd finished, Justin moved swiftly away. He was well out of range of her swinging fists before she managed to scramble to her feet.

Dyanna ground her teeth. No epithet seemed foul enough, no curse dire enough. She wanted to hit him, kick him, curse him to the deepest firepits of Hell. But in the end, all she could do was bite her lip against the tears of fury and mortification, and clench her fists to keep from rubbing the smarting flesh of her backside through her crumpled skirts.

"Let that be a lesson to you," Justin said quietly. "And let us hope it is not one you need to have repeated."

Dyanna said nothing as he turned on his heel and left the bedchamber. He was halfway across the sitting room when he heard a movement behind him. Turning, he found Dyanna, framed in the doorway, a porcelain shepherdess in her raised and trembling hand.

Their eyes locked and something in Justin's calm golden gaze seemed to start her bruised flesh aching all over again. A moment passed. Then another. The tortoise-shell and gilt clock chimed the hour. And then, slowly, haltingly, Dyanna lowered the shepherdess back onto the polished tabletop from which she'd taken it.

A glint of satisfaction glimmered in Justin's eyes. He allowed himself the smallest of smiles before leaving the sitting room.

He was not quite to the head of the stairs when he heard Dyanna's ear-splitting shriek of frustration and outrage. He paused, one hand on the bannister, waiting for the crash he feared would follow. But there was only silence. He waited a minute. Nothing. The pent-up breath he hadn't realized he was holding slipped out in a relieved sigh as he started down the long, elegantly curving staircase.

Chapter Nine

Seated at the gilt-bronze desk in his gold moiré-hung study, Justin looked up from his ledgers. Head cocked to one side, he listened to the sonata issuing from the harpsichord in the nearby music room. He could imagine Dyanna's face as she played, brow furled in concentration, small, pearly teeth tugging at her lower lip, frowning as she approached the passage that had been troubling her for the past hour of her music lesson. He held his breath as she began the passage, then smiled, shaking his head in sympathy as she once again struck the wrong keys. After a few moments' silence, she began again.

He could picture her tutor, the formidible Herr Kemmel, a florid-faced Viennese whose

Sandra DuBay

elaborately curled white wig sat atop his large bald head like snow atop a mountain. The man would be frowning and muttering, reminding Dyanna yet again that Mozart had written the sonata at eight, while Dyanna could not master it at almost eighteen.

Still, Justin had to admit, she was trying, persisting with a dogged determination he would not have expected of her, given her headstrong and volatile temperament. She hadn't even protested too loudly when he'd engaged Herr Kemmel. In fact, she'd seemed pleased by the prospect of resuming the music lessons she'd begun at Blaykling Castle. Now that he thought of it, she'd been almost meek in the few weeks since he'd given her that spanking.

He sat back in his chair, bathed in the early afternoon sunshine, waiting for her to begin that troublesome stanza. She had been—well, perhaps meek was stating it too strongly. Dyanna would never be docile; her very nature was too fiery for that. But she had been agreeable. She had not argued. She had not even protested his choices in the wardrobe he had ordered for her, even though he suspected she thought most of it too young and missish. It made her look younger than her years and perhaps, just perhaps, he admitted in the privacy of his own thoughts, that was his object. For he was constantly aware of her

112

beauty. It sometimes startled him when he came upon her unexpectedly in the library or the garden. Bathed in the light of an evening fire, she was breathtaking. The memory of the night they'd met at the Angel Inn was never far from his thoughts, however hard he might try to banish it from his mind.

A high-pitched scream of pure frustration tore him out of his reverie. From the music room came the jarring discord of Dyanna's fists descending onto the ebony and ivory keys of the delicate, intricately inlaid Italian instrument.

Justin rose from his desk as he heard the scraping of the harpsichord bench on the parquet floor. Leaving his study, he strode down the hall to the bow-windowed room where the harpsichord stood, silent and abandoned now, near a tall and graceful golden harp that had belonged to some time-shrouded ancestor.

Herr Kemmel, his white wig askew, his once crisp stock limp with perspiration, mopped at his reddened face with a damp and crumpled handkerchief. He did not look up until Justin joined him near the opened French doors which led out into the sprawling, informal garden behind DeVille House.

"Lesson over, mein herr?" he asked archly, gazing out into the garden where Dyanna romped with Clancy, one of the huge, adoring

113

Irish wolfhounds that lived in the stables beyond the tall hedges.

"*Ach*, this girl, my lord," the maestro said with yet another swipe at his moist brow. "She has no discipline. Practice! She must practice! This nonsense—" he waved his handkerchief in the direction of the garden"—should not be allowed."

Justin said nothing as his eyes followed Dyanna across the wide expanse of carefully manicured lawn. Her ruffled gown fluttered as she ran, its lilac satin streamers rippling behind her. Her hair, only moments before demurely wound into a twist at the crown of her head, had shaken free of its pins and fell in a tumble of glistening curls over her shoulders.

The wolfhound bounded toward her, a short, thick branch clamped in his massive jaws. He waited expectantly for Dyanna to grasp the stick and when she did, shook his great head and knocked her sprawling on the grass.

Justin chuckled, and Herr Kemmel turned accusing eyes on him. "You approve of this, my lord? This girl is your ward. Can you approve of this behavior?"

"She is young, *mein herr*," Justin replied, enchanted in spite of himself by the sight of Dyanna trying to wrest the stick from the dog's powerful grasp and by the soft, musical sound of her laughter. "She is high-spirited."

"It is this spirit which must be broken," the music teacher decreed.

"Broken?" Justin looked at him, appalled. "Surely you don't mean that."

"I do. A woman of breeding, of rank, should be retiring. Submissive. Not like—" Again he gestured toward the garden.

"I like a woman with spirit," Justin disagreed. "I've no patience with meek little milksops who hide from their own shadows. A woman is not a horse, *mein herr*, to be broken, to be forced into submission. She should have pride, fire—in short, spirit."

"In my country, it is not so. A young woman who behaved this way would be considered—"

"Take care, *mein herr*," Justin warned, his voice cold and filled with disdain, his very stance emphasizing the difference between him and the music teacher who was, after all, little more than a glorified servant.

Leopold Kemmel frowned. He could see that he was in imminent danger of losing a pupil. "Forgive me, my lord," he said. "It is only that she is not . . . " He faltered, groping for words that would allow him to extricate himself from the awkward situation.

"Go on," Justin prompted, "she is not . . . ?"

The musician said nothing, knowing there was no safe way out. He shrugged, bowing to the inevitable.

115

"I think my ward has had enough of music lessons, Herr Kemmel."

"As you wish, my lord," the Viennese acquiesced, realizing he had misjudged Justin's feelings for his ward. With a short, abrupt bow, he went to the harpsichord and gathered his music.

At the door, the music teacher paused and looked back. Justin stood, half turned away from him, gazing out toward Dyanna, frolicking in the sunshine. His feelings—the enchantment and fascination the lithe, silver-haired girl held for him—were all too apparent in his face as he watched her. Smiling, Herr Kemmel turned away, wondering as he went if the cool, elegant Lord DeVille was as yet aware of his own feelings and wondering, too, how long those emotions would be held in check.

Unaware of the Austrian's departure, Justin strode out into the sunshine. Dyanna had disappeared into the ornate little domed folly at the far end of the garden. It was there that he joined her, finding her seated on a marble bench, a blade of grass twirling in her fingers.

"Where's Clancy?" he asked, leaning against one of the marble pillars that supported the high, gilded dome.

"Off digging up one of the flowerbeds, I suppose." She glanced toward the house. "Where's Herr Kemmel?"

"Gone." Justin grinned. "I gave him the sack."

Dyanna's eyes grew round. "You didn't!"

"I did."

"But why?"

"I'm afraid he thinks you're something of a hoyden."

"A hoyden! Well! The sour old son of a—"

"Dyanna!"

She giggled, her eyes twinkling. "I'm glad he's gone! I like music, Justin, but I'm no prodigy. Why must I learn to play like one?"

"A lady is supposed to be accomplished."

"But I'm not a lady. Ask Herr Kemmel."

Justin smiled in spite of himself. For the first time, he realized that he had meant every word of what he said to the Viennese musician. If making Dyanna into the perfect young lady meant breaking the spirit that lent that sparkle to her eyes and that bounce to her step, he would rather see her remain a hoyden.

"Go have Charlotte put you back together," he told her, plucking a blade of grass from her tangled curls. "And I'll take you driving in the park."

Clapping her hands, Dyanna blew him a kiss and spun away. Lifting her billowing skirts, she ran toward the open doors of the music room while Justin watched, captivated.

It was not until she had disappeared from

117

view that he could bestir himself to go to the stables and order a carriage brought around.

Attired in the black mourning upon which Justin insisted when they ventured out in public, Dyanna viewed the world through the fine lace veil that swathed her black-plumed hat. But from the moment they entered Hyde Park, she forgot her somber attire and was breathless, excited at the prospect of seeing fashionable London on parade.

"Is that Mrs. Robinson?" she asked, jabbing Justin with a black-gloved finger. She nodded toward an exquisitely beautiful woman in pink and silver who held court from an open carriage. "They say she is the Prince of Wales's mistress."

"Do they say so?" Justin asked, amused that even a girl as insulated from public scandal as Dyanna had heard the gossip about the seventeen-year-old prince and the twenty-one-year-old actress.

"You know they do," she chided him. "Isn't it romantic? They say he fell in love with her at first sight."

Justin bit back a cynical observation concerning the prince's frequency of falling in love. "So they say," he agreed noncommittally.

"I do so long to see him. Is he as handsome as they say, Justin?"

"The very picture of a romantic young

prince," Justin admitted. "All the ladies agree."

Dyanna sighed. "I wonder if I shall ever meet him. I wish—"

Her wish was silenced by the approach of a round, disheveled young man on horseback. Tipping his hat, he bowed low to Justin before his eyes roved admiringly over Dyanna.

"My lord," he said, his eyes never leaving Dyanna's face. "I'd be obliged if you'd introduce me."

Justin smiled. "I might have known you'd be nearby. Very well, then. Charles James Fox—my ward, Miss Dyanna McBride. My dear, this wretch is Mr. Fox, whose name you've no doubt seen in the papers."

Though politics was not one of Dyanna's abiding interests, she knew of Mr. Fox, leader of the Whigs in Parliament. On a more personal level, she knew he was acclaimed a genius, a womanizer, and a compulsive gambler.

"Mr. Fox," she said softly, wondering that a man of his stature should not at least own a clean stock.

"Miss McBride," he returned. "Very much your servant. I knew your father, Rake—that is, Rayburn McBride. I was sorry to hear of his death. But I believe you were about to make a wish when I interrupted."

"I was wishing, sir, that I might meet the Prince of Wales."

"And so you may, my dear. It is said he will be at Cumberland House tonight. His uncle, the Duke, has persuaded him it is time he began coming out in society, even if his father, the King, does not think so."

"But I shan't be there," Dyanna pointed out.

"No?" Fox looked at Justin curiously. "But you were invited, were you not, my lord? I could have sworn your name was mentioned at Brooks' Club as one of those to be honored with His Royal Highness's acquaintance."

"The Duke was kind enough to invite me, yes," Justin confirmed. "And I do plan to attend."

"Justin!" Dyanna breathed. "We are to go to Cumberland House?"

"I plan to attend, Dyanna, alone."

Her face fell, but she said nothing, seething in silence as Justin made their farewells to Mr. Fox and turned the carriage in the direction of DeVille House.

Chapter Ten

"Justin!" Dyanna stood at the head of the stairs glaring down at her guardian who, dressed in black and gold brocade, was about to leave for Cumberland House. "It is unfair!"

He sighed. Taking his hat from Ipswich and submitting to a last once-over by Bertran, he waved a dismissal to his servants and faced his angry ward alone.

"The matter is not open to discussion, Dyanna," he said, his tone firm and weary with the quarrel that had been raging intermittently ever since they'd returned from Hyde Park.

"But I was invited! The Duke of Cumberland was a friend of my father's, was he not?"

Justin resisted the temptation to tell her that gambling and whoring together did not make men lifelong friends, particularly not when one of them was a Royal Duke, brother to King George III. Instead, he said only:

"I have told you, Dyanna, that Cumberland House is not a proper place for a young woman not yet introduced to society. The Duke of Cumberland is a roué and a rake. His duchess is considered by many an adventuress, and she is not received at Court. It would not do for you to be known to associate with them."

"You are associating with them."

He closed his eyes, his frayed patience nearing its end. "I have accepted the duke's invitation, my dear, for the opportunity of sounding out the Prince of Wales's opinions. The prince is chafing under the restrictions his father places upon him. He longs to be treated as a man, but is kept a boy. Cumberland thinks to build a rival court around the Prince, with Cumberland House as its base. I wish to know in which direction that wind is going to blow."

"And while you are out testing the wind, I must sit idly at home."

"Dyanna, you are not yet eighteen. You have not grown up in society. You should enter it cautiously, slowly. I have decided you would be better to wait until your year of mourning is over. You will be older then, more sophisti-cated. Wiser in the ways of the world.''

"A year!" she cried. "It is unfair!"

"This is where our discussion began," he observed, clapping his hat on top of his head, "and this is where it will end. Good-night, Dyanna."

Leaving her to glare after him, her hands gripping the gleaming bannister until her knuckles whitened, Justin turned and with a swirl of his caped cloak, was gone.

Later, in her room, with only the sympa-thetic Charlotte for company, Dyanna sulked.

"He means to keep me a prisoner," she complained her fingers snipping at the pale green ribbons threaded through the lace that frothed her leaf-green lawn nightdress.

"A prisoner," Charlotte repeated. "Like in a gaol?"

"Exactly like that!" Scowling, Dyanna leaned closer to her maid. She lowered her voice to a conspiratorial whisper, even though the two of them were alone in the room. "Do you know, Charlotte, I read something pre-cisely like this in a book?"

"Really, miss?" The maid's eyes were filled with wonder. She, too, loved to read, but she seemed to think every book was a true story.

"It was about a girl named Jenny Flynn. Her parents died and left her in the clutches of a guardian."

"Same as you and my lord DeVille!"

"Exactly so! This man's name was Greatrakes. Ebenezer Greatrakes. And do you know what he did? He shut her away in a gloomy old mansion and tried to steal her fortune!"

"He didn't! That monster!"

"And more than that! He seduced her! Ruined her. Robbed her of her innocence and virtue!"

"The beast!" Unconsciously, Charlotte pulled her drab cotton nightdress closer about herself. "Even my lord DeVille would not be so wicked as that!"

"Don't be too sure," Dyanna said cryptically, thinking of that night at the Angel Inn, but conveniently forgetting that Justin hadn't known she was his ward that night and that she had made no great show of resistance to his advances. Tonight she wanted to think him a beast and a rake. It suited her mood.

"What do you mean, miss?" Charlotte asked, enthralled and titillated.

"Nothing. Nothing at all." Dyanna was not about to reveal what had happened—or almost happened—between herself and Justin at the inn. And particularly not to a maid who was still, officially, a servant of the Marquees of Summersleigh. "Go to bed, Charlotte. There is no need for you to stay up with me."

"Are you sure, miss? I don't mind."

"I'm sure. You go to bed."

Obviously reluctant, the maid rose. After dropping her young mistress a curtsy, she left Dyanna alone with her private thoughts.

From a drawer in the night-table, Dyanna retrieved the book about Lord Lucifer Wolfe. She had read no more in it since Justin first brought her to DeVille House. The past few weeks had been quite pleasant. But now, angry at him as she was, she was willing to believe he had done precisely what Geoffrey had feared he might do—lulled her into trusting him.

Thoughtfully, she let her fingers stroke the finely worked leather of the cover. It was said that Lucifer Wolfe—or Sebastian DeVille if Geoffrey were to be believed—had had the power to fascinate women, to bind them to him by sheer animal magnetism. She wondered, suddenly, how much like his father Justin might be. Did they look alike? She thought of the portraits that lined the walls of the salons downstairs. Was Sebastian there, tucked discreetly between two forebears of less notorious reputation?

Leaving her room, Dyanna swept silently down the hall, only the soft hissing of her rippling nightdress marking her passing. Taking one of the candles from the candelabrum that burned on a table at the head of the stairs, she started down the staircase toward the red salon.

The house seemed abandoned. The servants had been dismissed; Justin seldom asked them to stay awake until he returned. Entertainments such as the one at Cumberland House could go on until daybreak. Even the faithful and vigilant Bertran, who often remained out of bed to help his master undress, was dozing in a chair in Justin's upstairs suite.

Crossing the hallway downstairs, Dyanna reached for the latch at the door to the elegant, red-walled salon that connected the library with the music room. Her fingers brushed the cold bronze, then froze, hovering in the air above the ornately scrolled latch. She had heard the sound of a horse's hooves on the gravel of the drive outside.

"Justin," she breathed, poised for flight. But no, it could not be Justin, her inner voice reasoned. It was far too early for him to return, and besides, he had gone in a carriage. The sounds in the drive were unmistakably those of a single horse.

Hurrying to the window, she peeked out. A soft gasp of surprise escaped her when she saw Geoffrey Culpepper about to ascend the stairs to the door.

"Geoffrey!" she hissed, her heart fluttering as his footsteps drew nearer to the door. She wavered, undecided. It was the height of impropriety for him to arrive unannounced and uninvited at such an hour, of course, and worse still when Justin was out and she was wearing her nightdress. And without so much as a maidservant hovering in the background —scandalous! Justin would be furious if he found out.

A frown creased Dyanna's brow. But Justin was not there, was he? No! Where was he? Out for the evening, enjoying himself at a soirée to which she had been invited but was forbidden to attend. He was selfish! He cared nothing for her pleasure, only his own! What harm could it do if she visited with Geoffrey for a few moments? He was the only suitor she had— thanks, again, to Justin! If her high-and-mighty guardian did not want her seeking her own pleasures, he should see that she had some happiness instead of devoting his time to his own enjoyment!

Feeling pleasantly self-righteous—and tantalizingly bold and defiant—she opened the door to admit her caller.

"Geoffrey," she said, smiling, "I could not imagine who might be arriving."

"I almost did not stop," he told her, laying aside his *chapeau bras*. He unfastened the clasps of his surtout and removed it carefully lest he disturb the impeccable white ramillies wig, whose silver embroidered bow matched the glittering fabric of his waistcoat. "I thought everyone was in bed."

"Most everyone is. Justin has gone out—to Cumberland House. He dismissed the servants when he left."

Geoffrey's eyes slid over Dyanna's diaphanous gown. Her hair, undone and falling softly down her back, gleamed in the light of her candle.

"Perhaps I shouldn't stay," he told her. "I would not want you punished because of—"

"No, please stay. I haven't seen you in so long. I thought you had surely forgotten me."

"As if I could." He offered her his arm and she laid her hand on his midnight-blue satin sleeve. "I hadn't the courage to call. Your guardian does not encourage potential beaux, you know."

"Well, my guardian is not at home, Lord Geoffrey," she murmured, casting a flirtatious sideways glance up at him. "And I've missed talking with you. Come, if we go into the small salon off this anteroom and are quiet, no one need know."

"It will be our little secret," he said, delighted that she should prove so amenable to thwarting her guardian's wishes. It was, he told himself, a good omen for his plans.

"Our little secret," Dyanna agreed.

Feeling deliciously defiant, Dyanna led Geoffrey to a tiny salon, hung in old ivory silk, that was little more than a glorified anteroom. Intended primarily for family evenings on winter nights before the fire, the room contained plain, unadorned furnishings which, while they might have lacked the gilded elegance of those found in the grander salons, more than made up for their lack of beauty in comfort.

"I'm surprised," Geoffrey began when they'd ensconced themselves on a worn wine-velvet sofa, "that I've not seen you about town. I looked for you at the theater, Vauxhall Gardens, Hyde Park . . ."

"Justin took me driving in the park this afternoon," she revealed, "but he brought me home as soon as Mr. Fox noticed me."

"Charles Fox? A brilliant man. A younger son of Lord Holland. He is a descendant of King Charles II, you know."

"I didn't know. In any case, he was most kind and admiring."

"It doesn't surprise me. There is a great deal about you to admire, dear Dyanna."

"It seemed to irritate Justin."

A tiny frown creased Geoffrey's brow. His compliment had passed unnoticed. Dyanna was too preoccupied with whether or not her guardian was irritated to take note of what he was saying. That did not bode well at all for his plans.

He decided to let it pass. "I do believe our fine Lord DeVille wants to keep you to himself, my sweet," he teased, keeping the tone light.

"It is worse than you know. He intends to keep me out of society until my year of mourning is over. If I'm fortunate, I may be able to wangle a trip to the theater or opera

129

out of him, but no balls, no private entertainments for the next year."

"Truly? So long?"

"Forever! I shall meet no one, Geoffrey! Go nowhere! Do nothing! I am his prisoner!"

"Poor darling," Geoffrey cooed. "Poor sweet little darling."

But secretly he was elated. So, DeVille intended to keep Dyanna on the edges of society for a year? So much the better. That meant there was less chance of some smooth-mannered, silver-tongued suitor slipping into the picture. And more opportunities for Geoffrey to persuade Dyanna that the best thing she could do was to defy her tyrannical guardian and place her delectable person—and her even more delectable fortune—in his hands.

He twined a strand of her hair about his finger and stroked the back of his hand along her silky cheek.

"If you were mine," he said, his voice low and velvety, "I would want to take you everywhere. I would want the world to see how fortunate I was that such a beautiful creature deigned to be my own. I would want everyone to share in the pleasure of your company."

"Justin wants only to lock me away from the world," Dyanna muttered sourly.

"DeVille's a fool." Geoffrey's voice had a hard, angry edge. It annoyed him beyond bearing that the speech he had rehearsed so carefully seemed to have passed by her without her even noticing. "He is a roué, a womanizer. Likely he's abed with one of the highborn harlots who frequent Cumberland House even as we speak."

He saw the shadow that crossed Dyanna's face and cursed himself for a fool. A vague sense of alarm blossomed inside him. It was apparent, from the look on Dyanna's face, that the notion of DeVille's being with another woman troubled her. Could it be she was starting to have feelings for her guardian? That would never do.

"Dyanna," he murmured, gently taking her hands in his. "Dyanna, darling. This is a delicate question, but one which I feel I must ask. DeVille has not—that is—he would not try to seduce you, would he?"

A hot flush flooded Dyanna's cheeks. Seduce her! Justin treated her as if she were nothing more than a troublesome child most of the time. If only he would treat her . . . But no, she refused to allow herself to explore such dangerous emotions.

"Oh, no," she whispered after too long a silence. "He has not done anything like that."

Geoffrey wondered at the odd tone of her voice, at the long hesitation before she'd answered. Could she be disappointed that DeVille had not touched her? But no. Of course that was ridiculous.

He pressed a kiss onto her fingers. "I could not bear it if he touched you. It would wound me to the quick."

Dyanna stared up at him. "Why?" she asked ingenuously.

"Why?" He felt a wave of frustration wash over him. What was wrong with this girl? He usually had them eating out of his hand by now. "Why?" he repeated, his voice rising. "Dyanna! I love you! Surely you know that. I want to marry you."

"Marry . . ." Her fingers trembled as she drew them out of his grasp. Rising, she backed a few steps away and stared up at him as if he were a stranger. "Marry me?"

"And why not?"

She shook her head. "Justin would never permit . . ."

"We could elope. Run away together. It would be so romantic, my darling. Think of it."

Elope! Run away with Geoffrey. The thought astonished her. And yet . . . hadn't she agreed with the old marquess that she should marry as quickly as possible to thwart the hateful terms of her father's will? Here was her opportunity. Justin was not likely to allow her to meet many other eligible men.

"Dyanna?" he prompted.

"I need to think about it. Please, give me time to think."

"Don't wait too long," he pleaded, fearful

that any budding feelings she might have for Justin DeVille might blossom into something far more dangerous to his plans.

"I won't," she promised.

"Let me kiss you, Dyanna. Let me hold you."

He came to her then, and she let him take her into his arms and tip back her head to receive his kiss. His lips descended on hers in a savage, punishing kiss intended to inflame her maidenly senses. In truth it did little more than make her wish she had never answered the door when she'd seen him arriving.

As soon as she could, she stepped out of his embrace. An awkward silence descended between them. To cover his angry frustration, Geoffrey made a great show of putting on his coat and retrieving his hat from the table near the door.

"You will consider my proposal, won't you?" he persisted as she accompanied him to the front door.

"I will," she promised.

He left and she sighed, relieved, as she heard the clip-clop of his horse's hooves fading into the distance. Climbing the stairs, her fast-dwindling candle clenched in her shaking fist, she replaced the candle in the candelabrum and retraced her steps to the cool, inviting darkness of her bedchamber.

She wanted only the blissful nothingness of sleep, but questions and images assailed her.

Sandra DuBay

Where was the passion she hoped to find in Geoffrey's kiss? Where was the delicious onslaught of emotions, the tantalizing feelings she'd found in Justin's arms? What magic did Justin possess that Geoffrey did not? What power did Justin DeVille hold over her senses?

She thought about marrying Geoffrey. How could she live with him dreading those times when he would want to kiss her, hold her, make love to her? Or would those feelings of love and desire come later? Could she take that chance? What if they never came?

Lost in her musings, she did not hear the sound of Justin's carriage rolling up the drive, nor his footsteps as he climbed the stairs and moved along the corridor. She did not hear him enter her sitting room. It was only when her bedroom door opened and he entered that she sensed his presence.

"Dyanna?" he said softly.

She said nothing, feigning sleep as he approached the bed. He stood between her and the moonlight flooding through the window, so that there was no silver glow to show him the way her lips trembled, or the slight fluttering of her lashes as she held her eyes tightly closed.

"Dyanna?" he repeated. "Are you sleeping?"

Still she said nothing. It was all she could do to keep from crying out when his fingers brushed her cheek. With infinite gentleness

134

he smoothed back a curl onto her pillow. Plucking at the lace-frothed coverlet, he tucked it more securely around her, his fingertips brushing her arm below the ruffle of her short nightgown sleeve.

Dyanna waited, breathless, wondering what he would do next, but he only stood there at her bedside for a long, silent moment. Then he turned and was gone as swiftly and as stealthily as he had come.

Her emotions in turmoil, Dyanna felt the trembling seize her. But it was not until she heard the sitting room door close behind him that she gave way to tears of confusion, frustration, and fear.

Chapter Eleven

"May I bring you anything, miss?" Ipswich asked Dyanna one overcast morning nearly a month after Justin's visit to Cumberland House.

She shook her head, her fingers idly toying with the keys of the harpsichord.

"Nothing, thank you, Ipswich," she replied listlessly. "Is his lordship in?"

"His lordship has gone out, miss," the butler told her. "He was paying a call on Lady Melbourne, I believe."

"I see. Thank you. I shall ring if I need anything."

Dyanna sighed as the butler left her alone with her gloomy thoughts. Lady Melbourne.

Beautiful Lady Melbourne. Twenty-eight years old and said to be admired by many men, including the Prince of Wales. Gossip had it she was already the mistress of Lord Egremont. Nor was she the only lady upon whom Justin seemed to dance attendance these days. There was the twenty-three-year-old Duchess of Devonshire, who lived not far away in Piccadilly. Not a day passed that Justin was not engaged to dine or at least call on some society beauty. It was only politics, he assured her when she'd dredged up the courage to ask him. But she wondered. Politics was the domain of gentlemen. What had these ladies to do with it? Was there more than that going on between Justin and these beautiful and sophisticated ladies?

"Justin," she breathed as a torturous series of images flitted through her mind's eye—pictures of Justin with this woman or that, ladies and duchesses, nameless, faceless women. She saw him laughing with them, dancing, talking, telling them everything she so desperately wanted him to tell her. Making love to them in the perfumed, silk-sheeted beds to which they would lead him.

Dyanna folded her arms on the cool, beautiful instrument and gazed out at the garden, still damp from a brief morning shower. If anything had changed between Justin and herself since that first night he'd gone to

Cumberland House, it was that he treated her even more coolly. There was more distance between them now than before. She ate in her sitting room, like a child relegated to the nursery, while Justin went out. He no longer even deigned to take her riding. On those rare occasions when she ventured forth from DeVille House, she went with Charlotte and Bertran, who she suspected was sent along as a watchdog with orders to report to Justin on anyone she saw or chanced to speak with, rather than as a guard against unwanted advances by gentlemen.

And yet . . . Unbidden, her mind swept back to that night when Justin had come to her room upon his return from Cumberland House. There had been tenderness in his voice, in the gentle touch of his fingers as he'd brushed back her hair, stroked her face. She hadn't imagined the tenderness. It had been there. How could it have been so real, so obvious, on that one night—for those few brief, precious moments, and never again?

Rising from the harpsichord, she went to the French doors. With a trembling finger, she wrote Justin's name in the condensation on one of the panes, then quickly wiped it away lest someone should see and report her folly to Justin. Leaning her forehead against the cold, wet glass, she bit her lip to hold back the tears that welled into her eyes.

It was foolishness, she told herself, this

feeling inside her. And yet it felt just the way she'd always expected love to feel. But what was this pain, this dull, agonizing ache that would not leave her? And how could she fight this growing dread that the day would come when he would meet a woman he would want to bring home? How would she feel when she was banished to her rooms while he entertained a woman scarcely older than herself in a candlelit dining room or softly scented salon?

Perhaps it would be better, she reasoned, to simply give in to Geoffrey's wishes and elope. Though they had not been able to meet again since that night, Geoffrey had sent her letters, which Charlotte had intercepted and brought to her. He swore his love again and again in a hundred flowery ways and implored her to marry him. He could not live without her, he vowed. They must be together and when they were, no one—not Justin or even the powerful friends he was fast aligning himself with—could come between them.

"Maybe I should marry him," she told herself. "At least I know Geoffrey loves me. And in time, if I am not near Justin, perhaps I will discover that what I'm feeling for my lord guardian is not love at all. It may be that I will discover true love as Geoffrey's wife."

Doubts and indecision assailed her, but she resolutely pushed them out of her mind as she wiped the dampness from her cheek with the back of her hand.

Near the hedges at the far edge of the garden, Clancy, the shaggy brown wolfhound, appeared. He stood, gazing hopefully toward the house, a stick clamped in his jaws.

Dyanna smiled. Here was a friend whose love and loyalty she need not question. Opening the doors, she went out into the gardens, where the sunlight that peeked through the clouds sparkled on the raindrops still clinging to the grass and the leaves on the trees and bushes. She waved to the huge dog and he bounded toward her, his tail whipping wildly.

By the time she was thoroughly exhausted from chasing Clancy through the gardens and trying to wrest the stick from his powerful jaws, the sun was halfway across the western sky. As she turned back toward the house, she noticed Charlotte waving to her from the music room door.

"What is it?" she asked, pushing back a tendril of hair from her damp forehead as she entered the room.

"A letter," the maid replied, holding out a folded square of thick white paper.

"From Geoffrey?" She hoped the maid did not notice the lack of enthusiasm in her tone. She was beginning to dread Geoffrey's letters. He never ceased to press her to give him a definite answer to his proposal. She supposed she had given him reason to believe that she too was eager to wed, but his constant entreaties were making her feel trapped.

"I don't think so, miss."

Taking the letter, Dyanna broke open the wax seal and unfolded the paper. Her eyes widened as she read:

> Lord and Lady Barkleigh request the
> distinction of Miss McBride's company at
> a masked ball to be held at Barkleigh
> House the evening of June . . .

"Charlotte!" Dyanna cried, thrilled. "A masked ball! At Barkleigh House! And they've invited me! *Me*! Not simply Lord DeVille and Miss McBride, but me especially!"

"I do think his lordship got one as well," the maid informed her.

"I'm not surprised. But that is just as well. After all, I need a gentleman to escort me, don't I?"

"I'm certain Lord Geoffrey would—"

"No doubt he would," Dyanna cut her off. It was all well and good for Charlotte to be loyal to the grandson and heir of the Marquess of Summersleigh; he was still, after all, her master, but Charlotte's endless campaigning on Geoffrey's behalf was becoming tiresome. "But Lord DeVille is my guardian and he should be the one to take me into society. There will be plenty of time for Geoffrey once I've become a part of it."

"I suppose," Charlotte agreed pettishly. "What will you wear?"

"Oh, Lord, I don't know. Something wonderful! I want to dazzle all of London. I want them to gape and gawk and whisper! We shall call in the best dressmaker in all London and order something fantastic!"

Going to the bell-pull, she summoned Ipswich. "Has his lordship returned?" she asked when the butler appeared.

"Some minutes since, miss," he replied. "He has gone to his study."

Dyanna turned to Charlotte, a sparkle in her eyes. "With any luck," she told the maid, "you and I will spend the afternoon choosing the most beautiful costume London has ever seen!"

Flushed with anticipation, Dyanna went to the gold walled room that was Justin's inner sanctum. The air there was redolent with the aromas of fine leather and fine tobacco; the deep, rich midnight-blue velvet draperies muted the glare of the afternoon sun and lent the room a dark, mysterious air.

She rapped gently at the heavily carved door. When Justin replied, she entered the room, her precious invitation to the Barkleighs' ball clutched in her hand.

Justin sat in a chair sheltered in the curve of the tall bow window. A book lay open in his lap, a pen was poised in his hand, and an ornate brass inkwell stood on a table beside him.

"Dyanna," he said, a smile softening the

lines of his face. "Have you been out romping with that dog again?"

"How did you know?" she demanded, wondering for a moment if he didn't actually have that crystal ball he had once teased her about.

"Your hair is all tumbled down your back and your cheeks are flushed. I'm afraid the Misses Pettigrew would not think I was taking very good care of you."

"Oh, pooh! Those old biddies." Dyanna dismissed them with a sour grimace, quite forgetting that she had once liked Abigail, even if she could not bear Adelaide.

"What's that you have there?" He nodded toward her hand.

"It is an invitation. Addressed to me."

"From Lord and Lady Barkleigh, I imagine." Justin waited for her nod. "I got one as well. They were connected to your family in some way, weren't they?"

"They were my mother's god-parents," Dyanna confirmed. "I've never even met them."

"You will, some day, no doubt," Justin predicted off-handedly, making a notation in his ledger.

"Some day? But Justin, they have invited me—"

"I will make your excuses. I'm sure they will understand."

Dyanna drew a deep breath, hoping she had

heard him wrong. "You sound as if I will not be attending this—"

"You won't."

"But . . ." the crisp invitation trembled in her hand. "But, Justin, surely in this case . . ."

Sighing, he closed the book and replaced the lid on the inkwell. "Dyanna, we've been through this too many times. You must complete your year of mourning before—"

"Sweet bloody hell!" she exploded, flinging the invitation to the floor. "You may be a hypocrite, my lord, but I am not!"

"And what does that mean, pray?"

"It means that I hardly knew my father. He left after my mother died, left me without a backward glance and, so far as I know, never spared me another thought. Even when my grandfather died and I was left alone, he could not tear himself away from his gambling and whoring long enough to see me. He had not seen me for twelve years when he died. He did not give a damn about me. But for him—for this stranger—I am to closet myself away for a year and grieve? Can you truly imagine that anyone believes I mourn him?"

"It does not matter what anyone believes," Justin said calmly. "But your life until now has been anything but normal, Dyanna. This is a new beginning and it is time you started going about things in the proper way."

Dyanna forced herself to breathe deeply,

145

trying to quell the growing rage inside her. Her hands curled into fists and her nails cut crescent gouges into her palms.

"It is not fair," she said tightly, shaking with the force of her scarcely repressed fury. "Since you brought me here, I have done as you wished, tried to behave as you wished me to behave."

"I have been quite pleased," he confirmed. "And, to be honest, not a little surprised."

"But what good has it done me? What have I gained?"

He held up a hand to silence her. "Do you mean to tell me that your behavior was merely a ploy to buy my permission to leave off mourning and enter society?"

"No. Well, yes. I thought if I did as you wished, then you might . . . Well, why not?"

He chuckled, shaking his head. "If I had known what all this meek obedience was about, Dyanna, I would have told you not to waste your time."

"You must let me go to this ball!" she cried.

"I said no."

"But you must! I will go!"

"You will not! And there's an end to it!"

Dyanna glared at him, her eyes burning with the blue-white fire of her fury. "You'll be sorry for this, my lord!" she snarled. "You'll rue the day you crossed swords with me."

He eyed her with lazy amusement as she whirled and stormed from the room. In the hall she snatched up her skirts and fled up to her room, where she threw herself across the bed and pounded the pillows with both fists, pretending they were her loathsome guardian.

"I hate him!" she screamed, flinging one pillow across the room. "I hate him! I hate him! I hate him! I'll show him he can't keep me a prisoner! I'll do as I please and be damned to the fine Lord DeVille!"

Chapter Twelve

In the days that followed Justin's refusal to allow Dyanna to attend the Barkleighs' ball, Dyanna watched his engagement book carefully, looking for a day when he would be out for most of the afternoon. When at last she found one, she alerted Charlotte.

As soon as Justin's carriage had passed between the gateposts of DeVille House and into the street, she and her maid slipped out a small, seldom used door and made their way to Piccadilly.

"Are you sure no one saw us?" Dyanna asked, not daring to venture a glance over her shoulder for fear someone might be raising an alarm.

"I don't think anyone did," Charlotte assured her. "Where are we going?"

"Summersleigh House." Setting off with a determined step, Dyanna started up Piccadilly, making for the first side street that would take them toward Grosvenor Square. "The marquess will know how to help me!"

By the time they reached Grosvenor Square, Dyanna had forgotten her fear that someone from DeVille House would come bearing down on them at any moment. She found herself delighting in the mad hustle and bustle that was London at that time of year. The sun shone down on her as she skirted Berkley Square and entered Mount Street. As she walked along, gentlemen in carriages and on horseback glanced once, then again at the pretty girl in leaf green whose silvery curls bounced as she walked and shimmered in any stray sunbeam that managed to make its way beneath the broad brim of her befeathered straw hat.

Like any well-bred girl, Dyanna appeared not to notice the attention she was attracting, but secretly she reveled in it. How delightful it was to venture out from behind the suffocating walls of DeVille House in something beside dull black mourning. How wonderful to feel the sun on one's cheeks rather than the tickling scratchiness of a concealing black veil. And how wicked and unnatural Justin was to deny her all of this!

"Here we are, Charlotte," she said as she turned into the short street that ran between Mount Street and Grosvenor Square. "It won't be long now."

And, in fact, it was only moments later that Dyanna was ushered into the delighted presence of the Marquess of Summersleigh.

"I do beg your pardon, Uncle Horatio," she said, casting a curious glance toward the room's third occupant. "The butler did not tell me you had company."

"I'm glad he did not, m'dear," the old marquess boomed. "I want you two to meet. Damme if that DeVille don't keep you shut up closer than some Newgate bird. Here now, say hello to Phoebe, Lady Hayward. Phoebe? Dyanna McBride. Granddaughter to my old friend, Lord Lincoln."

Dyanna dropped a shallow curtsy. "Lady Hayward," she acknowledged softly, her blue eyes skimming hastily over Lord Summersleigh's friend.

Phoebe, Lady Hayward, was a beautiful woman of, Dyanna guessed, thirty-five or forty. Her hair was a rich, gleaming sable brown and her eyes dark, luminous, and coquettishly uptilting at the corners. A purple riding habit was molded to her deep-bosomed, tiny waisted figure. There was about her, Dyanna thought, an air of worldliness, sophistication, and invitation.

"Miss McBride," Lady Hayward replied. "I have heard so much about you from Horatio and, of course, from Geoffrey. But to be honest, I found it difficult to believe such a paragon could exist."

"I am no paragon of any virtue," Dyanna assured her. "I am afraid Uncle Horatio and Geoffrey are prejudiced in my favor."

"As well we should be," the marquess asserted. "Now, m'dear, tell me how it is you have managed to come visiting sans guardian at long last."

"He does not know I am here," Dyanna admitted. "Charlotte and I slipped away from the house after he had gone to his afternoon engagements."

"And what brought on this sudden desire to slip away, after so many weeks of immurement?"

Dyanna hesitated, drawing off her gloves with more fuss than was necessary while deciding how much she wished to reveal in front of Lady Hayward.

"Perhaps I should take my leave," the perceptive lady suggested.

Dyanna threw her a look of gratitude, but the marquess clamped a restraining hand on the lady's arm, preventing her from rising.

"Nonsense, dear Phoebe, stay where you

are. I am certain Dyanna doesn't mind speaking plainly before you. Do you, m'dear?''

"Of course not," Dyanna murmured, resigned. She wished she could have been alone with the marquess but now, knowing it would be insulting to Lady Hayward to refuse to speak before her, she plunged on:

"I was invited to the Barkleighs' masked ball."

"It is going to be a splendid affair," Phoebe Hayward predicted. "The Barkleighs are superb hosts."

"They were also the god-parents of Dyanna's mother," the marquess informed her. He smiled at Dyanna. "They will be delighted to see how very like dear Elizabeth you are."

"That is the difficulty," Dyanna revealed. "Justin—Lord DeVille—has forbidden me to go."

"Forbidden!" the marquess blustered. "But why?"

"He says I must live in seclusion for a year—a year of mourning for my father."

"A father you never knew! A father not worthy of the title!"

"I do so long to go, Uncle Horatio. I am being driven mad at DeVille House. It is nearly as bad as it was at the Academy. Worse, perhaps, because at school I had lessons, loathsome as they may have been, to keep me

153

occupied. At DeVille House there is nothing. Justin is out all day, every day. Nearly every night."

"Lord DeVille does seem to be cutting a considerable swath through the ranks of fashionable London," Lady Hayward observed.

"While I sit at home, mourning," Dyanna sighed. "Oh, Uncle, it is not as if I wish to become this year's sensation—"

"You could be," Lady Hayward cut in. "You are very lovely."

Dyanna spared her a smile, then went on:

"I merely wish to attend one ball."

"I think you should," Phoebe Hayward decided.

"So do I," the marquess agreed. "It is settled, child. You shall go."

"I told you, DeVille has forbidden it. He is going. If I were to so much as show my face at Barkleigh House, he would bundle me into the nearest carriage and take me home." She grimaced, adding, "And probably give me a good spanking for my trouble."

"He wouldn't dare!" the marquess roared.

Dyanna simply shrugged, unwilling to reveal either to the scandalized marquess or the beautiful Lady Hayward that she had already felt the flat of Justin's hand across her backside.

"I fear he would dare," she disagreed. "He would dare that, and more. He takes his position as guardian most seriously."

"Who would have thought it?" Lady Hayward asked. "I knew Justin DeVille once. Oh, long ago. Just after his father was declared dead and Justin assumed the title. It seemed to me then that the last thing he wanted was responsibility for, or to, anyone. He went to sea as a privateer to restore the fortune several generations of dissolute, reckless Lords DeVille had dissipated. Ah, well. People change. Perhaps he's had enough of careless wandering and now relishes playing the foster papa."

"I might welcome him as such," Dyanna told her, "if I were eight or nine. But I resent it now."

"And so you should." The marquess's jaw was set stubbornly. "Phoebe is right. You should go. And you must."

"But how?"

"I will help you," Lady Hayward offered. "If you would let me."

"How?" Dyanna repeated. "It would be impossible."

"Nonsense. It would be the simplest thing in the world."

Bewildered, Dyanna looked from the marquess to the lady in purple and back again.

"Forgive me," she said, "but I don't see how it can possibly be as simple as you both seem to think."

"Consider, Dyanna," Lady Hayward said, "the nature of this affair. It is a masked ball.

The object is to conceal one's identity. No one is supposed to know who anyone else is. We have merely to design a costume for you and decide how best to smuggle you out of DeVille House and get you to Barkleigh House. And back, of course, before your guardian misses you."

"But the Barkleighs will know. Surely one must present one's invitation, identify oneself—"

"Simplest thing in the world," the marquess repeated. "I'll have a word with William or Louise Barkleigh. I'll get you an invitation in some other name. That's the ticket! An alias."

"French," Phoebe said. "We can put it about that she speaks little English. That way people won't keep trying to draw her into conversation."

"A widow, perhaps," the marquess suggested. "That way there won't be a question of husbands or escorts or chaperones."

"LaBrecque," Phoebe pronounced. "Madame LaBrecque. The widow of the Maréchal LaBrecque."

"Is there truly a Maréchal LaBrecque?" Dyanna asked.

"Oh, I doubt it. But it doesn't matter. After that night the lovely Madame LaBrecque will vanish. No one will investigate."

Despite her earlier reservations, Dyanna felt herself being caught up in their excitement. As the marquess and Lady Hayward made their plans, Dyanna found herself believing that she would, with their help, attend the masked ball whether Justin liked it or not.

"Tudor!" Lady Hayward cried. "You shall go as a lady of Henry VIII's court."

"Why Henry VIII in particular?" Dyanna wanted to know.

"The hoods, my dear. French hoods. They were all the fashion then. They covered the hair and would be much more comfortable than a wig or powder. And a mask could be attached to one so easily." Phoebe pressed a finger to her lips and smiled sheepishly at Dyanna.

"Forgive me," she said softly. "I'm getting carried away. I never even asked if you would like my advice on your costume."

"Oh, but I would," Dyanna assured her. "I hadn't decided on a costume. I didn't dare hope I would really be able to go!"

"Well, if we have anything to do with it, you will," the marquess promised. "And from experience, I can tell you that when Phoebe decides she wants something, she usually gets her way."

Phoebe laughed, slapping the marquess's wrinkled hand playfully. "Horatio, really! You make me sound like a scheming woman. But I will do anything I can to help you, Dyanna. I think it is a crime for a lovely young woman like yourself to be shut away, supposedly mourning a father you never even knew. Now, shall we get down to our planning? I know a perfectly wonderful dressmaker, talented and discreet, whom we can trust to carry out our designs. Horatio? Order some paper and a pen, if you please. We are going to design a beautiful gown for our lovely Dyanna."

For the next two hours, Dyanna watched in rapt fascination as Lady Hayward sketched variations on the Tudoresque costume she had in mind for Dyanna's dazzling, if incognito, debut in London society. Her dream was coming true before her eyes as Phoebe Hayward showed her sketch after sketch inviting her opinions on skirts, sleeves, necklines, hoods, even golden ornaments that would hang from a jeweled chain encircling her waist.

"It looks very expensive," Dyanna worried, holding a sketch of the final result, a gown of scarlet and gold brocade, the over-skirt open in front to show an under-kirtle of black satin. The wide, hanging oversleeves were lined with cloth of gold and the puffed under-sleeves, of black satin, were caught at the wrists into wide cuffs stiffened with embroidery and studded with pearls that matched the trimming banding the low, square neckline. The French hood was to be of gold tissue gathered into a pearl-encrusted gold coronet.

"No more expensive than anyone else's

costume," Lady Hayward assured her. "These are sumptuous affairs, dear child."

"Hang the expense!" the marquess cried. "Tell the dressmaker to send the bills to me."

"Uncle Horatio, you couldn't!" Dyanna protested.

"I can and I will," he vowed. "I'll not have you trying to wheedle funds out of that skinflint guardian of yours in order to pay for something he should have given you freely."

Dyanna opened her mouth to protest that Justin had never begrudged her anything in the way of material comfort since the day he'd taken her to DeVille House, but she bit back the words. It was mean of him to deny her a small pleasure such as this ball. Mean and selfish!

She allowed Phoebe to whisk her away to an upstairs bedroom where she stood in her chemise while she was measured for her costume. She could not, after all, expect to make her way to the dressmaker's shop for extensive fittings. The costume would simply have to be made to fit her measurements and they would have to hope for the best.

Dressed again, she was descending the stairs when the clock in the hall struck the hour. Dyanna gasped. "I had no idea it was so late!" she told Phoebe. "I must be going."

"What, so soon?" the marquess said from the foot of the stairs. "It seems you just arrived."

Sandra DuBay

"I have to be back before Justin returns. I could not bear for him to suspect a thing. He has a way of finding things out, you know. He told me once he has a crystal ball."

"Humph! A little demon to whisper in his ear, more like," the marquess muttered.

"Perhaps he inherited it from his father, the sorcerer," Lady Hayward speculated, smiling angelically as the marquess's pleased, malicious laughter filled the room.

Such talk made Dyanna more than a little uneasy, and she quickly took her leave of the marquess and his pretty companion.

Charlotte was summoned and, amidst profuse thanks, Dyanna tucked a copy of Phoebe Hayward's sketch in her sleeve. With her maid at her heels, she left Summersleigh House and hurried back in the direction of Piccadilly. As she went, she said a little prayer that she would manage to slip back into the house as discreetly as she had slipped out.

Chapter Thirteen

"Has he gone?" Dyanna asked as Charlotte let herself into Dyanna's sitting room.

"Just now," the maid replied. "He said that since you had retired, the servants were dismissed for the night. That should make it easier for us."

"It should," Dyanna agreed. Nerves made her stomach flutter. She was torn between excitement at the thought of attending a grand ball in a beautiful costume and fear that it was all madness, a foolhardy charade that would deceive no one. "How did Lord DeVille look?"

"I didn't see him. I thought it best to stay out of sight. I hid behind a door so I could hear what he said before he left."

"I wonder if I will recognize him at the

ball," Dyanna mused. "With everyone masked—"

"You'll know him at a glance," the maid predicted.

Dyanna nodded, resigned. "I suppose I will," she murmured, thinking there was no one like Justin. She could pick him out in a room with a hundred other men all dressed exactly alike.

"It is time you were leaving. My lord Summersleigh said he would have the carriage waiting at nine."

Dyanna glanced at the clock. It was three minutes past the appointed time. "All right. Fetch my pelisse. We'll go now."

A few minutes later, having slipped out of the silent house, Dyanna and Charlotte were in the marquess's closed carriage being driven to Summersleigh House, where Dyanna would dress, assuming the identity of Madame LaBrecque, beautiful young widow of the late Maréchal LaBrecque.

Dyanna wondered what excuse the marquess had used to procure an invitation from the Barkleighs, not that it mattered. They had been friends too long—Lord and Lady Barkleigh and the Marquess of Summersleigh —for either to question a request from the other.

"I hope this works," Dyanna breathed as the carriage entered Grosvenor Square.

"Why shouldn't it?" Charlotte wanted to

know. "My Lady Hayward promised she would see you home long before my Lord DeVille leaves Barkleigh House."

"I know. It is not Lady Hayward who worries me."

"Then what?"

"It's Justin. He seems to know things—private things. It is as if he can look into my mind. He haunts my dreams. He—"

The carriage rocked to a halt and Dyanna was snapped back to herself. A glance at Charlotte told her she had said too much. The maid regarded her with obvious bewilderment.

"Come along," Dyanna ordered shortly, annoyed at herself for revealing too many of her fears to the maid who, despite her undoubted loyalty to Dyanna, still gave her first loyalty to her master, Lord Summersleigh. Moreover, Dyanna steadfastly believed that Charlotte regarded Geoffrey Culpepper as Dyanna's fiancé in all but name.

It was Geoffrey who met them at the door. Pulling a plumed hat from his head, he swept them a grand courtier's bow.

"Welcome, Madame LaBrecque," he said, "or should I say *bienvenue*? Lady Hayward is upstairs waiting to help you into your disguise. I will show you the way and you can tell me how you like my costume."

Dyanna watched with bemused eyes while he turned in a slow circle before her. He was, it was apparent, supposed to be a Restoration Cavalier. Dressed in bright yellow satin, his costume was awash with rivers of ribbon in shades of green and oceans of silver lace that cascaded from his throat, his wrists, and his knees. Rings glittered on his fingers and diamonds sparkled on the buckles of his red-heeled shoes. An enormous blond periwig, whose gleaming curls tumbled to his waist, engulfed his head, making him look like some hapless creature caught in the jaws of a great, hairy animal.

"It is . . ." Dyanna groped for words. "Astonishing."

"Do you truly think so?"

"Beyond belief," she assured him.

Happy, Geoffrey offered her his arm and led her upstairs.

"Now you must promise me," he said as they approached the upstairs bedroom where Lady Hayward waited, "that you will dance with no one but me. You have all but broken my heart by refusing to answer my letters or even meet with me. Tonight you can heal some of those wounds by being mine and mine alone."

Dyanna sighed. Why was it that the men in her life seemed determined to hoard her, like misers hoarding their gold? She opened her mouth to protest, but Lady Hayward, having opened the door to admit them, saved her the trouble by saying:

"Don't be so selfish, Geoffrey. Poor Dyanna's been all but kept a prisoner by Justin DeVille. Now that she's managed to slip away for an evening's entertainment, you cannot spoil it for her. And what is more, in that costume everyone will notice you and, no doubt, recognize you. If you are seen to be dominating the mysterious Madame LaBrecque, it might attract unwanted attention. The last thing we want is for DeVille to become suspicious."

Dyanna threw Phoebe Hayward a grateful glance as she was whisked into the room. The door was none too gently closed in Geoffrey's face.

"Thank you," she murmured. "I was worried . . .."

"I know," Phoebe assured her. "But Geoffrey is simply afraid some other man will steal you away. I do believe he is in love with you."

"So he has said," Dyanna admitted wanly.

"Well now, we must get you dressed, mustn't we?"

Dyanna nodded, carefully averting her eyes from Lady Hayward's costume. Phoebe's costume, the Huntress, apparently meant to represent Diana consisted of a sheer and clinging silk tunic, golden sandals laced up her shapely, and shockingly exposed, calves, and a golden bow and quiver that lay across the bed shimmering in the candlelight.

Still, Dyanna reasoned as she was quickly

and efficiently undressed by two of the marquess's maidservants and then redressed in the beautiful, glittering costume Phoebe had designed for her, Lady Hayward had long been a fixture of London society. If she wished to appear so skimpily and scandalously clad at a costume ball, it must be permissible for her to do so.

And yet, Dyanna could not shake a certain feeling of scandalized astonishment that stayed in her mind even after she'd descended the stairs and followed Lady Hayward out to the carriage that would take them to Barkleigh House. Another carriage carrying Geoffrey and the marquess—who, eschewing royalty and deities, had decided to come as a pirate king complete with a bandolier of pistols whose weight made him walk at an alarming angle—followed discreetly.

Barkleigh House, all grey stone and pillars, lay in Kensington, not far from Holland House. The line of carriages that had earlier moved at a snail's pace past the entrance had thinned to a trickle. It was only a moment—a very short moment, Dyanna fretted—after their arrival that they were climbing the stairs to the ballroom while Lord Barkleigh's major-domo called:

"Lady Hayward. Madame LaBrecque."

Side by side they climbed the stairs toward the gold-railed balcony where an array of men and women dressed as kings and queens, saints and sinners, the famous and the infamous stood watching and discussing the costumes of late arrivals. At the head of the stairs stood Lord and Lady Barkleigh in the glittering, jewel-encrusted guises of Elizabeth I and her beloved Essex.

"My darling Phoebe," Lady Barkleigh cried, seeming not in the least put out by her ladyship's skimpy attire. "Welcome."

"Louise," Phoebe returned. "This is Madame LaBrecque, whom you kindly allowed me to bring."

"My dear," Lady Barkleigh murmured. Behind the silver mask she wore, her blue eyes were kindly. "We are delighted to meet you."

Dyanna murmured her thanks and exchanged greetings with Lord Barkleigh before she and Phoebe moved into the marble-floored ballroom beyond where an orchestra played from a gold-railed balcony high above the dancers.

"Does she know who I am?" Dyanna whispered.

"Not at all. Horatio simply told her you were a friend. He thought it best to keep the secret among us. But I daresay the Barkleighs would approve of your masquerade. I'm afraid they do not approve of your father's choice of guardian."

"Just as they did not approve of my mother's choice of a husband."

167

"Just so," Phoebe agreed. "I do not mean to slight your father, dear Dyanna, I met him only once or twice, but his reputation, even you must admit, is not of the best."

"Nor is my guardian's."

"Justin DeVille is beginning to make a name for himself among the leaders of the Whigs. I should not be surprised to see him begin to be heard in Parliament before too long. Unsavory though his family history may be, he seems to be bent upon redeeming his family name."

"I suppose that is commendable, but—" She stopped, icy fingers clutching at her heart as she spied him across the long, pillared room. "There he is."

Phoebe squinted toward the opposite end of the candlelit room. "Where?"

"There, near the far door, in black."

Phoebe laughed. "Darling, there are a score of gentlemen in black. Which—?"

"Near the settee, before the last window. Talking to that girl . . ." Dyanna's words trailed off as she forced her gaze away from Justin and toward the young woman on the settee. Dressed as the Queen of the Night, her simple, elegant gown of midnight blue silk was sewn with hundreds of glittering silver stars. In her upswept chestnut curls, a crescent moon of diamonds glittered with each movement of her head.

"Ah, that is Lady Arabella Bevis, eldest

daughter of the Duke of Gresham. My Lord DeVille is setting his sights high if he thinks to woo and win that lady. But then, they do say he's made himself rich as Midas with his pirating—"

"Privateering," Dyanna corrected without thinking.

"Your pardon, privateering. He would not be a bad match for our haughty Lady Arabella."

Paling, Dyanna turned away. She felt sick. Was that where Justin had been all those days and evenings when he told her he was attending to politics? Had he really been out courting that proud, beautiful girl? Dyanna forced herself to take a good look at the girl. She couldn't be more than nineteen. If Justin married her . . .

Dyanna pressed her fingers to her lips. If Justin married her, he would bring her to live at DeVille House with him—and with her, as a sort of foster mother. How could she bear to live at DeVille House with that haughty beauty as mistress? How could she lie awake night after night with Justin and that elegant creature abed but a few doors away? How . . .?

"Dance with me, Dyanna," Geoffrey asked. "You promised."

"Later, Geoffrey," she murmured, already moving away through the milling throng. "I want to sit down."

"Sit?" He tried to follow but they were soon

169

separated. "But I thought you came here to—"

Eluding Geoffrey in the crowd, Dyanna made her way to a settee in a far corner of the room.

"Why did I come here?" she asked herself. "What did I expect to see? What did I think to find! I should have known what he was up to all those days and nights!"

Despairing, angry at herself for putting herself in such a situation, Dyanna did not feel the heated, golden gaze that studied her from across the room. She did not sense the curiosity, the admiration, the attraction she aroused in the heart and mind of the tall man in black velvet, who left his charming companion and went to his hostess's side. She did not see him draw Lady Barkleigh away from listening ears and whisper urgently to her. She did not notice Lady Barkleigh's reluctance to discuss the lovely, mysterious lady in scarlet and gold who had secluded herself in the corner. And she did not watch as Lady Barkleigh found herself gently coerced into crossing the room to Dyanna's side to perform introductions for a gentleman of whom she disapproved but whose name she had had to include on her guest list out of deference to his growing importance in society.

"Madame LaBrecque?" Lady Barkleigh said, her eyes betraying her distress. "Madame—?"

Dyanna gasped, suddenly aware of them before her. Her eyes flew to Lady Barkleigh's face as the older lady bent over her.

"Madame LaBrecque," Lady Barkleigh repeated sharply, her very tone conveying her reluctance to introduce a female guest to one whose family name was steeped in scandal. "Lord DeVille begs to make your acquaintance. My Lord DeVille, Madame LaBrecque."

Unable to flee, finding it impossible to escape, Dyanna held out a trembling hand to Justin, who smiled down at her, golden eyes aglow with admiration.

Chapter Fourteen

Immediately, Dyanna averted her eyes, terrified that Justin would recognize her despite her disguise.

"Would you dance with me, madame?" he asked, one hand extended toward her.

"Oh, no, I—"

"Please, madame. I saw you from across the room and felt compelled to ask Lady Barkleigh for an introduction. I would be honored if you would allow me to partner you in this dance."

Not knowing how to refuse, and knowing that to do so would raise more questions, attract more attention than she felt she could afford, Dyanna laid her gloved hand in his and let him lead her to the midst of the dancers.

"I am given to understand, madame, that you are a widow."

Dyanna bit her lip. Her heart was pounding, hammering in her breast, filling her with a breathless giddiness that was half fear of discovery and half enchantment at being Justin's partner. She felt her hand resting in his, his fingers entwined with hers, his hand resting at her waist while their bodies moved in sensuous accord.

Raising her eyes, Dyanna ventured a single look at him. He seemed handsome as the very devil to her bemused eyes. All in black velvet, he wore a black velvet cap trimmed with pearls and black plumes on his tawny gold hair. The black silk mask that concealed the upper half of his face could not dim the enchanting sparkle of those bewitching golden eyes.

"Madame?" he prompted when she'd left his question unanswered for too long. "You are a widow?"

"*Oui*," she whispered, remembering suddenly that she was supposed to be French. "I am. Forgive me, *monsieur*, my English—" She lifted her shoulders.

He laughed softly, gently. "I fear my French is little better. But I think we may be able to make ourselves understood to each other."

"I hope," she began falteringly, "I fear—"

"You are very shy, madame," he observed, his tone as caressing as the warm look in his eyes. "That has not been my experience with Frenchwomen. They are generally very"—he searched for a way to say what he meant without causing offense"—animated."

"And have you so great an experience of Frenchwomen, *monsieur*?" she could not resist asking, carefully keeping her voice to a near whisper and its tone far higher than normal.

"I have known a few," he admitted. "But none so lovely as you."

"You speak prettily, *monsieur*, but how can you know if I am lovely? My mask conceals—"

"Your mask does not conceal everything," he assured her. "Your lips, your chin, your throat, your—"

He stopped and Dyanna felt a flush spreading hotly down her throat and over her bosom, which swelled above the low, square neckline of her gown.

"Please, *monsieur*, I beg of you." She tried to draw her hand from his. "You are too bold."

"I beg your pardon," he said, holding tight to her gloved fingers. "It is only that you seem to have fascinated me from my first sight of you. Such a thing has happened to me only once before."

"Indeed," she murmured, wondering with a twinge of jealousy what woman in his past had so captured his imagination.

He took her jealousy for offense. "I did not mean to anger you. I only wanted . . ." He sighed, knowing he was making a muddle of it all. "Won't you look at me, madame?"

Dyanna trembled, wishing the dance would end, wishing she were somewhere, anywhere, but there with him. She could not force her eyes up to his face, fearing he might recognize her. Wordlessly, she shook her head.

"*Monsieur,* I . . . "she began, and then, mercifully, the music stopped.

She tried to leave him, tried to draw her hand out of his too-tight grasp. But he refused to release her.

"Please, madame," he entreated. "I need to see—"

"No!" she hissed, jerking her hand free. "I must go!"

Before Justin could react, before he could plea for forgiveness for whatever offense he had apparently given her, or try to restrain her, Dyanna had caught up her brocade and satin skirts and fled, running blindly through the nearest door.

In the long, deserted hall outside the ballroom, she paused, shaking.

"Why did I come here?" she demanded of the emptiness that stretched before her. "I knew he would be here. I knew—"

Behind her, the latch was swinging downward, the door was opening. Instinctively, Dyanna knew it was Justin following her, pursuing her. Without a thought to where she it went, she went on down the long, narrow, candlelit hallway.

Again and again she paused, listening, and each time she heard his footfalls behind her, getting closer, advancing relentlessly, unerringly.

Near panic, she pushed open the last set of doors at the end of the hall. The room was dark, only the slightest sliver of moonlight finding its way between the drawn draperies at the tall windows. Unseeing, Dyanna groped her way around a table and a chair before her hands found the unyielding wall of a tall, carved armoire.

Trembling, she leaned against it, breast heaving.

And then, from outside in the hall, she heard the sound of footsteps approaching. She held her breath as they slowed, passed her door, then stopped and returned.

Dyanna took a step toward the door, cursing herself for not feeling for a key she could twist in the lock.

"Please," she whispered, eyes tightly shut, "oh, please, make him go back to the—"

The rest of her plea went unuttered as the latch shimmered, catching the moonlight as it was pressed down. As the door swung open on silent hinges, Dyanna shrank back into the shadows.

"Madame LaBrecque," Justin said quietly,

silhouetted in the doorway. "I know you are here. I need to see you, speak to you."

"Go back," she whispered into the darkness as he stepped into the room and closed the door. "Go back. Leave me alone."

"I can't. I'm fascinated by you. Tell me your name."

Squeezing her eyes tight, Dyanna whispered the first French-sounding name that sprang to her lips:

"Marie."

"Marie," he repeated, moving across the room toward her without hesitation, as surely as if the room were flooded with light instead of shrouded in shadows.

A shrill cry escaped her as his hand found her sleeve, closed about her upper arm. A shudder coursed through her at his touch— the touch she feared, the touch she'd dreamed of since that night at the Angel Inn when they'd come within a breathless kiss of becoming lovers.

"Marie," he whispered, drawing her to him. "I can't explain . . . I don't understand . . . but it is as if I have known you, needed you, desired you all my life."

His finger slipped beneath her chin and tilted her face up toward his. His lips touched her forehead, her cheek, her ear, before taking her mouth in a tender kiss—a lover's kiss. His arm slipped about her waist and pulled her against him. Her hands clutched at the soft black velvet of his sleeves as if they could not decide whether to push him away or draw him closer, ever closer.

Dyanna felt his hand pulling away the French hood that concealed her hair, tugging off the mask that hid her eyes, but she made no move to stop him. The darkness in the room was all-concealing and the burgeoning desire building inside her made her reckless, oblivious to anything save the growing, ravening hunger inside her.

Her head fell back as his lips traced the throbbing softness at the base of her throat and the tantalizing swell of her breasts above her jeweled neckline. The breathless, mewling moan that slipped between her parted lips fanned the flames of Justin's already raging desire.

Slipping a hand behind her knees, he swept her into his arms and carried her to the narrow, canopied bed she had not even realized stood in the opposite corner.

In the enveloping darkness, Justin laid Dyanna on the high, curtained bed. Trembling with fear and yearning, she felt Justin's hands upon her. The intricate lacings and hooks of her costume yielded beneath his fingers as if by magic. In a few scant moments she lay clad only in the undulating shadows of the night-dark room.

Caught in his sorcerer's spell, Dyanna quivered as his hands caressed her in long, lingering strokes that swept down her arms to the trembling fullness of her passion-tautened, rose-tipped breasts, over the slight swell of her belly to the valley of her ivory thighs. He teased her silken skin, his lips moving, bestowing fluttering kisses along her throat, his tongue stroking the place where her heartbeat throbbed wildly. Her flesh, her senses, had awakened beneath the enchanting ministrations of his fingers, his hands, his lips, his tongue.

She moaned, writhing on the satin counterpane, her hands clutching at him, drawing him closer, as he pulled off his own disguise. His passion had risen apace with her own and he could no longer deny its demands for release. He moved above her, hands stroking her thighs as he moved between them. His lips at her ear formed soft love sounds as his hands slipped beneath her hips and lifted her. Dyanna whimpered deep in her throat, aching for him, afire with the need that burned inside her, the need her mind denied even while her very blood boiled with it.

Justin took her then, quickly, savagely, unaware that the body into which he drove himself was untouched, virginal.

Dyanna's cry of shock, of pain, was smothered by his hard, penetrating kiss. She clung to him as he moved against her, within her, faster and harder, rising and falling, until at last they soared together, breaking free of the web of enchantment the night and their love had woven about them, caught in rapture's embrace.

Dazed, Dyanna lay beside Justin, her pulse still pounding, her limbs atremble. Her body still seemed to burn with the heated aftermath of their lovemaking.

Turning her head on the pillow, she saw him, nearly concealed in the deep-shaded darkness. His eyes were closed, his lips slightly parted as he slept. Beads of perspiration dampened his forehead and upper lip. His skin was sheened with it where the moonlight touched it.

"Justin," she whispered softly, longing to touch him just once more. Her hand came up and reached out to him, but she drew it back before it grazed his flesh. Much as she longed to stay, dearly as she desired to lie there beside him reveling in the sensations, the emotions, the pleasures she had just been awakened to, she knew she had to be gone when he awoke.

Slipping off the high bed, she groped in the darkness for her costume. It lay in a heap beside the bed, tangled with his. With shaking fingers made clumsy by nerves and the need for haste, she put it on, arranging it as best she could without the help of either sufficient light, a mirror, or a maid. Feeling her way across the room, she felt on the floor for her hood and mask. Finding them, she put them on, stuffing her hair into the hood's caul with short, nervous strokes.

When at last she felt presentable, she went to the door and opened it. A shaft of golden candlelight fell through the doorway. In its glow, she saw Justin lying on the bed.

"Justin," she murmured again, her eyes caressing the strong, masculine beauty of his naked body, committing the image to memory. "I love you."

Then, silently, without waking him, she slipped out the door and went to find Lady Hayward who, along with Geoffrey Culpepper and the Marquess, were frantically searching for her. Pleading illness, she begged them to take her home.

Dyanna awoke the next morning stiff and sore. But the aches that plagued her evoked such delicious memories that she could not help reveling in them. Surely, she told herself for the fiftieth time since returning home the night before, surely Justin had known who she was, surely he had seen through her disguise, surely he must have known who it was he held, kissed, loved. Surely he must love her as she loved him. Secure in the thought, she stretched her arms above her head and smiled, content.

But as she lay there in her bed, she heard

noises from the downstairs hall—the sounds of bustling feet and slamming doors.

Curious, she threw back the covers and climbed out of bed. Pulling on a pale pink wrapper, she left her rooms and padded barefoot to the landing overlooking the entry hall.

Justin appeared below her, dressed in bottle green and buff, handsome as always but dearer to Dyanna now. She shivered, her body remembering their lovemaking, remembering the feeling of that powerful body against her own as he strode across the hall. She watched, silent, as he opened the door and stepped back to allow a battery of footmen to enter bearing trunks and boxes.

From outside, a low-pitched purr of a feminine voice cried:

"Justin! Oh, my darling! I've missed you so!"

"Caro," Justin murmured in reply, holding out his arms. "Come inside."

Before Dyanna's bewildered, horrified eyes, a vision of golden beauty in heliotrope silk swept through the door and into Justin's arms. A heart-shaped face of breath-stopping perfection was tilted coquettishly toward his and two pouting, bee-stung lips were offered for a kiss that was bestowed without hesitation.

"Dearest Caro," Justin said tenderly, his arms drawing the girl tightly against him. "You're more beautiful than I remembered, impossible as that seems."

"And do you still love me?" she asked, long-lashed, almond-shaped eyes twinkling up at him.

"More than anyone in the world," he replied before lowering his head to kiss her once more.

The woman, Caro, laughed and said something more, but Dyanna did not hear. By then she was stumbling back toward her rooms, heart tearing in two, eyes half blinded by hot salt tears that spilled unheeded down her flushed cheeks.

Chapter Fifteen

After the storm of her tears had passed, Dyanna tried to collect her thoughts and view the situation rationally. There was no telling who this new arrival was, she reasoned. She might be a relative—that was it, a cousin, up from the country. Perhaps she was married with children of her own and Justin was no more than a favorite relation to whose house she paid a visit whenever she managed to escape the rustic seclusion of her country home for London.

"That must be it," she told herself, dabbing her eyes and peering into the dressing table mirror to assess the damage her little tantrum had caused her. "No doubt she's married to some ancient, doddering old peer who has a crumbling manor house in the wilds of Northumberland that is positively packed to the rafters with screaming, quarreling, colicky children who all look exactly like their faltering old father."

The image made her smile. She felt the weight of uncertainty and dread lifting a little from her shoulders.

"Of course she's happy to see Justin. Who wouldn't be relieved to see a handsome young man after having been shut up all winter with some crochety old curmudgeon? I'm quite certain she is a charming and sweet young woman and we will be friends."

She smiled, pleased and optimistic, at her reflection. A movement behind her caught her attention. She swiveled on the stool just as Charlotte came bustling into the room.

"Your bath is almost ready, miss," the maid announced. "Milord wishes you to come down as soon as you've bathed and dressed."

"To meet his guest, I suppose," Dyanna mused.

"Yes. Who is she, I wonder? She's very pretty."

"She is. She is some relative of Lord DeVille's, no doubt."

"I thought while you're in your bath, I'd try to have a word with her maid. Though she's a sour old puss by the look of her."

"That would be a good idea," Dyanna said.

"I daresay she is likely no more than a country cousin come up to the big city to enjoy a little taste of society under Justin's sponsorship."

"Speaking of society," Charlotte teased her mistress as she went to the dressing room to collect Dyanna's morning gown and accessories. "Did you enjoy the ball last night?"

Dyanna averted her face to hide the flush that stained her cheeks. "It was—enlightening," she admitted.

"Exciting?" Charlotte asked.

"More so than you can imagine," Dyanna murmured. Rising from her bench, she moved toward the sitting room. "Will you see if my bath is waiting now, Charlotte?"

Wishing Dyanna would tell her more about the ball, and curious as to why she was so closemouthed about it, Charlotte nevertheless left the room. Behind her, Dyanna frowned, thinking of the night before. She had been so certain that Justin knew who it was he had held in his arms at the Barkleighs'—who it was he had loved with such passion. But if that were true, wouldn't he have come to her last night or this morning? Wouldn't he have told her he loved her? That they would always be together? That last night was only the first of a hundred—a thousand—nights, the start of a lifetime of sweet, sensuous nights in one another's arms?

"He didn't have the chance," she reasoned

187

as she soaked in a tub scented with essence of hyacinth. "I was still in bed until the very moment his guest—whoever she is—arrived. Doubtless after she leaves . . . I wonder how long she's planning to stay?"

Later, dressed and seated before her mirror while Charlotte swept her hair into a mass of ringlets intertwined with blue ribbons that matched her flounced morning gown, Dyanna asked:

"Did you discover anything about Lord DeVille's guest while I was in my bath?"

Charlotte, who was bursting with her news, nodded vigorously.

"Her name is Naysmith, miss. Caroline Naysmith. Her mother is Georgiana, Lady Naysmith. Her father, Lord Naysmith, is dead. Apparently, he died when Miss Naysmith was but a babe in arms."

"Naysmith," Dyanna repeated. "It seems to me I've heard the name. Naysmith. Yes, I'm sure I've heard it but I cannot remember where."

"I talked to Tilden, Miss Naysmith's maid," Charlotte went on. "She doesn't mind a little gossiping, that one."

"I'm not surprised," Dyanna muttered, comfortably ensconced in her notions of who and what Caroline Naysmith was. "Being shut up in the country with a relic of a master and all those children."

"Master, miss? Children?" Charlotte was

confused. "But Miss Naysmith is not married. She has no children. Tilden says she was visiting at the country home of the Earl of Bittern and is now on her way home to Devonshire. Tilden says as how the Naysmiths' land borders on Lord DeVille's land. They grew up together from the nursery, so Tilden says."

"This Tilden is very open-mouthed about her mistress," Dyanna complained, annoyed at being stripped of all her pleasant misconceptions. "I hope you were not so forthcoming about my affairs."

"Oh, no, miss. Though I have to say she does have some odd notions about you."

"What kind of notions?"

"She seems to think you're a child. 'His lordship's little ward,' she called you. 'The child,' she said. Where do you suppose she got those notions?"

"I can't imagine." Dyanna sighed, remembering those notions she had conjured up about Miss Naysmith, which had given her so much comfort.

Charlotte stepped back as Dyanna rose. With a silk-fringed shawl drapped about her shoulders, Dyanna left her rooms, marching resolutely down the hall and down the stairs, unable to put off the moment of confrontation any longer.

On the stairs, she met Bertran. The Swiss valet smiled and made her a courtly little bow.

"Good morning, Miss Dyanna," he said softly.

"Good morning, Bertran. My maid said Lord DeVille wished me to come down as soon as I was ready."

"Ah, yes. Doubtless he wishes you to meet Miss Naysmith. They are strolling in the garden."

"In the garden? Perhaps I should wait for them to come back. I wouldn't want to interrupt . . ."

She let the thought die. Averting her glance from the valet's face, she did not see Bertran's look of amused fondness. But he said only:

"His lordship did ask that you join them as soon as possible, miss. I'm certain he would not wish you to wait in here for him to return from the garden."

"I see. Thank you, Bertran," Dyanna said.

Continuing down the stairs, she went out through the music room into the garden. In the distance, in the small, domed folly at the far end, she saw Justin standing over Miss Naysmith, who sat on a bench. Squaring her shoulders, Dyanna went to join them.

Caroline Naysmith's musical voice reached Dyanna's ears long before she reached the folly.

"Don't tease me, Justin," the girl entreated, laughing. "You know I always hated it, even as a child. You used to tease me unmercifully."

"I did not," he protested, smiling. "I can't help it if you were so gullible you believed every word I said."

"It was not gullibility, it was simple trust. I believed you meant every word." She pouted prettily. "I suppose you didn't mean any of it. Not even that you love me."

"I meant that, Caro," he said, his eyes tender as he gazed down at her. "You know that."

"And what about marrying me? You know you always told me there was no other girl in the world you'd rather have for a wife."

On the path, concealed from Caro and Justin by a tall hedge, Dyanna paused, holding her breath, waiting for Justin's reply.

"And I meant it, dearest Caro," he vowed. "From that day when I was ten and you were five, and I proposed to you there on the path near the bridge. Do you remember?"

"Of course I remember. And you know, I mean to hold you to it. I pity any woman who tries to steal you away from me. She'll be lucky to escape with her life!"

Justin laughed. "You're a ferocious little she-cat, Caro. But then, you always were."

His head came up as Dyanna appeared from behind the hedge. "Well! Here's our little lie-abed. Dyanna! I was beginning to despair of ever seeing you again."

"I slept in a little late," she admitted. "And

191

then I was not sure if I should join you. I thought perhaps you and your guest might like to be left alone at least for a while."

"Nonsense! I want you two to meet. Caroline, this is Dyanna McBride. Her father was the Viscount McBride. Her grandfather was the Earl of Lincoln. I believe I've mentioned her to you before."

"Indeed, you have." Caroline rose from the bench and turned to face Dyanna. The cool, golden beauty so evident in the hall when Dyanna had glimpsed her from the landing, was even more pronounced upon closer inspection. Like Justin's looks, Caro's beauty seemed an almost physical force that struck one and took one's breath away.

"Dyanna," Justin went on, "Miss Caroline Naysmith, daughter of Lady Naysmith and the late Sir Richard Naysmith. We grew up as neighbors. Caro's family's lands border mine in Devon."

"Neighbors! We grew up in one another's pockets!" Caro's copper-colored eyes skimmed over Dyanna. "Good God!"

A panic seized Dyanna. She wondered if she'd spilled something on her gown or might be wearing mismatched shoes.

"What is wrong?" she asked anxiously.

"Nothing, with you, my dear," Caro assured her. "It is Justin who will have to answer for this!"

"For what?" he demanded.

192

"For all those letters in which you spoke of 'little Dyanna' and 'my little ward' and 'the child'. Sweet heavens above, Justin, I expected a toddler!"

Justin laughed, equally amused by Caro's misconception and by the scarlet flush of embarrassment that flooded Dyanna's cheeks.

"I apologize if I gave you the wrong impression," he told her, not seeming in the least sorry. "But after all, Dyanna is very young. She is my ward. I am, in a manner of speaking, her foster father. Which makes her, also in a manner of speaking, my foster daughter."

"Balderdash!" Caro scoffed. Moving to Dyanna's side, she slipped her arm through Dyanna's. "Listen to him! I've never met a man so quick to justify his own mistakes. And with such imagination! I swear to Heaven, he could seduce a vestal virgin and excuse it by saying he thought she was a courtesan! Come away, dear. You and I must get better acquainted." Deviltry sparkling in her glistening copper-brown eyes, and she arched a graceful eyebrow toward Justin as she said:

"Let me tell you something, Justin. You may enjoy being someone's old papa, but once we are married, I refuse to play mama to a woman only two years younger than I."

"How many years younger?" Justin asked pointedly.

"Hush! Wretch!" Caro ordered, showing him the tip of her tongue for his impudence.

Laughing, she led Dyanna off in the direction
of the house, not noticing how pale and
shaken she had turned.

Chapter Sixteen

"When is that woman going to leave!" Dyanna demanded one morning a week after Caro's arrival. "Charlotte? Charlotte!"

The maid appeared from the dressing room where she'd been putting away some of Dyanna's freshly laundered gowns and underthings. "Miss?"

"Charlotte, can't you speak to Tilden and find out when Miss Naysmith is going to go home?"

"I can ask her, miss. I'm sure if she knows, she'll tell me."

"Then go and ask. Go now, Charlotte. I need to know."

The maid left and Dyanna rose and wandered into her sitting room. From the tall bow window, she could see the garden. Caro was there, radiantly beautiful in a gown of yellow silk flounced with lime green. She was calling to Clancy, who pranced near the shrubberies but refused to come any nearer.

"Good dog, Clancy," Dyanna muttered. At least the great, shaggy wolfhound was loyal to her.

A movement at the garden's edge caught her eye. Her mouth tightened into a strained white line as Justin appeared and crossed the garden toward Caro.

"Justin," Dyanna murmured, her eyes clinging to him as he walked along the sun-bathed path. They hadn't had a moment alone since his precious Caro had arrived. But even so, Dyanna had noticed him looking at her, a thoughtful, almost disturbed expression on his face. She felt certain that had it not been for Caro's presence, Justin would have come to her and told her he knew she had been 'Madame LaBrecque' at the Barkleighs' ball. But of course he could say nothing with Caro in the house. How could he broach so delicate a subject in front of an outsider? She would simply have to wait until the beautiful Miss Naysmith departed for Devonshire—if she ever would!

"Miss?" Charlotte had returned.

"Did Tilden tell you anything?" Dyanna demanded. Does she know when her mistress is planning to leave?"

"She said she did not know," Charlotte told

her. "She said Miss Naysmith had planned to stay only a day or two, but that Lord DeVille asked her to stay longer."

"That's impossible!" Dyanna snapped, refusing to believe that Justin was not as anxious for Caro's departure as she, Dyanna, was.

Charlotte lifted her shoulders. "I'm sorry, miss. That is what she told me."

"That may be what her mistress told her, but I know better."

Charlotte said nothing. There was nothing to say—nothing, at least, that Dyanna would hear without growing angry. From a pocket in her skirt, the maid drew a letter.

"This came for you, miss."

Dyanna took it. Turning it over, she recognized the familiar seal. "It's from Geoffrey. I'm surprised Justin did not see it in the morning post."

"It came by messenger. I happened to overhear him asking for you when one of the maids answered the door."

Listlessly, Dyanna broke the seal. Geoffrey had begun showering her with letters once more after the Barkleighs' Ball. She wondered, suddenly, why she had treated him so cavalierly. After all, at least he did not ignore her in favor of some simpering woman to whom he'd been attached since childhood.

Her eyes skimmed over the letter's contents. Meet him in the park, he entreated. They would walk and talk or, if she preferred a more private setting, go driving.

"I'll go," she decided. "I'll go and be damned to Justin DeVille and his fine Miss Naysmith!"

At precisely two o'clock that afternoon, Dyanna entered Hyde Park. Her face was shielded by a broad-brimmed straw hat and by a fringed silk parasol held aloft on a slender bamboo handle. Since receiving Geoffrey's letter, she had further fixed her determination to be agreeable to him. Justin had graciously agreed to take Miss Naysmith to the theater in Covent Garden that night. Of course Dyanna could not go, he'd decreed before she'd even had the chance to ask. As with all other things, her much-vaunted mourning precluded her appearing anywhere as frivolous and public as the theater.

"Dyanna?" A voice hailed her from the lane that ran through the park. "There you are! You came!"

Geoffrey was conservatively dressed—for Geoffrey. His suite of gold moiré was worn over a scarlet-and-white striped waistcoat and scarlet-and-white striped stockings. His cravat was of silk edged with delicate lace.

He bent low over Dyanna's hand as he reached her side. I did not dare hope," he declared fervently. "I have pleaded for your company so many times."

"I know, Geoffrey," she admitted. "I have treated you badly."

"I have put much of it down to DeVille's influence," he told her. "He can be very . . . persuasive."

Dyanna looked away. "Don't let's talk about Justin, please."

"Nothing would please me more. Shall we walk?"

"I would prefer to ride, if you don't mind."

Ever obliging, Geoffrey offered her his arm and walked with her to the lane where his carriage waited.

With Charlotte somewhat precariously settled next to the driver, and Geoffrey and Dyanna seated side by side on the tufted leather squabs within, the carriage set off. Geoffrey turned to Dyanna and said:

"They say your guardian has a houseguest. He has been seen squiring her about town."

"Yes," Dyanna admitted. "Miss Naysmith. Caroline. She is, I'm told, a neighbor of his from Devonshire."

"Caroline Naysmith! I'd say there is a deal more to their relationship than mere neighborliness."

"What do you mean?" she demanded.

He fixed her with a reproachful look. "Dyanna, Dyanna, do you pay no heed at all to the things I say to you? Have you been so fascinated with the dashing Lord DeVille that you have not spared me the slightest bit of attention?"

"I'm sorry, Geoffrey," she murmured,

blushing. "I admit I have been preoccupied with Justin and what is happening at DeVille House. Tell me again about why the name Naysmith should be familiar to me."

"That first night, at Summersleigh House, when we were in the library, I told you that Sebastian DeVille's mistress was named Georgiana, Lady Naysmith."

"That's right! I racked my brain trying to think of where I had heard the name. I should have remembered. Forgive me, Geoffrey."

"How could I not? But now, Lady Naysmith's daughter is a guest in Lord DeVille's home. It looks to me as though, since the mother could be no more than the previous Lord DeVille's mistress, the daughter is intent upon becoming the present Lord DeVille's wife."

"It certainly would appear so," Dyanna agreed wanly.

"And how will that make you feel? What if Caroline Naysmith becomes mistress of DeVille House?"

"It would be intolerable," Dyanna told him honestly.

"Then do something about it."

She eyed him curiously. "What can I do?"

Geoffrey sighed. "You know what you can do, Dyanna. I'm sure I've hinted at it a thousand times, but you willfully choose not to understand me."

Seizing her hand, he pressed smacking kisses onto the back from her fingers to her wrist. "I love you, Dyanna, and my love makes me bold; it gives me the courage to ask you to marry me once again. You can see now how your life is with DeVille. He keeps you a virtual prisoner. And if he marries Miss Naysmith—dear Dyanna, consider what I offer you. I will make you the belle of London, society's darling. Please, please say yes."

"I must consider, Geoffrey," she hedged. "After all, what you propose is an elopement. An illicit, backstreet affair."

"How sordid you paint it," he scolded. "I will procure a special license and find a proper clergyman. There will be witnesses. We will find the most beautiful country church we can. All will be as perfect as we can possibly make it. I do not mean for this to be a squalid business of which you will have to be ashamed. I mean it to be a romantic adventure of which you will be proud to tell our children and grandchildren."

"I will consider your proposal," she promised. "Truly I will. Of one thing I am positive; I cannot go on the way things are."

Amidst promises that she would seriously consider Geoffrey's proposal and that she would not wait too long before giving him his answer, Dyanna was let out in a street near Piccadilly. With Charlotte following, she

201

slipped back into DeVille House only moments before Justin's carriage turned off Piccadilly and rolled up to the front of the house.

"Dyanna?" Justin's voice echoed along the corridor outside her sitting room.

Positioning herself on the window seat, an open book in her lap, Dyanna assumed an air of complete innocence.

"In here, Justin," she replied, looking for all the world as if she had not stirred from her rooms all day.

He appeared in the doorway, tall and golden, dressed in a crimson coat with a buff waistcoat and oyster breeches. Dyanna felt a twinge of longing, of yearning, of desire at the sight of him. The memory of that night at the Barkleighs' was like a cloying ache in her very soul.

"Dyanna?" Justin repeated. "You're not listening to me."

"I'm sorry." She flushed, glad he could not know where her thoughts were straying. "What were you saying?"

"I was saying that I have decided to go to Devonshire to see how Wildwood is progressing. I had intended to go there as soon as I'd returned from America. But then all this business with your father's will and your guardianship cropped up. Now that all that is settled, I want to go."

"Devonshire!" Dyanna's smile was radiant. "Oh, Justin!" Casting aside her book, she ran to him and threw herself into his arms. Not noticing how he paled at the sudden contact of their bodies, she went on:

"I'd love to see Devonshire! And I'd love to see Wildwood! It must be beautiful! I just know it is!"

"Dyanna . . . Dyanna!" Justin interrupted, gently but firmly disengaging her arms from about his neck. "Dyanna, listen to me."

The smile faded from her face and Dyanna stepped back though her wrists were still imprisoned in his grasp. "What is it? What's wrong?"

"I didn't mean that *we* were going to Wildwood. I mean that I was going to Wildwood. I think it would be best for you to remain here in London."

"Stay here? To keep Caro company, I suppose?"

"No. Actually, Caro is leaving with me. She is returning home and she suggested I come see how Wildwood is getting on. It seemed sensible and—"

"I see." Dyanna jerked away from him. "You and Miss Naysmith are going to Devonshire. But I may not go. I must remain here, in this prison you call a home. In my plush gaol—"

"Dyanna," he sighed. "I don't know if the house is habitable yet. I may have to stay in rather primitive surroundings. I may even have to stay at Naysmith Court temporarily."

Dyanna turned her back to him to hide her emotion. "You must do as you think best, of course," she murmured.

"Don't take this badly. I—"

"Is there anything else you wished to tell me, my lord?" she asked coldly. "Because if there is not, I have a headache and I should like to lie down."

"No, there's nothing else. We'll be leaving on Friday."

"I see."

Faced with her cool silence, there was nothing for Justin to do but leave the room. The moment the door closed behind him, Dyanna called for Charlotte.

"Bring me paper and a pen and ink," she ordered. "I've a letter to write—a letter to Geoffrey Culpepper. You can deliver it to Culpepper House, Charlotte. I'll think of some excuse for you to leave. And then, after you come back, we'll have to begin planning what I will take with me."

"With you, Miss?" Charlotte asked.

"When I elope. Wish me well, Charlotte, I've decided to become Lady Dyanna Culpepper."

The maid started to leave the room, but Dyanna called her back. "Oh, and Charlotte? Find me that book—the one Geoffrey gave me about Lord Lucifer Wolfe. I've a mind to read it."

Chapter Seventeen

It was mid-morning of the following Friday. Dyanna, ensconced in a chair in her sitting room, closed the book she had been reading. She was tired of reading of the life and crimes of Lord Lucifer Wolfe—tired of wondering if the cruel, ruthless man portrayed in the book was actually Sebastian DeVille, tired of wondering how much like his scandalous father Justin might actually be.

A door slammed downstairs and Dyanna sighed. She knew without looking that the two traveling coaches drawn up before the house were being loaded in preparation for Justin and Caro's departure. She had not been downstairs that morning; she did not intend to go downstairs until her guardian and his beautiful traveling companion had left.

She was hurt by his callous dismissal of her, wounded by his unwillingness to take her with him. That he did not care for her company was obvious—hadn't he taken pains to spend time without her since her arrival at DeVille House? But then, she wondered, if he did not find her a pleasing or interesting companion, if he could not, as seemed the case, be comfortable in her presence—why did he not simply relinquish his guardianship to the Marquess of Summersleigh? She refused to believe it was her money he lusted for—he seemed to have money of his own in abundance. It could not be her person— despite her certainty that he had seen through her disguise at the Barkleighs' Ball, he had given her no hint that he knew she had been Madame LaBrecque. He had not come to her, not sought her out, not touched her. Their conversations had been so impersonal that a stranger overhearing them would never had suspected the intimacies that had passed between them in that shadowy bedchamber in Kensington.

Of course, she reasoned to herself, Caroline Naysmith had appeared first thing the next morning. Perhaps, if she had not come to stay . . . if Dyanna and Justin had been alone . . .

"No, he wouldn't have come to me,"

Dyanna muttered, resigned. "It would not have mattered a whit if Caro came or not. The simple fact is that Justin does not know I was Madame LaBrecque. I was simply a woman he lusted after and took." She glanced down at the closed book in her lap. If, as Geoffrey said, the story of Lucifer Wolfe was truly little more than an exposé of Sebastian DeVille's sins, then Justin DeVille's father's infidelities —primarily with Georgiana, Lady Naysmith, Caro's mother—had driven Justin's mother, the tragic Lady Barbara DeVille, to an early death. Whether she died accidentally, took her own life, or was pushed from the high tower of Castle DeVille, the fact remained that her husband's cruelties had made her life a hell on earth.

"There is much of Justin's father in him, I am sure. Much of that wickedness, those vices, that made them call Sebastian DeVille the Wicked Earl. I am, no doubt, fortunate that Justin does not love me. In that way I may escape the fate that befell Justin's mother. At least if Justin covets neither my fortune nor my person, history will have no chance to repeat itself with Justin, Caro, and me."

Leaning her head against the high back of the chair, she slipped off into a troubled doze, haunted by dreams of herself, poised at the window of a high, windswept tower. Footsteps —slow, measured, threatening—approached on the winding stone steps; Dyanna held her breath, waiting, watching, terrified, knowing that her fate hung in the balance, that her very life was in peril. And then, there he was— Justin, diabolically handsome in black velvet, the glow of bloodlust in his golden eyes. He approached, a slow, evil smile curving his lips. Dyanna backed away, pressing herself against the sill of the gaping window. She felt the cold wind at her back and knew, as he reached out to her, that he meant to kill her. His fingers brushed her arms, seized her, pushed her back . . . back . . .

"Dyanna?"

Dyanna awoke with a scream. Justin's face was above hers; his fingers dug into her shoulders.

"Let me go! Leave me alone!" she screamed. Scrambling out of the chair, she pushed past him.

"Dyanna," he said, laughing, "You were dreaming."

"You were . . . we were . . ." She pressed a hand to her forehead. She took a deep breath and noticed that Justin, dressed in brown and oyster, his black jackboots shining, had his hat clutched in one hand.

"You're leaving?" she said softly.

"I thought you would come down to say good-bye," he said, his golden eyes moving swiftly over her frilled, beribboned gown of jonquil satin before returning to her face.

"Come down to wish you a pleasant sojourn?" she countered. "Surely with such delightful company you will have no need of such wishes."

"Dyanna," he said, with more gentleness than she might reasonably have expected, "there are reasons for my leaving you behind . . ."

"Pray, my lord," she said, forcing a laugh she hoped sounded airy and carefree, "do not concern yourself. Don't forget, I spent all my life in the country. I am not so eager to return to it—particularly not to such a wild and remote part as Devonshire."

If he was at all taken in by her brave words, Justin made no sign of it. Instead, he merely shrugged, saying:

"I see you are in no mood to discuss this matter calmly. I'm sorry. I don't like for us to part with hard feelings between us. But I see it can't be helped. Goodbye, Dyanna."

Taking her hand, he lifted it to his lips and kissed it, his mouth lingering warmly, caressingly, on her skin as his eyes gazed deeply into hers.

A shudder shook Dyanna and she drew her hand out of his grasp. For a moment a look passed between them, a look that shook her to her very core. Before she knew what was happening, Justin bent and kissed her quickly, passionately, on the lips.

Then he was gone and Dyanna stood there,

fingertips pressed to her lips. She did not hear the clacking of the horses' hooves nor the rumble of the wheels as the two carriages— Caro's carrying Caro and Justin, and Justin's carrying the bulk of their luggage, Bertran, and Caro's talkative maid, Tilden—rolled out of the yard and disappeared into Piccadilly.

Charlotte was at the door almost immediately. "They've left, miss," she announced breathlessly, knowing what was arranged for an hour hence.

"Yes, I know," Dyanna murmured, her mind still full of Justin and his all-too-brief, bittersweet kiss.

The strange tone of her voice alarmed the maid. "You haven't changed your mind, have you?" she asked, her voice filled with apprehension, terrified at the thought of being cheated of the adventure of a lifetime.

Have I? Dyanna wondered. Has Justin, with that simple kiss, destroyed my resolve? Could he have such power that, with such a simple gesture, he could make me abandon the plans I have made with such deliberation? She closed her eyes. It's a trick! No doubt he senses something afoot and thinks that with a single kiss he can bring me back under his spell. Well, it won't work! I'm not poor Lady Barbara DeVille to be held in the thrall of some sensuous sorcerer!

"No!" she declared. "I haven't changed my mind. Are the bags packed?"

"Not quite. I didn't want to finish them until his lordship was safely away."

"Well, finish packing. I want to write Justin a note so there is no mistaking what has happened to me. By the time someone finds it and sends it on to him in Devonshire, Geoffrey and I will be married. There will be nothing Justin DeVille can do about it."

Relieved and excited, Charlotte went about the last of her packing. In an hour they would be on their way. In an hour, Dyanna would set her feet on the path toward becoming Lady Dyanna Culpepper and, one day in the future —the far future, she amended out of loyalty to the kind, elderly gentleman of Grosvenor Square—she would be the Marchioness of Summersleigh. It was a glittering prospect; it certainly dazzled Charlotte, who expected to accompany her young mistress on every step of the way.

When an hour and more had passed with no sign of Justin's returning, Dyanna placed the letter she'd written on her dressing table, where someone was sure to find it and forward it to Justin. Then, each carrying a carpet bag with their night things and a change of clothes, Dyanna and Charlotte set out.

With the master away, the atmosphere at DeVille House was one of easy informality. The staff, which normally bustled beneath the watchful eyes of Ipswich and Bertran, went about their chores with a lackadaisical air that made it easier than usual for Dyanna and Charlotte to slip away unnoticed.

"What if they miss you right off?" Charlotte asked as they slipped through the little-used gate in the high wall that had come in so handy on previous excursions.

"They won't," Dyanna told her confidently. "Luncheon is over. They are used to my spending my afternoons in my rooms reading. No one is likely to come up until suppertime. By then, we'll be well away and they will have no way of finding us."

Satisfied, Charlotte fell into step behind Dyanna as they marched resolutely along Piccadilly to where a maroon-and-black traveling coach awaited them, concealed around the corner in Half Moon Street.

"Dyanna, darling!" Geoffrey crooned as he sprang from the coach, a vision in baby blue and lemon. "You are just on time, though it seems I've been waiting here for hours!"

He bundled them into the carriage and then, seating himself beside Dyanna, ordered the coachman to set off.

"It is all arranged," he told Dyanna happily.

"All?" she repeated, suddenly seeing how foppish, how dandified he seemed next to— but no, she must not think of Justin, not now.

"The wedding! I have sent a messenger ahead to Patterton Park."

"Patterton Park?"

"My country home. I have notified the clergyman whose living I provide that he is to wait
upon our arrival. We will be married as soon
after we arrive as possible, and then spend our
honeymoon at Patterton."

Dyanna flushed and turned her face toward
the window. The thought of doing with Geoffrey the things she had done at Barkleigh
House with Justin aroused feelings in her she
could not afford to explore, given her circumstances.

"Is it wise, I wonder, to go to your country
estate? After all, should anyone come looking
for us, they would almost certainly look there
first."

"It does not matter. By the time they could
follow us there, the deed will be done. You
will be my wife. They will be powerless to
come between us." Geoffrey's beaming face
clouded a little. "Beside which, my mother
has declared she must be present."

"Your . . . mother?" Dyanna glanced at
Charlotte and surprised a look of unease on
the maid's face. Was the Dowager Lady
Culpepper such a dragoness, then?

"Yes. She resides at Patterton Park."

"So, we are to spend our honeymoon with
your mother?"

"Well . . . yes. But it is a very large house."

Sighing, fighting back feelings of panic and
misgivings, Dyanna concentrated on the scen-

ery passing outside the window and tried not to think of the possible folly of her actions.

Even as Geoffrey's coach passed out of London and entered the country, the coaches bearing Justin and Caro toward Devonshire drew into a coaching house and stopped before the vine-covered entrance.

"How perfectly lovely," Caro sighed, strolling toward a tumbling brook that passed behind the inn. Ducks waddled on the bank and a pair of swans glided gracefully beneath a charming Jacobean footbridge spanning the stream. "Oh, Justin, do let's stop here for the night."

Receiving no reply, she went to him and touched his sleeve.

"Justin?" she repeated.

The faraway, troubled look in his eyes gave way to attention. "I'm sorry, Caro. What did you say?"

"I said we should stop here for the night. It's so very lovely here. So peaceful."

He squinted at the sun, still high in the sky. "It's a little early to speak of stopping for the night, isn't it?"

Caro affected a much-practiced, much-admired pout that turned real when she noticed he had once more turned his attention to the faraway distance and away from her. They had been together so little since Justin had taken to his travels on the sea. She had thought this trip would bring a renewal of the closeness they had shared during their childhoods in Devonshire.

"Caro," he said softly, sending her hopes soaring. "I think—"

"Yes, Justin?"

"I think I should go back." He frowned, troubled by nagging, nameless doubts.

"Back? Back where?" she demanded harshly, all her feminine wiles abandoned.

"Back to London. You go on ahead. You have Tilden to keep you company and enough postilions to ensure your safety. I have the strangest feeling that something is wrong at home."

"Wrong with Dyanna?" she asked.

"Perhaps." Turning away, he went to Bertran and directed him to see that Caro's baggage was removed from his coach and placed in her own.

"If everything is as it should be with Dyanna," he told Caro, who had come to stand beside him, "I'll catch up with you."

Before Caro could speak, Justin and Bertran had climbed into his coach, and the gleaming black vehicle had turned and was heading back to London in a cloud of choking dust.

Chapter Eighteen

The first thing Justin noticed when he entered DeVille House upon arriving back in London just after nightfall was the almost preternatural silence of the great house on Piccadilly.

"Milord," Ipswich said, when at last he made an appearance in the entrance hall. "We did not expect you back. Cook has not prepared . . ." He exchanged an apprehensive glance with Bertran as his sentence trailed off into nothingness.

"Cook has not prepared what?" Justin demanded.

"Supper, milord. Excepting, of course, for the staff."

"Miss Dyanna wasn't hungry? She isn't ill, is she?"

"No, milord. She isn't ill."

"Then why didn't she want supper?"

"Because she . . . that is to say . . ."

"Out with it, man!" Justin roared. "Because she what?"

After the tiniest of pauses, the butler went on in a rush, "Because she is not here, milord."

"Not here! Where the hell is she, Ipswich! I gave no one leave to let her go out!"

From the pocket of his coat, the butler produced Dyanna's note. "This was found in her room, milord, when one of the maidservants went up to call her to dinner." From his other pocket, he produced a packet of Geoffrey's letters tied with a frayed satin ribbon. "These were found in her dressing table." By way of explanation he added; "I was looking for some evidence of where she might be found, milord."

"And do these provide evidence, Ipswich?" Justin asked coldly.

"I believe they do, milord," the butler answered quietly.

Without another word, Justin turned and disappeared into his study. As the door closed behind him, Ipswich gestured for Bertran to follow him to the butler's pantry, where he would explain the contents of the letters and the belowstairs speculations as to what might be in Dyanna's note.

In his study, Justin sank into a chair. The

packet of letters he tossed onto his desk. Dyanna's note he turned over in his hands. A part of him knew with dreadful certainty what it contained. Another part, perhaps more trusting, if less practical, hoped against hope that he was wrong.

At last, knowing it was foolish to delay the inevitable, he broke the seal and unfolded the crisp, heavy paper. Dyanna's flowing, ornate handwriting decorated the page. She wrote:

"My Lord DeVille;
By the time you read this note, I shall be Lady Dyanna Culpepper. After many long days and sleepless nights, I have come to the decision that this is the wisest and, in truth, the only course open to me. I am, as your ward, under your power until my twenty-first birthday or my marriage. But I cannot bear the prospect of three years and two months more of captivity, albeit in that most beautiful and luxurious of prisons—DeVille House.

Lord Geoffrey Culpepper vows that he loves me; you are aware of the long and close association of our two families. I believe we will suit well enough and pray we will find some measure of contentment together.

I pray you, my Lord, wish me well in my new life. I feel certain that once your initial surprise and, perhaps, anger, has

*passed, you will be relieved to find
yourself freed of what I feel certain has
been an onerous situation for you.
   I remain, yours respectfully,
   Dyanna McBride*

The letter shook in Justin's hand as he laid it on the gleaming desk top. Eloped! She had eloped with that foppish idiot, Geoffrey Culpepper. But how? They must have been laying their plans for months, he thought—how else could it have been arranged on such short notice? How else could they have been so ready to act the moment an opportunity presented itself?

His eyes fell on the packet of letters Ipswich told him had been found in Dyanna's dressing table. Reluctantly, he drew one from the top of the stack. Unfolding it, he read:

*"My own darling Dyanna;
Too many days have passed since last we
were together. My eyes long to behold
you, my fingers ache to touch you . . ."*

Scowling, Justin stuffed the letter back into the stack. That the others were like it he had no doubt. He had no wish to read more—no desire to see the images they painted in his all too fertile imagination. They must have been conspiring together from the very beginning. From the first she must have given Culpepper reason to believe she would marry him. What else had she given him? Her heart? Her love? Herself?

Anger and jealousy raged inside Justin, but as he gazed at the evidence of Dyanna's perfidy, those emotions faded before a heavy, aching sadness that filled his heart. Against all better judgment, in spite of the way he'd forced himself to keep his distance from Dyanna, to treat her, and train himself to think of her, as a child, he knew he was falling in love with her.

Love. It was not an emotion he'd had a great deal of experience with. He'd managed to avoid entanglements of the heart, preferring the easy freedom of light-hearted affairs with women no more interested in bonds and emotional ties than he was.

But now . . . Once he'd seen Dyanna, perhaps from the moment he had first held her that night at the Angel Inn, she'd been the only women in his heart, his mind. The only woman he desired—saving, of course, Marie LeBrecque. That night at the Barkleighs' Ball preyed on his mind, though he could not say why; the woman had been alluring in some way he did not understand. He'd wanted her as soon as he saw her, and it had saddened him to awaken in that shadowy bedchamber at Barkleigh House and find her gone. There was something about their lovemaking that nagged at the edges of his conscience. For all that she was supposed to be a widow, Madame LeBrecque had been somehow innocent, tentative, though passion had overcome her initial reticence. Still, there was something about her, an impression only, for it had been too dark in the room to see clearly what he thought must surely be the face and form of an angel, that reminded him of—

He shook his head ruefully and permitted a small, self-mocking smile to curve his lips. Even when he had, after so many weeks of self-imposed celibacy, taken a woman to bed, it had to be a woman who, for some unfathomable reason, reminded him of Dyanna. He might have known. He looked at the letters lying on the table before him and cursed himself for a fool. He should have known. When at last love had caught him—outwitted him in his efforts to elude it—it had to be with a willful little hoyden who had already given her heart to another.

"So be it," he muttered. With a sweep of one hand, he brushed the letters and Dyanna's note into a drawer. "I wish them the joy of each other. Though what joy she could find in the arms of that jackanapes is beyond me!"

Leaving the study, Justin bellowed for Bertran and, when the valet answered his master's summons, set him to the drawing of a bath and the laying out of Justin's evening clothes. He would go out and relax, perhaps gamble or dance or flirt, and forget that ungrateful chit whose aqua eyes and silvery hair danced all too clearly in his mind's traitorous eye.

Although he left DeVille House intending to go to one or another of the dinners, balls, or salons to which he had invitations, Justin ordered his driver to take him instead to Brooks's Club in St. James's Street. It was there that Charles James Fox waylaid him.

"Justin DeVille! Well met, my lord. I'd heard you'd left London for the wilds of Devon."

"A change of plans, sir," Justin replied, not particularly interested in the gossip of the brilliant, slovenly Mr. Fox.

"Ah. And how fares that beautiful ward of yours?" He kissed the tips of his fingers. "A goddess, my lord. I envy you her guardianship."

"She is well enough," Justin replied guardedly.

"What will you do with her? Once her mourning is over, of course."

Justin fought to contain his impatience. He had come to Brook's to try to forget Dyanna, if only for an evening, and here was Fox wanting to discuss her.

"I expect I'll marry her off," he said casually. He was unwilling to so much as hint that anything was amiss between his ward and himself. "Perhaps she'll wed Summersleigh's heir—young Culpepper. The families have been friends for generations, you know."

"Culpepper! Lord Geoffrey?" Fox laughed. "Hardly likely, my lord. I should think Culpepper's wife would take a dim view of that."

Justin was shocked out of his bored impatience. "His wife! But I thought he was . . . I never heard that he . . ."

Fox nodded, not surprised by Justin's astonishment. "It is supposed to be a secret. Young Culpepper believes, and rightly so in my opinion, that the old marquess, his grandfather, would disinherit him if he found out."

"Who is she? His wife?"

"She was an actress—on the boards with Perdita Robinson, in fact. Her name is Octavia FitzGeorge. One hears she gives herself grand airs and demands that her servants address her as 'milady,' for all that Geoffrey will not acknowledge her publicly as his wife. He keeps her in a house in Great Queen Street. He keeps her in great style, so they say, but they are always in debt. Only the prospect of Culpepper's becoming Marquess of Summersleigh keeps the duns away. Between us two, my lord, Culpepper is a reckless gambler and not above playing upon the advantage, if you follow me. It is bound to end badly, I fear, but he is desperate for money and cannot risk the old Marquess's questions by going to him for it. So, what is he to do?"

"What indeed?" Justin asked aloud, his

calm exterior belying the outraged fury building inside him. What is Geoffrey to do for
money but dupe a young heiress into eloping
—convince her to enter into what is, for him,
a bigamous union. And all in the interest of
getting his hands on Dyanna's fortune.

"My lord?" Fox prompted when Justin had
remained silent too long.

"I beg your pardon?" Justin said, suddenly
recalling his surroundings.

"I asked, my lord, if you would care to go to
the faro tables and try your luck."

"Thank you, Fox, but no. I have just recol-
lected an important appointment. Good
evening—and thank you."

"For what?" Mr. Fox wondered aloud, but
by then Justin was no more than a retreating
shadow.

Chapter Nineteen

The house in Great Queen Street to which Justin was directed was not grand or impressive, but it was elegant, and in the houses nearby dwelt, among others, the dramatist Richard Brinsley Sheridan.

Descending from his carriage, Justin mounted the steps to the front door and rang the bell. He waited some time, then knocked again. At last, after what seemed an eternity, his persistence was rewarded.

"What do you want?" a rough, masculine voice asked through the partially opened door.

"I wish to see your mistress," Justin told him. "It is a matter of some importance."

"'Er ladyship ain't in," the man snarled. "An' if yer tryin' to collect fer—"

"I am not a bill collector," Justin asserted coldly. "Tell your mistress I am here with important news about Lord Culpepper."

"'Is lordship? He ain't dead, is 'e?"

"No, he is not dead. Now tell your mistress Lord DeVille is here. I don't relish being left to dawdle on doorsteps!"

"Lord De—" Wide-eyed, the man pulled open the door, allowing Justin to step into a small, sparsely furnished entrance hall. "Yer pardon, milord! It's only—that is, we ain't used to the gentry callin'. I thought . . . I'll get 'er ladyship."

Justin had to smile as the man scurried away. If the butler was any indication of the servants Geoffrey had provided for his 'wife', he hadn't been extravagant. In fact, it looked as though he'd recruited them from the tap-room of the nearest inn.

"My lord?"

Justin turned as a door opened behind him. A woman stood there. She was little more than a girl, really—small, generously round-ed, with a spattering of freckles across a tip-tilted nose and wide, dark eyes framed in thick lashes the same strawberry blond as the piled-up curls atop her head.

"Madame," Justin said. He had come pre-pared to be stern and forbidding, but he found himself softening toward this gentle, young creature who had clearly been taken in by Geoffrey's grandiose promises. "Forgive my calling upon you this way."

"Not at all, my lord. Won't you come in? I am sorry Geoff—Lord Culpepper—is not here at present. If it is he you have come to see—"

"Actually, it is you I have come to see, madam. My business concerns Lord Culpepper."

Leading him into a salon whose sparse, worn furnishings belied Charles Fox's tales of the splendor in which Lord and 'Lady' Culpepper lived, Octavia FitzGeorge stopped in her tracks and fixed Justin with a frightened stare.

"Does he owe you money, my lord? I'm afraid I have none here to—"

"Calm yourself, madam," Justin soothed her, declining an offer of comfits with a wave of his hand. "I am not here to dun you. If you will but tell me where it is Geoffrey Culpepper has gone, I will be on my way."

The haunted, anxious look was back. "Gone, my lord?"

Justin smiled. "I know you are—or were—an actress, madam. But I beg you not to feign innocence. Surely you know where it was Lord Culpepper was going when he left London earlier today?"

"My lord, I do not think I should . . ."

His impatience getting the better of him,

Justin rose to tower over the diminutive Octavia. "You must understand, my dear, that this man does not deserve your protection. Though I will mention no names to you, I happen to know—and have proof—that this so-called husband of yours is at this moment eloping with a young woman of means."

The rosy blush of Octavia's round cheeks faded to a cold, dead white. "It's . . . it's not possible! He is married to me!"

"Are you certain? How do you know you are legally married?"

"He procured a special license."

"Did you see it?"

"No, but he said he had it. There was a priest."

"How do you know it was a priest? How do you know it was not merely some crony of Culpepper's dressed to look like a priest?"

"No! He did marry me! He did!"

"Perhaps," Justin allowed. "I do not say it is impossible. But I do know, my dear, that your Geoffrey has eloped with this girl—this heiress of noble blood—and he means to marry her."

"I don't believe you!"

"I thought you might not. Tell me, would you recognize his handwriting if you saw it?"

"Yes, but why—"

From his pocket, Justin drew one of Geoffrey's more lurid love letters to Dyanna.

He had taken pains to obliterate Dyanna's name and address from the letter, but Geoffrey's distinctive handwriting made it proof of Justin's words nonetheless.

Wordlessly, he handed it to Octavia, and wordlessly she read it. The truth was brought home to her, as her illusions about the man she loved were swiftly stripped from her, and she had to accept Justin's revelations. Shaking, she sank into a chair and raised misty eyes to her visitor.

"It's true," she whispered. "True. But he promised me he would take me to Summersleigh House. He promised I would one day be Marchioness of Summersleigh." A tear trickled slowly down her cheek. "He told me he loved me."

"It may be that he does," Justin told her, not believing it himself but loath to see her completely destroyed. "But he is badly in need of money—you know that yourself. And this girl is a great heiress. It may be she he intends to dupe."

Sitting down across from her, Justin leaned closer to the softly weeping young woman. "I want to stop this charade, my dear. It must be stopped, for all our sakes. If you know where he intended to go, you must tell me."

"He said he was going to Patterton— Patterton Park, his country seat. He said he was going to visit his mother, the Dowager Lady Culpepper."

"Patterton Park. Do you know where it is?"

"Derbyshire, he said. It is a great estate. And I was to be its mistress." She sighed, bereft, hopeless. "I suppose that was a lie as well."

"We must wait and see, madam. But now I will take my leave and trouble you no more. Good night."

Octavia walked beside Justin to the door and dropped him a graceful curtsy as he prepared to leave.

"I wish you well, madam," Justin told her, seeing in her a pretty young girl duped by a foppish nobleman who wanted only a mistress but could overcome her scruples only with deceit. "I hope this matter turns out as you wish it."

Octavia murmured her thanks, but the look in her eyes as she closed the door behind him was stark and filled with anguish. The pretty dream she had been living since Geoffrey married her had been shattered and she had awakened to a harsh reality.

Returning to DeVille House, Justin routed Bertran and ordered horses saddled.

"We're riding for Derbyshire," he told the valet.

"Tonight, my lord?" the Swiss servant asked.

"We've lost enough time. I can only hope Culpepper waits until tomorrow for the wedding. With any luck, he's enough afraid of his mother to wait until she can be present to see her son married. I've heard she is a martinet who kept her husband well in hand. Let us hope she is as overbearing with her son."

Even as Justin and Bertran rode out from DeVille House to begin a perilous night ride to Derbyshire, the carriage bearing Dyanna and Geoffrey toward their destination passed through the picturesque village of Newington.

"Look there," Geoffrey said, drawing Dyanna's attention to the ancient church that stood on the outskirts of the village. "In that church we will be married tomorrow."

Bleakly, Dyanna nodded. She had been so eager when they'd started out from London— so sure this was the right thing for her to do. But now it seemed she had a misgiving for every mile that separated them from London and the safety of DeVille House.

"You are fatigued, my darling?" he asked, lifting her hand to his lips.

"Very much so," she told him, drawing her hand from his and burying it in the folds of her pelisse.

"Then you must go to bed as soon as we reach Patterton. You will want to be well-rested for tomorrow—and tomorrow night."

The thought of tomorrow night—her wedding night—sent a shudder coursing through Dyanna. Resolutely, she pushed the thought out of her head as the carriage turned from the road onto a narrow, tree-shaded lane.

"Patterton," Geoffrey whispered, with a hint of awe in his tone.

Dyanna gazed out the window as they emerged from the trees and started up a long, curving drive that cut through the large park surrounding the house.

The mansion of Patterton Park was a long, low building of red brick with a low-hipped roof and a proliferation of chimneys—most in dire need of repair. In fact, Dyanna saw nothing awesome about the house, excepting perhaps the size of the investment that would be needed to restore it to something approaching its former elegance.

"Geoffrey," she said, "why doesn't your grandfather effect some of the repairs?"

"Dyanna." His tone was stern. "I beg of you, do not mention Grandfather in my mother's presence. They do not . . . they are not fond of one another."

"But why?"

"My grandfather, for some reason, blames mother for father's death."

"He thinks she killed him?"

"Nagged him to death, actually. He says father simply could not bear to live with her another moment."

"Oh, Geoffrey, she—"

"Please, say nothing about it," Geoffrey begged as the carriage rolled to a stop before the crumbling steps leading to a front door whose paint was peeling. "Mother is not so bad, but she is—well, strong-willed. Opinionated. But come, see for yourself."

Geoffrey descended from the carriage, then turned to Dyanna and lifted her down. Together they entered the mansion and were immediately led into the Dowager Lady Culpepper's formidable presence.

Draped in plum silk, Lavinia Culpepper was a daunting personage indeed. With a bosom like a shelf and three quivering chins rippling beneath her lantern jaw, she sat enthroned on a great gilded chair facing the door, awaiting the arrival of her son and his intended bride with the air of a queen granting an audience.

"Mother," Geoffrey said, kissing both of her lined, rouged cheeks. "I have brought Dyanna. We are to be married tomorrow."

"Come here, my dear," the woman ordered, lifting a pair of pearl-encrusted spectacles to her deep-set blue eyes. "Let me look at you."

Dyanna stood obligingly still as Lavinia examined her. She was polite, but her direct stare made it clear that she was not cowed by the older woman.

"You are very pretty, very pretty indeed. But then your parents were handsome people. I think you will do quite nicely. You may kiss me."

Dyanna came to the woman's side and pecked at the quivering cheek she was offered.

But when Lady Culpepper suggested they get to know one another over a late supper, Dyanna shook her head.

"Forgive me, madam, but I am very tired. I would prefer to be shown to my room. After all, we will have years to get to know each other, will we not?"

Lavinia eyed the girl, as if recognizing in her an adversary worthy of her mettle. Graciously, she inclined her head.

"As you wish. Geoffrey, show Dyanna to her room, then come back here. I wish to speak with you."

Meekly, Geoffrey took Dyanna and Charlotte up a long, twisting wooden staircase and along a dark corridor. He showed them into a bedchamber obviously newly cleaned and hung with cheery silk of lemon yellow shot with gold.

"Tomorrow night, this will be our room," he reminded Dyanna. Bending, he would have kissed her had not his mother's voice reached them from below.

"Geoffrey!"

Shamefaced, Geoffrey bade Dyanna goodnight and fled back to his mother's side.

Dyanna, spurning Charlotte's attempts at conversation, was quickly undressed and changed into her nightgown. Tucked into the high, canopied bed, she dismissed Charlotte and lay back against the enveloping pillows.

The cavernous room was filled with shadows that seemed to loom above her, taking on ominous shapes and undulating with the play of the moonlight through the silken draperies.

Lying there, Dyanna felt like the heroine of one of the Gothick novels she so loved. Caught between a suitor she did not love and a rapacious, uncaring guardian whom she adored, there was no escape. No matter which path she chose, the future stretched ahead bleak and unpromising.

Rising from the bed, she went to the window. The moon shone down on the tree-shaded lane that led to the entrance of Patterton Park. What wouldn't she give, she thought with a sigh, to be riding along that lane, riding away from Patterton Park, riding back to . . .

To what? Turning away from the window, she sank onto the slightly musty cushions of the window seat. To Justin? By now he must be in Devonshire, with Caro Naysmith. He didn't know she was missing from DeVille House; he didn't know she was about to marry Geoffrey Culpepper. He didn't even know that she loved him with all of her heart.

A small, tremulous, self-mocking smile quivered at the corners of her mouth. Would it make any difference to him if he did know? Or was his love for Caro so strong, so firmly entrenched after all their years of intimacy that no one and nothing could threaten Caro's place in Justin's heart?

Dyanna thought of her favorite heroine, Jenny Flynn. When she'd read that book, she'd thought Jenny's story the most heartwrenching she could imagine. But was not hers even worse? For not only had she fallen into the clutches of a heartless, unfeeling guardian, she'd had the misfortune to fall in love with him.

Chapter Twenty

The morning dawned grey and overcast, the air heavy with the promise of rain. It was not yet ten when two carriages set out from Patterton Park. One carried Geoffrey and his mother; in the other rode Dyanna and Charlotte. Their destination was the stark, grey stone, fourteenth-century church whose tall, crenellated tower dominated the village of Newington and stood like a sentinel over the churchyard filled with weathered and lichen-covered tombstones carved with names still borne by families in the village.

"It's not too late to change your mind," a sly little voice whispered inside Dyanna's head. "It's not too late . . ."

"No, I can't," she murmured softly. "I must do this. I must! I—" Glancing up, she found Charlotte staring at her. A flush bloomed in her cheeks and she turned her eyes toward the bleakness of the grey day outside the carriage window.

Her gloved fists were clenched in the folds of her flounced gown of ivory silk. It was the nearest thing to a wedding gown she could produce on such short notice, but it was not nearly grand enough to suit Geoffrey's mother. The Dowager Lady Culpepper had treated Dyanna to a harsh, cold stare when she'd descended the stairs that morning, ready to leave for the church. It was obvious that the older woman wondered if Dyanna was truly as rich an heiress as Geoffrey had led her to believe. If so, one certainly could not tell from her apparel.

The memory of Lady Culpepper's censorious glare sent a shiver of apprehension down Dyanna's spine. After they were married, Geoffrey had decreed, they would live for a while at Patterton Park—with Lady Culpepper.

An image, like a scene from one of Dyanna's books, flitted through her mind—an image of her and Geoffrey, lost in the dark, cavernous depths of Patterton Park, their days and nights haunted by the grim, disapproving countenance of Lady Culpepper.

I don't want to do this, she thought. I don't

want to live in that drafty, crumbling old house with Geoffrey and that mother of his.

But what would she do if she refused to marry him? Go back to London? Back to sit in DeVille House while Justin roamed the town courting this beauty or that? Go back to wait in London while he rode off to Devonshire to be with Caro who, no doubt, fulfilled the same function in his life that her mother did for his father? It was folly to love a DeVille—Dyanna had learned that for herself. Did not Justin's mother's love for his father drive her to her tragic end? No, the only course open to Dyanna was this marriage.

She bit her lip as they turned into the lane leading to the church. From her place in the open carriage, Dyanna saw the other carriage stop. Geoffrey, resplendent in sapphire silk and silver brocade, an elaborately curled, white-powdered wig atop his head, leapt out, then turned to help his mother descend. The door of the church opened and the pastor appeared. He was a tall, top-heavy man with thin, bandy legs made all the more noticeable by his knee-breeches and black stockings.

The moment her feet hit the ground, Lady Culpepper made for the Reverend Mr. Tuttle. She had very definite instructions to impart on how she wished the ceremony performed. Since Mr. Tuttle's living was in the gift of the Culpepper family, he was obliged to honor her wishes to the letter.

Charlotte stepped down from Dyanna's carriage and moved away as Geoffrey came to help Dyanna down. Steeling herself, Dyanna rose and held out her hands to him.

"What's that?" Charlotte asked, squinting into the distance at a cloud of dust rising from the rocky roadway just outside the village.

Dyanna and Geoffrey stared toward it. At first they could make out only two figures on horseback, both galloping hell for leather in their direction.

"Is it someone you've invit—?" Dyanna began. Then, all at once, she knew. "Justin!"

Geoffrey's face turned as pale as his white wig. Stepping up onto the carriage step, he stared. "It can't be!"

Something akin to bliss blossomed in Dyanna's breast. She felt as if she were being snatched from the very gates of Hell. "But it is," she breathed. "It is!"

"How did he know . . . ?" He turned accusing eyes on her. "You told him!"

"I didn't! I swear it. He was going to Devonshire. He had already left. Somehow he knew. Somehow . . ."

"He's the Devil! Just like his father! That's how he knew, damn his soul to hell!"

Jumping onto the carriage, Geoffrey pulled Dyanna down beside him. "Drive on!" he shouted. "Get us out of here!"

"Geoffrey!" Dyanna protested as she was thrown against him by the wild rocking of the carriage. "Geoffrey, no!"

"Shut up!" His eyes bored into her. "You're mine, damn you! Mine! DeVille can't have you! He doesn't even need your money!"

Braced against the wild pitching of the carriage, Dyanna stared at him. "My money! Is that what all this was about? You never really loved me, did you? It was all nothing but playacting so you could get your hands on my fortune!" Her rage flared inside her as he merely stared at her. "Damn you!" she screamed. "Damn you to hell!"

Careless of the dangerous bucking of the carriage, she pounded at his chest, his arms, his face with her balled fists. Then, without warning, the carriage wheel struck a rock whose sharply pointed surface lay half-concealed in the roadway. Dyanna felt herself falling, being thrown from the flying carriage. Hurtling toward the ground, she screamed, terrified.

Her shriek ended abruptly. There was a single, sharp pain in her head as her body struck the earth with bone-shattering impact. She moaned, softly, shortly, as the blackness enveloped her.

Justin reined in his plunging horse near her, throwing the foam-flecked reins to Bertran as he leapt to the ground. He knelt beside her, his hands shaking. A fury burned inside him; he wanted nothing more than to chase down the carriage that had so nearly overturned. But it was even then disappearing into the distance, carrying Geoffrey away. He wanted to kill the man who had taken Dyanna away; he wanted to watch the light of life die in his eyes.

But for now, there was Dyanna. Justin knelt in the tall weeds near where she lay, still and pale, her eyes closed.

"Is she hurt, my lord?" Bertran asked, coming to his master's side after tying the horses to a tree.

"I don't know," Justin whispered. His hands were shaking. He was afraid to turn her over—afraid, for he had seen the flecks of crimson staining the jagged rock near her head.

Together the two men eased Dyanna onto her back. Her head fell to one side. For all that Justin had seen in battles at sea—had, in his days as a privateer, seen men wounded by gunfire and swordthrusts and cannon shot; had, on occasion, seen a man lose a limb to the surgeon's saw—nothing had ever moved him, frightened him, sickened him like the sight of the crimson blood spattered around the grisly cut near Dyanna's temple.

"Go to the village. Find a doctor, an apothecary, anybody!" Justin rasped. "Hurry!"

Mounting his horse, Bertran galloped off in the direction of Newington, passing the Reverend Mr. Tuttle, who was hurrying up the road.

"Is she—? Merciful heavens!" he cried, turning a delicate shade of green at the sight of the blood marring the ivory flesh of

Dyanna's face and matting the loose, silvery curls at her temple.

"Is there somewhere I can take her?" Justin asked. "The church? A rectory?"

The clergyman lifted his arm and pointed. "There is—" The rest of his words were drowned by Charlotte's scream. Having followed Mr. Tuttle, she now saw her mistress for the first time.

"For Christ's sake!" Justin snarled, drawing a shocked gasp from Mr. Tuttle. "Shut up, woman!"

"I said, sir, the rectory is just up that path."

Gently, Justin lifted Dyanna's limp body into his arms. Her head was cradled against his chest, the sticky, thickened blood staining the dark brown cloth of his coat. With the clergyman leading the way, he started up the path.

"Stay here," he ordered Charlotte over his shoulder. "When Bertran comes with the doctor, bring them to us."

Tears trickling down her cheeks, Charlotte nodded. She watched as Mr. Tuttle and Justin disappeared behind a tall yew hedge. It was all so confusing. Why had Lord Geoffrey not come back? He must know Dyanna was hurt. He must! And even though Lord DeVille was here, Geoffrey should have returned. If he loved Dyanna . . .

A cloud of dust and the rumble of carriage wheels seemed to answer her hopes. But it was not to be. The second carriage that roared past and disappeared around the bend carried old Lady Culpepper who, uninterested in the fate of her would-be daughter-in-law, was off in hot pursuit of her fugitive son.

Mr. Tuttle held open the door as Justin carried Dyanna into the small, homey front parlor of the red brick rectory. As Justin laid her on a daybed near the windows, the reverend brought a coverlet which he draped gently over her. Without waiting to be asked, he disappeared into the depths of the house, returning shortly with a cloth and a bowl of tepid water.

Justin bathed Dyanna's cut gently, fearing to cause her more pain. But she did not stir, did not moan, did not seem even to breathe. Her stillness and her deathly white pallor, frightened him beyond measure, but he would not allow himself to consider that she might be any more than merely unconscious owing to the blow to her head.

The foyer outside the parlor was suffused with the bleak, grey light of the cloudy day as Bertran bustled in followed by a short, balding man and by Charlotte, who was still weeping.

"This is Dr. Stowe, my lord," Bertran said.

Justin moved away from Dyanna's side. "She was thrown from a carriage," he told the doctor. "She has not moved since. Her head struck a rock as she fell."

Bending over Dyanna, the doctor probed the cut. "It is superficial," he pronounced.

"Then why won't she awaken?"

Frowning through his spectacles, the doctor pressed his fingers to the side of Dyanna's throat. Bending, he pressed his ear to her breast.

"Doctor," Justin prompted, "if her wound is superficial, then why . . .?"

"The cut is superficial," the doctor corrected. "The wound—the blow to the head . . . I'm sorry, my lord, there is nothing to be done."

"Nothing . . . You can't mean . . ." Justin's normally ruddy complexion had gone nearly as white as Dyanna's.

"I'm sorry, my lord," the doctor repeated. "The lady is dead."

Chapter Twenty-One

The short and somber procession wound its way toward McBride Hall along tree-shaded lanes, a closed, black coach followed by two silent men on horseback, making their way through the countryside.

Bertran, riding alongside his master, followed behind the coach that carried Charlotte and the satin-lined coffin containing Dyanna's body. He watched Justin closely. He was worried for his master—worried over the taciturn blackness of mood that had settled over him since the doctor in Newington had pronounced Dyanna dead.

Burning for revenge, his golden eyes glowing with bloodlust, Justin had ridden to Patterton Park determined to kill Geoffrey

Culpepper. He had been met by Lady Culpepper and a host of Patterton footmen and told that Geoffrey had fled, his destination unknown. Whether it was the truth or not, Justin had no way of knowing. He had ridden away from Patterton, no less determined to be avenged on the man he blamed for Dyanna's death, but willing to defer his vengeance until Dyanna had been laid to rest.

Returning to the village, Justin had procured the finest coffin readily available, of black lacquered oak with silver fittings and a lining of tufted white satin. He had purchased a large black traveling coach, large enough to carry the coffin and Charlotte, who would not, even then, be parted from her mistress.

They had set out at first light riding toward McBride Hall where the great, grey stone family chapel that Rakehell had built to honor his wife waited on a hill behind the manor house. It waited now to receive Dyanna—the last of the McBrides.

Since then—since they had ridden away from Newington, taking with them their precious, tragic burden—Justin had not uttered a single word. He merely rode behind the coach, staring straight ahead, his full, sculpted lips set in a rigid line. And Bertran, before many miles had passed beneath their horses' hooves, had begun to worry for his master's sanity.

He hoped that once their unhappy business

was complete—once Dyanna had been laid to rest in the family mausoleum at McBride Hall—Justin would return to his senses and take up his life where he had left off those months ago when the fateful letter from his solicitors reached him at Portsmouth.

He was relieved when they left the main road and passed between the vine-shrouded, rusted gates guarding McBride Hall.

But as they emerged into the overgrown clearing surrounding the hall, Justin reined in his mount and stared at the ruin that was Dyanna's ancestral home.

Though faithfully cared for by trusted servants left by the Earl of Lincoln after he had come to take his young granddaughter away to Blakling, those servants had left after the old earl's death, when it had become clear that Rakehell McBride had no intention of paying his father-in-law's minions. Years of neglect, years of abandonment to the elements and to hoardes of squatters and vandals had followed, and had reduced the once proud gabled Tudor manor to a crumbling hulk. It's once sparkling, diamond-paned mullioned windows were, in large part, gaping holes in which only jagged shards of glass and fragments of lead remained. Much of the lead roofing had been stolen and the ancient stone lions that had guarded the iron-bound front door since the house was built had been decapitated. Tall, tangled weeds crept up the stone steps and ivy, wild and trailing, had wound its way up the walls and into the broken windows.

Dismounting, Justin walked up the broken steps and shoved open the door, which creaked a protest at having been awakened from its long, unbroken sleep. With Bertran following, he entered the once-beautiful hall, where the fine oak paneling had been carved by knives—inscribed with the names and sentiments of regiments of vandals, squatters and gypsies. The remnants of broken furniture—those pieces left when the rest had been smashed into kindling—littered the chipped marble floor with its tattered, moth-eaten wool carpet.

"I can't leave her here," Justin muttered, his eyes following the rise of the rickety stairs toward the dark, unpromising second floor.

Bertran sighed, daunted by the prospect of continuing their macabre pilgrimage across the countryside. Where would he decide to take her next? Blakling Castle? That would be another two-day ride, considering the speed at which the lumbering black coach moved.

"You would not be leaving her here, milord," he reminded Justin gently. "She would be in the crypt, beneath the chapel. With her parents."

"If the house has been ransacked this way," Justin replied. "Who is to say the chapel has not been similarly despoiled?"

"Perhaps, milord, as executor of Miss Dyanna's estate, you can see to it that no further vandalism comes to this place. Prevail upon her heirs—whoever they may be—to take better care of the estate in future."

"I suppose that is possible," Justin agreed, much to his valet's relief. "We will go and look at the chapel."

Leaving Charlotte and the coachman with Dyanna, Justin and Bertran rode out through the overgrown park to the mausoleum built by Dyanna's father to house the remains of his beloved wife.

The chapel, built above a crypt intended to be the final resting place of generations of McBrides, was a rotunda of dressed sandstone. A colonnade of Doric columns surrounded it and an enormous funerary urn stood as a finial high atop the soaring, domed roof.

Justin and Bertran let themselves in through the unlocked, iron-work door. Within, Bertran was relieved to see, the chapel was relatively untouched. The beautiful plasterwork was unbroken, the mahogany altar and pulpit unmarked. Even the fine, cherrywood pews were intact. There was an air of incompleteness about the place, Bertran reflected, owing, he supposed, to the sudden abandonment of the project when Rakehell McBride had thrown himself back into his life of reckless hedonism.

"It is a beautiful chapel," he told Justin hopefully.

"It should be finished," Justin decided. "There was still work to be done when Rakehell left for London."

"It could be finished—and quite simply."

A small, wan smile quirked the corner of Justin's mouth. "Are you trying to influence me?" he asked the valet.

"I admit that I am, milord," Bertran admitted. "So long as the chapel is in good order, there seems no reason to take Miss Dyanna any further. It will do none of us any good."

Justin sighed. "I suppose you are right. It will not bring Dyanna back and this"—he scowled in the direction of the ruined manor house "—this is her family home. Come, let's look at the crypt."

Bertran held his breath as they descended the stairs, which were guarded by a carved wooden rail and gate. At the bottom of the stone steps a filigreed iron gate opened into a chamber into whose walls niches had been made to receive the coffins of succeeding generations of McBrides. Two of the niches were filled—one with the beautiful rosewood and mother-of-pearl coffin of Lady Elizabeth McBride and the other with the plain, unadorned wooden casket of Raburn 'Rakehell' McBride.

Justin ran a hand over the plain coffin with its simple lead fittings. "It seems that the

254

executors of Rakehell's will wasted little money and less care on their client's funeral. I would they had waited until I could make the arrangements."

"There has been much unhappiness in this family," Bertran said softly. "Miss Dyanna's mother, estranged from her father because of her marriage; Lord McBride and Lord Lincoln, losing the wife and daughter they both loved; Miss Dyanna, losing her mother, abandoned by her father—"

"Yes," Justin agreed. "Too much unhappiness. There is much many could have done to make Dyanna's life a happier one."

Bertran stole a sideways glance at his master as they left the crypt and climbed the twisting stairs to the chapel. He thought he understood what Justin was feeling. Remorse —that he had not shown Dyanna the depth of his love for her. Guilt—at having kept her a near prisoner at DeVille House for the last months of her life. Helplessness—at being unable to alter the fate that ultimately awaited her. He wondered if it would comfort his master to know that Dyanna had loved him in return, then decided it would only compound Justin's heartache. The knowledge of the time and opportunities lost would serve only to drive the cutting edge of grief more deeply into his heart.

Returning to the house, Justin ordered the coachman to help him take Dyanna's coffin to the chapel, where it would rest overnight. In the morning the local clergyman would be fetched from the village and a funeral service would be held to lay Dyanna to rest with her parents in the crypt.

As afternoon gave way to evening, Justin, Bertran, Charlotte and the coachman worked to assemble enough furniture to allow them to pass the night in relative comfort in the crumbling hall. Once they had gathered together the best of what was left in the dust-shrouded rooms and coaxed a fire into life in the only parlor downstairs still possessed of intact windows, Justin dispatched the coachman and Charlotte to the village with orders to procure food for them all and to deliver a letter to the local clergyman containing Justin's request for his services in the morning at the chapel of McBride Hall.

Those errands run, Justin left the others and walked out across the park to the chapel. Darkness was gathering overhead—darkness caused not by the lateness of the hour but by the thickness of the deep grey clouds piling in the sky above.

Justin entered the chapel. What scant light there had been before—admitted through the half-dozen stained-glass windows set into the curving walls—was gone now. The chapel was deeply shadowed and eerily silent. Dyanna's coffin, resting on a makeshift bier that was, in fact, an ancient trestle table brought up from the house, stood before the altar.

Unable to restrain himself, Justin lifted the lid, which he had not been able to allow to be nailed in place. It was but a temporary measure, this black lacquered coffin. He would see Dyanna laid to rest in the finest mahogany, her beauty cushioned by the softest velvet, the finest lace. He would see her dressed in silk, adorned with jewels. There had not been time for such considerations before, but he would see them attended to before the crypt was sealed. She was, after all, the last of the McBrides. No other would be laid to rest in the crypt beneath the chapel. He would see the door bricked up after Dyanna was interred. The house and the chapel itself might be torn to ruins by the human jackals who preyed on such abandoned estates, but they would lay no hands upon Dyanna. That, he told himself, was the least he could do.

Gazing down at her pale skin, scarcely darker than the creamy muslin of the gown she wore, Justin felt his heart ache within his chest. He touched her cheeks with reverent fingers. The flesh, though still supple and soft, was disquietingly cool. Her lashes lay like sooty fans on her cheek, and Justin wished passionately that they might flutter and lift, that he might gaze once more into those aqua eyes that had the power to wreak such havoc inside him. Her eyes, her beauty, had always had overwhelming power over his senses. From the first moment he saw her, when he believed her no more than a simple tavern maid, he had been under the spell of her beauty. He had never been so enchanted by a woman—never been so enraptured by the simple act of gazing at her, nor ever desired a woman with such a ravening, relentless hunger. It had frightened him—he had spent his life running from such entanglements. He had avoided attachments of the heart, the way others avoided contagion. It had driven him from his home, driven him to immerse himself in the rigors of the season. He had paid casual court to a dozen young ladies, but not a one of them had been able to touch his heart, his senses, the way Dyanna had. He found himself at balls, surrounded by giggling young beauties and longing for nothing more than to get home so that he might tiptoe into Dyanna's room and gaze at her as she slept.

He felt a renewed twinge of guilt at having immured Dyanna at DeVille House. He had shut her away from society, away from the eyes of those eligible young men who might have been suitors for her hand, because he could not bear the thought of watching her courted, wooed, perhaps won by another man. He had driven her to Culpepper. His tyrannical selfishness had sent her fleeing into the arms of that cowardly fop.

A surge of hatred, a desire for revenge, flared in his heart but quickly died. Was he not as much to blame for Dyanna's death as Culpepper? He shared the responsibility for her death—perhaps even bore the brunt of the blame. Had he not intervened, Dyanna would be Lady Dyanna Culpepper, alive and well, instead of the late Miss Dyanna McBride, lying there in her coffin before the altar of her family mausoleum.

Bending, Justin brushed his lips across hers. A teardrop, warm and glistening, fell onto her cheek and lay there, unheeded, as he turned on his heel and left the chapel.

Chapter Twenty-Two

Night had fallen and with it the rain that had been threatening all afternoon. Outside the hall, where the fire in the parlor grate did little to dispel the chill and damp that had settled over the great, hulking ruin of McBride Hall, the overgrown garden bowed beneath the weight of the rain that fell, not heavily but steadily, and promised to do so all night long.

Inside the parlor, having finished their meager supper, Charlotte, Bertran and the coachman exchanged sympathetic glances as Justin rose. Lighting a candle from the flame of another that burned in a plain, tin candlestick apparently deemed unworthy of theft by any of the vandals and robbers that had called the hall home, he left the parlor and disappeared into the cavernous depths of the hall.

"It ain't 'ealthy," the coachman declared once he judged Justin to be out of earshot. "'E's pinin' fer that gel. Pinin' too 'ard, if ye ask me."

"Well, nobody asked you," Charlotte snapped, then added, "But he does seem grieved beyond what I'd have expected from him."

"Why should he not grieve?" Bertran wanted to know. "He has a heart, after all."

Charlotte compressed her lips in a tight white line. Bertran would defend him, she supposed, for he was Lord DeVille's servant and owed him loyalty. But she could not help but believe that if cruel fate had delayed the earl for but another quarter hour, her beloved Miss Dyanna would be Lady Culpepper now, alive and safe at Patterton Park, lying in her marriage bed rather than in a coffin alone in a chapel in a rain-drenched park.

To the horror and discomfort of the two men, the maid broke into loud, disconsolate sobs which she buried in the folds of her white muslin apron.

Above, having braved the rickety staircase with its broken treads, Justin had found a window seat cushioned with tattered velvet. Extinguishing his candle, he sank onto the seat. Outside the great oriel window in which he was framed, rain poured down. Justin watched it—watched the rivulets course down the window, stared at the rustling branches of the trees in the park outside. Further off, beyond the tangled garden where once Dyanna had toddled, chased by her nurserymaid, the chapel stood silhouetted against the cloudy night sky.

Dyanna was there, he thought. Alone in the cold, dank darkness of the chapel. A desire to go to her washed over him—a longing to touch her again, to gaze at her beauty once more, perhaps to hold her small, chilled hand between his own. Such thoughts were not healthy, he told himself. Dyanna was dead.

There! He had put the unthinkable into words. She was gone and would never return. Tomorrow she would be laid to rest. Perhaps he would abandon his plans for another, more splendid funeral. After all, what difference did it make? What difference could it make? Surely none to her. After tomorrow—after the service—he should mount his horse and ride away. He should leave the disposal of her estate in the hands of the solicitors and let that be an end to it.

Rising from the window seat, he started back downstairs, meaning to try to forget the chapel and the treasure it contained. But as he turned, his eyes darted toward the window for one last glance at the temple on the hilltop beyond the garden. It was then that he saw the glimmer behind the stained-glass window.

Frowning, he placed one knee back on the window seat and leaned closer to the glass. His breath clouded it. With one hand, he wiped the obscuring mist away. Was there—? Yes! There was a glow emanating from within the chapel. It had not been his imagination. It was there. There was no lightning with the rain to account for the light, nor was there a moon whose silvery glow might seem to illuminate the window when seen from a certain angle.

There was someone there! Someone in the chapel! But who? What? Not being of a superstitious nature, Justin did not, as some might, imagine a ghost to be roaming the night. No, this light was of no unearthly origin. It was all too real and it warranted investigation.

Not bothering to try to relight his candle, Justin carefully retraced his way down the stairs. In the hall, he clapped on his hat and donned his coat. Tucking a pistol beneath it, he threw open the door and ran out into the rainy night.

"Milord?" Hearing the commotion in the hall, Bertran came to the parlor doorway just as Justin flung open the front door.

"There's a light in the chapel," Justin shouted back. "Someone's out there."

The coachman came abreast of Bertran as Justin disappeared into the darkness.

"Resurrection men," he muttered knowingly. "Mark my words."

"Resurrec—? Body snatchers, you mean?" Bertran was appalled. It was common knowledge, of course, that such dastardly men provided medical schools with ill-gotten cadavers needed to fill the needs of research and dissection laboratories, but surely such a horrible fate would not come to Miss Dyanna!

The coachman shrugged. "It 'appens. But they might only be grave robbers. Was the lady wearin' jools?"

"She has pearls," Charlotte told him. "Eardrops. And a diamond necklace."

"Not any more, I reckon," the coachman said grimly.

"I'm going to help his lordship," Bertran told them, pulling on his own coat and taking up a second pistol. "They may be desperate men."

"Hurry! Hurry, please," Charlotte begged. "Don't let them touch Miss Dyanna!"

The chapel was dark and deserted when Justin reached it. In the shadowy depths, he could see Dyanna's coffin still lying on its makeshift bier.

He scowled, wondering if he could have been mistaken after all. Had he, in his grief, been deluded? Were his senses so addled that he had begun to see things that were not there? It seemed so.

With a heavy sigh, he turned toward the door. Then he stopped. Something was not right. He looked back toward the altar, staring for a long, puzzled moment before the realization struck him.

The black coffin lay as he'd left it—with one alteration. The lid, which he'd not been able to see sealed shut and which he'd left propped against the bier, was now firmly atop the oblong box.

Striding to the bier, he twisted viciously at the latches that secured the top to the black lacquered casket. One after the other, he freed them. When at last the final latch had given way, Justin flung back the lid. Inside, carefully spaced along the satin interior to provide the necessary weight to give the illusion of a body, were wet and shining stones, apparently brought from the rubble outside.

"Damnation!" he thundered.

Whirling, he ran for the door, nearly colliding with Bertran at the doorway.

"She's gone!" he shouted. "They've taken her!"

Together the men scoured the wet ground for some sign of the direction the villains had taken. In the mud and sodden grass they found evidence of booted feet. Bending low in the darkness, they followed the tracks, moving off into the night through the dripping undergrowth.

"Milord," Bertran hissed when they'd gone some distance. "I hear them!"

Justin paused to listen. Over the noise of the downpour, he could hear voices. His hand slipped inside his coat and wrapped around the butt of his pistol. Bertran, at his side, did the same, but Justin shook his head.

"Once we've caught them," he told the valet, "I will hold them and you must go for help."

"But if there are several, milord," Bertran protested, "might it not be wiser for the two of us to herd them all back to the Hall?"

Justin considered it. Truth to tell, he did not greatly care what became of the men. They were animals, scavengers who preyed upon the dead. They deserved to be shot, in his opinion, but the law did not agree. Though English law could, and did, hang children of seven or eight for a single act of petty theft, a body snatcher was merely imprisoned. A dead body, unlike gold or silver, was not regarded as an article of great value.

"Let us just get Dyanna back," he told the valet. "If one of them attacks, shoot him. Otherwise, do nothing."

As they came closer to their quarry, Justin realized that the men had stopped. Their voices were raised. They were quarreling.

"The doctor'll pay a pretty penny for this one," one of them was saying. "She's a little beauty, and fresher'n the others. We might get eight or ten pound for 'er from the right man."

"She's quality," a second voice pointed out. "It's not like the others. She ain't a drunkard

Sandra DuBay

or a whore or a derelict. It ain't like she won't
be missed by anybody."

"We put the stones in the box. They'll never
know the difference."

"But supposin' they do? Just take the necklace and the earbobs, I say, and be done with
it. Leave the body if you don't want to risk
takin' it back, but—"

"Shh! I hear somebody! There's—"

Justin stepped out of the undergrowth, his
pistol drawn. At the sight of the long, gleaming
barrel fixed on them, the two men shrank
back.

"I ought to shoot you where you stand," he
snarled, stepping over Dyanna as she lay on
the sodden ground, the rough, dirty blanket
thrown back, the rain pouring over her, soak-
ing her to the skin. "Filth, that's what you are.
You deserve to hang."

"Please, m'lord," the taller, dirtier of the
two begged. "We got to eat, you know, and
bodies, they ain't no use to no one ceptin' the
doctors. We got to make a livin'."

"You make a living selling the flesh of other
human beings—condemning them to dissection in some surgeon's theater. You—"

"My lord—" Bertran hissed from behind
him.

"Not now," he snarled, not taking his eyes
from the two body snatchers. "Stay were you
are, damn you!"

"Milord!" Bertran said again.

"Damn it all, man, I said not now!" Justin waved his pistol at the two men, who were stumbling backwards, their eyes wide with horror, their mouths twin open in shock. "I said hold your ground!"

But the two men, disregarding Justin's orders and the lethal weapon trained on them, whirled in the mud and stumbled off into the darkness.

"What in the hell—?" Justin began.

"Milord!" Bertran cried.

"What is it, man!" Justin turned. "You were supposed to help—"

His words died, strangled in a throat suddenly choked with shock and amazement.

On the ground, her clothes sodden, her hair hanging in lank, dripping rivulets, her face awash with the chilling raindrops that made her shiver, made her teeth chatter, Dyanna was half-sitting, half-leaning in Bertran's arms.

Her hand, atremble, was raised to her head; her fingers, bloodless, white, and icy-cold, probed the bruised cut that had caused her death-like unconsciousness.

His heart pounding in his chest, Justin came to her and knelt in the mud beside her. As his eyes searched her face, the droplets that ran down his cheeks were not entirely composed of rain.

"Dyanna," he whispered, still unable to believe the evidence of his own eyes. "Dyanna. Can it be? You're alive?"

"Who—who were those men?" she whispered. "What am I doing here?"

"Those men were body snatchers. They stole you from the chapel."

"Body snatchers? Chapel? I don't understand."

Justin smothered a smile; he felt almost giddy with relief. "The chapel at McBride Hall," he told her, pulling off his coat to wrap around her. "We were going to bury you tomorrow morning."

"Bury me? Bury me!" She shrugged out of the coat. "But I'm not dead!"

"But Dyanna, we thought . . ."

With Bertran's help, she struggled to her feet. "You were going to put me down there in that crypt—alive!" Her eyes were wide with horror. "You fiend! You inhuman fiend! I hate you! I'll hate you until I die! Why couldn't you have left me alone? Why couldn't you have let me marry Geoffrey!"

His face stony, his voice as cold as the chilling rain that drenched them all, Justin rose and said, "I wish I had, Dyanna. Then I would be well and truly rid of you!"

Turning on his heel, he strode off into the dark, rain-washed forest, leaving Bertran to help Dyanna back to the Hall.

Chapter Twenty-three

The great black traveling coach rumbled
through the countryside once more, resuming its travels, albeit at a far faster pace than
when it had been part of the sad little funeral procession. Inside, Dyanna reclined on
one of the wide, tufted velvet seats. Wrapped
in a fur rug, she tried to concentrate on the
book in her lap—a novel Justin had procured from someone in the village near Mc-
Bride Hall—tried, without much success,
to ignore Charlotte's stares. The maid gazed
at her raptly, as if she had indeed arisen
from the dead rather than merely from
unconsciousness caused by the blow to her
head.

"Dyanna? Are you getting tired?" Justin

asked, drawing his mount abreast of the coach window. He sat the great, thundering horse as if he and the beast were one, but Dyanna was in no mood to admire him.

"I'm fine," she snapped. "No thanks to you."

"You'll feel better after you've rested. I want a doctor to look at you once we're back in London."

"London," she muttered as he disappeared, dropping back to ride beside Bertran behind the coach. "Back to DeVille House. Back to watching the world pass by from the window."

Sighing, she returned to her book. She was over-dramatizing her plight and she knew it. But for the moment she enjoyed wallowing in the luxurious depths of self-pity. She'd forgotten for the moment how relieved she'd been to see Justin galloping toward her, rescuing her from a marriage she'd come to want desperately to escape. She'd forgotten that if it hadn't been for Justin, she'd be at Patterton Park at that very moment, at the mercy of Geoffrey's whims, under the censorious eyes of that domineering, critical mother of his. She would have been listening as they planned the restoration of their crumbling estate, watching as they plundered her inheritance to restore Patterton Park to its former glory.

All she knew at that moment, as she rode through the mauve and blue twilight toward

London, was that she was being returned to the silken prison from which she'd escaped only days before. DeVille House. She would be safe there, within those beautiful walls, safe from scheming fortune hunters like Geoffrey Culpepper. Her inheritance would be secure—but what of her heart?

Leaning forward on the seat, she looked out through the small, oval window in the back of the coach. Justin was there, riding beside Bertran. His strong, handsome face was set in grim, hard lines. His brown coat still bore traces of her blood—stains left there when he had carried her from the road's edge to the rectory where, according to what Charlotte had told her, the village doctor had pronounced her dead.

Dyanna gazed at Justin. He held the reins in his gauntleted hands with such assurance. The powerful, plunging animal beneath him was completely in his command.

A shiver coursed through her. Her senses, too, were in his command. A look from those gleaming, golden eyes could shatter her composure. A touch of his hand set her senses awhirl. The feelings he evoked inside her made the dreamy, romantic sentiments that passed for love in the novels she read seem pale and insipid. It frightened her to be so much in his thrall.

Inevitably, she took refuge in her daydreams, but even there, he haunted her. The

masterful, handsome heroes of her fantasies
all seemed to have Justin's face now. When
they spoke, it was in his voice. She could not
escape him, it seemed, in reality or imagination.

She was jerked out of her reverie when the
carriage slowed and turned, passing beneath a
stone arch barely wide enough to accommo-
date the massive bulk of the coach. Dyanna
looked out the window and saw a pretty,
vine-covered, half-timbered building. Above
the door, a sign proclaimed it to be The Black
Swan.

Dismounting, Justin came to the coach
while Bertran went inside to order accommo-
dations.

"It's getting dark," he told Dyanna as he
opened the door. "We'd better stop for the
night."

Drawing her pelisse about her, Dyanna
waited until Justin had drawn off his riding
gauntlets, then took the hand he offered to
steady her as she descended from the coach.

Inside the warm, fragrant inn, where the
smells of food cooking in the kitchen and
being served in the dining room welcomed
them, the hostess hurried up to them.

"Give you good evening, my lord," the rosy-
cheeked, aproned woman said, bobbing a
curtsy. Her wide, dark eyes lingered on
Dyanna, who leaned on Justin's arm as they
stood in the darkly paneled hall. "Oh! Is

milady ill? I can send my boy to fetch a doctor, milord."

"The lady is fine, madam," Justin replied. "She has been ill. What she needs most now is rest. And perhaps something hot from your kitchen."

"Right away, my lord," the woman promised. "I'll show you to your rooms at once."

Supported by Justin, Dyanna mounted the stairs. She felt weary; the lingering aftereffects of her ordeal seemed to have robbed her limbs of their strength. She leaned heavily on Justin as they climbed the steep, curving staircase.

At the top of the stairs, Justin paused and looked down into Dyanna's half-closed, fatigued eyes. With a gentle smile, he slipped an arm beneath her knees and lifted her. Then, as if carrying nothing more substantial than a down pillow in his arms, he followed the Black Swan's hostess to the rooms Bertran had bespoken for his master and his master's ward.

"My best room, my lord," the hostess said proudly as she stood back to allow Justin to carry Dyanna into a pretty chamber in which the four-poster was hung with pale spring-green brocade.

"Will the lady need help?" the hostess asked, watching as Justin carefully set Dyanna in a chair near the fireplace where a low fire had been kindled.

"Her maid will be along," Justin told her.

"Perhaps if you could see to supper? Nothing elaborate, something warm and simple."

With another bobbing curtsy, the proprietress left the room, passing Charlotte who carried both Dyanna's carpetbag and her own.

"She's almost asleep," Justin told the maid. "Get her into her nightgown and see if you can persuade her to eat something before she goes to sleep. The hostess has gone to fetch something for supper."

"Justin?" Dyanna murmured, as Charlotte coaxed her to her feet and began unfastening her gown.

"His lordship has gone to his room, I believe, miss," Charlotte told her. "I'm to help you into your nightgown. Supper will be here directly."

"I'm not very hungry." Dyanna's voice was muffled as Charlotte pulled her nightgown over her head and tugged it down into place. "But I'm suddenly so tired."

"It's not surprising after what you've been through," Charlotte decided. "And now, having to go back to London . . ." She shook her head mournfully. "And where, I'd like to know, is poor Lord Geoffrey?"

A knock at the door came as a welcome interruption for Dyanna, who had no desire to hear Charlotte prosing on and on about poor Lord Geoffrey. She remembered all too clearly Geoffrey's face as he revealed the truth of his supposed love for her—it was not Dyanna who was so irresistable to him, but her fortune.

"Please answer that, Charlotte," Dyanna asked coolly. She smiled politely as the door was opened and the inn's proprietress carried in a tray filled with wine, rolls, and steaming, fragrant stew.

"I hope this will please you, milady," the woman said, her envious eyes taking in every detail of Dyanna's flowing nightdress and wrapper of delicate lawn frothed with lace at the hem and banding the bottom of the satin-bowed, elbow-length pagoda sleeves.

"I'm sure it will," Dyanna told her. "Thank you, Mrs—?"

"Lambton, ma'am. If there is anything else . . ."

"I will send my maid with a message if there is anything I require," Dyanna assured her, ignoring Charlotte's look of chagrin at the thought of being sent downstairs like a lowly page.

"Very good, ma'am." With a last look at the beautiful young girl she thought must surely be wife to the handsome lord who had carried her upstairs, Mrs. Lambton started for the door.

"Mrs. Lambton?" Dyanna called as the door started to swing shut behind the woman.

"Milady?"

"Did my lord bespeak a room for Charlotte as well?"

Mrs. Lambton's reply drowned Charlotte's soft gasp of surprise and dismay. "He did, milady. Two doors up the hall on this same side. He said he did not know if you would wish your maid to stay with you or not, so he asked for the room to be sure."

"Thank you, Mrs. Lambton."

It was not until Dyanna sat down at the elegant little table and unfolded her napkin that she raised her eyes to meet Charlotte's hurt stare.

"Am I not to stay with you tonight, miss?" she asked plaintively. "What if you are ill in the night? What if you cannot sleep? What if—?"

"Oh, do hush," Dyanna insisted. "You will be two doors away, Charlotte. If I need you, I can call you." She sighed, seeing Charlotte's expression of woe deepen. "Oh, come and sit down. We'll have supper before you retire."

By the time their supper had been eaten and the dishes removed, Charlotte had made Dyanna feel sufficiently guilty that she allowed her to turn down her bed and brush her hair for far longer than it required.

"That is enough," Dyanna said at last, gently but firmly taking the silver-backed brush from the maid's hand. "I am very tired, Charlotte. I

278

want to sleep now. I will see you in the morning."

"And you will not hesitate—" the maid began.

Dyanna interrupted her wearily. "I will call you immediately if I need you," she promised.

Reluctantly, Charlotte left and Dyanna, relieved at last to be away from the maid's smothering concern, walked to the windows where the pale green draperies had been drawn against the night drafts that found their way through the window.

Her hands trembled as she drew her lawn wrapper tighter around her. She heard the door behind her open once more and scowled, thinking the maid's persistence was bordering on insolence.

"I said I would call you if I needed you, Charlotte," she said, an angry edge to her voice.

"It is not Charlotte," Justin said.

Turning in a swirl of lawn and lace, Dyanna found Justin standing just inside the door. Her sea-blue eyes met his gleaming golden gaze and were captured in their fathomless, captivating depths.

"I came to see if you were all right," he told her. "And to say good-night."

Dyanna nodded, her loosened, flowing hair shimmering like spun silver in the candlelight. "I am well," she replied. "Thank you."

Smiling, Justin toyed with the unbuttoned

Sandra DuBay

cuff of his rolled-up sleeve. He felt suddenly awkward, gauche as a schoolboy. "Well, I suspect you'd prefer I left so you can go to bed."

Dyanna hesitated. No! she wanted to cry. No, stay with me. Hold me, tell me that you followed me to Derbyshire, took me back from Geoffrey, because you love me and not merely because in the eyes of the law you are my master.

In the end, she only nodded. "I am rather tired," she murmured, eyes downcast.

"Well, then . . ." Turning, Justin laid his hand on the doorlatch. Over his shoulder, he gazed at Dyanna, so fragile, so beautiful. He'd come so close to losing her and now—now that she was back in life, he wanted to seize her by the arms and shake her, demanding that she tell him the truth.

Why did you run away with an arrogant, conniving fool like Geoffrey Culpepper! he wanted to shout at her. Why did you leave me? Do you love him? Do you want him? Did you give him the love I want so desperately for myself? But he said only:

"Good-night, then. There is no hurry for us to return to London. There is no need for you to get up early in the morning if you don't wish to."

"All right," Dyanna acknowledged, wanting nothing more than to run to him, to be enveloped in his arms, to press her face to those tight golden curls that frosted his tanned chest between the opened edges of his shirt front. She clasped her hands in front of her to still their trembling. "Good-night."

The door closed behind him, causing the flames of the candles to dance in the shifting air currents. Dyanna slowly circled the room, blowing them out until only the one beside the bed remained. When she climbed the little bedstep and crawled beneath the covers, she blew that one out as well and lay back in the darkness watching the waving pattern of tree branches in the moonlight outside her bedroom window.

The past few days had been bizarre beyond anything she'd ever read in any of her books. Charlotte had told her as much as she could bear to hear of how the doctor from Newington had pronounced her dead, of how she'd been taken to McBride Hall in a coffin and left before the altar in the mausoleum her father had built.

Dyanna shivered beneath the blankets. If it hadn't been for those men—the grave robbers—Justin would have sealed her in the crypt below with her parents. She knew full well it would have been unintentional—he'd truly believed her dead—But the thought . . .

Might she not have awakened there, in the crypt, in the coffin, sealed in, buried alive . . .?

With a deep, shuddering breath, Dyanna turned on her side and willed away those hideous, morbid thoughts. She could not bear them; they were too terrifying to be borne.

But she fell asleep with those thoughts lingering at the edges of her subconscious, waiting to make their stealthy way into her dreams . . ..

It was just past midnight that she awoke with a scream.

The images lingered with her—horrible, terrifying combinations of her own experience and every Gothick novel she'd ever read. Breast heaving, she clawed at the coverlet, her eyes searching madly in the darkness for some scrap of reassurance that she was safe, that it had all been merely a dream.

She gasped as the door opened and Justin appeared. In his room across the hall, he'd heard her cry out. Throwing on his velvet robe, he'd rushed to her room and found her sitting up in her bed, trembling violently, her aqua-blue eyes huge and haunted, glistening with unshed tears.

"Dyanna," he said softly. "What is it? What's wrong?"

Her fingers grasped at the soft velvet of his robe. Her eyes searched his face.

"I dreamed . . . I thought . . . I was in that place. That terrible place. I woke up and I was closed in, trapped . . ."

Realizing at once what she meant, Justin was overcome with remorse at the thought of what he had almost done to her—at the unspeakable fate he'd come so near to consigning her to.

"Oh, Christ," he muttered, sitting on the bed's edge and drawing her to him, cradling her against his chest. "Oh, Dyanna, I'm sorry. I'm so sorry."

Dyanna lay weakly in his arms. The enticing, masculine smell of his flesh, the warmth of his body, the strength of his arms about her, soothed her, tantalized her, reawakened all the yearnings she'd fought so hard to suppress.

She felt his hands on her back, her neck, her hair, felt the reassuring touches grow into caresses. His lips touched her hair, her forehead, her cheeks. Turning her face up toward his, she offered him her lips.

Their kiss was, by turns, tender and savage, passionate and gentle. When they parted, a soft sigh passed between them, filled with longing and desire.

"Dyanna," Justin breathed, his fingers caressing her face, her throat, no longer able to deny the force of his love for her. "You must know that I—"

"Miss!" Wrapped in a voluminous cotton gown, Charlotte stood in the doorway. "Miss! I heard you cry out! Are you sick? What is wrong? I—oh, my lord, I . . ."

Shaking with frustrated anger and suppressed desire, Justin rose from the edge of Dyanna's bed.

She reached out a hand to draw him back. "Justin," she rasped, "what must I know? What were you going to say?"

He hesitated, torn from the soft, cloying web of passion, thrust back into cold, harsh reality. "You must know . . ."

"Yes?" she prompted, sure he'd been going to reveal himself—his feelings, his emotions —to her at long last. "Yes?"

Justin gazed at her. He'd been about to lay his soul bare before her but now . . . was it the right thing to do? Perhaps not, and particularly not in front of the maid.

"You must know I did not mean to hurt you at McBride Hall," he said lamely. "It was a mistake."

The breath left Dyanna in a whoosh. That was not what he had been going to say. She was certain of it. But Charlotte had shattered the spell. Charlotte had destroyed the moment and robbed Dyanna of the knowledge of Justin's feelings.

"Yes," she agreed, even as Justin moved toward the door. "I know it was merely a hideous mistake."

"Then I'll leave you in the care of your maid."

He looked at Charlotte and, even in the faint light of the candle stub the maid held, she saw the bright, glittering light of fury in his golden eyes.

Resisting the temptation to flee from him,

Charlotte curtsied and sidled away from the door as he left the room.

"I had a nightmare," Dyanna said simply, coolly. "Nothing more."

"I'd better stay here with you," the maid said, already plumping the pillows in the armchair near the hearth. "In case it happens again. You don't want to disturb Lord DeVille again."

Wordlessly, Dyanna lay back and drew the covers up to her chin. It didn't matter, she told herself, still trembling and filled with the ache of unfulfilled desire, whether Charlotte stayed or not. It was unlikely that Justin would come back to her tonight.

Chapter Twenty-Four

It was nearly mid-day when the coach bearing Dyanna and Charlotte set out from The Black Swan and turned into the London road.

Dyanna was pensive. Her mind was filled with the scene in her room the night before. It had been almost worth the horror of the nightmare to find herself in Justin's arms. He had kissed her, caressed her. A shiver coursed through her at the memory of his lips against her, of his hands touching her, so warm, so strong through the thin lawn of her night-dress.

She sighed and Charlotte was immediately concerned.

"Are you all right, miss?" the worried maid inquired.

"I'm fine, Charlotte," Dyanna reassured her. "You must not be so quick to worry."

Retreating into silence, Dyanna turned and looked out at Justin riding, as he had the day before, behind the coach, the faithful Bertran at his side.

He too, seemed thoughtful. His look was faraway and almost wistful.

I wish he were thinking of me, Dyanna thought; I wish the tenderness of last night were there after the sun rose. How can he be so concerned, so gentle, so caring if he does not have some feeling for me beyond that of a guardian for his ward?

That he desired her, Dyanna had no doubt. But why did he keep that desire under such strict control? He had nearly unleashed it last night. If Charlotte had not come into the room, where might those kisses and caresses not have led? If only Charlotte had not interrupted . . ..

Sitting back in her seat, she fixed the maid with such a resentful glare that Charlotte recoiled, wondering what on earth she could have done to merit such a look. She dared not ask, and the rest of the trip to London passed in an awkward silence.

Their return to London filled Dyanna with memories, some pleasant, some unpleasant, and with a nervous anticipation of what was to come. Would things be different now? She hoped so. She could not bear the thought of returning to DeVille House and living under the same circumstances from which she'd fled after foolishly placing her faith and trust in Geoffrey Culpepper.

DeVille House loomed, gracious and elegant behind its fine iron gates, which were thrown open in anticipation of Justin's return.

Inside the house, Ipswich had lined up the maids and footmen to welcome their master and his ward home. There had not been the slightest doubt in any of their minds that Justin would succeed in retrieving Dyanna.

"Welcome back, miss," Ipswich said. "Welcome home, my lord."

"Ipswich," Justin said. "Are Miss Dyanna's rooms aired?"

"They are, my lord."

"Good." Removing his hat, gloves and coat, Justin draped them over the butler's outstretched arms. "I shall want to bathe and change. Dyanna, I wish to see you in the study in an hour."

"Yes, my lord," she murmured to his retreating back. Her hopes, her heart sank. Were they then to return to the same conditions that had made her flee before? Was Justin's tenderness of the night before merely an aberration not to be repeated?

Finding the eyes of the entire household staff upon her, Dyanna smiled and allowed Bertran to help her out of her pelisse.

"I shall want to bathe and change as well," she told the butler. "You will please see to it at once."

Ipswich bowed shallowly. "At once, miss."

With a smile for each of the servants who bowed and curtsied in turn as she passed them, Dyanna crossed the hall and mounted the stairs she'd thought, only a few days before, never to see again. How could she have imagined that she'd be back, still plain Dyanna McBride, when she'd had every expectation of being Lady Dyanna Culpepper by now?

But then, she reasoned to herself as she stepped into the beautiful sitting room and gazed toward the opened doors of her bedchamber beyond, how could she have known that Justin, whom she had thought safely removed to Devonshire, would return to London so quickly? How had he known that something was afoot? Could there, perhaps, be some supernatural power he'd inherited from his infamous father?

She allowed a small, self-mocking smile to curve her lips. Geoffrey had told her of Sebastian DeVille and his powers; Geoffrey had told her the book about Lucifer Wolfe was about Sebastian DeVille. But Geoffrey had lied about so many things. Perhaps the scandalous tales about Justin's father were only so many more lies.

Sinking into a chair, Dyanna rested her

chin in her hand. "So here I am," she said to the room. "Exactly where I was before I left. Well, perhaps not exactly. If nothing else, Geoffrey Culpepper has shown his true colors and I shan't be duped by him again."

"Miss?" Charlotte stood in the doorway.

"What is it, Charlotte?" Dyanna asked, feeling a little guilty for the bad temper she'd shown to the maid. Her timing the night before could not have been worse, but she had only been doing her duty.

"Your bath is waiting. What will you wear when you've bathed?"

"My primrose muslin, I think."

With a little curtsy, the maid left and Dyanna could see her feelings were still hurt by the treatment she'd received.

"Ah, well, she'll get over it," Dyanna told herself philosophically as she went to have her bath.

Later, bathed and dressed in a flounced gown of primrose muslin, her hair dressed in loose curls at the back of her head, Dyanna went down to the study as Justin had asked.

She found him there, devastatingly handsome in immaculate evening dress.

"You're going out?" she asked, a hint of reproach in her voice.

"To Brooks's," he confirmed. "After dinner. I must hear what's gone on since I've been away."

"I see." Dyanna averted her face, ostensibly

studying an engraved invitation to a ball that had been held the night before. She had hoped against hope that there would be a new beginning for them now that she was back. She had hoped that Justin's actions of the night before signaled a new phase in their relationship—that, having come so close to losing her, he might now be willing to show her whatever feelings he had for her. Obviously, she'd either been deluding herself or his feelings for her did not go beyond a few moments of ungoverned passion.

"What was it you wished to see me about?" she asked coolly.

From a drawer of the desk, Justin took the packet of love letters from Geoffrey Culpepper. He tossed them across the desk, and they and they landed with a soft thud in front of Dyanna.

Paling, she looked up at him with a mixture of indignation and embarrassment.

"They were found by Ipswich after you left. He was looking for some clue as to where you might have gone."

"And he sent for you? Efficient, isn't he?"

Sitting in his chair, Justin gazed up at her. "No," he said. "He did not send for me. I turned back before we were very far outside London."

Dyanna feigned an icy disdain she was far from feeling. "Caro must have been disappointed. She seemed to be looking forward to having you to herself in Devonshire."

"Caro is not the issue here," Justin reminded her sternly.

"And what is the issue here?" she demanded to know.

He pointed to the stack of letters. "Those are the issue. Geoffrey Culpepper."

Flushing, Dyanna half turned away to hide her face from him. "That's over," she told him.

"Is it?"

There was a challenge in his voice—a hardness, a ruthless anger. Dyanna returned his glare with one of her own.

"What are you asking?"

"I want to know what Culpepper was to you. A suitor?" There was a short, significant pause. "A lover?"

Dyanna's eyes widened; she drew a sharp, shocked breath. "How dare you ask me such a question?" she hissed. "You've no right—"

"I have every right!" Justin growled, rising to his feet to tower over her. "I am responsible for you! I have a right to know if my ward has been ruined. Do you expect any gentleman to wish to marry Geoffrey Culpepper's whore?"

"His—" Dyanna dug her fingers into the shining surface of the desk to steady herself. "You filthy-minded son of a—"

"Answer me!" Justin's golden eyes blazed. "Tell me the truth, Dyanna. Are you a virgin?"

Dyanna trembled beneath the heated weight of his stare. How could she answer his question? If he had merely asked if Geoffrey had been her lover, she could, in all honesty, say no. But to ask if she were untouched, virginal . . . Should she lie and say yes? If she told the truth—said no—he would assume she had taken Geoffrey to her bed. He would never suspect that he himself, had robbed her of her innocence, her virginity. He would not believe her if she told him that she had been the woman in his arms in that shadow-filled room at Barkleigh House that she had been Marie LaBrecque that night at the ball.

She swallowed hard. She could not tell him. That night was the most precious—and painful—memory she had. She could not expose it to his disbelief, perhaps his derision.

"I'm waiting, Dyanna," he prompted angrily.

"Wait all you like," she replied, chin held high. "I'll never tell you."

His eyes narrowed. Did her refusal mean she had been Geoffrey Culpepper's mistress? The mere thought of that good-for-nothing piece of scum so much as touching Dyanna roused a murderous fury in Justin's heart.

"I could have you examined," he reminded her. "I could call in a doctor or a midwife—."

Horrified, Dyanna took a step back. "You wouldn't!" she breathed, mortified at the mere thought.

A knock at the door made them both start violently.

"What is it!" Justin snarled.

Ipswich's face appeared around the door's edge. "Dinner is served, milord."

"We'll be there directly."

The door closed and Justin glared at Dyanna once more. "No," he admitted, addressing her fears. "I probably wouldn't. But since you will not answer my question, I can only assume you gave yourself to Culpepper. I had thought to right the wrong I committed before, that of keeping you here shut away from society. I had decided that there would be no harm in your going to the theater on occasion, or the park"—he saw the hope light Dyanna's eyes—"but that will have to wait now."

"But why!" she demanded as he would have left the room to go to the dining room.

"Because, my dear," he answered coolly, slyly, "before you can appear in polite society, I must be certain there are not unfortunate repercussions from your little escapade."

"Repercussions? What are you talking about?"

"Merely, my dear, that I must be sure you are not carrying Geoffrey Culpepper's child."

"Oh! How can you suggest such a thing!"

Justin lifted his wide shoulders. "You will not tell me if you are a virgin or not; how am I to know that you are not with child?"

"And if I tell you I am not?"

"I cannot afford to believe you. We will wait, Dyanna, and see. In the meantime, you

295

must keep to this house—unless, of course, you wish to answer my question concerning your innocence.''

Gazing up into those uncompromising golden eyes, Dyanna knew she could not expect him to accept her refusal to answer his question. Nor, however, could she answer it truthfully and fully. There was nothing she could do but bide her time. She was once again the prisoner of DeVille House.

"Are you coming to dinner?" Justin asked, holding the door open for her.

"I'm not hungry," she snapped, though, in fact, she was famished.

"As you will."

Turning, Justin disappeared out the door, leaving his fuming ward to glare after him, wishing him to Hades and the Devil and every foul place in between.

Rushing to the door in a swirl of muslin and lace, she shouted after him:

"I hate you, Justin DeVille!"

At the door of the dining room, he turned. A smile, coolly amused, curved his full lips.

"No doubt you do, my dear, but I am inclined to take that as a compliment. For if Geoffrey Culpepper is any indication, you have damned poor taste in men!"

Chapter Twenty-Five

"Where can he be going all the time?" Dyanna demanded one rainy afternoon when, while standing at her sitting room window, she watched Justin drive off in his closed carriage. "Every day he goes off in the morning or the afternoon. Sometimes he doesn't even come home for dinner."

"He's been going off in the evening very often as well," was Charlotte's unwelcome reminder.

"Perhaps—" Dyanna squelched the thought. She'd been about to wonder aloud if there was some woman Justin might be seeing, but she could not, would not allow herself to so much as consider the possibility. "Ah, well, I suppose he has a great deal of business to attend to. Particularly now that he's become such a crony of the Duke of Cumberland and his set."

Wandering back to her favorite armchair, Dyanna picked up the book Justin had given her when they'd begun their journey back from McBride Hall. Try though she had, she could not enjoy the book—the story of a rebellious girl who comes to realize that the man she regards as a tyrant is, in truth, a wise and just protector. It hit a little too close to home for comfort, and she suspected that Justin had chosen it more as a lesson for his errant ward than for her entertainment.

Laying the book aside, Dyanna left the room and·strolled up the hall. At the far end, a short, narrow passage led off the main hall to the attic stairs.

Dyanna peered down the passage. The door at the far end stood open. The steep, twisting attic stairs of bare, painted wood rose up, turning at a sharp angle and disappearing into the darkness of the enclosed stairwell.

At the top, she knew, though she had never climbed those stairs herself, were storage rooms and the servants' quarters—separate, dormitory-like rooms for the footmen and the maidservants. Only those servants at the very top of the household hierarchy—Bertran, the master's valet; Ipswich, the grand and imperious butler; and Charlotte, whose position as

Dyanna's personal maid set her apart from the ordinary maids—had their own rooms.

Going to the foot of the stairs, Dyanna heard voices from above. One she recognized as belonging to Ipswich. Curious, she climbed the stairs, holding tight to the railing, which had been worn smooth by the hands of hundreds of maids and footmen over the course of decades.

At the top, Dyanna followed the sounds to the men servants' dormitory. One side of the long, narrow room was taken up with beds jutting out from the wall, each surmounted by a shelf on which personal belongings could be stored. Opposite each bed was a tall, slim armoire where livery was kept both for daily wear and formal evenings.

Near the far end of the long room, Ipswich and two maidservants were grouped around the last armoire in the row.

The retort of Dyanna's heel on the wooden floor brought Ipswich to attention.

"Miss Dyanna," he said, bowing shallowly.

"What is happening?" Dyanna asked, craning to see that the maids seemed to be packing the contents of the armoire into a wooden crate.

"Tom, the young footman engaged shortly after milord's arrival in London from Portsmouth, has run off, I fear." The butler's mouth pursed in disapproval. "He took several pieces of silver, I'm afraid. Doubtless to sustain him in his idleness. He always was a lazy wretch. I blame myself for not turning him out."

"What will you do?" Dyanna asked, sitting on the edge of the bed while the maids folded young Tom's belongings and tucked them into the crate.

"Nothing, I fear, miss," Ipswich replied, unable to conceal his frustration. "I suggested to his lordship that the Bow Street Runners be set on the wretch's trail, but his lordship said he would not see a sixteen-year-old boy hanged for the sake of a few teaspoons."

"You don't approve, do you?" Dyanna observed.

"No, miss, I fear I do not. Such leniency will only encourage others to follow his unfortunate example. It may be commendable from a Christian point of view, but in the end it could prove disastrous."

With that, the crate containing Tom's belongings was trundled off to the storage rooms at the other end of the attic and Dyanna followed Ipswich back down the stairs.

That diversion at an end, Dyanna wandered downstairs to the music room. But even the harpsichord held no attraction for her. She'd forgotten how much she'd once enjoyed her music—she'd forgotten everything except her resentment against Justin for immuring her in DeVille House.

"Spite!" she announced to the gleaming

instrument that had lain silent since her flight with Geoffrey. "That's all it amounts to. I will not answer his question, satisfy his curiosity, salve his male pride, so he shuts me up here while he prances about the town. I hope he—"

Glancing up, she found Bertran standing in the doorway, a paper-wrapped parcel in his hand.

Flushing, she smiled sheepishly at the valet. "Good afternoon, Bertran," she said softly.

The valet grinned. "Good afternoon, Miss Dyanna," he replied. "You were, I believe, about to express some wishes with regard to his lordship's future?"

Her blush deepening, Dyanna shot him a shaming glance. "They can wait, Bertran. What have you there?"

The valet turned the parcel over in his hands. "His lordship sent me to the stationers, Miss, and while I was there, I saw this novel. Newly written and published, I believe. I thought you might find it diverting."

"Why, Bertran!" Beaming, Dyanna took the parcel from him and unwrapped it. Bound in green leather, the title, embossed in gold, read:

LADY FEVERSHAM'S SECRET

Opening the book to the first page, Dyanna's eyes skimmed the opening paragraphs:

"Feversham Court is abandoned now, its walls crumbling, overgrown with ivy, its windows merely gaping holes, like sightless eyes, staring out at the derelict gardens. The little door in the garden wall is hidden, concealed by the thick, thorny tangle of climbing roses that once framed it so prettily. Its hinges are rusted, the key and the lock now one, immovable, mute, giving no sign that they once, in the not too distant past, represented freedom for the beautiful, tragic mistress of the house.

Like the great manor that was once her home, Lady Feversham is no more. There is little to remind one of the roles she played: that of mistress of Feversham Court, wife of the brutish and tyrannical Sir Roger Feversham, and the other more exciting, if less honourable part she played beyond the little door in the garden . . .."

Dyanna beamed delightedly at Bertran, who seemed inordinately pleased to have given her such a welcome present.

"Thank you, Bertran," she said, leaning up on tiptoe to kiss his cheek. "I've been so dreadfully bored. You cannot imagine how I've longed for a new book to read."

"I am glad you are pleased, Miss Dyanna," he murmured.

Dyanna giggled delightedly at the sudden color that stained his cheeks. "Why, Bertran! I've made you blush!"

The color in his cheeks deepening, Bertran made her his best valet's bow and retired. Behind him, in the music room, Dyanna hugged the book to her bosom. Lifting her skirts in one hand, she hurried up the stairs to her sitting room where, ensconced in her favorite armchair, she began to read about Lady Feversham and her secret.

By the middle of the afternoon, Dyanna had made the acquaintance of Lady Anne Feversham who, having been forced into an alliance with a loutish and overbearing husband, one day discovers a long-forgotten door in the garden wall. Unable to bear the miseries of her marriage any longer, Lady Feversham, in various disguises, escapes through the garden door and seeks adventure in the countryside beyond.

In turn, as the chapters progressed, the audacious Lady Anne was a highwayman, a stableboy, a tavern maid, and, having decided to play the part of an invalid at home—the better to have long periods of privacy during which she could retire to her room and issue orders that she not be disturbed—escaped to London itself and went on the stage.

Dyanna was enchanted. Lady Anne was everything she admired. Her life—the dual roles she carried off with such enviable panache—was the stuff of Dyanna's fantasies. How she longed to lead such a life of excitement! But she, like Lady Anne, was the victim of a tyrannical master. In her present mood, she saw Justin as no less cruel, no less overbearing and harsh, than Sir Roger Feversham himself.

By the time she was summoned down to dinner, Dyanna could not bear to leave Anne Feversham and her adventures. Sending down word that she was not hungry, she remained in her room, even though Charlotte had told her that Justin was dining at home that evening—something he did rarely since their return from the country.

She was in bed, propped on half a dozen lace-frothed pillows, when Justin appeared.

"Are you ill, Dyanna?" he asked, sitting on the edge of her bed. "You didn't come down to supper."

She shrugged. "I wasn't hungry."

Justin's golden eyes lingered on the spill of her silver hair over her shoulders, on the pale perfection of her skin and the rosy tinge that just touched her cheekbones, on the inviting pout of her lips that reminded him all too keenly of that night at the Black Swan Inn when he had come so close to casting off all restraint and making love to her as he so longed to do. She was, whatever her faults, however reckless and wild her character, the most beautiful creature he had ever seen and to be near her was an exquisite torment composed of equal parts pleasure and pain.

For Dyanna's part, she could not deny, however much she might wish to, that he was like no other man she had ever known. Her heart, her senses leapt at the sight of him, at the mere thought of him. Even as they sat there, an awkward silence lying heavily between them, her fingers ached to twine themselves in the thick, tawny silk of his hair; her body longed in every fiber to feel his arms around her.

Taking a deep breath, she tore her eyes from his and shrugged. "I was reading. Bertran brought me a book this afternoon."

Justin lifted the volume from where she'd laid it on the coverlet. "Lady Feversham's Secret," he read. "What is her secret?"

"By day she is a dutiful wife. By night, she rides the highways, robbing and stealing. She's been a tavern maid and other things. It's very exciting."

"She won't find it so exciting if she's caught," Justin predicted. "They hang women, too, you know."

"Oh, pish! She won't get caught. She's too clever for that!"

Justin smiled fondly. "I hope you're right, sweetheart."

Rising, he allowed himself the luxury of

bending and softly, quickly, kissing that delicate, petal-soft cheek.

"You're going out?" she asked, checking an impulse to reach out to him and draw him back.

He nodded. "I have to see a man—on business."

Dyanna said nothing as he turned and left the room, but a troubled scowl creased her brow. It was still there when Charlotte appeared with a tray of Cook's most delectable sugared rolls.

"Lord DeVille said to bring these up to you," she said. "I passed him in the hall as he was on his way out."

Dyanna nodded. "He was just here. He says he has to see a man on business. But I wonder . . . Do you think he is seeing some woman, Charlotte?"

"I don't know, miss," the maid answered honestly. "It's possible I suppose."

Sighing, Dyanna reached for her book. "I wish there was some way of knowing for certain. I wish I could follow him some night and see where he goes." She laughed. "Lady Feversham would have done it. She would have dressed in disguise and slipped out through her little garden door and found out what she wished to know. She would have gone as a man, I suspect. For London is dangerous at night for a woman alone."

Charlotte nodded, a little mystified. She had

no notion of the plot of the book Dyanna was reading and so knew neither who Lady Feversham was nor why she should have resorted to disguises.

At a loss for anything to add to Dyanna's line of speculation, Charlotte changed the subject.

"Did you hear, miss," she asked, "about young Tom, the footman?"

"Yes. Ipswich said he ran off and took some of the silver with him. I was upstairs earlier today while Ipswich and two of the maids were packing away Tom's clothes—"

Dyanna drew a sharp breath. Her eyes flitted from Charlotte's face to her book and back again.

"Charlotte," she said thoughtfully, "Tom was not a very big lad, was he?"

"Oh, no, miss. He was rather small and thin."

"About my size, would you say?"

"Well—yes, about, I should think."

Lying back on her pillows, Dyanna's lips curved into a mischievous grin.

Watching her, Charlotte could not imagine what mad scheme was hatching in her all too fanciful brain, but she knew her mistress well enough to be filled with foreboding at the mere thought of what it might be.

Chapter Twenty-Six

It was long after midnight before Dyanna considered it safe to make her way up the steep and winding stair to the attics of DeVille House.

Creeping past the doors leading to the men and women servant's dormitory, Dyanna shielded her candle with her hand. She did not want any wakeful footman or parlormaid to notice the glow of the candle flame as she passed and come to investigate.

The room to which the errant Tom's belongings had been taken was low and dark, its slanting roof proclaiming it to be beneath the very eaves of DeVille House. Dyanna searched among the boxes and trunks for the one with the least dust—the one approached by a path of footprints in the thick grey dust that carpeted the floor.

Setting her candle on the lid of an iron-bound trunk, Dyanna lifted the lid of the crate and sorted through the garments inside. There were Tom's everyday and formal liveries, two pairs of breeches, a shirt, and a worn, brown cloth coat. A tricorne had been set atop Tom's chestnut-colored, pig-tailed wig, making it look eerily as if someone were still wearing it.

Dyanna sorted through the clothes. She could not, she knew, simply cart the whole crate down to her room—it had taken two maids to carry it into the storage room.

Burrowing her arms into the wooden box, she pulled out Tom's everyday livery, one pair of dark-blue cloth breeches, the shirt, and the coat. Studying what was left, she pulled out a pair of stockings and the wig and hat. A pair of shoes lay in the bottom of the box, but they were of no use to Dyanna. Although Tom had been a small, thin boy, his feet were far larger than Dyanna's. But she had a pair of scuffed leather slippers that would do well enough if they were not examined too closely.

Gathering the clothes into a pile, she scooped them into her arms and replaced the lid on the crate. With her bundle wedged between one arm and her hip, she took up her candle and started her stealthy retreat to her room.

Below, in the privacy of her bedchamber, behind the doors she only dared lock when Justin was out of the house, Dyanna pulled off her nightdress and kicked off her satin slippers. With a sense of delicious naughtiness, she pulled on the long white stockings, then the dark blue satin breeches that buttoned just below the knee with two big brass buttons. The white shirt, though too wide in the shoulders and too long by half, she tucked into the breeches and hid beneath the dark blue coat with its padded shoulders and high, stiff collar. The brass buttons that surmounted the vent in the back glittered prettily as she turned before the gilt-framed pierglass.

Delighted, Dyanna rummaged in her closet for her oldest black slippers. They would do creditably if one did not look too closely and notice the decidedly feminine bows on the toes. Well, that could be remedied. Tomorrow she would take a knife and cut the silken threads that fastened the bows to the slippers.

There remained only the matter of her hair to contend with. It was too long, too curly and of too unusual a shade to simply tie back in imitation of a man's. Her eyes went to the dark, rich brown wig whose curled pigtail was tied with a black grosgrain bow.

Skewering her hair atop her head, she fitted the heavy wig over her own silver curls and tugged it down into place around her ears.

Her image in the pier glass delighted her. She looked like a boy—albeit a young, exceptionally pretty boy. All that was needed to make her the perfect example of the young footman was the immaculate white gloves that completed the livery.

Where could they be found? The butler's pantry, no doubt. A sudden, mad impulse sent her venturing out from behind her locked bedchamber doors and down the grand staircase, a candle clutched in her hand.

From the entry hall she passed through progressively smaller and less grand chambers of DeVille House until she found herself in the butler's pantry. She was certain Ipswich would be mortified by this invasion of his inner sanctum, but it could not be helped.

Dyanna rummaged through cabinets and drawers until she found what she sought. In a drawer, separated by layers of tissue, lay the white gloves worn by the footmen on formal occasions.

Taking a pair, Dyanna closed the drawer and retreated to the entry hall. She had never before visited the depths of the house where the day-to-day business of running a great and extensive household was conducted.

In the entry hall, Dyanna put her candle on a table and drew on her gloves. They buttoned at the wrists and she drew the wrist frills of her shirt down over them and tugged the wide cuffs of her coat into place.

A mirror hung on the wall of the entrance hall, flanked with ornate sconces. The candles in them burned inside their crystal globes in anticipation of Justin's late return. In the golden glow of the flames, Dyanna regarded her reflection with utter enchantment.

So engrossed was she in her transformation that she did not hear the clip-clop of iron-shod hooves on the drive outside. She did not notice the crunching of the gravel beneath Justin's feet as he dismounted nor the retort of his heels on the steps outside the door as he made his way up them.

It was not until the door-latch rattled in his hand that Dyanna realized he was home. It was too late to flee—she could not even have reached one of the doorways that led off the hall in time. Trembling, she watched in terrified fascination as the door swung open.

Entering the hall, Justin pulled off his hat. Without looking, he dropped it on top of Dyanna's head where it dropped over her eyes; only her nose kept her face from disappearing completely. Unfastening the clasp of his evening cloak, he pulled it off in a fluid, swirling motion and draped it over her, making her stagger with its sudden weight.

"You didn't have to wait up, Tom," Justin muttered wearily, heading toward the stairs without a backward glance. "Just throw those over the chair and go to bed, there's a good lad."

Not waiting to be told twice, Dyanna dumped the cloak and hat over the chair and ran for the hall leading toward the kitchens—the hall from which the narrow back stairs led to the upstairs corridor and the safety of her room.

It was not until he was halfway up the stairs that Justin realized what he'd just done.

"Tom?" he said softly, remembering suddenly that the youngest footman had absconded. Pausing on the stairs, he looked back down into the entry hall. It was deserted. His hat and evening cloak lay draped over the arms of a tapestried chair near the door.

But there had been someone there. He had given his hat and coat to a footman the size of young Tom. Hadn't he?

Shaking his head, Justin resumed his climb up the stairs. He hadn't thought he'd had that much to drink. Whatever it was they put into the punch at Brooks's, it was more potent than he had realized.

While Justin was pondering the mystery of the disappearing footman, Dyanna was climbing the twisting, narrow, pitch-black staircase that seemed to rise forever into the darkness. She'd kicked off her slippers at the foot of the stairs and her stockinged feet made no sound on the wooden treads as she at last reached the top of the stairs and emerged through the door into the upstairs hall.

In the silent emptiness of the corridor she could hear the sound of Justin's footsteps nearing the top of the marble staircase.

Poised in the middle of the hall for a moment, Dyanna wondered if Justin would come to her room as he occasionally did upon returning from an evening out. It was as if he had to reassure himself that she had not run away again.

In the distance, his shadow fell across the corridor. In a moment, he would be in the hall and would see her there. Forcing her feet into motion, Dyanna ran for her room. The door of her sitting room had just closed soundlessly behind her when Justin appeared.

In her room, Dyanna tore off her wig and shoved it, along with her shoes and the rest of the clothes she'd pilfered from the attic under her bed. Then, her hair tumbling around her shoulders, she leapt into bed and jerked the covers up under her chin.

As she'd feared, the rattle of her sitting room door sounded hollowly in the darkened room. The thud of Justin's boots crossed the carpet approaching the bedchamber door.

Dyanna tensed as she heard the creak of the door latch beneath Justin's hand. The door swung open, a smooth, white shadow in the moonglow that shone through the diaphanous draperies.

"Dyanna?" Justin entered the room, his footsteps muffled in the thick pile of the carpet. "Dyanna? Are you awake?"

Feigning sleep, Dyanna waited until he had reached the bedside before she stirred and pretended to awaken.

"Justin?" she said softly. "Did you just come in?"

"Yes," he admitted. "I'm sorry I woke you."

"I don't mind," she told him truthfully. It rather pleased her that he came to her room nearly every night before retiring to his own chambers across the hall. "Is it late?"

"Nearly two, I think. Can I get you anything?"

"Nothing, thank you."

Though normally she enjoyed these intimate nocturnal visits, she was too frightened tonight that he would discover, beneath the demurely drawn-up covers, that she was fully dressed in the dark blue-and-white livery of DeVille House footmen. Drawing a deep breath, she feigned a yawn that seemed to make the top half of her head disappear.

Immediately, Justin rose from the edge of the bed where he was wont to perch during his visits.

"I'll leave so you can go back to sleep," he said softly. "Good-night, sweetheart."

Bending, he brushed his lips on her cheek and was gone as quietly as he had come.

Dyanna heard the bedchamber doors close

316

behind him, then the sitting room door. His footsteps crossed the corridor and the soft thud of his own door closing behind him echoed through the rooms. Even so, it was nearly a half hour before she was brave enough to climb out of the bed and go about the business of stripping off the livery and finding a safe hiding place for her new-found disguise.

Dressed in her nightgown, she climbed back into bed and settled into her pillows. Though she did not know where Justin went on his evenings out, and did not know whom he saw or what he did, she took some comfort in the fact that when he returned he generally smelled of fine liquors and tobacco smoke. She could not have borne smelling some anonymous woman's rich, cloying perfume on his clothes.

Chapter Twenty-Seven

Having been so nearly caught by Justin in her guise as a footman dampened Dyanna's ardor for masquerades during the next several weeks. More than once during the intervening weeks, in the dead of night while the household slept, she had taken out the small pile of clothing from its hiding place in the bottommost drawer of the cabinet at the back of her closet. She had examined them, mended them, slipped on the jacket of the livery or Tom's own brown cloth coat and stood before her pierglass wondering if she would ever have the nerve to venture out of her room, out of DeVille House, disguised as a young man.

It was true, of course, that she no longer

had such a strong incentive for risking disaster by venturing out alone into the bustling, dangerous streets and alleys of London. Justin, realizing that the oppressive atmosphere of DeVille House and Dyanna's near imprisonment behind its elegant walls had played a large part in her desperate flight to Patterton Park, had relaxed his restrictions on her going out. She was free to go as she chose, within reason and taking care to be accompanied by Charlotte and, when Justin was not available, Bertran. She went to the shops until they began to bore her. She went riding in the park, reveling in the stares of gentlemen, delighting in how frequently Lord This or Mr. That applied to Justin to be presented to his ward and enquired as to whether or not she might be courted.

Nor was she displeased by the way Justin gently but firmly discouraged potential suitors. It fired her hopes that he intended her for some other fate—namely, though even now she scarcely dared hope for it, of one day becoming Lady DeVille. It was her favorite fantasy—surpassing even that of escaping into the swirling anonymity of London in the guise of a boy.

The afternoon was fine. The late summer sunshine shone brightly in a bright azure sky dotted with great fluffy clouds.

Dyanna sat in the garden. She wished she hadn't thrown herself quite so enthusiastically into shopping when first Justin had said she might go. The shops now held little appeal for her—she had smelled too many scents, tried on too many bonnets, found herself draped in too many fine fabrics to take much pleasure in it anymore. The novelty had worn off.

Sighing, she leaned back against the tree that shaded her complexion from the sun. Charlotte had detected a pair of freckles flanking the up-turned tip of her nose that morning and had nearly had a fit of apoplexy. No more sun! had been her decree, and Dyanna had agreed, more out of a desire to hear the last of the subject than for any real concern about the whiteness of her skin.

Lost in her reverie, she did not hear Justin's approach. She did not hear him coming up the walk between the carefully tended flower beds; she did not notice him stop in the shade of a nearby tree and gaze at her. Had she, she would have surprised on his handsome face all the admiration, all the love, all the desire he took such exquisite care to hide from her.

When, at last, she did sense his presence and look up at him, he was prepared. His strong, regular features were composed in an expression of careful serenity that betrayed nothing of the havoc she wreaked on his senses.

"Justin," she breathed as he moved toward her. She sighed as he came toward her. There had never been a man like Justin, her heart whispered. There would never be another.

321

"Good afternoon, Dyanna," he said. His voice, low and rich, sent shivers down her spine, raising the fine silver hairs on the back of her neck.

"Good afternoon, Justin," she replied, a breathy, breathless tone in her voice that sent a tantalizing tingle through him. "I thought you would be going out after lunch."

"I was thinking of doing just that," he admitted; there was a pleased, mischievous smile on his face that told Dyanna he had something special in mind. "That is what I came here to ask you about."

"Going out?" she asked hopefully.

"I thought you might enjoy an outing, as the day is so fine. We could drive in the park, or visit some of the sights, or—"

"The lions?" Dyanna asked.

"What was that?"

"The lions. I should like to see the menagerie in the Tower."

Justin hesitated. He had been to the menagerie once, long before, and found it a thoroughly depressing place. The cages were cramped and the animals, for the most part, old and apathetic. And the place smelled abominably. Still, it was what Dyanna wanted.

"Very well, the Tower it is. Go have Charlotte get you ready. I'll meet you in the hall in fifteen minutes."

Taking the hand Justin offered, Dyanna rose. For a long, lingering moment, her hand lay in his, warm and trembling. Her gaze rose slowly, shyly to meet his until their eyes met, a melding of gold and aqua. Dyanna shivered. He was so tall, so strong, so handsome. She longed for him to take her into his arms and kiss her.

Justin swallowed hard. She was so beautiful with her silvery curls tumbling over her shoulders and down her back. There were roses in her cheeks, as pink and pretty as those painted on the soft rustling silk of her gown. Did it matter so much that she was his ward? Did it matter that she was the daughter of his friend? She was a beautiful woman, willful and reckless it was true, but docile, meek women had never held much attraction for him. Had they met under different circumstances, he felt sure he would have made her his own long ago.

"Dyanna . . ." he said softly, gently, his fingers threading through hers, "I . . . we . . ."

"Yes, Justin?" she prompted, her heart pounding, certain that this was the moment she had longed for, the moment when all the barriers between them would tumble down, when all the qualms he'd had over the feelings his beautiful young ward evoked in him had at last been vanquished by the power of his love for her. In a moment they'd be in one another's arms. "We . . .?"

From the end of the garden, near the back of the house, Charlotte's voice shattered the enchanted tension that held them both in thrall.

"Miss Dyanna? Miss Dyanna! You're not out in the sun again, are you?"

"Damn!" Justin hissed, his golden eyes flashing as he glared toward the maid.

"What were you going to say, Justin?" Dyanna prompted almost desperately. "We what?"

He hesitated for a long, agonizing moment, but the spell, for the moment at least, was irreparably shattered. "We'd better hurry if we're going all the way to the Tower. Go along now and have Charlotte get you ready."

Turning on his heel, he moved off in the direction of the stables to order the carriage brought around to the front of the house.

In the shade of the tree, watching him go, Dyanna felt as if she would cry. She wanted to scream, to curse—most of all, she wanted to kill Charlotte!

Snatching up her skirts, she stalked toward the house. She'd be ready to leave in fifteen minutes all right; but she intended to spend ten of those minutes giving Charlotte the tongue-lashing of her life!

Contrary to Justin's hopes, the menagerie in the Tower had not improved since his previous visit. He was only too glad when Dyanna quickly decided she'd seen enough and they emerged into the sunshine of the day once more.

They were strolling toward their carriage when a shrill, unpleasant voice hailed them. They turned and Dyanna's eyes rounded at the apparition that was approaching.

"Christ," Justin muttered. "It's Rawley!"

Dyanna stared. The man was seventy if he was a day. His face was painted to a ghastly pallor with white lead, then rouged until stark patches of red stood out on the sharp, jutting bones of his cheeks. His lips had been carmined into an obscene cupid's bow that twitched at the corners as his deep-set eyes flickered over Dyanna. He was dressed in black satin and white silk and a gleaming white wig perched atop his head, its black-bowed pigtail trailing to the middle of his back, made his head seem far too large for his whippet-thin body.

"My lord DeVille," he drawled, bowing first to Justin, then to Dyanna. "I pray you, present me to this vision of loveliness."

Justin hesitated, clearly loath to bring Dyanna into contact with this relic of the decadent past.

"Lord Rawley," he said tightly, resigned to making an introduction. "Allow me to present Miss Dyanna McBride, my ward. Dyanna, Viscount Rawley."

"McBride?" Lord Rawley's red-rimmed, kohled eyes made another slow perusal of Dyanna's body. "Surely not Rakehell Mc-Bride's little daughter. Damme, I'd no idea how long it's been. What a little beauty you are, my love. And DeVille, why've you been hiding this glorious creature?" He smiled and Dyanna could not take her eyes from the curving, blood-red lips. "I knew your father well, my dear—better, I dare say, than your guardian." His eyes slid to Justin's face and back again. "What a pity you were not left in my care. What a pity indeed!"

Dyanna shivered, feeling a sick quivering in the pit of her stomach. Involuntarily, she edged closer to Justin. The thought of being left at the mercy of this painted, leering old man made her flesh crawl. For the first time in many years, Dyanna felt a surge of gratitude for the father who had deserted her before she was out of leading strings. If nothing else, he had left her in the care of a man not worn out by his vices nor so riddled with debauchery as to see her as nothing more than a succulent treat for his lusts.

"If you will excuse us, my lord," Justin was saying, feeling Dyanna's trembling as she pressed close beside him. "We were just leaving."

"Of course, forgive me," Lord Rawley said, making them both another courtly bow. "I look forward to meeting you again, my lovely Miss McBride . . . under more pleasant circumstances." His dark black eyes glittered. "Oh, yes, I look forward to furthering our acquaintance."

Before Dyanna could react, the foppish old reprobate had taken Dyanna's hand and lifted it to his carmined lips. When he released it, its delicate white skin bore a perfect imprint of his mouth.

With another leering smile, Lord Rawley moved away and Dyanna pulled out a lace-edged handkerchief and scrubbed at the red imprint on her hand.

"Who was that man, Justin?" she asked as he handed her into the coach. "He made my skin crawl!"

"As well he might," Justin agreed. "He was an intimate of Sir Francis Dashwood, one of the Friars of Medmenham. Now he confines himself to practices more discreet but no less loathsome."

"What practices?" she demanded, craning her neck to watch the fantastic old man disappear around a corner.

Receiving no answer, she prompted: "Justin? What practices?"

Justin said nothing. Poised to climb into the carriage, his foot on the step, he was staring off in the other direction.

Dyanna leaned down so she could see out the opposite window. In the distance, a woman returned Justin's gaze—a pretty, petite creature with strawberry-blond curls. She seemed distressed, but made no move to approach.

"Barnes," Justin said, addressing the coach-

327

man as he stepped backward and closed the carriage door. "Take Miss Dyanna home."

"Justin!" Dyanna protested, reaching a hand toward him as if to hold him back. "Where are you going?"

"I have to talk to someone. I'll see you at home later."

"But Justin!"

Without another word, Justin moved away in the direction of the pretty blonde who smiled tremulously as she saw him approaching.

From the window, as the carriage rolled away, Dyanna watched, torn between anger and chagrin. She hung out the carriage window, watching as Justin went to the woman in jonquil silk, watching as he reached her, as he put out a hand and touched her elbow.

The last sight Dyanna had before the carriage bore her away was of Justin and the pretty blonde, whose befeathered bonnet barely reached the top of Justin's shoulder, walking with their heads close together, deep in some intimate, obviously private conversation.

As the carriage rolled through London, making its slow way along the crowded streets toward Piccadilly and DeVille House, Dyanna determined to discover the identity of the strawberry-blonde Justin found so fascinating and exactly where she fit into Justin's life.

Chapter Twenty-Eight

Even as Dyanna was being borne away under protest, Justin made his way to where Octavia FitzGeorge stood.

"Ma'am," he said, lifting his hat as she dropped him a little curtsy.

"Good day, my lord," she replied softly, flushing prettily as Justin fell into step beside her.

"I was wondering, ma'am, if you had heard anything from Lord Culpepper."

A distraught look crossed her pretty, round-cheeked face. "Oh, my lord," she bleated. "I was going to ask you the same thing!" She sighed, sinking onto a stone bench beside the path. "I suppose he has married the young woman of fortune you spoke of when you visited the house on Queen Street." Tears glittered in her great dark eyes. "I am lost. Utterly lost."

Sitting down beside her, Justin took her hand in his. He felt compassion for her. He was, and had always been, easy prey for pretty, tearful women. He could captain a privateer, fight any man to the death with sword or gun, but he could not bear the sight of tears in a pair of fine eyes.

"He did not marry the young lady," he revealed. "The marriage was prevented in time."

Octavia's relief was as obvious as it was enormous. "Thank God!" she breathed. "Oh, thank God. Was it you, my lord? Did you prevent his wedding the lady you mentioned?"

"It was," Justin admitted, unwilling to say more on the subject.

"Oh, my lord, how am I ever to repay you?" Her tears dried, Octavia gazed up at Justin with rapt admiration.

"Your gratitude is quite enough," Justin told her, though he believed in his heart of hearts that the pretty young woman before him should not be too pleased that Geoffrey's plans had been thwarted. For one thing, he sincerely doubted that Geoffrey's marriage to the former actress was a lawful one. It seemed only too likely that she was no more than his mistress for all she believed otherwise. Her disillusionment had merely been postponed.

It would come eventually—of that he was certain.

"What I cannot understand," Octavia went on, "is why, if he has not married this young woman, he has not returned to London."

Justin thought he could better understand Geoffrey's continued absence. Surely the wretch must know that Justin was not done with him. The wrong he had attempted to do to Dyanna must be avenged. Justin had vowed to make Geoffrey Culpepper pay for what he had tried to do, and he had not changed his mind simply because Dyanna was restored to him safe and sound.

"I expect he will return—eventually," Justin assured her. "Though, if you will forgive my frankness, ma'am, I believe you would be far better off to begin making preparations for your own maintainance. I would not, if I were you, depend upon Geoffrey Culpepper for your future welfare."

A great sigh welled up in Octavia's plump bosom. "I suppose you are right, my lord, but what can I do? I cannot bear the thought of returning to the stage—To stand up there while the world laughs at me for an abandoned wife. Lady Culpepper, the future Marchioness of Summersleigh, trodding the boards? You must see how impossible that would be."

Justin felt a sudden, almost unendurable desire to throttle the pretty, dense creature before him. Could she, having seen Geoffrey leave her to elope with another woman, still believe that he cared for her? Could she truly imagine that she would one day reign at Summersleigh House? If nothing else, did she actually believe that London society would accept her, a base-born woman who had once exposed herself on the public stage, as one of them?

It would be a kindness, Justin believed, to discourage Octavia's self-deceiving beliefs. But one look at her dreamy face, her faraway gaze as she imagined the exalted position she would one day occupy, told him that any such attempts on his part would be futile. She would see the truth one day; Geoffrey himself would force her to open her eyes and see herself for what she truly was—his mistress. Until then, it was useless to try to change her mind.

"I expect," Justin went on, growing anxious to end the conversation and be away, "that Geoffrey will not stay away from town for much longer. Everything he most prizes is here, after all."

He had meant, of course, Dyanna and her fortune as well as the gaming hells Geoffrey so loved to frequent. But Octavia chose to believe Justin had meant her and dimpled prettily.

"Oh, my lord, how you do go on!" she gushed. Then her dimples faded as her delighted smile was replaced by an exaggerated expression of worry and woe. "Although, I fear if he does not return soon, he will find little to greet him. I vow, I am quite worn to a frazzle. The servants, excepting my dear maid Eliza who was with me in the theater, have all run off. Well, who could blame them? I had no money to pay them. There is scarcely enough food to eat and we must needs sit in near darkness in the evenings, for candles are prodigiously dear, you know. But I must not tire you, my lord, with a recitation of my troubles."

Raising a gloved hand, she pressed a trembling fingertip to the corner of her eye.

Justin resisted the impulse to smile. He was not surprised the girl had not succeeded spectacularly on the stage, for she was no great actress. But it did surprise him that she had not succeeded in finding a more considerate, generous, and important protector than Geoffrey Culpepper, for she was feminine to the tips of her fingers. Had he not so completely lost his heart and his senses to Dyanna, did he not know of her connection with such a loathsome wretch as Culpepper, he might have been tempted to take the girl under his own protection—for a time at least. He had no doubt her charms would pall quickly.

"If I did not fear you would take my offer amiss," he told Octavia, knowing already what she would do and say, "I would take it upon myself to offer some aid to you in your distress. But of course—"

"My lord," Octavia breathed. "You are kindness itself. How can I ever repay you?"

"By sending me a message when Lord Culpepper at last makes his appearance," he answered, rising and offering her his arm.

Slipping her hand into the crook of his elbow, Octavia looked worried. "You do not mean my lord any harm, do you, sir? I could not bear to be the means by which harm came to my dear, dear husband."

Justin ground his teeth. Did the woman actually care so much for the man who had used and abandoned her, or was she merely playing a role? He weighed his words carefully before he said:

"I have unfinished business with Lord Culpepper, ma'am. You may rest assured that I mean to give Lord Culpepper nothing he has not earned to the fullest extent."

Octavia squinted up at him. She did not understand all the implications of what Justin had said, but it sounded vaguely as if Geoffrey was in line for some sort of reward. He would like that, she decided, brightening. She threw Justin her most dazzling smile and told him:

"I will agree, then, to your terms, my lord. You shall be the second to know when dear Geoffrey returns. The first of course"—she giggled—"will be me."

"Very well, then," Justin agreed. "Shall we go somewhere quiet and discuss finances?"

The afternoon passed with agonizing slowness for Dyanna. The memory of the sight of Justin striding so purposefully toward the pretty strawberry-blonde in the yellow gown tormented her. It would not be banished; her efforts were useless. Even the book about Lady Feversham held no charm for her now.

She could not concentrate. Where was he? she asked herself. What was he doing? No, on second thought, she did not want to know what he was doing. The possibilities were too hard to bear. He'd been so eager to see the woman. He'd sent Dyanna home alone like a child who had misbehaved on a Sunday outing in order to be with that woman.

"Who is she?" she asked aloud, not for the first, nor the tenth time that afternoon. "Has he been seeing her all along? All those nights he's been out on business, as he says, has he been with her?"

"Perhaps she is his mistress," Charlotte suggested. "Had she a look of breeding about her? Did she strike you as a lady of quality?"

"Oh, I don't know," Dyanna sighed. "She was pretty. She had blond hair with a reddish cast and a pretty, plump figure. She was beautifully dressed. Very feminine. But as to her breeding or lack of it, I don't know. How is one to tell? A single ride through Hyde Park of

Sandra DuBay

a Sunday afternoon can show you great ladies who look and act like trollops and trollops who look and act like great ladies. One has scarcely to look further than one's own neighborhood. The Duchess of Devonshire"—she gestured toward a great house not far away in Piccadilly—"and her sister, Harriet, Viscountess Duncannon, have had more lovers than even they care to count. At the same time, Mrs. Robinson, no more than an actress, had to be wooed by the Prince of Wales as though she were a princess of the blood royal."

"What will you do?" Charlotte wanted to know.

"I don't know. I don't suppose there is anything I can do if he wishes to be with that woman. But oh, Charlotte, it is the not knowing that is the hardest to bear—the mystery, the wondering. I have to know the truth. Only then will I know what there is for me to contend with."

A scratching at the door interrupted them and Dyanna motioned for Charlotte to answer it.

A maid appeared in the doorway. Curtsying, she said:

"Your pardon, Miss, but supper will be served in half an hour."

"Oh, I'm not really very hungry," Dyanna said. "I don't suppose my lord DeVille is back?"

336

"Oh yes, Miss. He came back quite an hour ago and more."

Dyanna sat up. "He did? Well, then, tell Ipswich I will be coming down to dinner after all."

Later, as Justin held Dyanna's chair for her, she could not wait any longer to broach the subject that had been on her mind all afternoon.

"Justin," she said after the maid and footman who had served them had departed, "who was that young woman you were in such a hurry to speak to this afternoon?"

Sipping his wine, Justin lifted his shoulders. "Simply an acquaintance."

"Have you known her long?"

"A month—perhaps a little longer."

Dyanna thoughtfully chewed a morsel of roast duck while she studied him. "What is her name?"

"Dyanna," Justin said, laying down his fork and blotting the corners of his mouth with his napkin. "She is just an acquaintance—a casual acquaintance. I am sorry you even saw her. Please, just forget her. She is no one you need concern yourself with."

He went on with his dinner, but Dyanna found she had lost her appetite. Why was he being so evasive? If the woman was truly no more than a casual acquaintance, why couldn't she at least know her name?

337

Sandra DuBay

She broached the subject no more—she knew Justin would tell her nothing. It was very likely, in fact, that any further inquiries would only anger him and ruin their evening.

But though she said no more about Justin's mysterious acquaintance, his reticence only fired her curiosity. She would find out who the woman was. She would discover her name and exactly what her relationship with Justin amounted to. And she would find it out whether Justin liked it or not!

Chapter Twenty-Nine

Life went on as usual at DeVille House in the weeks that followed. Summer gave way to autumn, but Dyanna scarcely noticed the changing of the seasons. She was obsessed—she thought of nothing, it seemed, but the strawberry-blonde she had seen with Justin that day at the Tower.

Justin, as she'd known he would from the start, said no more on the subject. He came and went as he pleased, talked with Dyanna on any subject—saving that of his mysterious acquaintance—teased her and escorted her to the park, the shops, and on rare occasions, to the theater. It was only on that one subject, that one forbidden topic, that he was silent.

And it was only that one subject that Dyanna was truly interested in.

"Are you going out tonight?" she asked one evening in early September when she noticed Justin descending the stairs dressed in deep blue brocade and an elegantly embroidered, white satin waistcoat.

"Yes," he admitted. "I have an engagement."

Dyanna said nothing and he glanced at her, finding her aqua-blue eyes filled with melancholy and gentle reproach. Sighing, he reached out a hand and stroked her cheek.

"Would you rather I stayed home with you?" he asked, a tender, fond smile curving his lips.

Shrugging, Dyanna moved out of his reach. "If you have an engagement, my lord, pray do not let me keep you from it. I am not a child, after all, who needs to be sat at home with. I am perfectly capable of entertaining myself."

Justin sighed, hesitating before taking the hat and gloves and cloak which Bertran had brought to him. He knew what was troubling Dyanna—what had been troubling her ever since that cursed day when Fate brought them to the Tower at the same time as Octavia FitzGeorge. But he could not tell Dyanna who Octavia was. He could not tell her that Geoffrey had kept a mistress—a mistress with whom he had gone through some form of marriage to overcome her scruples. Not yet, at least—not until he had had his revenge on Geoffrey for what he did to Dyanna. For now, however, whatever the cost to Dyanna's curiosity, he had to maintain the secrecy he thought essential to lull Culpepper into a false sense of security that would encourage him to venture once more into London.

"Dyanna," he said, trying to placate her but not knowing how to do so without giving himself away. "There is something I have to do—some unfinished business I have to conclude. Once that is taken care of, we will go away from London. Just you and I. Perhaps we will go to Wildwood. You said you wished to see it, remember?"

"Wildwood," Dyanna repeated. "And what will you do at Wildwood? Visit Caro Naysmith?"

"Oh, Dyanna," Justin moaned. "I was not even thinking of Caro. I can see you are in no fit frame of mind to discuss this matter tonight. Once my business is concluded, I will explain everything to you and you will see how very foolish and groundless all these suspicions of yours are."

"Will I?" she asked. "Are you sure?"

With his fingertips, he traced the delicate line of her jaw. "Yes, I am quite sure. Can't you simply trust me for a little while?"

"Very well," she acquiesced, not a little moved by the gentle touch of his fingers on her skin. "I will say no more on the subject."

"Thank you, darling," he said approvingly. "I'll see you tomorrow."

"You're not coming home tonight?" she asked, following him toward the door.

Laughing, Justin tugged one of her silvery curls. "Yes, I am coming home tonight. But it will likely be after your bedtime. Now remember, you promised to say no more about my business."

"I won't," she assured him, smiling vapidly as he strode out the door toward the carriage that waited at the bottom of the front steps.

She stood in the open doorway, watching, and heard him instruct the coachman:

"Brooks's first."

The coachman nodded, and the moment Justin had settled himself inside the carriage, it was set into motion with the crack of a whip over the heads of the matched bays that drew it.

Dyanna watched as the carriage rolled out between the opened gates and disappeared into the traffic of Piccadilly. Then, snatching up her skirts, she ran for the stairs and the privacy of her room.

"You're mad!" Charlotte objected. She sat on the bench of Dyanna's dressing table and watched incredulously as Dyanna pulled on

Tom's clothes and wig. "You can't go out at night! Alone! Dressed in breeches!"

"Dressed in breeches is the only way I can go out," Dyanna said, tucking up the last stray silver curl beneath the chestnut wig. "I heard Justin say he was going to Brooks's first. If I go there and wait, I might be able to follow him to his ultimate destination—likely the home of that woman. I may be able to learn something."

"I don't like it," Charlotte decided. "It's dangerous."

"Don't be such a simpleton," Dyanna snapped. "In *Jenny Flynn*, Jenny dressed up in boy's garb all the time in order to make her way about."

"Didn't she ever get caught?" Charlotte asked.

"Well, yes, but that's not the point. Oh, Charlotte, don't worry. I'll be fine. After all, I came to London alone, you know, and nothing happened."

Except, of course, the voice inside her head whispered, that you were held up by a highwayman and nearly seduced by your own guardian in an inn.

She forced those traitorous thoughts out of her mind. Not only were they unwelcome, but she feared they would undermine her determination and erode the confidence she needed to venture out into London by night.

Clapping her tricorne atop the black bowed

wig, Dyanna examined herself in the pierglass. She could not help being pleased. She felt confident that no one she passed on a darkened street would suspect for a moment that beneath the brown coat, white shirt, and black breeches was a young woman of birth and breeding who made her home in an elegant mansion in Piccadilly.

"Wish me luck," she told Charlotte as she moved toward the door. "I'll be back before Justin."

"I hope so," Charlotte breathed, but she knew better than to try to stop Dyanna from doing exactly as she pleased.

Letting herself out through the music room doors, Dyanna crossed the moonlit garden and emerged in Piccadilly.

Taking a deep breath, she steeled herself against the impulse to retreat into the luxurious security of DeVille House. Justin had said he merely had to conclude whatever business had been occupying him of late and then they would be off to Wildwood together. Perhaps she should take him at his word and simply try to be patient.

She looked back toward DeVille House. Its windows glowed, beckoning her back inside. But what if Justin were merely trying to lull her into complacent placidity? What if he thought he could calm her fears enough to allow him to do as he pleased while she sat at home meek and unquestioning, week after week, month after month?

No! She had to carry out her plan. She had to at least try to discover where it was he was going—what business consumed so much of his time and required such secrecy.

Squaring her shoulders, she set off down Piccadilly toward St. James's Street, in which was located Brooks's Club.

St. James's Street ran from Piccadilly to St. James's Palace. As Dyanna turned into the street, she felt herself being infected with the tantalizing excitement of being alone on the night-shrouded streets of London. They were little less bustling at night than during the day, though the people seemed somehow more glamorous, the women more beautiful, the men more rakish, almost dangerous. Bejeweled ladies and evening-clothed gentlemen rode by in elegant carriages. Gentlemen alone or in pairs alighted from carriages and disappeared into the clubs and private houses that lined the street.

Dyanna made her way along St. James's with little trouble. Everyone, it seemed, was going somewhere. They moved purposefully with little time or thought to spare for a thin young man who hurried along the street toward Brooks's.

Justin's carriage, Dyanna was pleased and relieved to see, stood waiting for him—a sign, she thought, that he would soon be leaving and she could discover his final destination for the evening.

She took up a position across the street and a little toward Piccadilly, for Justin's carriage was facing in that direction and she imagined his destination must lie that way. Behind her, set within a high iron gate, was a private club, its windows heavily curtained. Its members arrived in closed carriages, descending beneath a stone porte-cochère which concealed their identities in its black shadows.

As she waited, watching, a carriage passed her slowly. It turned into the drive of the house behind her and rolled into the shadows beneath the porte-cochère.

Curious, Dyanna watched over her shoulder as a black-clad footman sprang to open the door. Two men descended, silhouetted in the darkness. One spoke to the footman, pointing toward the street, and Dyanna knew she was the object of their conversation.

The footman left the shadows and approached her. Dyanna, certain they had taken her for some loitering footpad or vagrant, stood poised for flight at the first sign of trouble. But the footman stopped within a few feet of her.

"Milord wishes a word with you, boy," he told her.

Dyanna hesitated. The footman looked like

no other footman she'd ever seen. Heavy, with a pocked face and hands like hams, he looked more like an inmate of Newgate. His eyes were small and cruel. Dyanna thought she would not like to cross swords with him even if she were truly a man.

"Come on, boy," he repeated, his voice a low, gravelly growl. "Don't keep milord waiting."

"I . . ." Dyanna lowered her voice as much as she could. "I am waiting for someone—my master is in Brooks's. I daren't miss him."

"Monck?" A shrill, grating, unpleasantly familiar voice echoed from the shadows. "What is taking so long?"

"Come on," the footman insisted. "Your master will wait. And milord only wants a little of your time"—a sneering leer contorted his already ugly face—"and mayhap a little of your fine, soft flesh."

Dyanna gasped. Looking past the footman, Monck, she saw the two men who'd descended from the carriage emerge from the shadows. One she'd known from his voice—the ghostly, painted face of Lord Rawley seemed to glow in the silvery moonlight. The other was no less familiar, but more of a surprise. Geoffrey Culpepper stood beside the painted old fop.

Dyanna stared, astonished. But the crushing grip of the footman's beefy hand on her arm jerked her back to reality. Struggling frantically, she tore her arm free of the man's grasp and fled up St. James's toward Piccadilly. Behind her, the footman chuckled softly; then, painting an apologetic expression across his round, florid face, he went to report his failure to the disappointed old roué.

In the shadows halfway to Piccadilly, Dyanna leaned against a tree and gasped, trying to catch her breath. Rawley and Geoffrey! What a pair! And what had the footman meant when he'd said old Lord Rawley wanted a little of her 'fine, soft flesh'? What kind of man was he? Oh, how she wished she could ask Justin, but—

Justin! Her eyes went to the façade of Brooks's club, but Justin's carriage was nowhere to be seen.

"Damn. Damn!" she muttered. "Thanks to that old reprobate, I've lost Justin. Damn him to hell!"

Shoving her hands in her pockets, Dyanna returned to Piccadilly and started back toward DeVille House. There was no point in searching for Justin. The streets of London spread out around her, like the tangled strings of a spider's web, in every direction. It was hopeless. She would simply have to wait for another night.

With a muttered curse for Lord Rawley and one for Geoffrey for good measure, she marched toward DeVille House. She was angry and disappointed. But under it all, she was curious as to what might go on behind the shadow-shrouded walls of that house on St. James's Street and what hideous Lord Rawley and Geoffrey Culpepper could possibly have in common.

Chapter Thirty

Justin stepped out of his carriage and climbed the steps to the front door of the house on Great Queen Street. The footman Octavia FitzGeorge had hired with some of the money Justin had given her opened the door as he approached. He was expected.

A summons had reached him at DeVille House just after dinner. It had had an air of panic about it—a tearful quality he'd come to recognize as uniquely Octavia's. He hoped the woman was not going to try to wheedle more money out of him. She was fast losing her fragile, helpless femininity and becoming rapacious.

As he gave his hat and cloak to the footman, Justin had to smile. The woman was not even his mistress—their arrangement was purely business, as he had made clear from the start—but it seemed she could not resist trying to cajole gifts and favors out of him as a mistress would from her rich lover.

His golden eyes scanned the saloon as the footman led him into it. When first he'd come here, it had been dark and dingy, poorly furnished with a collection of threadbare pieces that seemed to have come from some impoverished nobleman's servants' quarters. Now, thanks to him, it was pretty and bright, the furniture new and of good quality. And for what? he asked himself. Every time he sent to inquire, he received the same answer: No, she had neither seen nor heard from Geoffrey Culpepper, but oh, yes, my lord, she would certainly tell him the moment the wretch showed his face at her door.

A glimmer of impatience crossed Justin's face. Perhaps it was useless. Perhaps Culpepper had gone abroad and all Justin's efforts were good for nothing saving the continued maintainance of Octavia FitzGeorge.

"My lord?" a small voice squeaked from the doorway behind him.

Justin turned. A pretty, calico-gowned maidservant stood there eying him with something close to awe.

"Where is your mistress?" he asked.

"Upstairs, my lord. She asks that you attend

her there, as she is too distraught to leave her bed.''

Justin hesitated. He'd been summoned before to bedchambers by ladies who pleaded indisposition. It generally turned out to be a ruse and the lady's only indisposition was the desire for a new lover. But he'd made it clear to Octavia that he was not interested in a mistress and all her subtle attempts at seduction had been gently, but firmly, declined.

"Very well," he told the maid, gesturing toward the door, "lead on."

He followed the girl up the stairs and along a corridor to a room at the northwest corner of the house. Curtsying, she opened the door, then closed it behind him when he'd entered.

The room was walled in pale pink silk that gave it a rosy tinge in the glow of the candles. The furniture was gilded and tapestried and the bed that dominated the room boasted a golden coronet fastened to the ceiling from which draperies of rich gold brocade cascaded to the floor.

Octavia FitzGeorge lay sprawled across the bed, her shoulders heaved and her broken sobbing filled the room.

Justin winced. Not tears—anything but tears. He could almost feel her delicate fingers working their stealthy way into his wallet.

"Octavia?" he said softly, going to the bed and pulling up a chair beside it. "Octavia, stop this and tell me what's wrong."

To his surprise, the sobbing subsided and she pushed herself up to a sitting position. Sniffling, she wiped her eyes with the back of her hand.

"It's . . ." She faltered. "It's Geoffrey."

Justin leaned toward her. "He's back? He's been here?"

She nodded, catching a little, shuddering breath. "He was here earlier. Oh, my lord! He was so cruel! So heartless! He knows I've been seeing you—I told him there was nothing . . . that you had been kind to me. But he was so angry! He said he wants nothing more to do with me. He said I must be out of this house tomorrow! He says I must deny that we were married and if I do not . . ." She shivered, her eyes round with fright. "He says he'll see himself made a widower! Oh, my lord! The look in his eyes! I truly believe he would kill me! I'm so frightened, my lord!"

"Did he say where he's staying in London?" Justin asked.

She shook her head. "No, my lord. Oh! How could he do this to me! I hate him!"

"Do you?" Justin asked. "Truly? Would you be avenged on him, if you could?"

"I would!" she declared. "But how can I? I cannot even prove we were married. Geoffrey took the license." Her eyes misted with tears of fear and humiliation. "Do you think he would harm me, my lord?"

Justin nodded, hating to frighten her more,

but truly believing Geoffrey capable of eliminating the wife who stood between himself and his goal—namely, Dyanna's fortune. If Octavia held her tongue, he might let her alone. But if not . . . it was all too possible she might meet with an accident some dark night.

She gazed at Justin over the wadded handkerchief. "What will I do, my lord? Geoffrey has cast me into the street. He says he can give me nothing. He says I must go back on the stage and earn my keep. That may be possible, but how will I live in the meanwhile? I am lost! Utterly, hopelessly, lost!"

Rising, Justin went to the window and gazed out. He felt responsible, at least in part, for her plight. He supposed that was precisely the response she hoped to evoke in him. On the other hand, it might be handy to have Geoffrey Culpepper's wife, legal or not, in his debt. He might need her later, to prove Geoffrey's treachery in eloping with Dyanna.

Turning, he said, "Dry your eyes, madam. I'm certain something can be arranged for you—just until you are able to make other arrangements, you understand."

"My lord!" she breathed, hands clasped theatrically to her bosom while she gazed at him in rapturous delight. "How kind you are!"

Justin sighed. If that was any sample of her acting, her return to the stage would be a long, long time in coming.

Sandra DuBay

"Come along, Octavia, call your maid. Have her bathe your eyes and dress you to go out. We shall find you a place to stay—temporarily."

Waving aside her gushing thanks, Justin left the room. Passing Octavia's maid in the corridor, he scowled, irritated that it should have come to this. All he'd wanted to know was when Geoffrey Culpepper returned to town. Now, he found himself supporting an out-of-work actress! He thought of Sheridan, the playwright, whom he knew through Charles James Fox and the Prince of Wales. He had a lot of influence in the theater—perhaps he could help him find something for Octavia FitzGeorge to do.

Cheered, he was in a far better frame of mind as he and Octavia set out in search of a suitable—and reasonably priced—place for her to live.

Candles dispelled little of the gloom of the grand saloon of Lord Heneage Rawley's town house in Harley Street. Reclining on a rug-covered Turkish divan, the grotesquely painted viscount eyed Geoffrey Culpepper through an ornate quizzing glass as he paced angrily up and down the darkened room.

"DeVille!" Geoffrey was ranting. "That bastard is the bane of my existence! First he comes between me and Dyanna's fortune, and now he wheedles his way into Octavia's life—and who knows what else!"

Lord Rawley rang a bell and a pretty young boy in oriental silks appeared with a bottle of absinthe on a tray. When the boy was gone, Lord Rawley sipped from his glass and turned an apathetic eye on Geoffrey.

"He does have an unfortunate way of turning up when and where he is least wanted. I saw him at the Tower not long since and asked to be presented to Miss McBride. If looks could kill, my friend, I would be dead and gone today."

"He seems to have appointed himself her guardian angel," Geoffrey sneered. "He has delusions of being some sort of knight who charges about being chivalrous to women. Well, he can be chivalrous to Octavia. I've turned the little bitch out into the street."

"How can that help?" Lord Rawley wanted to know.

"It will help," Geoffrey assured him cryptically. "You must trust me, my dear Heneage. Everything has its purpose. Everything advances our cause."

Setting his empty glass aside, Lord Rawley toyed with the quizzing glass that hung on an ornate gold chain around his neck. "Tell me, Geoffrey," he said idly, "is there more to your determination to have Miss McBride than merely her fortune?"

"Not at all," Geoffrey assured him. "I care nothing for the girl. She's a spoiled, headstrong, willful little hoyden. But rich—good God, what a fortune! The estates of the McBrides and those of her grandfather, Lord Lincoln. She could use Blaykling Castle for a summer house."

"Then you intend to marry her?"

"If I must," Geoffrey admitted. "But there might be another way. I'm looking into it."

"And if there is no other way?"

"You're driving at something, my lord. What is it?"

"Oh . . ." Lord Rawley waved a pale, perfumed hand. "I was only thinking what a pity it would be if such a beautiful young girl as Miss McBride were to meet with an accident."

"Yes." Geoffrey smirked. "It would be a pity, wouldn't it? Particularly if she had just been married—if she had her whole life before her."

"What would be even more pitiful," Lord Rawley went on, his red-rimmed eyes gleaming, "would be if she took her own life. There is, you remember, a tendency in her family to wildness. Perhaps in her it takes the form of an unbalanced mind."

"I suppose it's possible," Geoffrey allowed. "It doesn't really matter what happens to her, so long as the end result is the same."

"Dyanna McBride out of the way and her

fortune in your pocket," Lord Rawley drawled.

"Precisely," Geoffrey agreed.

Making a steeple of his bony fingers, Lord Rawley pursed his lips and eyed Geoffrey askance. "Tell me, my boy, if I agree to help you—if I agree to conceal Miss McBride for as long as it takes to convince her to agree to your plans for her, what will be my reward?"

"Once Dyanna's fortune is mine," Geoffrey told him, quickly averting his eyes from a shrunken head, one of the less grisly items in Lord Rawley's macabre collection, "I will be able to give you whatever you ask."

Pushing himself to his feet, the black-clad viscount crossed the room. With one finger he toyed with the blood-red, heart-shaped patch placed high on his white-painted right cheek.

"It is not money that I desire," he told Geoffrey, his narrow back to his visitor.

"Then what?" Geoffrey wanted to know.

Rawley turned to him, an almost diabolical gleam in his eyes. "I want her to myself for a time. Alone. With no interference from anyone. At the end of that time, she will be yours to do with—or dispose of—as you please."

Geoffrey's dark eyes met the sly, unwavering gaze of Lord Rawley, and he felt the fine hairs on the back of his neck stand up.

"What are you planning to do with her?" he asked, fully aware of Lord Rawley's less palatable interests and tastes—knowing all about the room upstairs and its contents and purpose.

"Does it matter?" the Viscount countered. "You don't love her, remember? And perhaps, when I am through with her, she will be more docile, more pliable. You might even decide you'd like to keep her for a while."

Geoffrey hesitated, wondering if he truly hated Dyanna enough to throw her into the clutches of a man so truly and utterly perverse as this decadent nobleman.

"Tell me, my lord," he asked carefully, "are you still in correspondence with your imprisoned friend in France?"

"The Marquis de Sade?" Rawley said, smiling. "Oh, yes!"

Chapter Thirty-One

Weary and irritable, Justin let himself in when he returned to DeVille House that evening. It had taken some time, but he had at last been able to secure a modest house in Gracechurch Street for Octavia. She'd pouted a little, of course. Gracechurch Street was far removed from her quiet former neighborhood. Running between Cornhill and Eastcheap, it was not so very far from the Tower of London.

Still, Justin had pointed out to her, it was better than being tossed into the street, and if she'd a mind to try her luck elsewhere she was welcome to. That had quieted Octavia somewhat and in the end she'd seemed satisfied with the six-month lease Justin had taken on the house and the letter of credit he'd given her to pay her expenses during that same six months. By the end of that time, he'd warned her, she would be expected to fend for herself. He hoped she would find employment on the stage—since that seemed to be her only ambition so far as work was concerned—but he rather suspected she would prefer to find herself another rich, if not noble, protector.

Still, he thought as he relinquished his cloak and hat to a footman, he'd seen her provided for the present. He'd repaid her for what little information she had provided about Geoffrey. And that, as far as he was concerned, was an end to his association with Miss Octavia FitzGeorge.

"Where is Miss Dyanna?" he asked Ipswich, who had hurried to the entrance hall when he realized that his master had returned at last.

"She was in the music room when last I saw her, milord," the butler replied. As Justin turned away, he asked, "Will you be wanting dinner soon, milord?"

"No, Ipswich. I ate while I was out. Has Miss Dyanna had hers?"

"Oh, yes, milord, some time ago."

Nodding, Justin went to the music room and opened the door. Across the room Dyanna sat at the pianoforte. It was closed and her arms rested on the inlaid cover protecting the keys. Her cheek rested on her crossed wrists and she gazed out at the mist gathering in the twilight-blue garden.

Lost in her musings, Dyanna was unaware of Justin's arrival. She did not hear the click of the doorlatch, nor did she know that even at that moment he was standing in the doorway watching her. Her mind was faraway and filled with thoughts of Geoffrey Culpepper.

She should tell Justin, she thought, thrusting a fingertip into her mouth and biting at the nail. She should tell him that Geoffrey was back in town. But what then? She knew Justin hated Geoffrey and longed to be avenged on him—she could hear it in Justin's voice when he spoke Geoffrey's name. But how could she tell him? Where could she say she saw him? Certainly she could never admit that she was out at night alone, disguised as a boy. What would he think if he knew she had tried to follow him last night? He would be angry. And also, perhaps, a bit smug that she should care so much about where he went. Would he enjoy knowing how much she minded his having a mistress? Probably. She would not give him the satisfaction of knowing how much it bothered her. And she could not— would not—be the cause of more strife involving Geoffrey Culpepper. No, she would simply let the matter die. So long as Geoffrey left her alone, she would say no more about him.

"Dyanna?" Justin said. His voice was low, but the sudden shattering of the perfect silence of the room made her start violently.

"Justin!" she cried, pushing herself away from the instrument and smoothing her gown. "I did not know you had come home."

"A few minutes ago," he told her. "Ipswich said you've already had your dinner."

She nodded. "I didn't wait. I didn't think you'd be home. You've been away a great deal lately."

He said nothing and she knew that if she pressed him for details of the business that kept him away so long it would only end in an argument. Clasping her hands before her, she watched as he went to a loveseat and sat down.

"Justin," she said, crossing the room toward him, "I never had the chance to ask you before, but . . . who was that horrible old man who spoke to us that day at the Tower?"

A grimace of distaste flitted across Justin's face. "Rawley," he said. "Viscount Heneage Rawley. He's an old reprobate. The things they say he's done make Sir Francis Dashwood and his Friars of Medmenham Abbey look like children at play. They say he experiments in black magic, alchemy, sorcery, necrophilia. . . . There are rumors that young boys in his service disappear. He says they've gone to work at his country estate, but no one ever sees them there. Young women hired as maidservants complain of cruelty. They say he whips them for the slightest transgressions. And seems to enjoy it. But I shouldn't be telling you all this. It will give you nightmares."

"He already gives me nightmares," she admitted. "That dead-white face and those eyes! The way he looked at me made my skin crawl."

Against her will, she remembered his ghastly pale face in the moonlight the night before. He had thought she was some loitering boy with nothing better to do than stand on the pavement waiting for a handout or the offer of a job. If what Justin said was true, she might have become one of the hideous Lord Rawley's victims. Thank God she had been wise enough to run away from the hulking footman, Monck!

Shivering, she wrapped her arms about herself. "Why don't they do something about him? Why isn't he clapped in gaol or something?"

"For one thing, my pet, he is rich as Midas. For another, he has many powerful connections. I don't say friends, you understand, but connections. The truth of the matter is that in his youth he was an intimate of many men who are very powerful today. Like most young men, they committed youthful follies that could prove embarrassing if they were made known. In many cases, Lord Rawley not only

Sandra DuBay

knows the particulars of these follies, he has
letters and journals to prove the veracity of his
tales. You might say that Heneage Rawley is a
collector of the skeletons from other people's
closets. So long as he doesn't commit high
treason, they believe the safest course is to
simply leave him to his own devices—or
should I say his own vices?"

Dyanna didn't smile. She had come too
close to sampling the viscount's vices first
hand to find Justin's puns amusing.

"Dyanna"—Justin held out a hand to her—
"there's nothing to fear from Heneage
Rawley. Even he can't be foolhardy enough to
prey on a young woman of breeding and
quality. His prey are the children of the streets
who are helpless and alone, powerless to fight
against him."

Dyanna reached out to take Justin's hand
and saw her own tremble. Justin saw it too
and, with a soft murmur of concern, drew her
onto the loveseat beside him and held her in
his arms.

"You really are upset about that old lecher,
aren't you?" he asked.

She nodded, and suddenly the feelings and
nerves of the past weeks overwhelmed her.
Burying her face in Justin's shoulder, she
dissolved into tears.

Justin felt himself melting inside. Octavia's
tears had been bad enough, but he was powerless against Dyanna's. Each glistening tear

was a trial to him; each of her sobs was like a needle plunged into his heart.

"Hush, Dyanna," he murmured. "Please, don't cry anymore. Please."

"I'm sorry," she managed haltingly, sniffling, the back of her hand wet where she'd wiped away her tears. "I don't know what's wrong with me."

"It's all right," he assured her, holding her close. "Why don't we just spend a quiet evening here? Maybe that will help. What do you say?"

She looked up at him, her lashes bedewed with her tears, her cheeks prettily flushed and dewy. "You'll stay home tonight? You won't go out again?"

Smiling gently, he nodded. "I don't think I shall be going out as much anymore," he told her. "One part of my business was completed today."

"Oh, Justin," she breathed, winding her arms about his neck. "I'm so glad! Can we go away soon? Can we go to Wildwood?"

"Very soon, I should think," he agreed.

Smiling, she nestled her head against his shoulder. Surely if he was so willing to go away with her, that woman, whoever she was, couldn't hold much appeal for him. Perhaps everything was going to be all right after all.

Justin held her against him. He loved the sensation of having her in his arms, her body next to his, warm and soft. The sweet scent of her hair, her skin filling his nostrils, stirred his senses.

His hands went to her hair and drew out the pins that held it. It tangled in his fingers as the silvery skeins tumbled down over Dyanna's shoulders. Twining his hands in its thick, luxuriant mass, he pulled back her head until her face was turned up to his.

"Justin," she breathed, her eyes on the sculpted fullness of his lips. She closed her eyes, shivering, as the tip of his tongue traced the outline of her petal-pink cupid's bow mouth.

Gently, Justin eased her back on the loveseat until she lay half beneath him on the striped silk that covered it. Her eyes were slitted, her lips parted. At the base of her throat he could see the quick fluttering of her pulse.

His head fell and his lips touched the silken, translucent flesh of her breasts above the lace edging of her gown. Dyanna gasped; beneath the thin muslin of her gown, her nipples hardened into tight coral buds that ached for his touch, his kiss.

She buried her fingers in his rich golden hair and arched her back, offering herself to him shamelessly, eagerly. She longed for him, ached for him; she thought she would die if he did not touch her, kiss her, take her. She shuddered as she felt his hand, warm and strong, finding its way beneath the tangle of muslin and lace, stroking the soft pale flesh of her calf, the tantalizing hollow at the back of her knee, her thigh.

"Yes, Justin," she breathed, a catch in her voice that echoed the frantic fluttering of heart. "Justin, please, please . . . !"

Sliding to his knees beside the loveseat, Justin pushed her skirts and petticoats aside with angry impatience. He slid a hand down the long, slender length of her leg and pressed his lips to the warm, velvet-soft flesh of her thigh above her lace and ribbon garter.

A cry of surprise and pleasure welled in Dyanna's throat; too late she tried to smother it with the back of her hand. Justin lowered his head once more; his kisses were like touches of fire on her flesh. He pushed her petticoats higher, higher, and then . . .

"Miss Dyanna?" Charlotte's voice was muffled through the thickness of the door. "Miss Dyanna? Are you there?"

"I'll kill her!" Justin snarled, thrusting himself to his feet while Dyanna pushed down the yards of muslin and lace. He glanced back at Dyanna, fury and frustration lending an unearthly glitter to his golden eyes. "Say goodbye to her, Dyanna. She's a dead woman!"

In spite of herself, Dyanna giggled. Rising from the loveseat, she stumbled—her legs felt strangely weary and her senses still seemed madly jumbled—and hurried past him, gesturing for him to let her answer the door.

Opening it a crack, she saw her maid standing outside. "What do you want, Charlotte?" she asked.

"You asked me to remind you, miss," the maid said, "that you wanted to get to bed early tonight so you could be up in the morning and go to the milliners."

"Oh, yes. Thank you, Charlotte. I won't be too long."

With a curtsy the maid left and Dyanna closed, and locked, the door.

"See how easy that was?" she asked. "And no one's dead." Smiling flirtatiously, she played with the buttons on Justin's coat. "Mrs. Bond, the milliner, said she is getting a shipment of bonnets from Paris. I want to be there early to get my pick of them."

"Send Charlotte," Justin told her, all humor gone from his face. He did not want to risk letting Geoffrey Culpepper get near Dyanna.

"I don't want to send Charlotte. I want to go myself."

Justin hesitated. He didn't want her to know that Geoffrey had returned. He told himself it was because he didn't want to alarm her, but in reality he was not certain what her reaction would be. He shook his head.

"I'm serious, Dyanna. Send Charlotte. I think it would be a good idea if you did not leave the house for a while."

"But why!" she cried, wondering for a

frightening moment if he had somehow learned about her sojourn of the night before.

"Because I said so, that's why," he snapped. "Don't forget, I am your guardian."

"You seemed mighty unconcerned about that a few moments ago!" she snarled, and instantly regretted her words.

Justin's face hardened. "Forgive me. It won't happen again."

Dyanna felt perilously close to tears as he brushed past her and started for the door. "Justin!" she called, raising a hand in a feeble gesture to stop him.

He turned. One questioning brow arched.

"Don't do this to me," she pleaded. "Don't make me a prisoner in this house again. I beg of you."

"It won't be forever," he told her. "Just for a little while."

"But why!" She watched, devastated, as he left the room. "Why!" she shouted after him, but her only reply was the fading sound of his footsteps.

Justin could hear, as he walked away, the sound of Dyanna's renewed sobbing, but he steeled himself against the impulse to go back and try to comfort her, just as he tried to steel himself against the ravening desire for her that wracked his body, his heart, and his very soul.

Chapter Thirty-Two

"I know why he's doing this!" Dyanna told Charlotte early the next morning.

"Because of Lord Geoffrey?" Charlotte suggested. Dyanna had told her, upon her return from her failed attempt to follow Justin, that she'd seen Geoffrey in St. James's Street.

Dyanna laughed unpleasantly. "No doubt that would be his excuse if he cared to give me an excuse. But that's not the truth. The truth of the matter is that with me shut in here at DeVille House, he is free to squire his pretty little mistress about town. He needn't worry about meeting me in the park or the shops. Depend upon it, Charlotte, our fine Lord DeVille is playing the gallant, attentive swain to that little strawberry-blond trollop!"

Sandra DuBay

Charlotte cast a glance at the clock. She had looked forward to seeing the new Parisian bonnets at Mrs. Bond's shop. But now that Lord DeVille had forbidden Dyanna to go out. . . . Disloyal as it seemed, she hoped Dyanna's immurement did not mean that she was to be shut away as well.

As if reading her thoughts, Dyanna sighed and said, "You'd better hurry if you're going to have first choice of the bonnets at Mrs. Bond's, Charlotte. You know the colors I want. Have Mrs. Bond send the bill to Justin."

Beaming, Charlotte curtsied and ran for her pelisse. She was going to escape from DeVille House before Dyanna decided she wanted someone to share her incarceration.

Dyanna had never expected Charlotte to sit at home with her simply because Justin refused to allow her to go out. But by the middle of the afternoon, when Charlotte had not returned, she was feeling resentful about what was beginning to look like Charlotte's flaunting of her freedom.

When she heard the carriage returning, bearing her wandering maid home, Dyanna told Ipswich to send Charlotte up to her sitting room the moment she set foot in the house.

Charlotte appeared. From her tentative expression, it was obvious she was expecting the worst.

"Where did you have to go for the bonnets, Charlotte?" she asked coolly. "Paris?"

"I'm sorry, miss," Charlotte replied meekly, her eyes fixed on the carpet. "I went to Mrs. Bond's and chose several very pretty bonnets. I'm sure you will be pleased with them. Lady Hayward was there."

"Lady Hayward?" Dyanna remembered the beautiful widow with whom the aged Marquess of Summersleigh was keeping company. "Phoebe Hayward?"

"Yes, miss. She asked after you. She said she was sorry she had not seen you lately. She said the marquess heard about your eloping with Lord Geoffrey. He was very upset with the way things turned out."

Dyanna sighed. She could well imagine that Lord Summersleigh, who had wanted her as a wife for his grandson from the beginning, would be upset that their elopement had ended in nothing—had, in fact, very nearly ended in tragedy—but for her own part, she saw now that it would have been the greatest mistake of her life.

"I would like to see Lady Hayward again," she admitted. "She was so kind to me; she helped me go to the Barkleighs' ball."

"We spoke for quite some time," Charlotte went on. "Lady Hayward is very knowledgeable about what goes on in London."

"I suppose she has all the newest gossip," Dyanna said, smiling.

"Oh, yes, miss. She knows everything. About everyone."

Dyanna could see from Charlotte's expression and the look on her pretty, round face that there was something she was dying to tell her.

"Sit down, then," she invited. "And tell me what is going on in the world."

Relieved and eager, Charlotte took the chair opposite Dyanna. Smoothing her titian curls into something resembling order, she weighed her words before beginning.

"The latest piece of gossip in London," she said carefully, "concerns Lord DeVille."

"Justin?" Dyanna grimaced. "Are they talking about me? Does everyone know he's shut me up like a child?"

"Oh, no, Miss. It's not about you. It seems . . . that is . . . the rumor that is spreading about London is . . ."

"Oh, for heaven's sake, Charlotte," Dyanna hissed impatiently. "What is it!"

"They're saying that my Lord DeVille has taken a house. They're saying he has set up an establishment for"—she took a deep breath —"for his mistress, miss."

The breath seemed to leave Dyanna's lungs in a rush and the room swam in and out of focus. "His mistress," she whispered. "But who . . . who is she? Did Lady Hayward know her name?"

"FitzGeorge, Miss. Octavia FitzGeorge. Lady Hayward said she was an actress."

"Octavia FitzGeorge." Dyanna murmured the name, once, then again. "Octavia FitzGeorge. I wonder if it was . . . that day at the Tower . . ." She glanced up at Charlotte. "Did she say what this—lady—looked like?"

"Small, miss. Very pretty. They said she has red-blond hair and great dark eyes. She was at Drury Lane, so they say. Before she left the stage at her lover's request."

"Her lover . . ." Dyanna closed her eyes but maddening pictures of Justin and his pretty blonde danced in her mind's eyes. Octavia FitzGeorge. Now that face had a name. Now her worst fears were proven true. She felt limp, drained, sickened.

"Can I get you something, miss?" Charlotte asked. "You're so pale."

"Nothing, thank you, Charlotte," Dyanna said weakly. "I'll be fine in a moment."

"Oh, I should not have told you," Charlotte mourned. "I should not . . ."

"No, you did right to tell me," Dyanna assured her. "I'm glad you told me. I'm going to confront Justin with it. I'm tired of all these lies."

Sighing, Dyanna leaned back in her chair. Perhaps it was a mistake, she told herself desperately. Rumors got started in London all the time and many proved to be false. Perhaps

377

this, like so many others, was the result of some silly misunderstanding. Perhaps this Miss FitzGeorge was the mistress of some friend of Justin's, but because they had been seen together gossip painted them as lovers.

It was little more than wishful thinking, she knew, and she was grasping at straws to try to avoid facing the fact that Justin had a mistress. But she had to put off the moment of acceptance as long as possible. She could not face the truth. Not yet.

A madness started inside her—a driving, desperate need to see this house, this mistress, for herself. Only then, only when she had seen the house, seen the woman, and seen Justin with her would she be forced to accept rumor as fact.

"Do you know," she asked Charlotte, "did Lady Hayward know where this house is?"

Charlotte hesitated. She knew full well why Dyanna was asking. She knew that once Dyanna knew the location of the house she would want to slip out of DeVille House and seek it out. She hesitated, frowning as if weighing two equally disagreeable courses of action in her mind.

"Charlotte?" Dyanna prompted. "Do you know where the house is?"

"Gracechurch Street," Charlotte said softly, a guilty flush staining her cheeks. "It is in Gracechurch Street."

Rising, Dyanna went to her desk and pulled

out a fresh sheet of notepaper. Opening the inkwell, she held out a pen to her maid.

"Do you know where Gracechurch Street is?" she asked.

"Yes, miss," Charlotte admitted, then immediately wished she had said no.

"Come over here, then and draw me a map. I've a mind to go and see this house and this mistress Justin thinks so highly of."

"Please, miss," Charlotte entreated. "Why not just leave well enough alone?"

"Because there is no 'well enough.' I must see the truth for myself. Now come, Charlotte, I have asked you to do something."

Charlotte hesitated. It was on the tip of her tongue to tell Dyanna everything, but she could not. In the end, tears in her eyes misting her vision, she went to the desk and, taking the pen, began to draw.

It was just after dinner when Justin went out. Twilight had not yet darkened into night and so Dyanna waited—waited for the concealing darkness that would cover her escape from DeVille House. There was no need to follow Justin tonight, after all. She knew what his destination would be.

Her lips tightened as she pulled on the disguise that had served her on her previous foray into the London night. The map lay on the desk; it was detailed enough, and she had studied it long enough, to give her a thorough knowledge of the distance and direction she must travel to reach Gracechurch Street and the home of Octavia FitzGeorge.

"Please don't go, miss," Charlotte pleaded. "Please!"

"What's wrong with you, Charlotte?" Dyanna muttered crossly as she carefully positioned the chestnut wig atop her head.

"I've got a bad feeling about this, and that's the truth of it," the maid insisted. "Wait until tomorrow night if you must go. Or let me come with you."

"No, I cannot wait—and wonder—another night. And I must go alone. I'll be fine, truly. You mustn't worry."

With another reassuring smile for the troubled maidservant, Dyanna crept down the stairs and let herself out into the night-shrouded garden. The map was safely folded in her coat pocket, though she didn't think she would have to consult it. Grimly determined to discover the truth—however painful that might be—she set out for Gracechurch Street.

Chapter Thirty-Three

By the time she reached St. Clement Lane in the Strand, Dyanna thought she could surely not go another step. All around her the night-time bustle of London ebbed and flowed, and had she not been so determined to reach her goal, had she not had Charlotte's map securely tucked in her pocket, she felt certain she would have panicked long ago and retreated to DeVille House.

But she went on. She was nearing St. Paul's when a carriage stopped in the road beside her and caught her eye. Unlike most others, no footman rode on the back of this vehicle. It was too tempting. Just as the carriage started up, Dyanna darted into the road and jumped onto the back of the carriage, curling herself into an inconspicuous ball between the great, yellow wheels of the yellow-and-black chaise. Closing her eyes, she massaged her aching calves through her smudged white stockings. It was bliss to be riding after walking for so long. She had to remind herself to watch carefully so that she might leap off the back of the carriage in time. After coming so far, it would not do to miss her destination and be carried into some unfamiliar part of London from which she might have trouble finding her way back.

When the carriage slowed to turn into St. Swithin's Lane, Dyanna took a deep breath and launched herself off the back of the carriage. Hitting the pavement, she lost her balance and tumbled into the gutter.

"Damn!" she muttered, pushing herself to her feet and knocking some of the dirt from her coat and breeches. Still, it wasn't as bad as it might have been. Had it been raining, the gutter would have been streaming with stinking sewage and refuse.

Straightening her clothes, she set off toward Gracechurch Street, which was not far away.

Following Cannon Street, she came to the corner of Gracechurch Street and Eastcheap. Her courage wavered, but she pushed the doubts from her mind. Pulling Charlotte's map from her pocket, she looked for the number of Octavia FitzGeorge's house, then resumed her trek.

When she found the house, she stood for a

long while gazing at the lights that glowed through the elegantly curtained windows. Justin's carriage was nowhere to be seen. Dyanna did not know whether to be sorry or relieved that he was not there. On the one hand, she knew her courage, her determination, would have been fired by the sight of his carriage—by the knowledge that he was there, with his mistress, when he was supposed to be, so he said, out conducting business. On the other hand, she knew he would be furious that she had gone to such lengths to find him, and she could not bear the thought of being shouted at—humiliated—before his paramour.

Stealthily, she crept toward the house. She wanted to peek into the window, try to see Octavia FitzGeorge, to prove to herself that she and the strawberry-blonde Justin had seen at the Tower were one and the same.

Her mind occupied with the matter at hand, Dyanna did not sense that she was not alone in the darkness; she did not hear the soft footfalls of her stalker. It was not until the arm snaked around her waist that she realized that she, and not Octavia, was the night's prey. Twisting around, she caught a single glimpse of an all too familiar face before the blow was struck and darkness descended.

Hearing a commotion from downstairs, Charlotte looked up from the book she was reading in Dyanna's sitting room.

Perhaps, she thought hopefully, Miss Dyanna had come home. Perhaps she had realized how foolish it was for her to—

"Dyanna!" Justin's shout echoed up the stairwell.

Charlotte froze. Lord DeVille! But he wasn't supposed to be home until much later.

"Dyanna?" He was closer now, mounting the stairs.

Charlotte stood in the middle of the room. She couldn't decide whether to hide in the bedchamber or flee to the servants' quarters in the attic.

By the time she'd made her decision, it was too late. Justin stood in the sitting room doorway.

"My lord," Charlotte breathed, sinking into a deep curtsy.

"Where is Miss Dyanna?" he asked, glancing around the room.

"Well, my lord, she . . . that is to say . . ."

"Spit it out, girl," he ordered.

"She isn't here, milord." Charlotte's hushed whisper was barely audible.

Justin's golden eyes narrowed. "What do you mean, she isn't here? Where is she?"

"She went out, milord. She—"

"Out!" Justin's cry seemed to shake the very walls. "What in hell do you mean, she went out!"

Terrified and guilty, Charlotte burst into

tears. "I tried to stop her, milord. I swear to God I did!"

"Oh, Christ!" Justin ran a hand through his hair. "Doesn't she know the dangers for a girl alone in London by night?"

"Beggin' your pardon, milord, but she's not a girl. . . ."

"What are you talking about?" he demanded.

"She's dressed as a boy. She went up in the attic and got some of Tom's clothes. You know, the footman who ran—"

"Yes, yes," Justin interrupted. "She's out there disguised as a boy? But why?"

"She's looking for you, milord. She thinks you've got a mistress. She thinks you won't let her out of the house because you don't want her to see you with your—with your ladyfriend."

His mind awhirl, Justin sank into a chair. "That little fool! It's nothing to do with another woman. I didn't want her out and about in London because Culpepper's back in town."

"She knows. She saw him."

"I was afraid if she knew, she would be frightened into doing something foolish or—" He looked up as Charlotte's words sank in. "What do you mean? How could she have seen him?"

"She went out before dressed in Tom's clothes. She said she saw Lord Geoffrey get-

385

ting out of a carriage. He was with—I don't know his name—that old man with the painted-up face Miss Dyanna met at the Tower."

"Lord Rawley."

"Yes, milord."

Justin cradled his head in his hands. How Dyanna could do anything as stupid as this, he couldn't imagine. He wanted to throttle her. He had to find her, bring her back safely to DeVille House—so he could kill her!

"I can't believe this," he muttered. "I don't believe any of this."

"But it's true," Charlotte insisted, thinking he truly did not believe her. "She has Tom's livery in here as well."

Before Justin could stop her, she'd run into the bedchamber and burrowed in the closet to find Dyanna's hiding place. Returning with a wooden box, she set it on the floor before him and whipped off the lid.

The contents of the box blazed scarlet and gold. Charlotte gasped; in her haste she had seized the wrong box.

Justin shoved her hand aside as she was about to replace the cover. A shudder of recognition coursed through him, shaking him to the soles of his feet.

"Marie," he whispered. He looked at the stricken expression on the maid's face. "It was Dyanna that night, at the Barkleighs', wasn't it? Dyanna was Marie LaBrecque?"

Tearful, Charlotte nodded. "Yes, my lord. She wanted to attend that ball so much. My Lord Summersleigh and my Lady Hayward helped her."

"Summersleigh! Damn all these Culpeppers to Hell!"

Unable to help herself, Charlotte started to weep. Her head buried in her hands, she did not see Justin wander thoughtfully from the room.

"Marie," he murmured to himself as he walked slowly down the corridor. "No wonder I was so attracted to the mysterious Madame LaBrecque. I should have known—how could I not have known! The shyness, the hesitancy I found so beguiling were, in fact, innocence. My God!" He stopped, paling. "I took her virginity! My own ward! How could I—"

And yet, in his heart, he knew that the attraction had been there from the first. Had they not been interrupted, he would have made love to her at the Angel Inn the first time he saw her. He had thought her but a tavern maid then, but still, she had been the most beautiful creature he had ever seen.

And then, when he had taken her to live at DeVille House, her presence had tormented him. She'd thought him cruel to leave her alone so much, but he could not bear to be near her without wanting her, touching her, loving her. Nor could he bear the thought of giving her to some suitor, though as her guardian his duty was to see her settled in life.

He had left her alone at DeVille House in order to spare himself the torture of being near her, but that had not kept them apart.

The memory of that enchanted night at Barkleigh House rose in exquisite, erotic detail in his mind. Her skin, her hair, the scent of her, feel of her, taste of her . . . There was no one like her. The thought of her out there, alone in the London night, made him wild with worry.

He returned to Dyanna's sitting room, determined to discover if Charlotte had any inkling of where Dyanna might have gone.

Her head pounding, the room swimming in and out of focus, Dyanna fought her way back to consciousness. Her shoulders ached; she didn't know why until she opened her eyes and found that she was bound, her wrists tied to the thick, spiraling posts of a fourposter hung in blood-red velvet.

Nothing in the dark, shadowy room gave her a clue as to her whereabouts. The draperies, of the same gold-braided red velvet, were drawn across the window. Candles burning in tarnished silver candelabra did little to dispel the lurking shadows that filled the chamber. The golden frames of paintings on the walls glimmered in the wavering light. Dyanna squinted at them; they seemed, every one of them, to be filled with naked bodies in exotic, erotic poses.

"Do you like them?" a horribly familiar, unpleasantly shrill voice asked.

Dyanna stared into the darkness at the foot of the bed. There, in the light of a single candle, seated in a great, carved, high-backed chair, his deathly pale face seeming to glow in the candlelight, sat Lord Rawley. An evil grin split the horrible skull-white face and the red-rimmed eyes sparkled with unholy glee.

Dyanna's head fell back on the pillows. Her worst fears, her worst nightmares, had come to pass. Her scream shattered the unearthly silence of the room, drowning Lord Rawley's malicious laughter.

Chapter Thirty-Four

Dyanna's screams echoed through Lord Rawley's house in Harley Street. Below, the few servants whom the decadent old viscount had managed to keep shook their heads. It was not unusual to hear such sounds and they knew better than to interfere, but it was nothing that one ever grew accustomed to.

But there was one in the house who could not ignore the screams, however little he professed to care for Dyanna.

"What the hell is he doing to her?" Geoffrey demanded as he reached for a glass of wine poured by the young boy in his Indian silks.

"Could be anything, milord," the boy replied.

Sandra DuBay

Rising, Geoffrey climbed the stairs and hurried along the dark corridor to the scarlet-walled, velvet-draped chamber.

Bursting through the unlocked door, he found Rawley calmly seated in his chair at the foot of the bed, a diabolical smile creasing the thick white paint on his face, watching as Dyanna wept and struggled against her bonds.

Through her tears, Dyanna caught sight of Geoffrey.

"Geoffrey!" she cried. "Oh, Geoffrey, please, don't let him hurt me. Please!"

"What have you done to her?" he demanded of his accomplice.

Rawley shrugged. "Nothing. The imagination is the most powerful weapon, and one all too often turns it against oneself. She woke up, saw me here, and began to scream. Interesting, is it not?"

"Geoffrey," Dyanna entreated again. "Let me go, please. Untie me. I can't bear this."

Geoffrey's gaze swept over Dyanna. In her stockings, breeches and thin white shirt, nothing of her beauty was hidden from him. Her silvery hair cascaded over the pillows, shimmering in sterling waves on the blood-red coverlet of the bed. Her wrists, bound with silken cords, were rubbed red and raw by her struggles, and he could not help wincing at the sight of that creamy flesh being bruised and scraped.

"Please, Geoffrey," she said again, taking

hope from his hesitation. "Don't let him hurt me. Please!"

Rawley's kohl-darkened brows arched as Geoffrey moved to the bedside and bent to release Dyanna's arms.

"What are you doing?" he demanded crossly. "We had a bargain, if you remember, sirrah!"

Scrambling off the bed, Dyanna threw herself into Geoffrey's arms. Wrapping her arms about him, she buried her face in the soft velvet of his coat.

Automatically, Geoffrey's arms encircled her. Through the thin cotton of her shirt, he felt her breasts pressing against his chest; his hands rested at the small of her back and his fingers lay on the gentle swell of her buttocks, separated only by the worn cloth of her breeches.

Dyanna pressed closer to him. She could feel the effect her body was having on his and, much as she loathed it, knew that only Geoffrey stood between her and whatever vile fate Rawley had in mind for her.

"Please, Geoffrey," she breathed, turning her face up so her lips brushed his throat, just below his ear, as she spoke. "Please, keep him away from me. Take me away from this place, and I'll do anything you say."

"Anything?" he asked, his voice growing husky, his breathing uneven.

"It's a trick!" Rawley snarled, furious that

his amusement was being denied him. "Don't believe her! Leave her to me!"

"Anything," Dyanna sighed.

"Will you marry me?" he asked. "Will you come away with me, somewhere that damned DeVille can't find us, and marry me?"

Touching her lips to his jaw, Dyanna moved provocatively against him. "Oh, yes," she breathed, wanting to weep. "Let's go now, Geoffrey. Let's leave tonight."

"Hah!" Rawley shouted. "You're as great a liar as she is! Don't go with him, girl. The wretch already has a wife!"

"What?" Dyanna, startled out of her play-acting, stared at Rawley, who had thrust himself out of his chair and was pacing the floor in his fury and frustration.

"Damn you, Rawley!" Geoffrey snarled. "Shut your mouth!"

"Ask him about her!" Rawley insisted. "Ask him about his pretty little wife—the wife he abandoned in order to cast his net for an heiress!"

"Geoffrey . . . ?" Dyanna murmured, drawing a little away from him.

Thrusting her aside, Geoffrey advanced on the old viscount. "Say one more word, you decrepit old bastard, and I—"

"Yes?" Reaching back, Lord Rawley snatched up the riding crop he had intended to use on Dyanna. "What will you do?"

As Geoffrey advanced on the viscount, Dyanna cast surreptitious glances toward the door. What, she wondered, were her chances of escaping while the men were engaged in their quarrel?

Face grim with worry and anger, Justin left the little house in Gracechurch Street and strode toward his carriage. He had questioned Charlotte and learned that Dyanna had set out to find Octavia's house and discover whether the rumors linking Justin and the former actress were true.

There were discrepancies in her story; he had his doubts as to whether the rumors that had sent Dyanna out into the night had truly come from Lady Hayward. He suspected another source but determined to investigate those suspicions later—after he had recovered Dyanna.

Octavia swore she had not seen Dyanna at all. Justin was inclined to believe her, for she was not so good an actress as to be able to lie convincingly. It followed then that Dyanna had never reached Gracechurch Street or, if she had, had been waylaid before Octavia had discovered her presence. Although it was not impossible that Dyanna had simply run afoul of the cutpurses and footpads who preyed on solitary innocents abroad in London by night, Justin suspected a different culprit. Geoffrey

Culpepper was abroad in London and Justin felt certain he had something to do with Dyanna's disappearance.

With this in mind, he made his way to the house in Great Queen Street from which Octavia had just moved. The house belonged to Geoffrey, after all. It followed that he might have taken possession of it after his wife's departure.

But the house was dark and deserted. There were no signs that anyone had set foot in it since the last of Octavia's belongings had been removed.

Returning to his carriage, Justin sat back against the wine leather squabs and gave himself up to thought.

He was convinced, now, that Geoffrey must have Dyanna. But where? Certainly he had not taken her to Summersleigh House. Or had he? The marquess certainly wanted Dyanna for his grandson.

"Barnes!" he called up to the coachman.

"Milord?"

"Summersleigh House. Grosvenor Square."

Dyanna winced as Lord Rawley wielded his crop with practiced accuracy. A red welt dotted with pinpricks of blood appeared on Geoffrey's cheek.

Hissing, Geoffrey fell back, one hand pressed to his cheek. "I'll kill you for that, you

396

old bastard!" he snarled. "By God, I'll kill you!"

Frightened, Lord Rawley scrambled away from Geoffrey's grasping hands. For a moment, the path to the door was unblocked and Dyanna dashed for it.

But as she seized the latch and rattled it, she realized that it was locked—that Geoffrey, unnoticed by her, had twisted the key as he'd entered.

Panicking, she pounded the door with her fists, but it was hopeless. Lord Rawley's servants knew better than to interfere in their master's pleasures.

Turning, her back pressed to the locked door, Dyanna watched in horrified fascination as Geoffrey advanced on the terrified viscount.

"You haven't seen him at all?" Justin asked the old marquess, who sat in his small salon wrapped in a brocade banyan, a tasselled fez atop his head.

"Not at all," the marquess assured him. "I didn't know he'd come back to town. "What's the trouble, sir?"

"Dyanna's disappeared," Justin told him. "I've reason to believe Culpepper's kidnapped her."

"Kidnapped her?" The marquess smiled. "Perhaps they've eloped again. I was sorry about the way the last attempt ended."

"I was more than sorry," Justin replied grimly, "Dyanna was nearly killed!"

"Even so, she was not killed. And I still cherish hopes of that charming girl being my granddaughter-in-law someday."

"And what," Justin could not resist asking, "do you plan to do with your grandson's current wife?"

"Eh?" Shocked out of his pleasant musings, the marquess sat forward in his chair. "Explain yourself, sir!"

Arms sheltering her bowed head, Dyanna sat huddled against the locked door trying hard not to hear the viscount's shrieks. It had been no difficult task for Geoffrey to wrest the riding crop from the old man's hand. Now, driven to a fury by the lashing blows the aged roué had managed to land on his face and body, Geoffrey had backed Lord Rawley into a corner and was whipping him unmercifully.

Geoffrey's face was nearly unrecognizable; it was contorted with his fury, his mindless, unreasoning rage, and Dyanna could not help wondering what he would do when he'd had done with punishing the viscount.

Justin climbed back into his carriage after having left the Marquess of Summersleigh. He almost regretted having told the old man of his grandson's greatest bit of folly—that of marrying an actress.

But Justin's attention was soon diverted

398

from Lord Summersleigh's chagrin and back to the problem at hand. He'd remembered Lord Rawley's attraction to Dyanna at the Tower and Charlotte's telling him that Dyanna had seen Rawley in Geoffrey's company during her first foray into London by night.

"Harley Street," he called up to the coachman. It was not unlikely that Geoffrey had taken Dyanna to Rawley's house and Justin could not suppress a shudder at the thought of Dyanna in the clutches of that vice-ridden old satyr. God only knew what was happening to her at that moment.

As the carriage left Grosvenor Square and rolled up Brook Street, Justin's hand stole beneath his coat and fingered the silver-inlaid butt of the pistol he'd brought from home.

The room had suddenly fallen silent. It was an ominous, fearsome silence and Dyanna's eyes were filled with fear as she looked up from where she crouched near the door.

In the shadows across the room, Geoffrey loomed over the still form of Lord Rawley, who lay at his feet. The crop dangling from his fingers, Geoffrey turned the old man over with the toe of his boot.

A moan, anguished and filled with terror, escaped from Dyanna's lips as the candlelight illuminated the old man's face. The stark white paint of his face was striped with bloody welts. His eyes, wide open and staring, gazed into the darkness that shrouded the ceiling.

She raised her horrified gaze to Geoffrey's face as he turned toward her. "You've killed him!" she moaned. "Murdered him!"

"Who are you going to tell?" Geoffrey demanded. "How do you plan to get away?" An evil grin contorted his face. "I think, dear Dyanna, that I cannot afford to let you go."

Heart pounding wildly against her ribs, Dyanna scrambled away from the locked door. Fleeing across the room, she yanked at the window, but it too was locked. Below, in the street, she saw a carriage drawing up. Frantic, she pounded on the glass with her fists, trying desperately to attract the attention of the coachman or whoever might be inside the carriage.

She screamed as Geoffrey's arm snaked around her waist and tried to drag her away from the window.

Justin stepped down from the carriage and gazed up at the house. As he did, the shadows flickering in an upstairs window caught his eyes. Fists pounded at the glass, hands clutched at the dark draperies which were torn down as the person was dragged away from the window.

Drawing his pistol, Justin ran up the steps and pounded on the locked front door.

The young boy in his Indian silks opened it and was thrust aside as Justin pushed his way into the house. The boy was alone on duty— the few other servants in the house had long since retired to their rooms, not wishing to hear the screams that issued from the locked room upstairs.

"Where is your master?" Justin demanded.

The boy's wide eyes were fixed on the pistol in Justin's hand. He was not inclined to offer himself in defense of a master who had often beaten and abused him. Lifting his arm, he pointed up the stairs.

"Third door down, on the right."

Bolting past the boy, Justin thundered up the stairs. Dyanna's screams, echoing down the hall, spurred him on. He could hear her begging, pleading, but not with Rawley. She was calling Geoffrey's name. Culpepper!

Justin rattled the latch. The door was locked. Backing away from the door, he launched himself against it and, splintering the wood of the door and the jamb, crashed into the room.

Dyanna lay sprawled across the bed. Geoffrey, one knee on the bed, the other foot braced on the floor, loomed above her. With one hand, he held her throat in a choking grasp; in the other gleamed a long, curving Turkish dagger.

The crash of the broken door startled them both, and Dyanna took advantage of Geoffrey's loosened grip to scream. But his hold on her tightened quickly, and he brought the cold, razor-sharp edge of the blade to rest beneath her right ear.

"You're too late, DeVille!" he snarled. Wild, horrible laughter filled the room. "I'm going to kill her! Now!"

Dyanna moaned, but the sound was drowned by the blast of the pistol as Justin pulled the trigger. The knife nicked Dyanna's flesh as Geoffrey fell across her, crimson blood spreading from the ragged hole in his coat.

Justin dragged Geoffrey off Dyanna and frantically searched her for wounds. The cut on her throat was slight. He daubed it with a handkerchief and satisfied himself that she was not hurt.

"He killed Lord Rawley," Dyanna whispered, trembling in the circle of Justin's arm.

Justin glanced at the body. "I can't say that's any great loss." He looked at the startled, staring faces of Rawley's servants, who had gathered in the broken doorway. "Your master is dead," he told them. "Lord Culpepper has killed him."

Like magic, they disappeared and Justin led Dyanna from the room.

They met no opposition as they descended the stairs and left the house. The servants were too busy looting their dead master's house to care who came and who went.

Climbing into the carriage, Justin held Dyanna in a comforting embrace as the carriage rolled away down Harley Street.

402

Chapter Thirty-Five

The entire household gathered in the entrance hall to welcome Dyanna home and congratulate their master on his recovery of her.

In short order, Dyanna was handed over to Charlotte to be bathed and put to bed. Dyanna remained silent throughout, deciding not to confide the horrors of the night to the girl, who was almost as distraught as her mistress. Dressed in a nightdress of delicate silk, Dyanna lay in her bed, scarcely daring to believe that she was safe, rescued from the clutches of Geoffrey and Lord Rawley. Justin had come for her, saved her, brought her home. How tender he had been as they'd rode home from Harley Street! How gentle and solicitous of her well-being. Surely his feelings for her must be more than merely those of a guardian for his ward.

She caught her breath as she heard the click of the sitting room doorlatch. Footsteps crossed the sitting room floor, paused at the bedchamber door, then entered.

Looking up, she found Justin beside the bed. His velvet robe swirled around him. The moonlight shone on him, gleaming in the golden depths of his tousled hair.

"How are you feeling?" he asked, sitting on the edge of the bed.

"Well," she answered. She shivered with remembered horror. "Geoffrey meant to kill me, Justin. He would have if you hadn't come —I'm convinced of it."

"So am I," Justin agreed. It puzzled him, for he had always thought Geoffrey's object must be Dyanna's fortune. But he was obviously willing to see her die; he hadn't seemed concerned about her when she'd fallen from the carriage in Newington, either. There was more to this than he knew, and he meant to get to the bottom of it. But not now . . . not now . . ..

"You made a very fetching boy," he teased her, tugging at one of her silvery curls. "Very fetching indeed."

"Thank you, milord," she said, giggling.

"But I must say, I think you looked far more lovely in your other disguise."

"Other disguise?" she repeated, wondering

if he'd realized that she had been the footman in the hall that night.

"Yes. At Barkleigh House, as Madame LaBrecque."

"Who . . . how do you know?" she whispered, stunned.

He explained Charlotte's mistake in bringing the wrong box from the closet, and Dyanna could not help smiling, imagining Charlotte's chagrin over her mistake.

Justin stroked the delicate line of her jaw. "I should have known that night," he said softly. "I should have recognized you. God, how I wanted you—from the first moment I saw you. I've never wanted anything the way I wanted you that night—the way I want you now. . . ."

Dyanna trembled, seeing the fire of desire in his golden gaze. "No," she whispered, but she knew at that moment it was inevitable.

"Yes," he replied, and then she was in his arms, held, cradled, caressed.

Dyanna gazed up at him, her beautiful aqua eyes filled with the wonder of his face above hers. She was fascinated by him, caught in his spell, drawn to him—the moth drawn too near the flame of his passion.

For a long moment they lay there, frozen in time, as if afraid the magical web of desire they had so effortlessly spun about themselves might shatter like crystal if either moved, if either spoke.

Sandra DuBay

Dyanna's hand quivered, lifted, hovered for a moment in the air like a timid, fluttering butterfly, then touched his cheek, brushing it, caressing it, before her fingertips gently explored the sculpted contours of his full lips. Justin kissed her fingertips, his tongue darting out to caress them, tease them. Their eyes met and held, and his lips came down to cover hers softly, briefly, gently, in a lover's kiss of heart-stopping tenderness.

He moved away from her and she reached out a hand to draw him back.

"Justin," she whispered, her fingers aching to touch him again, her arms to hold him. Every part of her yearned for him, craved him with a hunger she could no longer deny. Whatever had passed between them before, whatever problems might face them in the future, mattered not at all at that moment. He was desire incarnate and she was not complete without him.

Taking her outstretched hand, he drew her up. They stood together beside the bed and Dyanna shivered to see the burning desire, the longing in his eyes that matched, even exceeded, her own. She stood, trembling, while his fingers moved over her, unfastening her gown, drawing it off her shoulders, letting it fall. It seemed only a moment later that she stood before him, her skin flushed and warm, tingling with anticipation of his touch.

When his robe had joined her nightdress on

the floor, they stood together, his hands cupping her face. Eyes as gold as the sun and as blue as the sea gazed into one another. Their love had been inevitable—they were destined for one another, born to share a love that neither time nor treachery could destroy.

"Justin," Dyanna whispered, her head falling back as his mouth sought the warm, scented softness where her throat and shoulder met.

His arm slipped behind her knees and he swept her up and laid her back on the bed.

Dyanna trembled as he touched her, caressed her, kissed her, awakening all the passion within her, making her want him, need him with the same raw, primal desire that burned inside him for her.

He waited, still he waited, reining his desire, until her arms went around him—until she opened herself to him, offered herself to him, until her desire demanded him.

And then they were one, moving together, giving and taking, finding together a paradise so exquisite that nothing they had ever known, not even the breathless, shattering climax of their love, was more beautiful.

Dyanna awoke with the dawn, feeling drowsy and sore and wonderful. She stretched beneath the sheets and turned on her side. As she did, her eyes met Justin's. He lay beside her, propped on one elbow, watching her.

Sandra DuBay

"Justin!" she cried, blushing. "How long have you been watching me?"

"Not long enough," he replied, bending to kiss her shoulder above the drawn up sheet. "I want to talk to you, Dyanna," he said seriously.

"Just talk?" she cooed, twirling the golden curls on his chest with her finger.

"For now," he said, taking her hand and lifting it to his lips. "I want to talk about Geoffrey . . ." He laid a finger on her lips as she would have protested. "And about Octavia FitzGeorge."

As they lay there, the morning sun glowing behind the drawn draperies at the windows, Justin told her the truth about Octavia FitzGeorge, Geoffrey's relationship with her, and Justin's reasons for setting the woman up in the house in Gracechurch Street. When he'd finished, Dyanna sat up in bed and fixed him with a curious look.

"So there was never anything between you and Miss FitzGeorge—or Lady Culpepper as the case may be?"

"Never," he insisted. "Now, I want you to tell me something. Tell me what in the world gave you the notion of dressing up in Tom's clothes."

Slipping from the bed, Dyanna retrieved her books from the table across the room. "In this one," she told him, "Jenny Flynn disguises herself as a boy. And so does Lady

408

Feversham in this one." She shrugged. "It seemed like a good idea."

"What about this one?" he asked, picking up the book about Lucifer Wolfe. A shadow crossed his face when he saw what it was.

"Where did you get this?" he asked, "No, don't tell me. Geoffrey Culpepper. Right?"

She nodded. "He told me it was really about your father and mother and Lady Naysmith, Caro's mother."

Sitting up in the bed, Justin flipped through the book. "I suppose they might have been the inspirations for these characters," he admitted. "My father shared the common interest in alchemy popular at that time. Lady Naysmith was his mistress, and my mother did die in a fall from the tower of Castle DeVille. My father perished in the fire that destroyed the castle. That, it would seem, is the basis for this book, but the rest—the sorcery, the cruelty, the murder—these are all products of the writer's imagination. All right?"

Dyanna nodded, feeling foolish for having taken the story so much to heart, and for having placed so much trust in a lying wretch like Geoffrey Culpepper.

"All right," she agreed.

"What do you say," Justin went on, "to leaving today for Wildwood?"

"I'd love to," she agreed wholeheartedly.

"In a few hours I shall go to the authorities and explain my part in Geoffrey's death and tell them what I know of Lord Rawley's death. When I come back, we'll go."

"In a few hours," Dyanna repeated. "And what, my lord, shall we do in the meantime?"

Reaching for her, Justin drew her to him and kissed her lips, her throat, her breasts, as he drew her down beside him in the bed.

"I think we can think of some way to wile away the time," he murmured, his tongue teasing the soft creamy flesh around her navel. "Don't you?"

Chapter Thirty-Six

It was late afternoon when the lumbering black traveling coach rolled up the long, curving drive to the sparkling new front of Justin's home—Wildwood.

Dyanna leaned out of the window to gaze at it. They had been traveling, it seemed, forever, and she longed to reach their destination. Justin smiled as an exclamation of admiration sprang to her lips. He had created a beautiful home there, on the land that belonged to his ancestors for generations.

Of grey stone, the house was an elegantly simple block with a steeply pitched roof pierced by six dormer windows. Centered on the west front was a pedimented portico supported by four fluted columns.

A tall, stately woman in brown merino, her greying hair covered by a close-fitting cap, hurried to meet them as they descended from the carriage.

"Good afternoon," Justin said. "You must be Mrs. Stour. I hope everything is ready for us?"

"Indeed it is, my lord," the housekeeper assured him. As had all the servants, she had been engaged by Justin's estate baliff. "We were prepared for your arrival before, but Miss Caroline told us you would be delayed."

"Yes. Unavoidably delayed." Justin gazed around the hall with a critical eye. Though he had been assured that the house was progressing as planned, he'd had no notion it was so close to completion. He was relieved to find the house itself finished—the furniture he'd purchased delivered and uncrated—and only the landscaping of the wooded park still to be accomplished.

"This is Miss McBride," he told Mrs. Stour. "Miss Dyanna McBride. My ward."

The housekeeper curtsied. "If you will follow me, miss, I will show you to your rooms."

Dyanna exchanged intimate, lovers' smiles with Justin, then followed Mrs. Stour across the hall and up the splendid oak stairway whose newel posts boasted carved urns and fruit in a credible imitation of the exquisite work of Grinling Gibbons.

Above, the housekeeper showed her into a large and airy chamber with pale yellow walls and a canopy bed hung with cream and yellow French toile.

"Will this room be satisfactory, miss?" the housekeeper asked, stepping back as footmen carried in Dyanna's trunks.

"It will do very well," Dyanna assured her.

"If you need anything, the bell is there, next to the fireplace."

"Thank you, Mrs. Stour. I'll ring."

Curtsying, the housekeeper followed the departing footmen out of the room. As the door closed behind her, Dyanna slumped into a chair near one of the two tall windows that illuminated the room with afternoon sunshine.

"Would you like to try on the new bonnets now, miss?" Charlotte suggested, eager herself for Dyanna to try on the delectable new creations she had been sent to fetch before they'd departed from London.

"No, I don't think so," Dyanna replied, shaking her head. "Perhaps later." She looked up at the maid curiously. "You were gone a long time, Charlotte. Weren't the bonnets ready?"

"There were a great many ladies at Mrs. Bond's shop," the maid replied, evading the question. Turning away, she hid the guilty flush that suffused her cheeks.

But Dyanna, tired of sitting so long in the carriage, did not notice as she rose from her chair.

"I feel like exploring," she told the maid. "I

wonder if Justin would mind if I looked around a little outside."

Leaving her rooms, she went downstairs and met Mrs. Stour in the downstairs hall.

"Where is Lord DeVille?" she asked.

"His lordship is gone," the housekeeper revealed. "He rode away almost as soon as you arrived."

"Rode away? Where to?"

"Why, to see Miss Caroline. Naysmith Court is only a short distance away, miss."

"Miss Caroline," Dyanna repeated dully. An image of the gold and pink beauty of Caro Naysmith flashed into Dyanna's mind. "Thank you, Mrs. Stour," she said, forcing a friendly smile. "I think I shall go out and walk a bit."

The housekeeper tied her bonnet ribbons while Dyanna drew on her silk-fringed paisley shawl. Going to the door, Mrs. Stour held it open as Dyanna stepped out into the late afternoon sunshine.

Lost in her thoughts of Justin and Caro, Dyanna was upon the ruins before she realized it. Overgrown with vines and ivy, they seemed to have grown up out of the very ground and were now sinking back into it. They were jagged, blackened, and, to Dyanna's fertile imagination, romantic.

One tower remained of Castle DeVille — one tower that had not completely escaped the conflagration which had consumed the once-proud, crenellated structure. It rose, square and solid, its windows long since broken, though whether by the heat of the fire or the ravages of time, Dyanna could not tell. She circled the tower, fascinated. It was like something out of a fantasy—or one of the fanciful Gothick novels she so delighted in.

A gasp of surprise escaped her when she saw the door. Of weathered wood bound with rusted iron, it stood a little open. The invitation was as clear as it was irresistible.

Laying both hands flat against the splintered wood, Dyanna leaned against the door, pushing with all her might. Its rusted hinges creaked as she shoved, and she was rewarded when the door opened before her.

The light flooding through the door showed her a curving stone staircase leading up inside the very walls of the tower. Dyanna's heart thudded heavily in her chest as she started up. She pressed her hands against the stone walls to steady herself, for there was no rail, no bannister to catch her if she fell. Iron rings in the wall suggested there might once have been a rope handrail, but it was long gone, rotted away from the damp and the rain that fell through the broken windows spaced along the length of the steep and winding stairs.

Driven on by fascination and curiosity as to what might lay at the top, Dyanna went on. The stairs seemed to rise before her in an endless spiral. Dyanna followed them up and up until at last her persistence was rewarded by the sight of an open door above her.

As she stepped through the door, Dyanna braced herself. The room she'd entered was at the very top of the tower—windows on all four sides presented her with a panoramic view of the countryside. They also admitted the winds that buffeted the tower, and the rushing currents of air through the room took her breath away and threatened to sweep her off her feet.

With a shiver, Dyanna gathered her shawl tighter about herself. She felt suddenly cold, alone, and vulnerable. There was a loneliness about the place that made her uneasy, almost frightened.

With one hand clasping her shawl and the other skidding along the rough stone walls, she descended the winding stairs. As she stepped out through the open door into the dappled sunshine of the forest, she sighed, relieved to be outside once more.

After standing for a moment to regain her bearings, she started back for Wildwood, eager to put the grim, lonely tower behind her.

It was that night, at dinner, before she could broach the subject of her afternoon's discovery. Caro was there. She had come back with Justin and now sat at the end of the long mahogany table in the pale grey dining room with its gaily colored Turkey carpet. The seating arrangement irked Dyanna, for Justin and Caro sat opposite each other like the master and mistress of the house, while Dyanna sat to one side like a child.

She was busily scowling at Caro when she realized that Justin was speaking to her.

"Did you rest from the long ride this afternoon?" he was asking.

Dyanna shook her head as she set down her goblet of wine. "I went for a walk. The countryside hereabouts is very different from London, isn't it?"

"Very," Justin agreed. "But surely you didn't walk so far that you saw much of the countryside."

"Oh, I saw it from the tower in the forest."

Caroline, at the far end of the table, gasped and began to cough. Taking a drink, she fixed Dyanna with a wide-eyed gaze, horror plain in her large, luminous, copper-colored eyes.

"What tower?" Justin asked tightly, capturing Dyanna's attention from Caro.

"The tower in the forest. I thought it was part of Castle DeVille. The ruins thereabouts seem to have been burnt."

"It is part of the castle," Justin admitted. He brought a fist down with shattering force on the shining tabletop, causing both Dyanna and Caro to jump in their seats. "Damn it all! Why didn't I have that god-forsaken tower pulled down!"

His golden eyes flashed as he leaned toward

Dyanna. "You are never—never—to go near that place again! Do you hear me? Never!"

"But why?" she demanded, forgetting Caro's presence. "The view from the top is—"

"The top!" he hissed. "You went to the top! What's wrong with you? Are your brains addled? Couldn't you see it wasn't safe?"

Dyanna drew back, hurt and bewildered. "I don't see what harm it did. You've no call to shout at me—"

"You don't see what harm—!" Justin ground his teeth. "Shout at you! You little fool! I should turn you over my knee for going up in that tower!"

Shoving back her chair, Dyanna thrust herself to her feet. "Don't speak to me that way!" she snarled. "And don't you dare lay one hand on me! Oh! I hate it here!"

Feeling the hot flood of tears in her eyes, she rushed from the room.

Behind her, in the dining room, Justin leaned back in his chair. He had reacted too violently, he knew, but he couldn't help himself. He started to rise to go after Dyanna, but Caro's gesture stayed him in his seat.

"Let me go, Justin. I'll speak to her."

Directed by Mrs. Stour, Caro found Dyanna lying across her bed, weeping as though her heart had broken.

Caro tapped at the door jamb to get Dyanna's attention. "May I come in?"

Dyanna sat up and wiped at her wet cheeks with the backs of her hands. She'd been embarrassed to have Justin shout at her, threaten to spank her, in front of Caro. Now, to be found weeping like a child completed her humiliation.

"As you wish," she murmured grudgingly.

Coming into the room, Caro sat down in a yellow moiré chair and settled her azure silk skirts around her.

"Justin wanted to come and explain why he was so angry," she said, "but I told him I would come instead."

Dyanna eyed her suspiciously. Was Caro truly concerned, she wondered, or did she merely wish to keep Justin from coming to her? She said nothing, however, and Caro went on:

"Tell me, Dyanna, what do you know of Justin's family? Do you know how his mother died?"

"In a fall," Dyanna replied. "From a tower of Castle DeVille."

Caro nodded. "She fell," she acknowledged. "It was a terrible, hideous accident, though there were those—her husband's enemies—who claimed it was suicide. But that is beside the point. The tower you climbed today was, as you surmised, once part of Castle DeVille. It was from that tower —from the room at the top where you were today—that Lady DeVille fell."

Dyanna was seized with a fit of trembling. To fall from that high, windswept tower . . .

"How horrible," she whispered.

"So you can understand the aversion Justin feels for that place. You can see how upset it must have made him to think of you there, where his mother died."

"Yes," Dyanna nodded. "I can see."

Rising, Caro smiled gently at Dyanna. "I hope you are not so angry with him now. He would be very sorry, I think, if he thought he had hurt you, however little he meant to."

Curious, Dyanna gazed up at the beautiful, tawny-haired woman. "Why are you doing this?" she asked. "I should think you would like to see Justin and I angry with one another."

"Whyever would you think that?" Caro asked, genuinely surprised.

"Why, because you . . . you and he . . . I thought you and he . . ."

Caro's musical laughter filled the room. "Justin! And me!" She laughed, but then her smile faded. "He hasn't told you, has he?"

"Told me what?" Dyanna asked.

Resuming her seat, Caro shrugged. "Justin is my brother."

Dyanna was stunned. "Your brother! But—"

"My half-brother, actually. My mother and his father were lovers. This was after his mother's death and my father's. I expect he didn't tell you because he thought it would embarrass me if you knew I was his father's—well, natural daughter."

"But I heard you talking with him in London. You said he proposed to you when you were children."

Caro laughed again. "So he did. We didn't know we were brother and sister until we were older. But it was all only children playing—pretending."

Dyanna sat gazing at the beautiful woman before her. The resemblance in their coloring was plain. Justin's sister . . .

"Justin loves you, Dyanna," Caro went on. "He was only angry because the thought of you there, where his mother died, frightened him."

There was a noise in the doorway. Both women turned to find Justin standing there, just inside the door. Wordlessly, Dyanna rose from the bed and went to him. Smiling, he wrapped his arms around her and held her close, his lips against the shining crown of her head.

Tactfully, Caro rose and left the room, closing the door behind her.

Dyanna rolled her eyes as Charlotte appeared before her, an all too familiar look on

Sandra DuBay

her face. She knew what was coming. Ever since Charlotte had heard about Dyanna's discovery of the tower, she had been badgering her to go and visit it. Charlotte had gone out several times, and stayed away for hours on end, but she always returned claiming she had not been able to find the ruins of Castle DeVille.

"Justin does not want me going up in that tower," Dyanna explained yet again. "I told you that, Charlotte. I'm not going to make him angry just to satisfy your curiosity."

"We don't have to go up in it," Charlotte persisted. "I only want to see it."

Expelling her breath in an impatient sigh, Dyanna tossed aside the sheet of music she'd been studying. She wished the library at Wildwood was stocked, but it wasn't yet and the only book she'd brought with her was the Lucifer Wolfe story—and that only as a souvenir.

"Oh, I suppose you'll give me no peace until I take you there," she sighed.

"None!" Charlotte agreed excitedly.

"Very well. Get our shawls and bonnets and let's be done with it."

Picking their way among the rubble and overgrown weeds, Dyanna and the maid approached the tower.

"Be careful, Charlotte," Dyanna warned. "There are some holes about. You don't want to turn your ankle."

She waited for a reply, but none was forthcoming. Looking around, she saw no sign of the maid.

"Charlotte?" she called, moving in the direction of a thick copse at the edge of the ruins. "Charlotte? Where are you?"

Still she heard nothing. She called Charlotte's name, but to no avail. When she looked back, a black-clad figure stood before her, sword gleaming in his hands.

A shrill little scream tore itself from Dyanna's throat. Turning, she lifted her skirts to flee. But the sword flashed before her, and its point was driven into the soft bark of a young tree, cutting off Dyanna's escape. She shrieked again.

"For Christ's sake," a masculine voice growled. "Will you stop that bloody screaming!"

Dyanna's silver-blond brows arched as she turned wide, aqua-blue eyes toward the man who held the sword.

"Why, Geoffrey!" she cried. "You're alive!"

Chapter Thirty-Seven

Geoffrey's hand closed tightly around Dyanna's upper arm, restraining her even after he had tugged the point of his sword from the bark of the unfortunate tree.

"Yes," he agreed, without a trace of humor. "I'm alive. No thanks to your precious Lord DeVille. His concern for you must have thrown off his aim. It was only a graze. It's so touching, his devotion."

"But why didn't he tell me you were alive! They must have told him when he went to speak with them about Lord Rawley!"

"He probably didn't want to worry you," Geoffrey sneered. "He's so considerate."

"Unlike you! I despise you, Geoffrey!"

Geoffrey's eyes narrowed. "DeVille has

everything now. You, the inheritance. He's even turned my grandfather against me. The bastard told him about Octavia. I've been disinherited!"

Dyanna gaped, astonished. "The Marquess of Summersleigh has disinherited you? But how could he? You are his only heir! To whom will he leave his estates?"

"You may well ask!" Geoffrey snarled. "It seems grandfather is going to remarry. His bride, so I am told, is already, as they say, in the family way. I am to have a new little uncle or aunt thanks to Lady Hayward."

"Phoebe? Phoebe is going to be the Marchioness of Summersleigh?"

"She is pregnant with a child she claims belongs to my grandfather," Geoffrey sneered.

"Doubtless the child is your grandfather's," Dyanna insisted, offended by his disparaging air. "Uncle Horatio might be old, Geoffrey, but he is not dead! And he seemed exceedingly fond of Lady Hayward."

"Fond enough to give what is rightfully mine to her child!"

"It is your own fault," she said, trying without success to pull her arm from his bruising grip.

"Well, something will have to be done."

"That is between your grandfather and yourself. I'm not going to help you! You tried to trick me into an illegal marriage! Then you gave me into the clutches of that horrible old man! I hope they hang you for killing him!"

"They won't," Geoffrey stated. "Too many powerful men are glad he's gone. I told them what happened and they ruled it self-defense."

"Too bad," she snapped. "But after what you've done, you can't expect me to help you with your problems!"

"Oh, yes you will!" he snarled, shaking her, his fingers digging painfully into her arm through the thin silk of her dress.

"No, I won't," she argued, trying to pry his fingers off. "You let me go! Let me go or I'll send Charlotte for Justin!"

"Let me go or I'll send Charlotte for Justin!" Geoffrey mimicked cruelly. "You won't sent Charlotte anywhere because Charlotte's first loyalty is to me!"

Dyanna turned to stare at the maid, who had suddenly reappeared. Charlotte dropped her gaze guiltily, unable to meet Dyanna's eyes.

"Charlotte, is that true?" she demanded.

The maid shrugged. "Lord Summersleigh is my master, and he did so want you to marry Lord Geoffrey."

"You deliberately brought me here, didn't you, so Geoffrey could find me? And before, in London . . ."

"I didn't see Lady Hayward at the hat shop,"

she whispered. "I saw Lord Geoffrey. He told me about the house in Gracechurch Street."

"Oh, Charlotte . . . . You don't know what he tried to do to me!"

"Enough of this talk," Geoffrey snapped. "I'm tired of it! Come along with me, Dyanna."

Bracing her feet, Dyanna resisted with all the strength in her. "No! I won't go anywhere with you! I won't marry you! You can't force me to!"

"I haven't asked you to marry me," he reminded her. "It would be foolish, now that you know I already have a wife, wouldn't it?"

"Then what are you going to do? Kidnap me? Hold me for ransom?"

"Nothing so tiresome." Geoffrey's eyes glinted darkly as he pressed the sharp edge of his sword against her throat. "Now, come along, Dyanna. All will be revealed in due course."

Resolved to play along with his madness until she could find a means of escape, Dyanna allowed Geoffrey to drag her along with him. She shot an accusing glare back at Charlotte, but the girl studied the ground with a hurt, shamed air and would not look up at the mistress she had betrayed.

On the other side of the forest, Justin returned from his morning ride with Caro. Now that Dyanna knew who Caro was, he felt sure the two women could be friends.

"Mrs. Stour?" he called, standing in the hall with Caro beside him. "Mrs. Stour?"

"Coming, my lord," the housekeeper called, hurrying in from the housekeeper's wing of the house.

Justin pulled off his riding gauntlets and tossed them onto a table. "Where is Miss Dyanna?"

"She went out, my lord," the housekeeper told him. "Some time ago." Smiling, she dropped a little curtsy to Caroline. "Good morning, Miss Caro."

Caroline smiled. "Good morning. Miss Dyanna did not go out alone, did she?"

"Oh, no, Miss. She went out with her maid." Mrs. Stour's eyes went back to her master. "A parcel came for you while you were gone, my lord. From London."

"Ah, yes. I asked to have some papers sent to me before I left London. Where is it?"

"In the morning room, my lord."

Justin turned to his half-sister. "Will you excuse me for a few minutes, Caro? If this is what I think it is, I'd like to see it immediately."

"Go ahead," Caro told him. "If I know you, you won't be fit to live with until you've seen your letter."

Tweaking his sister on the cheek, Justin

Sandra DuBay

turned and strode away. Caro and Mrs. Stour watched until he was out of sight, then Caro turned to the housekeeper.

"Have you any idea where Miss Dyanna might have gone?" she asked.

"Her maid's been pestering her to see the ruins of the old castle, miss," Mrs. Stour told her. "I hope they don't go near the tower. The master would be furious."

"I'm sure Dyanna would not do that," Caro assured her. "I think I'll go and try to find them. If Justin finishes, tell him where I've gone, won't you?"

The housekeeper promised she would, and Caro disappeared back out the grand front door.

In the morning room, Justin's golden eyes skimmed over the thick sheaf of papers his solicitors had sent him from London. It was what he had hoped for—a copy of the Last Will and Testament of the Earl of Lincoln, Dyanna's maternal grandfather.

Justin had sent for it in hopes it would shed some light on Geoffrey's behavior. After all, why would he have gone through all the trouble of convincing Dyanna to elope with him when he already had a wife? He would have known the marriage would be invalid— he would have known all claim on Dyanna's fortune would be revoked when the knowledge of his marriage to Octavia FitzGeorge became public. Something must have convinced him that it was to his advantage to have Dyanna in his possession. For some reason he must have thought he could get and keep her fortune if only he had her in his power. But what on earth could have made him believe such a mad scheme could succeed? There must have been . . .

Justin skimmed over a paragraph, lost in his own musings. Then a word, two, caught his eyes and he returned to the lines above and read again, carefully.

"Good Christ!" he muttered, when the import of the words sank in. "The bastard! The scurvy son of a whore!"

Filled with a murderous fury that clouded his vision and muddled his thoughts, Justin flung the sheaf of papers away and pushed himself to his feet. The last piece of the puzzle fell into place with terrifying clarity.

In the forest, halfway between Wildwood and the eerie, overgrown ruins of Castle DeVille, Caro's attention was captured by a soft, pitiful moaning.

Frowning, she followed the sounds to a little-used path, no more than a trail, that snaked through the forest to the tower.

There, cushioned by the carpet of leaves and undergrowth, Charlotte lay. Her face was ghastly pale, her lips blue. Her simple calico gown was stained crimson with the blood that flowed from a wound in her side.

431

"My God!" Caro breathed. She went to kneel beside the fallen girl.

Feeling Caro's hand on her cheek, Charlotte opened her eyes. Tears welled in them, trickling down her cheeks and falling on the leaves beneath her head.

"I tried to stop him, Miss Caro," she breathed, her every word harsh and gasping. "I didn't know . . . I swear I didn't know . . . ."

"Stop who, Charlotte? Who did this to you?"

"Lord Geoffrey, Miss. I thought he loved Miss Dyanna. That's why I helped him. But I didn't know . . . I swear I didn't know what he meant to do. Now he's taken her . . . forced her to go with him. Oh, Miss Caro, I know he means her harm!"

Caro hesitated, torn between running on to catch up with Dyanna and Geoffrey and running back to Wildwood to fetch Justin and help for Charlotte. Finally she decided in favor of the latter.

Pulling off the long coat of her crimson riding habit, she covered the shivering girl.

"I'll be back, Charlotte," she promised. "I'll bring help for you and for Dyanna. Don't you worry, now."

With a last, comforting caress of the girl's alarmingly cold cheek, Caro lifted her skirts and ran back through the forest, following the trail that would take her back to Wildwood— back to Justin. Surely he would know what it

was the girl was talking about. And surely he
would know what to do to help both Charlotte
and Dyanna.

Chapter Thirty-Eight

Summoned by Caro, Justin, Bertran, Mrs. Stour, and two footmen retraced Caro's hurried steps to the place in the forest where Charlotte lay.

"She's not . . . Justin, is she . . .?" Caro whispered when they found the maid lying unnaturally still on her bed of leaves.

Justin pressed his fingers against Charlotte's throat. "She's alive," he announced, to the relief of all. "But just barely."

Mrs. Stour, aided by Bertran, opened Charlotte's gown and inspected the wound left by Geoffrey's sword.

"It's deep, my lord," Bertran told him. "But I don't think it's pierced anything vital."

"We'll take her back to the house," Justin decided, "then send for a doctor."

As they prepared to lift her, Charlotte moaned softly. Her lids fluttered, then opened. She raised pain-filled eyes to Justin.

"My lord," she whispered. "Forgive me, I . . ."

"Charlotte," Justin said soothingly. "You should not speak too much. Just tell me where Dyanna has gone."

"She is with Lord Geoffrey, my lord."

"Culpepper!" Justin spat.

Charlotte trembled. "I'm sorry, my lord. I helped him—from the first. That is why my Lord Summersleigh sent me to DeVille House with Miss Dyanna."

Justin's golden eyes narrowed angrily. For months he had harbored the instrument of his betrayal beneath his own roof. "But why, Charlotte? Are you so loyal to Lord Summersleigh? To Culpepper?"

"I thought he loved her, my lord. He told me he loved her—he told me you meant her harm. That's why I helped him." Tears glittered in her eyes. "But it wasn't true! He didn't love her! *He* meant to do her harm. Sweet Jesus, I think he means to kill her!"

"Where are they, Charlotte!" Justin demanded. "Do you know where they've gone?"

"I thought he meant to carry her off to be married, my lord," the maid gasped. "When I realized . . . when it became clear what he really intended . . . I tried to stop him. He ran me through. I shall die with Miss Dyanna's blood on my hands!"

Justin resisted the impulse to shake the girl. "You're not going to die, Charlotte. We're going to get you a doctor. Now tell me. Tell me! Where is Dyanna!"

"The tower, my lord. He's taken her to the tower."

Sword in hand, Justin left them, running off into the forest, determined that the matter would end today one way or the other.

Halfway up the worn, winding stone steps of the ancient tower, Dyanna clung to one of the iron rings set into the wall. The rust ground into her hands, her whitened knuckles ached, but still she braced herself, resisting Geoffrey's efforts to force her farther up the stairs.

"Damn you!" Geoffrey hissed. "Let go of that ring and get up those steps." He brandished his sword before her eyes. "Or do you want some of what that damned, meddling maidservant got?"

The memory of Charlotte brought the tears flooding back into Dyanna's eyes. Unable and unwilling to release the ring to wipe them away, she shook her head and tried to wipe them away on her sleeve.

"You killed her, you bastard!" she hissed, lashing out ineffectually with one foot.

Geoffrey shrugged indifferently as he lifted

Dyanna's skirt and wiped Charlotte's blood on it. "She should not have interfered."

"She tried to help you!" Dyanna argued. "She's always been on your side! It was only when she realized you meant to kill me that she tried to stop you."

"Therein lay her mistake," Geoffrey snarled. "Her fatal mistake! It is one she will not make again."

His smirk infuriated Dyanna beyond bearing, beyond good judgment. Pulling the ring free with one hand, she brought it slashing through the air, flat against his cheek, staggering him back.

With a roar of outrage, Geoffrey seized the moment and forced her up a few more steps with sheer, brute strength she would not have suspected he possessed.

Desperate, Dyanna caught the next of the rings. But it was weak, rusted through, and snapped off in her hand. Off balance, she fell, gasping as she struck the edge of the stair on which she landed.

"Damn you, Geoffrey," she cried, gasping at the pain in her side and her shoulder. "I hate you! Hate you!"

"Get up," he ordered, jerking her to her feet without regard for any injuries she may have suffered.

His larger body against hers, he forced her farther up the stairs until she managed to catch hold of yet another of the rings.

"I am losing what little patience I had for this business!" he growled.

"You mean to kill me anyway!" she cried, beyond fear, feeling a giddy recklessness come over her in the face of certain death. "Why don't you just run me through the way you did poor Charlotte and be done with it!"

"I've another plan for you," Geoffrey told her. "I mean for you to be found at the bottom of this tower. Just as your precious DeVille's mother was found there."

Dyanna felt the blood run cold in her veins. "You can't be serious!" she hissed. "You can't really think anyone would believe I took my own life!"

"Can't I?" He smiled, a cold, pitiless smirk that sent a shiver down Dyanna's spine. "Think about it, Dyanna. You eloped with a married man. You run around London at night dressed in boy's clothes. You are obsessed with books about ghosts and curses and adventuresses. Don't think that sort of thing is not remarked upon, discussed with great relish, among the servants. They like nothing better than to sit in the servants' hall and rake their betters over the coals. Any peccadillo of anyone residing abovestairs is eagerly seized upon. You may take my word for it, dear Dyanna, the opinion belowstairs is doubtless that your brains were addled when you fell from the carriage in Newington and hit your head on the rock."

"You're mad!" Dyanna screeched. "Mad! You're the one whose brains are addled!"

"Am I? I am the one who will walk away from this tower. Not you."

"You may well walk away," she admitted, for though she had racked her brains, she could not begin to think of a way to overcome his superior strength and escape. "But you will not get away with this. When they find Charlotte's body, they will know—they will know—that she was murdered!"

"You're quite right, of course. But I have thought of that." Geoffrey flicked his thumb across the sharp edge of his sword. "I will leave the sword near your poor, broken body. Everyone will think you murdered your maid. Perhaps she tried to stop you from seeking your own demise, brave girl, and you ran her through for her trouble. There, now Charlotte will have died a heroine's death. Does that make you feel better?"

"My God! You really are mad!"

Seeing the gleeful light in his eyes, Dyanna fought against the rising panic inside her. She was afraid of dying—she harbored no fool-hardy pretenses to a bravery she did not feel—but even more, she hated the thought of being branded a madwoman, a suicide, and a murderess.

"Why are you doing this to me, Geoffrey?" she hissed. "You must hate me! Once you said you loved me . . ."

"I do love you, dear Dyanna," he cooed, lifting back a lock of her tumbled hair with the point of his sword. "I love your beauty. I love your spirit. But most of all, I love your fortune!"

"My fortune! You love my fortune, so you are killing me? that makes no sense. You cannot have my fortune if I am dead!"

Geoffrey opened his mouth to reply, but the voice that filled the twisting stairwell was Justin's.

"Yes, he can, Dyanna."

A wave of purest bliss washed over Dyanna as she saw Justin in the stairwell below them.

"Justin! Justin, help me!" she whispered.

With a vicious shove, Geoffrey took advantage of her inattention to push her up the remaining stairs to the square, wind-swept room at the top. She sprawled on the rubble-strewn floor as Geoffrey turned to face Justin, his sword clenched tightly in his blood-stained hand.

"Yes, DeVille," he taunted, "help her—if you dare! I would as soon kill you as well."

"You're not man enough to kill me, Culpepper," Justin taunted. "No, you're only man enough to kill women and old men."

With a scream of purest rage, Geoffrey rushed down the stairs that separated them and steel met steel as their duel was begun.

Chapter Thirty-Nine

Up and down the tortuous, winding steps, Justin and Geoffrey fought, each grimly determined to overcome his adversary or die in the process. The sounds of their battle echoed in the narrow stairwell. The clanging of steel on steel, the ringing as one of the other of them sent his weapon smashing into the stone wall, was deafening in the confines of the twisting passage.

At the top of the stairs, in the square, wind-swept room at the apex of the ancient tower, Dyanna sat, crouched in the farthest corner, longing to help Justin but fearing to do anything that might break his concentration and give Geoffrey, even for a moment, a temporary, but potentially lethal, advantage.

Sandra DuBay

She held her breath, drawing her knees
close up under her chin, as Geoffrey appeared
in the doorway. Pursued up the stairs, he
backed into the chamber, his eyes fixed on his
adversary who was still out of Dyanna's line of
vision. With a ferocity Dyanna would not have
expected to find in Geoffrey, he fought on.
Their battle was a dazzling, deadly dance, a
lethal, graceful melody of feint and parry,
lunge and thrust that could end at any moment with the death of one or the other.

A moment's indecision, an instant's inattention and the blade would drive home; a single
mistake would cost a life.

Dyanna watched, pulse pounding, nerves
taut, waiting—waiting for the moment she
knew would come. It was upon them before
any of them realized it. Geoffrey, stepping
back, missed his footing and fell. But before
Justin could move upon him, he had scooped
up a handful of the dust lying on the floor and
thrown it into Justin's eyes, blinding him.

For an instant, Justin's guard fell. Dyanna
saw the flash of Geoffrey's blade and
screamed as it sliced through Justin's coat, his
shirt, his flesh . . . .

Justin reacted instantly, recoiling, falling to
one knee, his hand pressed to the place in his
side where the dark, crimson blood was already beginning to well.

Like a deadly predator in the deepest jun-
gle, Geoffrey sensed weakness in his oppo-

nent. He had drawn Justin's blood and it had whetted his appetite for more. Swiftly, sword raised for the coup de grâce, he was on his feet and closing the short distance between them.

And then, in an instant, it was finished. From below, Justin drove his sword upward. It pierced Geoffrey's chest, impaling him, its bloodied point emerging through the back of his black coat.

Eyes staring, mouth agape, Geoffrey staggered back. He stared, unbelieving, as Justin's sword drew free of his body. His eyes, huge, glassy, saw the scarlet blood on the cold blue steel.

Before Dyanna's horrified eyes, he stumbled back toward the window. Before she could rise, before anyone could move, he fell, disappearing out the window, falling to the rubble-strewn ground so far below.

Dyanna clasped her hands over her ears to shut out the sound of his scream—to block out the sickening thud as his body hit the ground.

Across the chamber she saw Justin push himself to his feet. He loosely clasped his sword in one hand. With the other, he tried to stem the blood flowing from the wound in his side, which oozed up between his fingers at a frightening rate.

"Justin," Dyanna breathed. "Oh, Justin!"

She ran to him and, heedless of his wound,

embraced him, weeping with relief that he was safe, knowing, even though Geoffrey's sword had pierced his body, that he would live.

"We've got to get you back to Wildwood," she told him. "I'll run back and have Bertran come with a horse and cart."

Justin chuckled, then winced at the pain in his side. "I can make it back on my own," he insisted. "It's only a flesh wound."

Dyanna looked askance at the blood that seemed to be flowing too fast. "Are you certain? Perhaps you should wait here and I'll bring back a doctor. I—"

"Dyanna," he said sternly, the soft fondness in his eyes belying his tone, "if we stand here arguing about it, I'll no longer need a doctor. Now come, help me down the stairs. With any luck, the doctor has come to help Charlotte and he can treat me at the same time."

"Charlotte!" Dyanna stared up at him. "She's not dead?"

"No." Justin gasped as they started down the steep, winding staircase. "Caro found her in the forest. She told us where Culpepper had taken you. You have her to thank for your life."

"And you," Dyanna murmured.

Justin smiled wanly. "And Culpepper's poor swordsmanship. He could land a thrust, but his aim was damned bad."

She shot him a quelling glance. "How can

446

you laugh about such a thing?'' she demanded.

He chuckled, then groaned at the pain it caused him. "Carefully, my love," he teased. "I can laugh very carefully."

Back at Wildwood, the doctor who had dressed Charlotte's wounds saw to the cleaning, stitching, and bandaging of Justin's wound as well. When he'd left, Justin sat in the morning room with Dyanna.

With one finger, she traced the stark white bandage across the tanned, golden-haired expanse of his lower chest.

"You knew Geoffrey was still alive, didn't you?" she asked. "They must have told you when you went to speak about Lord Rawley's death." She frowned when Justin nodded. "But why didn't you tell me? Geoffrey made a joke of it. He said you probably didn't want to worry me. Why didn't you tell me?"

Justin grinned. "I didn't want to worry you."

"Wretch! But what I still don't understand in all this," she went on, "is how Geoffrey thought he could get my fortune by killing me."

Justin nodded. "I wondered about that as well. It didn't make sense for him to gull you into that false marriage. You could have exposed him and reclaimed your inheritance. The marriage would have been declared inva-

lid in any court in the land. He was not so
stupid as to think you would merely sit at
Patterton Park and let him ruin you in London. There had to be another motive. There
had to be something he knew that we did not.''

''What could it be?'' she wondered. ''Have
you figured it out?''

''I think I have.'' He gestured toward the
table on the opposite side of the room. ''In the
drawer of that table, you will find a packet of
papers. Bring them to me, will you?''

Obediently, Dyanna went to the table and
brought back the papers he desired. Curious,
she watched while he shuffled through them,
searching for the clause he had noticed earlier.

''What this is,'' he told her at last, ''is a copy
of your grandfather's—your mother's father's
—Last Will and Testament. Have you ever
seen it?''

Dyanna shook her head. ''All that was han-
dled by solicitors,'' she told him. ''My grandfather's will and, I suppose, my father's as well.''

''Well, your father cannot have been too
pleased if he saw it. You know your maternal
grandfather, old Lord Lincoln, detested your
father. He was determined that Blaykling Castle and the other properties and monies
should never fall into your father's hands.''

''As they would have if I had died before my
father,'' Dyanna commented.

''Indeed. Your grandfather inserted a clause

448

bypassing your father if you predeceased him. If you died without issue, the properties and income belonging to the Earldom of Lincoln, were to pass, in their entirety, to—"

He handed the paper to Dyanna, one finger pointing to the relevant clause.

"To—" Dyanna read. "To Lord Geoffrey Culpepper, grandson and heir of Horatio Culpepper, the Marquess of Summersleigh, my oldest and most beloved friend . . ."

"If you died without children," Justin told her. "Geoffrey inherited everything."

"But I don't understand," she insisted. "Why the sham marriage? Why didn't he just kill me and be done with it?"

"Too risky," Justin told her. "The greatest fortune in the world will do him precious little good if he's hanged for murder. It had to be in a remote place, out of London. How else could he get you to go away with him but with an elopement?"

"But he went to all the trouble of procuring a special license and—"

"Did you see it?" Justin inquired.

"No," she admitted.

"And I'll wager it never existed. No, what he needed was a remote spot with no witnesses. His mother, I suspect, knew what he was about. But I have no proof of that. The Reverend Mr. Tuttle was as duped by Culpepper as you were, I expect. He, no doubt, thought he was being asked to perform a legitimate marriage. And, within a short time, he would have been asked to perform a funeral service— yours."

Dyanna shivered. As she gazed out the window, she saw a cart bearing Geoffrey's body to the village, where it would be prepared to be sent on to Patterton Park for burial. Without feeling either regret or remorse at Geoffrey's death, she turned away.

"I suppose he would have arranged an accident for me."

"Doubtless. There would have been a quick, private funeral, then he would have returned to London and resumed life with Octavia FitzGeorge, albeit on a grander scale."

He must have been delighted when I fell from the carriage in Newington," she said softly. "When the report reached Patterton Park that I'd been pronounced dead, he must have been overjoyed."

"His plan would have succeeded without his having to lend a hand to your death," Justin agreed. "It must have been a great shock to him when he heard you were still alive."

"And then in London . . . Do you think he enlisted Lord Rawley's help in a second attempt?"

Justin frowned. "I think Lord Rawley was as much a victim as you. I suspect Geoffrey meant for Rawley to kill you but then, I think, he always meant to kill Rawley. That way, he could plead self-defense—which he did, successfully—and say he killed old Rawley while trying, in vain, to save you. He was cunning, if too impetuous."

Rubbing her arms, Dyanna sat on the footstool near Justin's chair. She raised troubled eyes to his face and said:

"I don't want to believe Uncle Horatio had anything to do with it. He was so kind to me, so caring—and yet it was he who brought Geoffrey and I together. From the first he was promoting a marriage between us."

"I don't think he had any part in it," Justin told her seriously. "I told him what I knew— that Geoffrey had married Octavia FitzGeorge and yet had tricked you into eloping. I told him my suspicions. He already had suspicions about his grandson. He disinherited him, you know."

"Geoffrey told me. He said his grandfather was going to marry Lady Hayward. I hope they're happy together." A frown wrinkled her brow. "But, oh, Justin, I don't like to think of someone plotting my death. This whole business frightens me. I can't quite believe it's over."

"It is over, sweetheart," Justin insisted, taking her hands in his. "And a happier time is beginning. Once we are married—"

"My lord!" Dyanna cried, standing. "I don't recall your proposing marriage."

His eyes twinkled. "If you want me to get

451

down on my knees, minx, you'll have to wait for my side to heal. And who knows? By then, I may have changed my mind."

"Wretch!" she hissed, balling her fist and delivering a gentle punch to his arm. "If you change your mind, more than your side will have to heal!"

"Ah, there speaks the true daughter of Rakehell McBride!" he laughed.

"And don't you ever forget it!" she ordered. "Now, I'm going up to see how Charlotte is. While I'm gone, you think about someplace splendid for us to go on our honeymoon."

Leaving the morning room, Dyanna climbed the stairs and went to Charlotte's room high on the third floor, almost directly above her own. The doctor had told her that although the maid had lost a good deal of blood, she was a healthy, strong girl and would recover quickly.

"Charlotte?" Dyanna said softly, opening the door. She hoped she would not awaken the maid if she were sleeping. "Charlotte . . .?"

Dyanna's face flamed crimson when she found Charlotte propped up in her bed looking very pale and pretty with her thick, titian curls tumbling about her shoulders. Seated on the bed facing her, his lips pressed to hers in a kiss as tender as it was fervent, was Justin's valet, the wry, ever-vigilant Swiss, Bertran.

The couple drew apart as Dyanna appeared in the doorway. Charlotte's face darkened with a blush no less hot than Dyanna's own, and Bertran, obviously mortified, dropped Charlotte's hand and rose to his feet.

"I beg your pardon," Dyanna murmured. "I had no idea. That is to say, I never imagined . . .."

"Please, mademoiselle," Bertran said quickly, "allow me to explain. Charlotte and I—we love one another. We would like to marry. But we know many people do not want their servants to marry. Neither of us has the private means to support a life outside service. But if we could save—"

"Bertran," Dyanna interrupted. "Bertran, please, you need say no more. For my part, I should be delighted to see you and Charlotte married. And I would not turn either of you out of service. I cannot speak for my Lord DeVille, although—and you are the first to know—he and I are to be married as well . . .." She blushed with pleasure as they both exclaimed joyfully. "In any case, I think if you were to speak to your master about it, you would find him perfectly amenable to having a valet who was the husband of his wife's lady's maid."

Beaming, Bertran pressed another brief kiss on Charlotte's forehead. Then, with a bow for Dyanna, he rushed out of the small chamber.

Sandra DuBay

Dyanna, going to the doorway, called after him: "He's in the morning room, Bertran."

Then, with Bertran dispatched on an errand she felt certain would end happily for all concerned, Dyanna went to Charlotte's bed and perched on the edge, eager to offer her thanks for Charlotte's help in sending Justin to rescue her and to inform Charlotte, though she suspected Bertran already had, of how the matter had ended. To all this, she added her warmest congratulations and her most heartfelt wishes for Charlotte and Bertran's future happiness.

Chapter Forty

The new, smart, dark blue-and-black traveling coach moved along the dusty roads drawn by a matched pair of gleaming white horses. Inside the coach, the Earl and new Countess DeVille sat, the Countess snuggled against her husband, dozing.

"Dyanna," Justin said softly, nudging her awake. "Dyanna?"

"Hmmm?" Dyanna sat up and rubbed her eyes with her fingertips. "What is it?"

Justin pointed out the window. There, framed in an opening in the trees, was a sight that could never fail to bring a rush of warmth and pleasure to Dyanna's heart.

The winding river stretched away, crossed

by a triple-arched bridge of golden stone. Beyond lay the village of Wykehurst and above, built on a rock ledge jutting from the high hillside, lay Blaykling, looking for all the world as if the huge building, with its many towers and turrets and fanciful, twisted chimneys, were floating somewhere near the clouds.

Dyanna sighed. "I wonder if Charlotte and Bertran have everything ready for us."

Justin laughed, thinking of the newlywed valet and lady's maid who had gone on ahead to await their master and mistress's arrival.

"They will if they can leave each other alone long enough to see to their work."

"They have no self-restraint," Dyanna sniffed, feigning airy disapproval. "Thank heavens we are not like them."

Justin's golden eyes twinkled as he pulled her into his arms and kissed her. "Yes," he agreed when at last his lips left hers. "Thank heaven we are not like them—or we wouldn't have set foot outside DeVille house for another month!"

Dyanna laughed, then frowned, curious, when Justin rapped on the roof of the carriage, signaling the coachman to stop just as they were passing over the bridge.

"What are you doing?" she demanded, bracing herself as the carriage rocked to a halt.

"Something I should have done long ago,"

he told her. From a compartment built into the carriage wall, he took Dyanna's copy of *The Life and Death of Wicked Lord Lucifer Wolfe*.

"Justin?" Dyanna called as he climbed down from the coach. "What are you going to do with—? Justin! Wait!"

But by the time she had scrambled down from the coach, he had dropped the book over the balustrade. Leaning over, Dyanna watched the volume float out of sight beneath the bridge, then ran to the other side to wait for it to reappear. But it did not; somewhere beneath the bridge, on the bottom of the slow-flowing river, the notorious book now rested.

"Why did you do that?" she demanded, following him back to the coach.

"It was hardly the kind of souvenir I'd have you keep to remind you of our courtship," he told her. "A love letter or a pressed flower would be more conventional."

"You never wrote me a love letter," she reminded him, "and you've never given me flowers. And, I need hardly tell you, our courtship was not precisely conventional."

"Neither will our marriage be if you persist in reading books like that."

Dyanna frowned as Justin pounded on the roof, setting the coach into motion once more. "But I like to read books like that," she protested.

Justin sighed. Twining one of her silky, silvery curls about his finger, he told her fondly, "Your imagination is too fertile, my love. You have only to read about a ghost and you start hearing the moan of tortured spirits and the rattling of phantom chains. You need only to read about a curse and you begin to feel symptoms. If you read about a haunted house, you begin hearing voices in empty rooms." He laughed as she punched him in the arm. "I'm sorry, my pet, but it is true. If you have to read, please, read gentle romances or history or something that will not fire that imagination of yours."

Lifting her chin, Dyanna pouted prettily as they rode on toward Wykehurst.

In the village, Justin once more stopped the coach.

"There are a few things I want to get before we go up to the castle," he told Dyanna, helping her down. "I'm going to the haberdashery there, across the street."

"I think I'll go look at the bonnets in Mrs. Riber's shop," Dyanna decided.

Dyanna watched as Justin crossed the street and disappeared into the shop of the Messrs. Eyesham and Flyte, Haberdashers. When he was lost to view, she turned, fully intending to look at Mrs. Riber's bonnets. But the pretty, bow-fronted shop of Mr. Digby, Printer, beckoned irresistibly.

The little brass bell over the door tinkled cheerfully as Dyanna entered the shop which served Wykehurst as a printers, stationers, and book shop.

The proprietor, Mr. Digby, was a short, stout man whose boisterous spirits made him the joy of the monthly balls. His round, ruddy face lit up with pleasure as he emerged from the back room, wiping his inky hands on a cloth as he came.

"Miss Dyanna!" he cried. Then his eyes widened and his mouth became a horrified 'O' as he realized his mistake. A roughish grin spread across his face as he made her as grand and low a bow as his girth would permit.

"Your pardon, my Lady DeVille. Allow me to offer you my congratulations on your marriage, my lady."

"Thank you, Mr. Digby," Dyanna answered, dimpling.

"Your lady's maid was here a few days since. She said her master and mistress would be following directly. Will you be living at Blaykling now?"

"For a while. Perhaps you and Mrs. Digby could come to dinner some evening while we are here."

"Nothing could give us greater pleasure. Would you, by any chance, be looking for a book to read?"

"Well . . ." Dyanna remembered what Justin had said. Several volumes lay on the table

Sandra DuBay

nearby and among them Dyanna noticed slim, light romances and works of deep, scholarly interest. Either would probably win Justin's approval; neither stirred the slightest interest in Dyanna.

"The reason I ask," Mr. Digby went on, "is that there is a new book, published not long since. A Gothick novel in two volumes which I think cannot fail to stir your ladyship's interest."

Dyanna felt the familiar pricklings of excitement that the prospect of a new story never failed to evoke in her. "I don't know if I should . . ." She hesitated.

"I think you will be interested in this. Once your maid said you were coming, I put a copy aside especially for you. It was written by a man whose grandmother was once housekeeper at Blaykling, and it is based, so they say, on tales she told him as a child."

"Tales?" Dyanna asked. "What sorts of tales?"

From beneath the counter, the printer drew two books bound in green leather, the names of the book and of the author, a Mr. Philip St. Aubyn, in shining gold letters.

Dyanna took Volume I from Mr. Digby. *"The Secret of Blaykling Castle,"* she read aloud. "Blaykling! I didn't know Blaykling had any secrets."

Mr. Digby laughed. "According to my wife, there are many, quite startling revelations

460

recounted in the story. Of course, they must be nothing more than the imaginings of an enterprising author."

"I suppose," Dyanna allowed, "but would he use the actual name of the castle if his story was not based in truth?"

"I should not imagine so," Mr. Digby agreed. "Still, only your ladyship can vouch for the accuracy of his descriptions of the castle and its history."

"And I could only do that after reading the book," Dyanna observed, laughing when the printer had the grace to flush. "Well, I will buy it. If only as a curiosity."

Surely, she told herself as she paid for the books and waited for Mr. Digby to wrap them, even Justin could not disapprove of her buying such an item of interest.

Still, after she left the print shop, she tucked the volumes deep down in the carpet-bag she'd brought in the carriage to hold her personal necessities. Then, so she could not accuse herself of lying to her husband, she darted into Mrs. Riber's shop and tried on several bonnets.

It was there that Justin found her.

The hour was late when Dyanna lay beside her husband in the enormous, century-old bed hung with scarlet Spitalfields silk. She could not sleep, despite feeling warm and drowsy, lost in the heated afterglow of Justin's lovemaking. Her mind was engaged in speculating about what secrets of Blaykling Castle might be disclosed in the book Mr. Digby had sold her that afternoon.

"Damn you, Mr. Digby," she said softly. "I should have known better than to let you sell me that book! I should have known myself well enough to know I could not resist reading it."

With a glance at Justin who slept beside her, she slipped out from beneath the coverlets and felt around in the darkness for her shift.

Slipping it over her head, she stood a few feet from the bed, torn between retreating to the sitting room to steal a glance at a few pages of the book and being a dutiful wife and climbing back into bed. At last, as she had been almost certain it would, her curiosity won out and she tiptoed into the sitting room and went to the writing desk where she had hidden the books and took out Volume I.

Lighting the candles in a three-branched candelabrum, she carried it to a table beside a comfortable armchair.

For a few more moments she hesitated. It was not too late, she told herself, to remain an obedient wife. But then, throwing caution— and obedience—to the wind, she opened to the first page of Volume I and began to read:

CHAPTER I
"It was quite by accident that I

happened upon the first clue to the secret
of Blaykling Castle. I had come there in
answer to a summons from the Earl of
Lincoln and his Countess, who were in
need of a housekeeper, their previous
housekeeper having retired after years of
good and faithful service.

But though my position entailed the
overseeing of a regiment of servants, I
prided myself on attention to detail. It
was this attention that drew me to the
massive, ornate, intricately carved marble
inglenook that was the chiefest attraction
of the great, barrel-roofed drawing room
at the north end of the first floor.

The intricacy of detail made it the
bane of every housemaid's existence, for
it seemed impossible to remove every
speck of the dust that covered it with
distressing regularity. It fell to my lot to
inspect it and discover those nooks and
crannies which some parlormaid's
negligence had overlooked.

It was while engaged in this tiresome
activity that I discovered the secret
passage. I had noticed a neglected film of
dust within the deeply carved wing of the
fat cherub who cavorted nearest the left
corner of the mantelpiece. Taking out the
cloth I carried in the pocket of my apron,
I wiped away the dust to reveal the
dark-veined, cream-colored marble.

Because of the depth of the carving, I was obliged to press harder than is my wont. As I did so, the wing seemed to lift, as if the cherub was about to take flight. I had no sooner recovered from my wonder at this than a harsh, grating sound filled the room and a panel at the back of the yawning fireplace slid out of sight to reveal the gaping mouth of a passage I had not heretofore suspected might exist . . .."

Dyanna closed the book, her finger marking her place. A secret passage! In the drawing room! She knew the room well—the author had certainly described the inglenook with an accuracy that suggested he had either seen it or known someone who had. But a moving cherub wing? A secret passage? Surely that could be nothing but the figment of an over-active imagination. There could not be any such thing. She would have discovered it during the happy years she lived at Blaykling. Wouldn't she? Some one of the servants with whom she was on terms of affection and friendship would have told her if any such passage existed. Wouldn't they?

Mentally, she chided herself for reading the book in the first place. Justin had been right. It had done nothing but fire her imagination. It was just a story, after all, written by someone with a more foolish imagination than her own and with the impertinence to name Blaykling as the setting for his imaginings.

Still . . . What if it were true? There could not be any harm in looking. And then, when she had proven to her own satisfaction that there was no truth to Mr. St. Aubyn's book, she could lock it away and think no more of it.

Just this once, she promised herself, lighting a candle in a brass chamberstick from one of those burning in her candelabrum, just this once she would be so foolish as to investigate Mr. St. Aubyn's claim. And then she could abandon the book and Justin would never know of her foolishness.

Her way lit by the golden glow of her single candle, she tiptoed down the elegant, soaring main staircase to the great hall with its magnificent, fan-vaulted ceiling, and into the drawing room where the massive marble inglenook that had been her grandfather's contribution to the home of his ancestors, gleamed in the shadowy darkness of the room.

Reaching it, Dyanna consulted the book once more before abandoning it on one of the high-backed settles beneath the wide overhang.

"The cherub nearest the left corner of the mantelpiece," she reminded herself, holding the candle close to the corner in question.

Well that, at least, was accurate, she thought, finding the fat dancing cherub. Her fingers touched the deeply carved wing. It seemed of a piece with the background. She pressed it with her fingers; it would not move. Leaning closer, she placed the heel of her hand against it and pressed upward with all her might. To her astonishment, the wing grated, then swung upward.

Almost immediately, there was a rasping, scraping sound. Dyanna leaned over and saw, to her amazement, that where once there was only the soot-blackened back of the fireplace, there was now a gaping hole. Tattered cobwebs hung there, moving gently on a breeze that had its beginnings at the other end of the passage.

Stunned and delighted, Dyanna moved the cherub's wing back into place, then stooped quickly to watch the panel slide back, leaving no hint of what lay behind.

"It's true!" she marveled. "The story was true! I can't believe it!"

Thrilled by her discovery, Dyanna swung the wing upward once more and once more watched, breathless, as the panel opened.

In her excitement, she forgot Justin's warnings, forgot what trouble her imagination and impetuous nature had led her to in the past. Without thinking of the consequences— without wondering if, perhaps, it might be wiser to read the rest of the book and discover what secrets lay at the other end of that dark and mysterious passage—Dyanna took up her candle and stepped inside.

The brick tunnel stretched before her, dank and black, festooned with cobwebs both new and old. Every few feet it widened into niches on either side that looked like bricked-in arches. Dyanna wondered if there had once been a labyrinth of tunnels beginning here and leading through the walls, honeycombing the great castle.

Her footsteps shuffled on the brick floor; she tried hard not to notice the rats that skittered in and out of the golden circle of light her candle cast. She started at their every squeak, gasped at the sudden movement of a lacy web caught in the air currents.

Nervously, she glanced back toward the end of the tunnel and wished she had lit some candles in the drawing room.

It was then that the powerful arm snaked about her waist, then that she was jerked off her feet and brought hard against someone— or something—warm and far larger than herself.

"Justin!" she screamed, the candlestick dropping from her fingers and rolling across the narrow tunnel. "Justin!"

"Yes?" an all-too-familiar voice breathed in her ear.

Twisting around, she found herself gazing up into a pair of laughing golden eyes. Justin stood in one of the niches, obviously pleased with himself.

"You!" she cried. "But how—when—?"

"I saw you coming out of Digby's shop with a package," he told her, retrieving her candle and leading her back out of the tunnel. "Then, when you were in your bath tonight, I found the book." Outside, beneath the overhanging inglenook, he pushed the cherub's wing back into place and watched the panel slide across the tunnel. "I knew you couldn't possibly resist coming down here to see if the tunnel actually existed. While you were in the sitting room, reading, I came down to wait for you."

"You weren't asleep at all when I got up, were you?" she accused him, balling her fist and punching him hard in the chest.

"No." He laughed, catching her wrists and pulling her into his arms. "Ah, Dyanna, I love you very, very much. But I can see I'm going to have my hands full."

Turning her face up to receive his kiss, Dyanna did not disagree.

CASSIE EDWARDS . . . ROMANCE AT ITS FINEST

Fans of Cassie Edwards will love **Secrets of my Heart**, a favorite in Leisure's classic romance collection.

SECRETS OF MY HEART. Orphaned on the long trail West, Lenora Adamson found her savior in rugged James Calloway. Convinced that she had met the man she would one day marry, Lenora gave herself to him body and soul, not realizing that James was a foot-loose wanderer who could be tamed by no woman.

_____2525-6 $3.95 US/$4.95 CAN

AUTOGRAPHED BOOKMARK EDITIONS

Each book contains a signed message from the author and a removable gold foiled and embossed bookmark.

PIRATE'S LADY Robin Lee Hatcher. Lady Jacinda Sutherland found herself captive on a pirate ship bound for white slavery in Constantinople—unless she surrendered her innocence to its dashing captain.

_____2487-X $3.95 US/$4.95 CAN

SCARLET SURRENDER Sandra DuBay. A fiery novel of ultimate passion that sweeps the reader to the decadent salons of Second Empire France, where a beautiful woman surrenders to a devilishly seductive hero.

_____2555-8 $3.95 US/$4.95 CAN

LOVE FOREVERMORE Madeline Baker. Loralee had a difficult task before her as the Fort Apache schoolmarm—and an even tougher task quelling her desires for a fierce Indian renegade.

_____2577-9 $4.50 US/$5.50 CAN